RETRIBUTION

By John Frame

 New Generation Publishing

Rhodesia

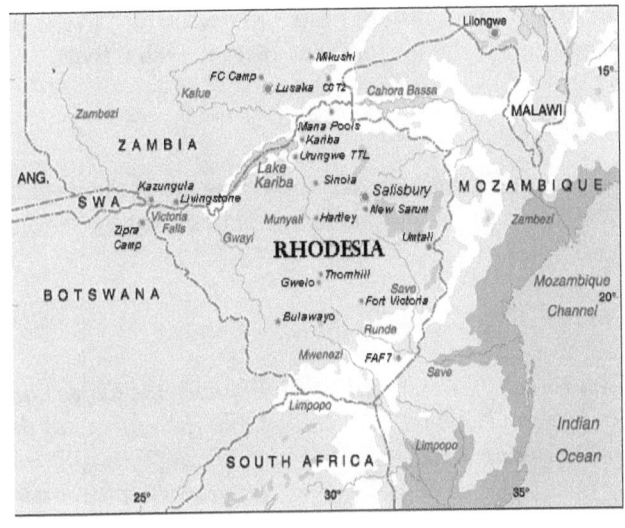

For my wonderful family.
In memory of my father George and my mother Lorraine, and John and Elvie, who lived in Rhodesia for the majority of their married lives.

***

Abbreviations and Glossary of Terms are at the back of the book to assist with understanding some phrases and words used.

***

We look with tired eyes
at the sun slowly waning
painting the skies
with colour raging

Masasa trees burning red
herald in another season
Yet already so many dead
in the name of freedom
Are we being misled
and will this conflict deepen?

The battle raging around us
has no end in sight
This scorched land has had enough.
Or is its destiny to witness this continued fight?

CHAPTER ONE

September 1978

The ZIPRA guerrilla heard the sound of the plane before he saw it.

A gentle breeze swept across the Zambezi Valley carrying light relief as the heat of the day disappeared as fast as the sun sank towards the horizon.

The guerrilla, raising his hand shielding his eyes from the sunset, searched the cloudless north western sky that was painted with an orange hue.

Aw I see it.

The plane climbed skywards in the distance. It would be overhead within a minute. Timing was critical.

Months of arduous weapons training automatically kicked in. Moving quickly to remove the weapon he carried on his back, he knelt down to take off its protective cover. After activating the power supply to the missile's electronics he looked up anxiously to see where the plane was. His pulse raced. It was making ground on him. The plane with its four turbo-prop engines was clearly visible.

He wiped his sweaty hands against his jacket before looking to see if the gyros had stabilised. They were. Remaining kneeling and oblivious of his comrades who were standing nearby encouraging him to speed up the process, he lifted the canister holding the missile and placed it on his right shoulder.

"The plane is near. Hurry comrade!" shouted one of them.

He searched for the plane through the sights but could not find it. Looking up, the blue and white tail markings and the name emblazoned on its side, '*Air Rhodesia,*' were clear as the plane soared overhead.

Looking back through the sights he tracked his target before slowly pulling on the trigger until there was resistance. The electronics activated locking the missile onto the target. A red light came on in the sighting mechanism. His heart pounded in his ears. Beads of sweat ran down his forehead. The buzzer sounded a moment before the green light came on. Then he pulled the trigger hard.

The rocket left the canister with a whoosh as it streaked skyward. The comrade saw the missile flash out of the tube before he lost his balance and reeled backwards.

The booster burned out as it left the launch tube. The two forward fins on the missile unfolded to assist it steer towards the plane. The four rear stabilizing fins engaged. Its self-destruct mechanism activated. The rocket's sustainer motor fired and the missile leapt to four hundred and thirty metres per second.

At this point the plane was doomed. The missile's passive infra-red seeker head had detected the radiation emanating from the plane's engines. Speeding skywards the missile developed a wobble as its seeker head calculated the navigation co-ordinates for all four engines. The wobble sped up as the missile neared the plane.

The five guerrillas emerged from a clump of trees and gathered around their fellow comrade as he clumsily tried to get up off the ground.

"Aw. Look at it go to the sky. It will hit the plane!" shouted a guerrilla with eager anticipation as he pointed his AK 47 rifle towards the plane.

The bang was audible when the SAM missile struck an inner engine near its exhaust. Instantaneously flames poured out of the engine changing its sound and the mortally wounded plane began to fall earthwards.

Elated, the comrades stamped their boots on the ground, chanting their revolutionary songs, their AK's held above their heads. All the while they watched the plane disappear over the line of hills leaving a sad trail of black smoke to mark its final decent.

"Shall we go and find the plane now?" queried one comrade. "We must see what damage we have made."

"It will be dark soon. There will be fire where the plane hit the ground. We will be able to find it tonight," said another.

"No! We must move away from this place," commanded their leader, the one who pulled the trigger. "The Rhodesians will come to the place the plane hit the ground. They will be angry. They will want to find us and take this weapon." He held it above his head. "It is a powerful weapon. It will bring us victory over the settlers and their sell out puppets. This weapon must not be lost to the Rhodesians."

Disappointment replaced elation. After such a long period of training in a camp in Angola, followed by the arduous month of survival in the harsh winter landscape of the Zambezi Valley, always vigilant to avoid contact with the Rhodesian Security Forces, they were to be denied savouring the moment of glory by seeing the wreckage, to make sure the plane had crashed.

"How will we know the plane hit the ground?" queried a comrade.

"When we get back across the border we will know. It will be reported that it has been destroyed and we will be heroes. No more talk now! We must move fast this night to get far away before dawn. Get ready to move."

The leader put the weapon back into its cover and threw it over his shoulder. He collected his AK assault rifle and back pack that he had left under a small thorn tree. His comrades filed off northwards, their rice-fleck uniforms blending into the fading light of the surrounding bush.

Before he set off for the Zambian border the ZIPRA guerrilla looked back towards the hills where the plane had disappeared. There was only a faint trail of smoke in the sky that flashed red to mark the end of another day.

That plane was hit in its belly, he thought to himself. *This will put fear into the hearts of the settlers. My forefathers will be proud of what I have done. I am a true Ndebele warrior bringing punishment to those who stole our land. The liberation struggle is victorious and we will reclaim our lands. My comrade leader will be very pleased.*

CHAPTER TWO

October 1954
They squatted under a Masasa tree that was resplendent in its spring bloom. The new foliage flashed amber and wine red in a blaze of colour that contrasted sharply with the dusty brown land. The old tree, twisted and weathered, leant precariously with half its exposed roots clinging to the rocky soil.

While little shade was offered by the sparse foliage, heavy clouds blocked out the sun. The cumulonimbus clouds had turned grey threatening an afternoon thunderstorm.

The father spoke to his young son in their native tongue, Ndebele. It was a special time for them. It was a time of learning where traditional knowledge was to be passed from one generation to another. The boy was eager to learn listening intently as he stared deep into his father's eyes searching for inflections.

His father called him 'Bhekizizwe', a man to '*look after the nation*', a name for someone destined to become a great warrior. He was excited because his father had explained his heritage to him for the first time.

He was amaNdebele, born of the noble tribe of warriors who lived in the district of Matabeleland, a large land area that occupied the western forty percent of Rhodesia. He was a descendant of the great warrior Mzilikazi who had separated from the Zulu King, Shaka, over a hundred seasons ago. The Zulu nation that occupied the southern part of Africa was revered for its warriors and was feared far beyond its borders.

Mzilikazi's military prowess shone at an early age and he soon became a close lieutenant of the King. But

8

a quarrel with the King led to a rebellion, the punishment being ritual execution. To avoid that fate Mzilikazi fled northwards taking his tribe of around five hundred with him. Shaka sent the Zulu warriors in pursuit to find and kill him.

Fleeing the pursuing Zulu warriors fed urgency to the journey northwards. Along the way they encountered other tribes whom they fought to gain the rites of passage through their territories. Mizilikazi's warriors were highly skilled fighters with their distinctive cow hide shields and short stabbing spears. These northern tribes proved no match as they were progressively defeated. After many months Mizilikazi settled in a place he called Mhlahlandlea and there his tribe enjoyed a long period of peaceful respite. But suddenly the Boers arrived with their ox drawn wagons. They too had experienced a tough journey as they fought with many African tribes on their way northwards from the Cape in their quest to get away from the British.

Mzilikazi's warriors clashed with the Boers, but their stabbing spears and hide shields were no match against the guns used by the Boers. Many warriors were lost before Mzilikazi decided that he must take his people further away from the Zulu homeland and these Boers. He assembled his people and led them northwards once more to cross the great river, later to be called the Limpopo.

In the land north of this river his warriors easily overwhelmed the pastoral Kalanga tribes. Mzilikazi removed all opposition in the lands that were occupied. He remodelled his new territory to suit his Ndebele nation in what became known as the Mfecane, a terrible time characterised by scorched earth, devastation and murder on a grand scale. It forged his nation out of blood to become the true masters of this land.

So it came to pass that Mzilikazi was a King holding sovereignty over the region between the two great rivers, the Limpopo to the south and Zambezi to the north, and between the desert of the Makgadikgadi salt pans to the west and the realm of Shoshangana, the Save River to the east. The great King set up his capital on a plateau surrounded by huge granite boulder hills and he called this place Gubulawayo.

When Mzilikazi died his eldest son Lobengula assumed power over the Ndebele. He continued the tradition of amassing cattle from the constant raids against the lesser tribes to the east. Allowing for the 'blooding' of the new warriors with their first kill of another human, these annual raids, regarded as sport for the Ndebele, were burned into their culture.

Bhekizizwe's father ended his tale by saying that Lobengula was a great King, with many cattle and many wives. His warriors were fearless and the spirits favoured them.

"Then tell me my father why the Ndebele are no longer great warriors? Why are the Ndebele not the rulers of this land?"

His father wrestled to find the right answer. He paused to think through how he should answer while his son waited patiently, his big dark coloured eyes eagerly seeking the response.

Both of them looked skywards as thunder rumbled overhead echoing across the vast land as it did so. The sky turned darker as the clouds grew heavier.

His father, a simple man, earned his living driving a truck for a furniture factory situated in the light industrial area on the outskirts of Bulawayo, the second city of Rhodesia. His wages ensured his family were well provided for with regular meals and clothing. Living in a township reserved for black Rhodesians situated adjacent to the industrial area, he rented a small one bedroom brick house. The rent was subsidised by the local municipality who built and maintained the township. The small bedroom led off a combined living space and kitchen that allowed for an open fire to cook food. An outside toilet and basin for washing was attached to the house. He shared a communal single water tap with five other houses. There was no electricity.

His father also possessed a traditional hut in his extended family's kraal which was situated in a Tribal Trust Land about one hundred and eighty kilometres north west of Bulawayo. This was where his three wives and his eleven children lived. He visited them once or sometimes twice a year when he got leave from his employer.

Bhekizizwe lived at the kraal with his mother, his brothers and sisters and went to a mission school run by a Catholic priest and two nuns. He had to walk five kilometres through the bush to go to and from school each day. It could be a dangerous journey especially for a young child. Children had been taken by wild animals, Leopards being the main culprits. Aware of the danger as he walked through the bush he instinctively listened to his sixth sense which had matured early in his youth and which he had realised would protect him from danger.

A keen student and eager to learn, his enquiring mind stimulated what otherwise would be mundane days of teaching for the nuns. They found his interaction challenged them to go more deeply into topics that ordinarily they would not do.

After his first visit to Bulawayo he was left in awe at how the city folk lived. Big houses made of bricks and tiles made the round mud huts with thatched pitched rooves in his kraal look inadequate. The cars and trucks, the streets with shops and so many people

11

all overwhelmed his senses. Upon his return to the Tribal Trust Land he had more questions for the nuns than there were answers for.

He queried first with his father and then with the nuns at his school what made some people more prosperous than others. On reflection it seemed to him that both his father and the nuns said the same thing in different ways. The answer was to work hard. Hence he figured that if he worked hard at school he would become prosperous and therefore afford the big houses and motor cars that he saw the white people had in the city.

He had already accepted that being a convert to the Catholic faith meant he had to forego his traditional culture. He learned that as a Christian one had to forgive ones enemies rather than shoving a short stabbing spear into their gut, or to turn the other cheek so both cheeks could get whacked and that if you give away everything you have to those in need you will get what the nuns called 'salvation with eternal happiness'. He gathered that God would ensure that by doing this kind deed he would not become one of the needy as a consequence. Rather he would become rich.

He learned that all men were created in the image of God and all men were equal. This particularly appealed to him. He understood this meant he was equal to all others including the white people. But knowing this also troubled him deeply. This meant the Bakalanga, the tribe to the south east, were equal to the Ndebele. This even applied to the Karanga, Manyika and the hated Zezuru tribes who were the natural enemies of the Ndebele.

His mother, who was the second wife of his father, spat on the ground and stamped her feet on the spittle when he told her what the nuns said.

"Ha! We are not equal to those Zezuru and Karanga dogs. We are the great Ndebele who piss on those dogs. Do not speak of such nonsense again!"

That had ended the discussion on this topic with his mother.

He broached this topic with his father when he visited the kraal. That was when his father realised it was time he spoke with his son. He took his son into the bush to his favourite Masasa tree. It was the tree he had spent many hours over the years thinking about a multitude of things. It was here he would start teaching his son the wisdom of his tribe.

"That question you ask me my son is very difficult to answer. It takes much thinking to understand."

As he continued to search for a simple way to answer his son's question he noticed ants attacking a large grasshopper, crawling all over it so it was overwhelmed and rendered immobile. Then he heard the distinctive sound of the honey eater in the near distance. He knew how to answer his son.

"My son, can you hear the honey guide?"

"Yes my father, but what has that bird got to do with my question to you?"

"Patience my son. I will explain this problem to you and answer the question you ask of me. The honey guide comes to the Ndebele and troubles him much. He flies around and around making a big noise. If the Ndebele ignores the honey guide then it makes even more noise. It wants something from the Ndebele and will not go away until the Ndebele gives it what it seeks.

The Ndebele follows the honey guide, sometimes for a long time and the honey guide takes the Ndebele to a tree. In that tree is the bee nest and in that nest is honey and grubs. The honey guide shows the Ndebele the way to the honey in exchange for the Ndebele

13

giving it some of the honey and to open the bees nest so it can feast on the grubs. The honey guide and the Ndebele give to each other what they both want and they go on their way to live as before."

"I know this my father. You have taken me with you before to find the bee nest that the honey guide asks you to find."

"Yes my son, but knowing this is important to what I now tell you. The honey guide that came to the great King so long ago was not a bird but white men from far away across great water. The King did not want anything to do with these white people and told them to go away. But like the honey guide they kept coming back. They wanted to look in the earth for rocks. They said that if they found the rocks then they would give the King great wealth. Like the promise the honey guide makes to the Ndebele, so the white men made to the great King.

The King gave the white men permission to look for the rocks and they came in their wagons to look at the ground in many places. But unlike the honey guide my son, more white people came. They moved into where the Zezuru and Karanga lived in the east and they built towns. But when they found the rocks they searched for, the rocks we know as gold, silver, they did not give the share they promised to the great King. Unlike the honey guide that does not ask for more than its own share and does not linger, the white men settled and kept asking for more. The great King was very angry at the settlers for lying to him. His warriors wanted to attack and chase them away, but the great King kept his warriors away from the settlers because they had guns and he remembered his father telling him about how he had lost many warriors when he fought with the Boers.

Then one day the great King's pride was insulted by the Karanga dogs. He sent a raiding party of several thousand warriors to bring these dogs to heel. The raiding party destroyed many kraals killing the Karanga dogs and they took what was their right. They took their cattle.

It was then that the honey guide, those white settlers, turned on the Ndebele. The white settlers attacked the Ndebele who fought bravely in many battles. But it was an unfair fight with guns against the stabbing spear. The Ndebele was defeated just like the Zulu were in South Africa and the white settlers took everything."

Bhekizizwe saw his father wipe a tear from his eye. He looked sad and Bhekizizwe felt his own tears well up in his eyes.

"My son, you must remember that the Ndebele are a great tribe and great warriors still. We share this land now but only for a fleeting moment. It will return to us one day and the Ndebele will rejoice once again."

The sky grumbled and a lightening flash struck the earth in the distance. The sky had turned dark grey. Rain fell on the distant hills.

"But when, my father? How will the land return to us?"

"Because we have more Ndebele than the white settlers and ... like those ants my son ...." he pointed to their nest where they were pulling the large grasshopper down the hole, " ... those ants overcome the larger grasshopper because they have more ants. Like the ants one day we will over-run the white settlers and take back this land."

Another louder crack of thunder followed a lightning strike.

"Now we must return to the kraal. The storm is upon us."

As they set off through the knee high grass towards their compound Bhekizizwe grabbed his father's hand and held on tight.

My father is a wise man indeed. One day all this land will belong to the great Ndebele again, thought Bhekizizwe.

CHAPTER THREE

August 1963

The early morning mist covered the landscape like a tea cloth.

The Ring Necked Doves monotonous and high-pitched crooning sound, 'Cooka-loo', flooded the silence of the morning as the farm workers slowly began to gather at the tobacco barns. The cold of the morning cut into the gathering crowd who milled around stamping their feet and rubbed their hands together in an attempt to stay warm.

The time was fifteen minutes to six. Farm life started in earnest at six when the tractors carrying the workers on the trailers headed off to the fields.

"Robert you must be very careful today. Remember that you have to make sure you know where your companions are and they must know where you are at all times. You must look after Richard. Remember he's a city slicker and not used to handling guns like you and Simon are. Okay?"

Robert's father clambered up on his Massey Ferguson MF 35X Multi-power Diesel Tractor. There were only five of these in the country. The 35X Multi-Power was fitted with the up-rated 44.5 three cylinder diesel engine. Multi-Power was a new change-on-the-move system which had a hydraulic clutch controlled by a switch on the instrument panel giving a thirty percent increase or decrease of speed in each gear.

Robert's father was protective of his new tractor and consequently there was a tug of war going on between him and Herbert, the head tractor driver on the farm. Herbert longed to get his hands on the new acquisition, but after two months he was yet to drive it. He thought

17

he may have had a chance a few weeks ago when Robert's father was ill with a head cold, but his hopes were dashed when he refused to succumb to the illness.

"Ya dad. I will take care of Richard."

Robert looked painfully at his father. It was a repeat lecture of what his father had said over dinner last evening. It embarrassed Robert then and now he was doubly embarrassed as Simon stood next to him. Robert looked across at Richard and caught a glimpse of him smirking. He diverted his eyes back to his father hoping that was the end of the lecture.

It was. His father was instructing Herbert to crank the engine and as he did so, the tractor roared into life. In an instant his father had mentally moved from caring parent to farmer.

The farm workers clambered onto the trailers attached to the two tractors. The women with babies had them attached to their backs with folded cloths tied in a knot in the front. The men loaded up the farming utensils, long handled spades, pick axes and three pronged rakes. Several pots and tin containers were also stashed onto the trailers. They contained the ingredients for the morning and midday meals that were to be prepared in the fields.

The workers began singing as soon as the two tractors set off in convoy down the gravel road. The sound of the singing faded as the tractors disappeared around the corner. The mist was beginning to lift as the sun's rays brought warmth to the earth.

Robert, Richard and Simon set off at a sprint to the main farm house situated two hundred metres away.

"Morning small baass," said Wellington as the boys burst into the kitchen, his face beaming a welcome for Robert. "I will have food ready just now for you."

"Hello Wellington," said Robert puffing. "We will need to have a big breakfast today as we are going hunting."

The large kitchen was situated at the back of the substantial house. Light flooded through two big windows onto the bench top that ran the length of the wall. Shards of light bounced off the smoothly polished stone floor.

The three boys lingered near the back door entrance where the Glenwood K wood burning stove was situated. The heat emitted from the stove was welcome relief from the cold outside.

"The big baass told me that you will be hunting today with the other small baass and ... him." Wellington looked suspiciously at Simon. "He said you must be careful and ..."

"Ya I have already been told by the boss thank you Wellington," interjected Robert not wanting to receive yet another lecture on the topic of gun safety in front of his pal Richard, especially by the cook.

Whilst he waited for the eggs and bacon to cook, Wellington set two places at the long solid wooden table situated in the middle of the kitchen.

"We need three places thanks Wellington," informed Robert.

"Ow! He will have some sadza outside," barked Wellington giving Simon a filthy look of disapproval.

"No, he must have the same as what we have Wellington. Simon will eat with us here in the kitchen."

Robert met Wellington's glare of disapproval. The seventeen year old boy was facing off against the cook who, at this stage, was still well up on the jousting score between the two over a twelve year period. However, the odds of winning future jousts were now stacking in Robert's favour as he grew into his late teenage years.

Simon grinned, thinking on the balance of probabilities Robert would win the joust this time and consequently he would soon be eating bacon and eggs rather than sadza. Wellington deliberately avoided looking at Simon so as to avoid the smirk he knew would be on his face.

"The madam will not approve," retorted Wellington in an attempt to regain the high ground in this standoff. "The African workers are not allowed in the main house and must not eat in it."

It was in Wellington's interest to ensure the right social order was maintained within the farm society. Being the cook for the farm owner and his family entitled him to a privileged status in the workers compound. His hut was larger. He was issued with a crisp white uniform. He had tennis shoes to wear and commanded much respect from the household staff and most others in the workers compound. Simon was at the bottom of the ladder as far as Wellington was concerned. He was a gangly youth, the third son of his nemesis, Herbert. The on-going power struggle between Wellington and Herbert remained unresolved with both staying misaligned on the question of whether the chief tractor driver held equal status as the main household cook. Robert's father wisely avoided adjudication in the matter.

"Well the madam is not here. She is in Salisbury. The boss is out in the fields and so I am in charge. And I say the three of us will eat breakfast here in the kitchen."

Wellington set a third place muttering his disapproval to himself loud enough so that the others could hear. He reached over to pick up two more eggs and cracked them open, pouring the contents in to the pan. He sliced off two rashers of bacon and threw them into the other pan. He manhandled the two pans roughly in an attempt to show his disquiet at the instruction Robert had given.

When the food was ready the three youths sat down and tucked into the breakfast of eggs, bacon, tomato and slices of fried potato. Toast followed with butter and an assortment of jams before strong coffee, mostly with Chicory in it, was served. All the while Wellington stewed in the background audibly muttering disapproval to himself.

Once they finished ravishing their breakfast, the boys filed out of the kitchen making their way to the study. A Kudu skin on the wood floor, a trophy from a safari his father had undertaken many years ago, complemented the large twisted horns from the animal that were mounted on a polished teak backing hanging above the stone fireplace. A large heavy set desk that faced the room was prominently placed in front of windows that overlooked the front gardens. It was covered with papers, farm magazines and books such that its Oak top was invisible.

Earlier that morning Robert's father had taken three .22 guns and a box of ammunition out of the metal gun cabinet which was bolted onto the wall next to a row of dark wood book shelves. Rob gave Richard and Simon their rifles before picking up his own rifle and the ammunition box.

"Okay, let's get going," announced Rob.

The sun shone on the silver 1961 Triumph 3TA motorcycle that stood proudly in the front driveway. It had been modified to attach a sidecar to it. The motorbike with its 350cc engine, which could pick up considerable speed, was Rob's pride and joy. He spent endless hours in the school holidays and weekends riding it along the sandy roads around the district. He would then spend even more time polishing it afterwards.

"I'll drive. Ric can go in the side car and Simon on the back with me."

Richard longed to have a go at driving it but so far Rob had not relented. Richard decided not to ask again. He did not want to be declined in front of Simon. Simon never asked, but he did enjoy riding as a passenger, especially to show off to the farm workers and other children. Once he was so involved in waving to the farm workers he fell off backwards landing unceremoniously in a cloud of dust. It caused much hilarity in the farm compound which took many months for the novelty of that event to fade.

The guns were stashed in the side car with Richard along with a bag that contained drinks and some homemade biscuits that Wellington had prepared and left on the motorbike. Rob kicked started the motor which roared into life as a deep throbbing sound and they set off towards the western part of the farm leaving a dust cloud as they went.

After ten minutes Rob turned off the main farm road onto a secondary track that led past a freshly ploughed field before veering off into an elevated wooded area. This was the location where Rob decided to leave the motorbike before setting off on foot to track down their prey. Alighting from the motorbike they each took their weapon and loaded them. Excitement built up quickly between the three boys as the reality that the hunt was about to commence took hold.

"Okay, that's where we must head off towards; that kopje over there."

Rob was clearly in charge. He pointed towards a rocky outcrop that was covered with small trees and shrubs located less than half a kilometre away. The boys stood on the edge of a ridge looking over a sweeping shallow valley. Between them and the kopje was mildly undulating ground covered with waist high grasses with the occasional clump of young trees.

"Dad said that the pigs will be resting up at that kopje. He says there are about six of them. One is a big bull."

"So how are we going to find them in that grass?" queried Richard.

"Dad says they have a nest or something that is up against a sheer rock."

He took the binoculars out of their leather case.

"Look to the left of the gomo …. there, can you see a big rock face?"

He passed the binoculars to Richard who scanned the area while adjusting the focus.

"Okay. I see it. So what do we do?"

Richard passed the binoculars to Simon.

"We will walk in single file …. quietly …. towards the gomo and when we get to a hundred metres from it we will fan out. In a line."

Rob looked across to see Simon struggling to find the target. He went over to Simon and took the binoculars off him. Looking through the binoculars he could see that the focus was out so he adjusted it before giving them back to Simon. He then stood behind him to help him with the direction.

"Can you see it now?" he asked.

"Yes, I can see it."

Simon passed the field glasses back to Rob.

"So when we are a hundred metres from it we will fan out. Okay? Simon you go left and Richard you go right. I will take the centre and give instructions." He paused and then after thinking he added. "We need call signs."

"What is call sign?" queried Simon.

"It's a name we will use when we are in the hunt."

"But my name is Simon. You know that, Rob."

"Yes I know but ..." Rob looked exasperated. " .... when we are in a hunt we need different names. So we can know who's who."

Simon looked unconvinced.

"I'll be called ...." He searched for a title. "Hmmm ... I'll be called Combat Leader. You are Combat One Richard and you're Combat Two Simon."

"Comat Two Simon?" queried Simon.

"No! No Simon, it's Combat. Combat Two."

Simon looked unconvinced.

"I am Combat One. Fine. Okay let's get going already," said Richard impatient to get the hunt underway.

"All right ... but first let's understand that we must not make a noise and also we must know where each one is at all times. So keep looking left and right? I'll give the instructions. Dad will kill me if one of us kills one of us."

"If we have to stay quiet then how are we going to get your instructions Rob?" asked Richard.

"Combat Leader!"

"What?"

"I'm Combat Leader. Not Rob from now on. We have to get that right. Okay?"

"Okay. Okay. Enough already."

"Hand signals. I'll give hand signals and I will only speak when I have to and when I do speak you have to reply, but only like 'yes Combat Leader' or 'no Combat Leader'. We must not have conversations. Okay?"

Richard nodded his acceptance. Simon shrugged his shoulders remaining unconvinced.

They set off in single file through the grass, guns at the ready. Rob was in the lead and every so often he would stop and hold his left hand up to halt those behind him. He would scan ahead and listen, then move forward signalling with his hand to his companions to

24

follow. When Rob was about a hundred metres from the kopje he saw a small anthill off to his right. He signalled the others to stop and stay. He moved to the anthill and scampered up the small mound. Once on top of it he took out the field glasses and looked intently through them.

Where are the damn pigs, he wondered. *There's the rock face where dad said their hide would be. So if I look down .... ah there they are.*

Rob rushed over to his two friends. He was grinning and excited.

"I spotted them. The damn pigs. They are where dad said they would be. I dunno how many there are but I saw them moving about by that rock," he said in a whisper.

"This is good. Are we going now to shoot them?" asked Simon keen to take a pig back to the workers compound this evening to show them his prowess as a hunter.

"Yes Combat Two. We will now split up to move in. Combat One that way to my right and Combat Two over there to my left."

Simon looked at Rob blankly until he recalled he was Combat Two.

"Geee wiz we are going to shoot them," reaffirmed Richard to himself.

Other than a few doves that he had shot with a pellet gun in the past he had never actually shot at another animal before. When Rob had said they would be going hunting for pigs a few days ago he wondered how that would play out and how he would feel about it. Rob had said the pigs wrought havoc with the maize crops and so they had to be culled. Rob's father planned to go out and shoot the pigs but Robert had persuaded his father to let him and his friends do it. Rob was a good marksman having accompanied his father many times

25

on similar hunting expeditions which had tilted his father's decision in his favour.

"Ya, now shush. Go thirty metres then stop and look to see what my hand instruction is. Keep in eye contact. Move together and don't get ahead of the line. Don't shoot towards a person okay?"

They split up to form a line and once in position they all moved forward cautiously after Combat Leader signalled with his hand above his head to advance. Time passed slowly as the three boys inched forward but after twenty five metres Combat One was ahead by ten metres.

Damn. Ric is getting ahead of us. I had better tell him to wait up, but… bugger it he's not looking around to see where we are as I told him to do. How do I catch his attention?

Combat Leader gave a whistle that he tried to make sound like a bird in the hope it would attract Combat One's attention. It did not sound like any bird that lived in Africa. Combat One carried on regardless. By the way he was moving forward with the gun at the ready to fire, his head bent forward and chin thrust out, it was obvious to Combat Leader that he had become transfixed on what was in front of him and oblivious of anything else.

"Combat One," Combat Leader called out in a whisper.

Combat Two heard him and looked across to see.

"Yes Comat Lead," called out Combat Two.

Jesus, why is Simon calling out?

"Shush," Combat Leader put his left index finger to his mouth indicating to Combat Two to keep quiet.

Combat Two acknowledged. But when Combat Leader looked back he saw that Combat One was more than twenty paces ahead and still moving in.

Damn. Richard is screwing this up. He's too far ahead. Why doesn't he look around? Stupid prick.

Combat Leader picked up a small rock and threw it at Combat One. It landed short of him but was enough to give him a start, snapping him out of his transfixion. He swung around to his left, as did his rifle.

Shit! He's pointing the bloody gun at me.

Combat Leader made a snap decision. That of self-preservation over that of covertly approaching the pig hide. He broke silence and shouted.

"Don't shoot! I threw a rock."

Richard looked up and across to where Rob was. He was hyped up having been intently focused on what was ahead of him.

"Don't shoot. It's not the pigs," shouted Rob once again.

"Okay. Why the hell did you throw the bloody rock then?"

"Because you are too far ahead man. Jesus. You are supposed to stay in line Ric. Ah .... Combat One. Now you've buggered it up," said Rob aggressively.

He was right. The squealing from the pigs soon became audible followed by the sound of hooves on the ground.

"Rob, they come," shouted Simon.

Thirty metres ahead of him and to his right the long grass moved as a pig rushed through to make its escape.

"They come towards us," he added.

Simon lifted his rifle to his right shoulder, closed his left eye and pointed the barrel towards where the grass was moving ahead of him. His heart pounded. He could not see the pig. He squeezed the trigger.

Thew!

He fired the shot into the waist high grass. He quickly reloaded the gun.

Richard saw the movement before Rob did. Distracted by the shot Simon had let off Rob was not concentrating. The grass parted as the pig ran at speed towards Rob. Richard lifted his rifle towards the movement and fired a shot.

Hearing the shot go off to his right Rob swung round to see Ric pointing his gun towards him.

"Jesus Ric! I said don't bloody shoot. You are shooting towards us," yelled Combat Leader.

It was then that he heard it, a laboured grunting sound. The grass parted ahead of him as a pig, a big female, burst out. Rob dived left and the pig turned slightly to its left catching Rob with its shoulder. It vanished into the long grass as quickly as it had appeared.

Thew!

Scrambling to his feet Rob looked around to see Simon shooting his rifle away to his left. Looking right he saw Richard running towards him.

"Are you okay Rob?" queried Richard anxiously. "Did the pig get you?"

"Jesus you nearly shot me. I told you not to shoot at me. Fuck it!"

"I didn't shoot at you. I shot at the pig coming at you. I tried to kill it before it whacked you," Richard replied in his defence.

"I have killed the pig," yelled Simon. "A big fat pig."

Suspending their spat, the two boys ran to where Simon was. He was dancing around in circles holding his gun above his head. At his feet was a large bull pig. Dead with a bullet hole above its one eye. A perfect head shot dropping it stone dead instantly. Elated Rob and Richard both hugged Simon who beamed with a grin from ear to ear. This was truly a significant kill for them. Rob was relieved as this turned their hunting expedition from as sad debacle into a success.

"How are we going to get this back to the farm house? We can't even pick it up between us, can we?" queried Richard.

"Good point," responded Rob. "Hmmm .... I had not thought about that."

They stood around the carcass and pondered the problem for a while.

"I tell you what. I'll go back on the bike to where dad is working the field and they can bring the tractor and trailer to load it up and take it to the compound." Patting Simon on the back he added. "The workers can have a feast thanks to old Simon here."

Simon nodded his approval as he contemplated how he would leverage his prowess when the story was told to the others in the compound. This would improve his standing generally as it would the relationship with a particular young teenage girl he fancied. This was a milestone event to be milked for all its worth.

The boys left the dead pig to make their way back to the motorbike and their refreshments. They quenched their thirst and devoured the biscuits before Rob set off on the bike to find his father.

Finding a tree to sit under to shield them from the hot sun Simon and Richard chatted together about farm life and school. Simon asked about Richard's schooling at Prince Edward Boys High School. He was interested to see if Richard was taught different subjects to those he was taught at his school. Simon attended the local district school run by the Department of Education. Their subjects differed and Simon was relieved to learn he was not being subjected to mathematics and physics, or having to learn another European language. The conversation meandered along and eventually got onto girls. A topical subject for adolescent boys, Richard who was awkward around girls particularly wanted to hear about the young girl Simon fancied pressing him to find out about 'how far' they had gone. He had manoeuvred Simon to a point of tell all when he spotted movement in the field off to the left of where the dead pig was.

"Hey what's that? Where are the field glasses?"

Richard got up and looked around for the glasses. They were not to be found.

"Rob must have taken them with him. Do you see .... there?" he queried.

"It's a Jackal. They are looking for the dead pig."

"Well we will have to stop them, Simon. Otherwise they will start eating it."

Simon had got up to fetch his rifle.

"I think there is more than one over there. I thought I saw two Simon."

Simon signalled to Richard to follow as he made his way down the ridge and towards where the animals were.

"Hey once we get into the grass we will not be able to see them."

"They are in the shorter grass over that way. I will show you how to hunt these dogs. Come. But we must not talk loud or they will run away."

"That's what we want isn't it? To chase them away?"

"No we must shoot them. They are bad. They attack the young cattle."

Richard accepted this view and followed Simon through the grass. Checking their weapons as they went to make sure they were loaded it was not long before they emerged from the waist height grass to where the grass was knee high.

Damn. Just as I thought. We still can't see them.

Simon came up close to Richard and whispered into his left ear.

"You must do your whistle when I say so."

Richard looked puzzled. Seeing his expression he added.

"I will show you tricks. When I say, then you whistle."

Richard had mastered a sharp whistle by putting two figures in his mouth up against his tongue. Simon moved off a few paces to his left to where the ground was slightly higher. He raised his rifle and pointed it in the general direction where they both thought the Jackals were.

"Now whistle," he said.

Richard put his finger and thumb together at his mouth and blew. A shrill whistle pierced the silence.

Two heads popped up out of the grass about forty metres away. Simon swivelled his rifle towards them before pulling the trigger. Both heads disappeared once the shot rang out.

"Jesus that's amazing," exclaimed Richard. "They looked to see what the whistle was. Let's do it again. Are you ready to try shooting again?"

"They will not look again. This trick works one time," said Simon. "We must go to see if one of the dogs was killed."

Ha not likely, thought Richard as he followed Simon.

"Look!" exclaimed Simon excitedly.

Lying in the grass was a dead Jackal. Shot in the head and a meter beyond that was another animal lying prostrate. It was a pig.

"How about that?" said Ric stunned that Simon had hit the Jackal. It seemed impossible he could have done that.

31

How the hell did he shoot the Jackal and the pig with the same bullet?

"Is the pig dead?" he asked Simon.

Simon gave the pig a nudge with his rifle, standing cautiously ready to bolt if it got up. Nothing moved. He moved closer and saw blood in its mid-section. A bullet had hit it damaging its vital organs before it fell.

"Yes the pig is dead also. It must be one that I shot at after I killed the big bull one. I am a great hunter."

The two boys hugged each other in celebration. In the distance they heard the sound of a tractor coming towards them.

***

Wellington proudly entered the dining room amply filling a white chef suit with an ill-fitting white cap balancing on his mostly bald head. He carried a serving platter stacked with a side of beef, roast potatoes, carrots, beans and cauliflower.

"Ah Wellington that looks terrific I must say," said Robert's father who sat at the head of the dining table.

Rob sat to the right of his father and across from him sat Richard. Wellington placed the serving platter in front of Rob's father and promptly left the room to fetch the condiments and gravy. The meal was served up by Rob's father onto bone china plates made in the UK. The boys were famished and as soon as the plates were passed to them they tucked in.

"Slowly boys. Snouts in the trough and all that. Just because your mother is not here Rob does not mean dining table decorum disappears."

The boys slowed down marginally but ate without conversation. Second helpings were dished out, just as large as the first had been.

"So young hunters, you bagged two pigs and a Jackal. That was terrific indeed." Robert's father broke the silence having waited until the boys were well nourished. "But you say all kills were down to young Simon. How astounding."

"It's only because Richard didn't listen and nearly shot me that I was distracted. Otherwise I would have shot the pig coming towards me," retorted Robert carefully avoiding the glare from Richard.

"You will have a nasty bruise on your leg from where the pig bumped you son."

The point of impact was swollen and turning a bluish colour.

"I did not nearly shoot you, Robert," protested Richard in his own defence. "I shot at the pig rushing towards you because I thought it was going to whack you. It did anyway," he added with satisfaction. "I am sure the one we found later with the Jackal is the one I shot. It had a bullet wound on its left side exactly where I shot at it."

"It can't have been. The pig near the Jackal was far too far away from where we were to be the same one. No, the two pigs were bagged by Simon. And the Jackal."

Rob preferred to attribute the kills to Simon rather than concede that Richard accounted for one while he himself shot nothing. At least he would not have to put up with Richard telling all his mates about it at school next week. With both boys not having a kill attributed to either of them there would be no bragging rites. At least that is how Rob reasoned it.

"It was the one I shot, I know it and besides I helped Simon kill the Jackal."

"Ya by a whistle ...."

"Okay you two. It is best that you both agree to disagree on this. There is no way we can prove it either way. Let's have our pudding shall we."

Rob's father had been subjected to the bickering between the two boys for several hours and was tired of it. He picked up the bell and rang it. Instantaneously Wellington appeared and immediately started clearing the dishes away ahead of bringing in the dessert.

"Robert I spoke with your mother before dinner. She asked me to tell you to make sure that tomorrow you pack up all your school kit. She said she put all the school kit you need on the chest in your bedroom. I will take you and Richard to Salisbury tomorrow after lunch. We will drop Richard off at his home then I will take you to the school. Senior boarders have to check in by five is that right?"

"Ya," said Rob sadly.

He was not looking forward to going back to boarding school. The school holidays had been fun. School was tedious with its rules and regulations. His 'M' Level exams were coming up at the end of the year and these were important examinations. He preferred his sport to his academic studies.

"Why is Mum staying with Aunty Mary anyway?"

"Your Uncle Bill has been called up by the Police Reserve and Aunt Mary did not want to be alone. It's difficult time right now. The Africans are being stirred up by the Unions and have started rioting in the African townships. Quite a few have been killed in the riots. It's all got quite political and violent actually and so the Police have called up the Reservists to restore order. Bill is a Police Reservist and has gone to the townships."

"What are the Africans rioting about?" asked Richard.

34

"It's complicated and I am not entirely sure myself. But I think it's got to do with the political unrest in Northern Rhodesia where the nationalist movement are pushing for the independence of Northern Rhodesia from Britain. It's stirred up political opportunism with some Africans here in Southern Rhodesia. The African nationalists here are stirring it up and.... well some Africans like the idea of setting fire to buildings and killing others from different tribes. So it's quite easy to get unrest in the townships going. It is all rather silly really if you ask me. What do you think Wellington?"

Rob's father had noticed that he had lingered to listen to the conversation.

"It is very difficult baass. The tootsies make big trouble. It is not good. Many people are hurt in the townships. My brother is in Harare Township and says it is very, very bad. The tootsies are steeling everything and killing Ndebele. This is not good time baass."

Rob's father saw the sadness in Wellington's face. He was unaware of the emotion this topic would generate within Wellington who was Ndebele. He decided to change the subject.

"So Wellington .... all of you will be feasting well in the compound on pig. I believe the women are roasting them on spits tonight."

"Yes Baass. The women are cooking the pigs. There will be much beer also."

"Just as well tomorrow is Sunday then. A day of rest to get over sore heads. Simon will be a hero now I suspect. His shooting ability was outstanding."

Rob's father remained impressed with how quickly Simon had learned to shoot. Wellington smiled a wry smile. He suspected Simon's ego would torment him for longer than he ever hoped.

CHAPTER FOUR

September 1963

He was fourteen when it happened. And it was to have a profound long term impact on his life which would dramatically change the lives of many others, albeit they were not to know it then.

It began when he was invited to visit the priest's house one Saturday. The house was merely a square brick building with white washed painted walls and a rusting tin roof situated adjacent to the Mission school. Both buildings, plus the other one that housed the nuns who taught at the school, were unspectacular. A fence made from wire strands attached to crudely sawn timber stakes surrounded the houses in an unsuccessful attempt to keep the goats from eating the vegetable garden, while a small wall made from stones and inadequate mortar bordered the school grounds.

Bhekizizwe approached this day with excited anticipation for he was to meet the Bishop from South Africa. The nuns had told him that it was a great honour to be specially selected to meet the Bishop. They had spent many hours grooming him for this day.

Finding it difficult to sleep, Bhekizizwe woke very early to get dressed in his best clothes and his new shoes that his father recently bought from the city. His mother ensured he washed himself the evening before and she had crudely trimmed his curly hair as they sat around the cooking fires.

Setting off well ahead of time on his long walk from the kraal to the Mission school so as to ensure he would not be late, he imagined what the experience would be like. He pictured a kindly, soft spoken man, knowledgeable on all subjects who would be benevolent and graceful. He anticipated engaging the Bishop in a conversation where he would demonstrate his intellectual understanding of many issues.

Bhekizizwe enjoyed his schooling at the Mission, proving to be a diligent student, always showing a keenness to learn more. The nuns had counselled him how he could progress his study further by going to a Catholic school in Bulawayo. Arrangements were yet to be made for the required application to the Church authorities, but they were pretty certain that he would get acceptance based on his academic standing. The nuns intimated to him that this meeting with the Bishop was a very important step in this process of him progressing to higher education next year.

Bhekizizwe arrived at the Mission school to be greeted warmly by three young girls. They were sweeping the gravel area around the school with brushes that were crafted from straw tied together and attached to wooden pole by twine. They jostled to engage him in conversation, each hoping to make an impression. The attention being plied by the young girls was neither unexpected nor unwelcomed as he was a strong, good looking boy. He played along to pass the time.

When he thought it time for his meeting with the Bishop he left the girls giggling together. Tentatively knocking on the front door of the priest's house, he nervously waited for it to be answered. The priest opened the door and greeted Bhekizizwe by using his European name. The priest asked Pieter to wait outside explaining that he would come to fetch him in a short while.

Pieter elected to sit under an old tree situated close to the house to get some relief from the sun. He noticed the grey coloured Austin Cambridge parked next to the house and thought it probably was the car of the important person he was to meet.

"Pieter," called the priest, standing at the front door of his house. "Pieter, come now."

The priest walked towards him. His cassock, which scraped along the ground, had a dirty brown skirt to it, hiding his sandalled feet. His Collarino looked as if it had seen better days. Pieter looked closely at the priest noticing that his pronounced stoop meant he shuffled which made him look far older than he actually was. The sun's rays on his narrow face and receding black hair accentuated the furrows on his forehead.

"I want to introduce you now to a big boss from Johannesburg. I have told you he is very important. When I ask you to tell the big boss if you like it here at this school I want you to tell him how well you are taught here at the Mission school. Okay?"

Pieter nodded his agreement. It was what the nuns had explained to him previously.

"So understand this Pieter, when I ask you if you like the school what will you say?"

The priest's face was very close to Pieter's so he could smell the lingering stale tobacco scent on his breath.

"I am to say that the teaching here is very good and that I have learned much."

"Excellent! Very good Pieter. Now only speak if you are asked to. Do you understand this? We will go in now to see the big boss of the Church and you will behave well. Yes?"

The priest looked for assurance which Pieter gave him with another cautious nod.

The priest, followed by Pieter, entered the room where two people sat. One was dressed in a purple robe. His blue eyes set close together in his square face were framed with metal rimmed glasses. The rings on

38

many of his fingers were ornate, if not gaudy. The other younger man was wearing a cream coloured safari suit. He held a file in his hand that was headed '*Ministry of Education*." He was a Government person.

Although there were unoccupied seats in the lounge room the priest told Pieter to sit on the floor in front of the two men. The man in the purple robe sat on a three seat couch and the other man on a chair to his left. The priest sat down on a stool next to Pieter.

Pieter listened to the man in purple speak about God, the Church and its mission. When he had finished he asked Pieter some bland questions which Pieter answered quickly. He sensed that the Bishop was not interested in hearing the reply. The man in purple smiled a lot while the other man did not. The questions and dialogue soon dried up and the priest told Pieter to leave.

He left the house disappointed with the experience which was nowhere near what he had thought it would be. Dragging his feet he went a short distance from the house before realising he had left his small bag with several pennies in it on the floor in the lounge. He had planned to visit the local store down the road from the priest's house to buy a Pepsi before returning to his kraal. He hesitated for a moment pondering if he should disturb the important people, but he decided that the need to buy a Pepsi outweighed the chance of getting told off by the priest, so he returned. The front door was open and without thinking he stepped inside. Realising he had not waited to be invited back in the house, he stood in the short hallway thinking about his next move.

"They are natives Excellency," said the priest. "We try to treat them with grace and teach them about being civilised, but it's an uphill battle."

"That young native who you just brought in, what's his name…?" The Bishop searched for the name.

"Pieter," responded the priest.

"Ah yes Pieter. Well he seemed to be ... how can one put it? He was less native than most. He was polite and you appear to have taught him manners and respect for the Church. He must be getting some benefit from our Mission surely? Tell me has he truly converted?"

"Ja, I like to think he has converted. At least he appears to have, but Excellency, these natives are not honest and they are entrenched with their witch doctor doctrines and tribal spirits. I have made some in-road while I have been at this Mission, but again I implore you that I would be used for the betterment of the Church if I was reassigned to a school in the city back in South Africa where I can teach our white children. They have more intelligence. I can make more progress for the Church there than I could ever do here."

The Bishop frowned holding the folds of skin of his chin between his fingers. He turned to the Government official.

"What is your assessment of the progress here at this Mission Mr. Brown?"

"The Church has made a valuable contribution here and the Ministry of Education certainly appreciates this contribution. We encourage that the Church persists with this Mission school and not reduce its presence."

The priest glared at him. Reassignment to a city school back in his home land of South Africa and away from what he saw was purgatory in the wild bush was the desired outcome.

"The nuns can remain Excellency," interjected the priest who felt his argument was waning. "They do a good job and ... and they are better equipped to deal with the frustrations of having to teach basic knowledge to dim-witted savages who are not long out of the trees."

"The Church does not subscribe to the Darwinian theory of evolution, but the point is taken and well noted," said the Bishop.

The laughter from the three men cut through Bhekizizwe as he stood in the hallway. Tears wheeled up in his eyes and ran down his cheeks leaving trails where the moisture marked the dust on his face. He turned and bolted from the house. He ran until he was exhausted, crashing onto the ground next to the sandy path that led back to his kraal. He lay there a long time weeping loudly.

He did eventually re-attend the Mission school, but only after a period of weeks where he chose to stay away so he could sit under the old Masasa tree to reflect on what he had heard. Looking at the world around him very differently, he decided that the teachings on religion were of no use to him. Rather he decided to fill the void in his brain left from expelling his religious knowledge with other information which he planned to use to advance himself in what he progressively saw as a hypocritical and imperfect world.

He learned to cunningly mask his true beliefs from the nuns and the priest.

CHAPTER FIVE

April 1966

"Chimurenga!" shouted Vhukile in Shona, the native tongue of the recruits, as he punched the air enthusiastically with his new Soviet AK 47.

"Chimurenga! Chimurenga! Chimurenga!" chanted the forty seven Guerrillas assembled in a bush clearing.

"Comrades your training has lead us to this day. Our destiny is to take back the land that the settlers stole from our forefathers. Our destiny is to free the masses from the heavy chains of oppression they carry. Today you become heroes when you enter the land that rightly belongs to us to kill the settlers."

Of the forty seven men assembled, twelve had recently been trained at the Nanking Military College situated near Peking in Communist China. The others received their less intense training in a make shift camp to the east of Lusaka in Zambia. The weapons they carried were a motley mixture of PPSH sub machine guns, Sten guns and Tokarev pistols supplied by the Chinese. Packed in green canvas back packs were explosives and twenty land mines.

"My eternal sorrow is that I will not come with you on this day comrades. I hold much sadness in my heart that I cannot share your glory. I must stay here and train other comrades to follow you."

Vhukile had been a willing recruit to the liberation cause when he first attended a rally in the African township of Harare. He joined the Zimbabwe African National Union the next day. ZANU was led by Ndabaningi Sithole, an ordained Methodist minister turned nationalist. Vhukile was immediately impressed with the orator, Sithole, being attracted to the message to overthrow of the minority white dominated government in Southern Rhodesia and to replace it with black Zimbabwean rule.

Born of a peasant farmer, Vhukile had no formal education, having been recruited at a very young age to assist with the chores around the kraal and then, at the age of seven, to work the fields and herd the goats. The conditions were harsh with many droughts causing severe food shortages. Three of his siblings had perished from disease by the time he was fifteen, the age when he left the land to find work in the city.

After violent rioting across the country left hundreds dead, the Rhodesian Government banned ZANU, arrested and jailed its leadership. Sithole was caught in the Police drag net. Vhukile, a rising star in the ranks of ZANU, was in China when the leadership was arrested. Upon hearing the news, he returned to Zambia to join with other ZANU members to continue the liberation struggle from exile.

The declaration of unilateral independence from Britain announced by Prime Minister Ian Smith on 11th November 1965 stirred a glimmer of hope for Vhukile that the political impasse with Southern Rhodesia would crystallise and that the economic sanctions imposed by the United Nations on the land-locked country would quickly bring the end to the white minority government. Vhukile and his ZANU comrades anticipated that Britain would take decisive action and invade Southern Rhodesia. The strategy adopted by those ZANU leaders in exile was to let Britain do the heavy lifting to terminate the Rhodesian Government. ZANU would then step in to fill the political void.

But as days turned to months after the declaration of independence, it became obvious that Britain was not going to take up arms against Southern Rhodesia. The nationalists, being impatient for political advantage, revised their strategy to take the fight up to the Rhodesians themselves through armed struggle. They planned to leverage off the 'Cold War' dynamics by engaging their communist friends in Peking and Moscow to help them.

Vhukile planned this first military insurgency into Rhodesia. He assessed the probability as low that all the guerrillas launching the insurgency raid would all return back to Zambia. The safe return of the insurgents was not the main priority. He saw this insurgency operation as a tactical step to put a mark on who would lead the liberation war amongst the nationalists, while being a shot across the bow of the Southern Rhodesian Government.

Vhukile's plan was for the guerrillas to split into two groups once across the Zambezi River and into Southern Rhodesia. One group would move east towards Umtali, a town on the border with Portuguese controlled Mozambique, where they would blow up the pipeline that fed oil to Southern Rhodesia from the sea port of Beira. The Southern Rhodesian economy was dependent on this pipeline for its total oil supply. That group of guerrillas would also kill white settler farmers in the Eastern Highlands before making their way back to Zambia along the border with Mozambique.

The second group of guerrillas was designated to infiltrate tribal trust lands south of Fort Victoria, a town in the southern part of the country. Their prime objective was to recruit fresh manpower and to assist them to exit Rhodesia, via Botswana, back into Zambia so they could undergo military training.

"Comrades it is time for you to depart on your historic mission. Chimurenga! Chimurenga! Chimurenga!"

The forty seven ZANLA guerrillas made their way the short distance to the point on the Zambezi River where the crossing was done without incident using small inflatable boats. Once in Southern Rhodesia they only moved in the late afternoon and early mornings or at night when there was a moon to give some light. Uncertain what level of local support they could expect from Africans inside Southern Rhodesia they deliberately set out to avoid detection.

Unbeknown to Vhukile, the Southern Rhodesian Special Branch had infiltrated a 'mole' in the group. From the moment the insurgents crossed into Southern Rhodesia a two man SAS team tracked them.

After a week into their mission seven of the comrades spontaneously decided one moon lit evening to blow up electricity pylons they had stumbled across the afternoon before. These electricity pylons took power from the Kariba dam, situated on the Zambezi River between Southern Rhodesia and Zambia, to Salisbury, the capital of Southern Rhodesia.

"This will stop the lights and put fear into the settlers," said the one comrade whose idea it was.

Without a clear command structure the insurgents debated this plan for over an hour remaining divided on its merits. Some of the insurgents believed this unexpected action would only alert the Police to their presence. Others felt restless believing it was time to do something. Regardless of the objections by the majority, the splinter group set off on their mission.

They stumbled though the bush for several hours in single file before they came upon the pylons where they hurriedly packed explosives at its concrete base before setting the fuses and fleeing the scene. Nothing happened. The explosives failed to detonate. The insurgents hesitated. To go back to see what had occurred may mean they get blown up, but then to return to reset the explosives may mean a successful mission. The early morning light creeping over the horizon settled the inconclusive debate. All seven insurgents, fearing they could be caught in the open when the sun came up, abandoned the plan and set off at a jog to return to where they left their comrades. The sun was edging into the morning sky when they arrived exhausted, to discover that the larger group were not where they had left them.

The larger group of insurgents not wishing to be caught in the vicinity of any explosion which they knew was bound to bring the Police to the area had elected to move away. They set off that evening making their way south eastwards to put plenty of distance between them and the explosion.

The seven insurgents found themselves on their own. The initial plans for this mission were now in tatters. The SAS who had tracked these seven insurgents notified the Police about the explosives. The Army were told and they removed them the next day.

The Police Commander monitoring the insurgency situation decided it was time to arrest the seven terrorists. The Air Force tasked to assist the Police deployed three helicopters to Sinoia, a provincial town that was close to where the SAS identified the insurgents were in hiding. Police Reservists, called up to swell the ranks of regular Police were transported to the vicinity in Army Bedford trucks.

The Superintendent disseminated the quickly formulated plan for the arrest of these seven terrorists to his men. Three distinct Police groups were assembled with one manning a stop line along the main Sinoia to Salisbury road. The second group was tasked to sweep in towards where the terrorists were camped while the third group would act as a stop line along a river that ran parallel to the road. The trap anticipated to catch the terrorists in the middle.

"Let's get this show on the road chaps," announced the Police Superintendent speaking into his radio handset. "The helicopter will fly at six thousand feet to observe the area and report information to me on the ground. I will direct the entire operation from the ops Land Rover."

A helicopter lifted off with its two man crew to make its way towards the early morning sun, the pilot following the coordinates supplied by the SAS. The other two helicopters remained on standby.

"Task Group One, please confirm the stop line on the main road is in place," asked the Superintendent.

"Confirmed Super," was an excited reply.

"Good show chaps. Please confirm the stop line at the river end is in place."

"We're in place Superintendent."

"Right then. Task Group Three. Start your advance. Confirm that."

"Righty oh. Task Group Three on the move."

With that confirmed the line of Police regulars and Reservists edged forward across the rough, lightly treed ground.

"Task Group Leader, this is Air Force One."

The radio crackled startling the Superintendent.

"Hello Air Force One. This is the Task Force Leader. Over."

"Ya, we have visual on the CT's," informed the chopper pilot. "I think we have been clocked. They are on the move. Moving south, south west."

Bugger that. This means a revision to the plan. Where's the bloody map.

The Superintendent fumbled to open the maps on the bonnet of the Land Rover. He reviewed his options.

47

"Air Force One, this is Task Force Leader. We will need the other helicopters to assist redeployment of my men. Please get them over here pronto. I will give directives on where I want them moved to in a tic."

The two helicopters soon arrived to redeploy some of the Police Reservists a kilometre further west before they withdrew a short distance. Air Force One remained as the operation observation platform to feed intel on the movement of the terrorists to the Superintendent. The pilot completed a wide sweep around the operational area when he observed a dangerous situation emerging.

"Task Leader. AF One. There's a problem. Your one group sweeping north is walking right into the group we've deployed."

The Police wore dark blue overalls. The terrorists wore black clothes. Dark blue and black was virtually indistinguishable and the probability the Reservists would see the other Police as terrorists was high.

Recognising the problem immediately and realising the mistake, the Superintendent sent urgent messages over the radio to the commander of the sweep line. Not all the Police had radios and with the sweep line over two hundred metres long it was difficult to get any messages relayed quickly.

Watching with increasing anxiety as the potential catastrophe unfolded the pilot made the decision to break his distance and he brought the chopper in to hover above the Reservists. The gunner leant out gesticulating as best he could to alert those on the ground of the impending danger. With the chopper above them, the downdraft from its rotors swirling dust and loose vegetation all over the place, the Reservists became distracted and confused. It looked like a fiasco and it was.

Suddenly a terrorist broke cover from a clump of trees and ran into flat grassland. He started firing at the helicopter. The pilot saw small puffs of smoke exiting his weapon. Nothing hit as the pilot shifted the helicopter sideways before taking the aircraft into a wide circle.

"We have contact. We have contact!" shouted the pilot over the radio. "AF Two and Three. Need you here to assist pronto."

"Roger that," came back a laconic reply.

The terrorist paused to reload his weapon before continuing to fire at the helicopter while it flew in a large circle around him. Within a minute the second chopper came in low behind the terrorist. The pilot swivelled port to give his gunner a field of vision. The gunner opened up with the 7.62mm MAG machine gun, but its crude mounting with no sighting mechanism impeded accuracy. Bullets ripped into the grass all around the terrorist as the gunner adjusted his firing line after observing where the tracer rounds hit. Realising he was under fire, the terrorist bolted. He managed six large strides before bullets ripped into his back. The flesh of his back was shredded and he went down dead.

As the noise from the contact abated, Police Reservists were taken aback when another terrorist came bounding out of the long grass towards them, his eyes wide open and his weapon held in his left hand by its leather strap. The comrade tried to stop when he saw the line of Police ahead of him, but his momentum carried him forward long enough for a policeman to pull the trigger of his shotgun. The blast hit him in the chest stopping him in mid stride. He fell backwards, his shirt blood stained. The Police did not stop to see if he was dead. The body had a hole it its chest and the conclusion was obvious. The helicopters moved away so as not to complicate the situation on the ground.

When the Police Reservists arrived at the initial contact zone two terrorists rose from their cover behind a large rotting tree trunk with the intent to engage in a gun battle. They were both shot dead in a hail of bullets. Then two other terrorists who were using a large earth ant hill for cover engaged the Reservists. One discharged his revolver firing towards the Reservists while the other attempted to throw a hand grenade. As he swung his arm above his head to throw the grenade, he was shot in the shoulder. The grenade dropped at his feet before exploding, killing him and his companion.

The seventh terrorist broke his cover from behind a tree in an attempt to flee towards the east but was cut down by rifle shots before he had taken five strides.

***

"Well done chaps," said the Police Superintendent. "Fine job done to get these bastards. This marks the first kill of CT's."

Standing on the back of a Police Land Rover he looked out over his men gathered around him. Lying off to one side in the flattened long grass were seven dead terrorists. Neutralizing this terrorist threat so quickly in a successful first contact with ZANLA was a relief.

"But chaps our job is far from over. The other bunch of bastards has moved on and we must arrest or kill them before they get to do their evil deeds. We will get information from our Special Branch soon enough on where these bastards are and then we will deal with them like we have this bunch."

CHAPTER SIX

May 1966

Gumbashuma looked over the wide valley from his vantage point high up in the kopje. Smoke meandered skywards from the cooking fires in the farm workers compound. Beyond that was a clump of blue gum trees that distorted his view of the main farm house, the farm sheds and tobacco barns.

In the three weeks since Gumbashuma split from the seven comrades he had successfully navigated his men to arrive at Nevada Farm in the Hartley district to the south of Salisbury. They needed to refresh their supplies of food and Gumbashuma thought the people he knew at the farm would readily assist. He also wanted to give his men time for rest while seeking out local knowledge on the whereabouts of the Police before they set off towards Fort Victoria.

Gumbashuma was demonstrating his leadership capabilities. He had a canny sense of bush orientation and was skilled in avoiding detection, essential for his mission to be successful. He had persuaded the other forty comrades to leave the camp when the seven comrades skulked off with their explosives. He thought it was a stupid plan that would only result in attracting the Police to their presence. Believing they needed distance between themselves and any explosion as quickly as possible to avoid follow up detection from the Police, he assumed command without resistance from the others. Having completed his training in China with Vhukile, he commanded a higher degree of respect amongst his fellow combatants.

According to their overall mission plan, a larger group had splintered off heading eastwards with the objective to find the oil pipeline and blow it up. The SAS soldiers had tracked this group which had the SB informer. This meant the section led by Gumbashuma was lost to the Rhodesian Security Forces.

"Hello my friend," greeted the elder when Gumbashuma strode casually into the farm workers compound in the early evening. "I see you Gumbashuma. My old eyes see you have changed."

"I see you too my friend. Much has changed. I must talk to you about this."

They spoke in Shona, both being of the same tribe.

Gumbashuma was invited to sit with the elder near his cooking fire to share in the meal that was being prepared by the women. He was famished and eagerly partook in the sudza and meat stock gravy. The second large helping offered him was not rejected. Noticing Gumbashuma was hungry by the way he attacked his meal, the elder refrained from asking any questions of him but rather he took the time to give a brief account of the current goings on at the farm and surrounding district.

After he had eaten, the elder invited Gumbashuma to explain what he had been doing for the past eighteen months since he last saw him.

"Since leaving the district I went to Harare Township and met with others. The Zimbabwe African National Union arranged meetings which were held with much secrecy so the Police would not know. Much was discussed about the nationalist cause to give us Government in our country. Much trouble happened there as the settlers tried to stop the nationalist movement. The Police arrested and beat many of our comrades. The movement set plans for many of us to be taken to Luzitu Boma, on the Zambezi near Chirundu. One night we crossed the river and went by truck to a camp in Zambia."

A woman carrying a pitcher of beer arrived and offered some to the two men. It tasted like honey to Gumbashuma. It had been a long while since he had enjoyed the taste of beer.

Gumbashuma explained the weapons training that he undertook over many months. He explained how he was sent to China by aeroplane. The elder was intrigued by the aeroplane part of the story finding it incredulous that people were transported through the air in a metal tube. The hardship Gumbashuma endured at the camp in China both impressed and saddened the elder. Impressed by the sheer physical endurance Gumbashuma had shown, but saddened by what he saw as unjust mental and physical pain being inflicted on his friend. Gumbashuma outlined the content of the lectures he attended. But the communist doctrines taught by the Chinese instructors proved too complex for the elder to comprehend. His friend then listened intently while he explained the purpose of his visit. They talked until it was nearly dawn and before they parted the elder agreed that Gumbashuma's men could stay in their compound.

He met with his old friend each evening to talk while they sat around the cooking fires. More men joined the gathering as the news spread through the district of their presence. Not all those attending the gathering agreed with Gumbashuma's views which gave way to lively albeit long winded debate. On the forth evening one topic was raised by the farm workers that had universal appeal amongst all those present. In venting their discontent with the farmer who employed them the discussion took a particular circuitous route as it explored the causes. The following evening this topic was debated again with increased emotion on what was acknowledged by most as unjust treatment of the workers. The farm workers explained to the comrades that Mr. Botha, the farm owner, was a hard task master showing little respect for the workers, short changing them on wages and their meal rations. Gumbashuma readily related to this sense of injustice. It fitted with his present mission founded on the cause to liberate the nation of the white settlers who were exploiting the Africans.

The discussion about Botha's treatment of his farm workers stirred up discontent with the comrades and they pressed Gumbashuma to take action against the white settler farmer.

"If we do anything here in Hartley district this will bring the Police," argued Gumbashuma. "Our mission is to get to the Victoria district to recruit members for the liberation war. It is not to attack this settler."

"Are we liberation fighters to rid this land of these settler pigs or are we cowards skulking around the darkness like hyenas?" retorted a more vocal comrade. "I say we must go and kill this pig and show the masses that we are liberating them from the chains of slavery. Our teaching was that comrade Marx rose up in support of the masses and he killed those who trod unjustly on the workers. We must do this here Gumbashuma."

As this debate raged on during the day Gumbashuma realised that the majority of the comrades were restless from the lack of action and that unless they did something definitive here and now their overall morale and discipline may disintegrate. The collective decision was made that afternoon to do something.

A half-moon shone brightly in the cloudless sky. It was mid-May. Winter was setting in. Gumbashuma and six of his men walked cautiously along the side of the dirt road that led to the unlit farm house. It was one o'clock in the morning.

Gumbashuma signalled one of his men to stop and stand guard at the gate to the farm homestead. The other six comrades moved quietly together along the drive way. A night owl shrieked and took off from a nearby fence post. It was searching for a rodent to feed on when the comrades disturbed it.

He directed two comrades with a whisper to the rear of the house to deal with anyone exiting the back door. One comrade stopped by the parked vehicles to prevent any escape by road. Gumbashuma and two others moved purposefully to the front of the house. They went up the steps to a veranda that wrapped around the homestead.

They were tense, their adrenalin running. Looking at each of his comrades searching for reassurance, Gumbashuma banged on the front door with a clenched fist. A dog barked shrilly from inside the house. He banged again.

A light came on casting a yellow glow out of the window at the right corner of the building. A few moments later another light came on sending a shard of light through a side window near the door.

Gumbashuma heard the farmer muttering loudly to himself. His heart raced in his chest as the bolt on the door clicked and the handle turned. He sweated profusely. The comrade standing next to him began to shake slightly. The third comrade had backed off to one side. They concealed their weapons under their black corduroy jackets.

"Ready," Gumbashuma whispered.

The door opened. A man carrying too much weight around his gut stood in front of them. He fiddled with the tie rope on his royal blue dressing gown.

"Ja, what is it man," he yelled in English.

His wife shouted something.

"It's some kaffirs at the front door. I'll deal with them," he said in Afrikaans.

He glared at the two black men standing on his front door noticing that their hostile facial expressions were mottled by beads of sweat.

"So what do you kaffirs want hey? You don't come to my front door. You use the back door and ...."

"You have stolen our land white settler," yelled Gumbashuma. "You have taken the land of my ancestors Maningi!"

Spittle sprayed from Gumbashuma's mouth. Botha, taken by surprise, instinctively took a step back to avoid the spit. A black man had never spoken like that to him before.

"Hey kaffir what is that you say!" shouted Botha's wife who, dressed in a pink dressing gown, emerged beside her husband.

"You have stolen our land Maningi and we have come to take it back."

Gumbashuma brought his PPSH sub machine gun out of his jacket. His comrade did the same.

Botha saw the barrel of the machine gun and involuntarily raised his hands as he stepped backwards bumping into his wife. He opened his mouth to say something at the same time Gumbashuma pulled the trigger. Whatever he said was drowned out by the noise of the gun. The second comrade also fired his weapon. Both the farmer and his wife flailed about for a moment as the bullets hit them both in the chest and upper abdomen before they fell heavily to the floor.

The two freedom fighters stood in the doorway staring in silence watching the pools of blood spread on the floor around the two bodies. These were the first people they had killed. The reality of what had occurred took a few moments to sink in before exhilaration swept away the nervous anxiety.

"Chimurenga! Chimurenga! Chimurenga!" shouted Gumbashuma releasing his nervous tension

Their other comrades joined them on the front lawn and together they yelled into the night sky. One fired a burst from his Sten gun. Others contemplated to do the same but Gumbashuma stopped them. He reminded them that they must conserve their ammunition. There was no resupply other than from stealing weapons or ammunition which may not be a viable option.

"We must go now, away from this place. The Police will come and we must be far away," he said leading them away from the homestead to rendezvous with the other comrades waiting near the farm workers compound.

***

Bonnyface started work early each morning to tend the gardens around the homestead. He awoke at four to start his duties at five. He would stop for his morning meal at seven then work to noon when he would have a short break before working through to six in the evening.

He started this morning as he did each work day by fetching his garden tools from the shed next to the carport at the back of the house. He put his garden tools into a metal wheelbarrow and pushed it to the front of the house where he continued tilling the garden beds that he had worked on the previous day. A simple uncluttered soul, he whistled happily while he worked.

He stopped whistling when he stubbed his bare foot with the rake. As he bent down to examine the extent of the injury he heard crying coming from the homestead. Looking around there was no one to be seen. It was too early for the cook to arrive. He looked back at his foot to see blood oozing from where he had cut it and pondered what he should do about it. The crying persisted. Wondering why the children were crying he decided to investigate. After a short while he ascended the steps onto the veranda. As he came to eye level with the floor he could see through the open door.

***

The Police arrived fifty minutes later in two Land Rovers carrying six black and two white Police officers. The Inspector was the first to enter the house. The bodies of the two victims lay where they had fallen. The blood splatter on the walls had dried and the pools of blood around the bodies congealed. Bonnyface was in the lounge room bouncing the nine month baby girl up and down on his knee. She was giggling. Her brother Bakkie was lying on the carpet playing with a dinky car. He was three and a half.

"We will need to get the neighbours over here to look after the children Sergeant," said the Inspector. "The victims' relatives will have to be contacted. Cordon off the house. Get on to that now, will you?"

The Sergeant rushed from the house barking orders.

"This looks like automatic weapons were used here," William observed. "Look at those pock marks on that wall. And the wounds on the poor souls?"

"Yes. The pattern looks that way all right. This has ominous signs of not being a local murder."

"Sir." The Sergeant re-entered the hallway. He carried some papers in his hand. "These are found outside."

He passed the papers to the Inspector.

"Bloody hell. This is ZANLA propaganda. This is a CT attack!"

He passed the papers to William.

"ZANLA has commenced the second Chimurenga to take back the land stolen by the white settlers. The masses will rise up against the settlers .... Each Zimbabwean must kill a settler......"

"Draw weapons from the Land Rovers Sergeant and secure the perimeter of the farmstead. Tell the crew to be alert that armed CT's may still be lurking. Get reinforcements in quick smart .... five officers .... no make that ten and they are to be armed. Arrange for the workers compound to be secured. No one in or out from the farm. And ..... get these poor souls covered."

"We need to call this in ASAP," informed William, the Special Branch officer.

They left the house to go to the Land Rover to use the radio. A Policeman covered the bodies with a canvas sheet.

CHAPTER SEVEN

June 1966

The Umfuli River meandered through the Zowa Tribal Purchase area on its unhurried way northwards towards the Zambezi River. It was early June and the flow of water slowed daily. Soon it would stop altogether leaving a dry sandy river bed except for some larger pools that would survive the winter months. The next rains were five months away.

Gumbashuma and his comrades set up a camp along the banks of the Umfuli. They chose a secluded section where the river took a sharp turn. The bank where the river cut into the soil was steep but there was a gentle slope on the opposite side with a sandy beach. The vegetation that backed onto the beach was lush. It was ideal for a secluded camp site. The river attracted animals seeking green feed and water which was ideal to supply meat for the comrades. A large pool of water would remain in the bend as the dry season progressed. Ideal for water supply. Gumbashuma chose the place well.

A father of a comrade owned a farm in this district. The young comrade had been away from his home for over eighteen months while undergoing insurgency training in a camp in Zambia. He was anxious to see his family again and had enticed Gumbashuma to the location suggesting a warm welcome would await them at his kraal. At first they were welcomed by the local farmers and their families and were offered traditional hospitality and courtesy. It seemed that the connection between the young comrade and his family helped to ease Gumbashuma and his gang into the district. But soon their extended presence disturbed the local people and their welcome waned. After three weeks the comrades found they were being progressively shunned.

"We are freedom fighters here to liberate the masses from oppression and yet these people show us little respect. Why is that?" Gumbashuma demanded of his comrade. "Go and ask your family why they treat us with no respect and suspicion."

The young comrade sauntered off to his father's kraal. It was early evening when he arrived and being a Saturday the family was preparing for the celebration of the end of yet another hard week working the fields. The maize crop grown during the summer had harvested good yield and the storage huts were overflowing with maize cobs.

Home brewed beer flowed freely as the evening meal progressed, so did the conversation.

"The news of the killing of the farmer has brought much sadness to the district," announced the father. "We must drink to recognise such a sad event that has occurred."

The group that sat around the large open wood fire raised their mugs.

"Why do you say it is a sad matter father?" said the young guerrilla loudly. He had consumed a large quantity of the brew. "That white pig deserved to be killed. He stole our land and oppressed our people."

"He was a farmer like us my son. We work the land and have a bond that unites us. Killing is evil and against the teachings of Jesus. It must be condemned and ..."

"And what? Did Jesus weep when our forefathers were killed by the settlers? Did Jesus help our people when our lands were stolen? Our people are oppressed by this white settler regime, they exploit us and the liberation movement is here to stop that."

61

"With violence?" shouted his father. "By spilling blood? By disregarding the teachings of the bible?"

"Yes father by all those things and more. The bible is a piece of shit. The liberation movement has started the new Chimurenga. The freedom fighters will bring the revolution here to rid this land of the white settlers so we can own our land once again."

"I own this land. And this man sitting across from you owns his land that he farms. So what is this revolution to us? We do not seek the changes you talk of."

"You talk through your ass father." He stood up and threw down his mug. "I was with my comrades who killed that white pig. I saw him and his bitch squeal for mercy before we shot them. The Chimurenga is here with us all now."

"My son! How can you say such things? How can you ... God forgive you," sputtered the father as tears welled up in his eyes.

"I don't seek your white God to forgive me. You must decide. All of you must decide." He pointed to each one while trying to steady himself. "Join the liberation struggle or ... or ... you are against it." He staggered backwards, tripped on an exposed tree root and fell heavily. Dusting himself off, he continued his ranting as he staggered off into the darkness.

His deeply religious Methodist father wrestled with the righteousness of his son's actions. The revelation distressed him greatly to the point he was unable to sleep for two days. He reported his son to the Police in Hartley.

The Police acted quickly. Already on heightened alert due to the murder of the Botha's, the Police Inspector at Hartley immediately set up surveillance near the father's kraal. Several days passed and nothing happened. Then one late afternoon, the young comrade strolled down a pathway through the bush making his way towards the kraal. He was oblivious of his surroundings, chewing on a succulent piece of grass, his Sten gun across his right shoulder.

He did not see the Police ambush until he was in the middle of it. By then it was too late for him to get away. He needed to make a snap decision to surrender or fight. He vacillated between the two options until the decision was made for him when a black policeman shot him before he could get his weapon off his shoulder.

Howling in agony from the one shot which hit him in his upper left arm he sank to his knees before three Police officers descended on him. They flipped him onto his front, his face pushed into the stony soil as they wrenched his arms together before placing handcuffs on them. One officer placed a wad of cloth on his wound to try to stem the blood loss before he was un-ceremonially dragged with his feet scraping along the ground and roughly thrown into the back of a Land Rover.

He lay face down on the metal floor weeping with fear and pain, when four Police officers clambered into the back, two kicking him hard several times in the torso with their steel capped boots. They put their feet on him as the Land Rover bounced along the dirt road. They all suspected what fate lay ahead of him. Murderers were hanged in Southern Rhodesia.

Later that day the young terrorist squealed like a stuck pig when he was put in a small room with two Special Branch officers. Believing they were about to kill him, he begged for his life. As the rough interrogation progressed he was led to believe that he could trade his life for information on his fellow comrades. Little did he know then Special Branch lied about the trade-off.

Armed with the detailed location and the number of terrorists at the camp, Special Branch briefed the Police HQ. Four sections, two made up of Reservists and two of regular Police, were rapidly mobilised. The Inspector who attended the Botha farm murders was placed in charge of the operation against the terrorist camp planned to be executed the next day.

The sun rose swiftly into the cool morning sky. The Police task force that had assembled overnight were ready to be deployed at sunrise but were delayed in leaving Hartley because one of the Bedford trucks assigned to transport the Reservists would not start. The Inspector commandeered a truck from the local garage. It was for sale in the second hand car lot and while its cream colouring was not ideal, it was of the right size required for transporting the Reservists.

The Police got as near to the site as they could by road before debussing.

"Okay chaps. Listen up. This is it. You have received your briefing on this one. Section One will form the sweep line and move towards the river on my order. Section Two, three hundred metres to the north of the camp. Section Three, the same distance to the south. Section Four will deploy across the river to cut off any CT's who try crossing the river. You'll have twenty minutes to deploy. Radio contact will be limited. I don't want us to give the game away. We only have one radio per section so keep in eye contact with your colleagues left and right. The section commanders who will be in the middle of each section will receive my orders and pass them along the line verbally. Is that understood? Right then, let's go and nail these bastards."

The section of Reservists tasked to form a stop line at the northern end of the river made good time and were in place sooner than anticipated. The other two

64

sections found it tough going through difficult rocky terrain to get to their designated points.

Okay it's time to sweep in, thought the Inspector looking at his stop watch. *The stop groups have had plenty of time to get in position.*

He gave the order for the sweep group, Section One, to advance.

A shirtless terrorist sauntered out of the camp to relive his bowls in a thicket. As he unbuttoned his trousers he caught a glimpse of movement through the trees. He paused to look more closely and was surprised to see blue uniforms coming towards him. Panicked, he ran at full speed back towards the camp, crashing through bushes as he went. Police who saw this terrorist dash across their sweep line were startled. Without hesitation one instinctively shot off a round. The bullet shot well past the terrorist. Others in the sweep line took the lead, firing their weapons as well. None hit anything other than a few trees.

Gumbashuma squatted near the fire he had lit earlier that morning preparing the maize meal for their breakfast when he heard the crashing sound and a shot ringing out. He dropped the bowl of maize flower and dashed to fetch his PPSH machine gun which was leaning against a stump close by. As he reached for the gun more shots rang out at the same time a comrade came bounding through the undergrowth into the camp site.

"Police! Police!" shouted the comrade as he ran past Gumbashuma. His face distorted by sheer fright.

With the alarm raised, the other comrades scampered frantically to get their weapons. Then all hell broke loose as the Police fired relentlessly, bullets zipping into the trees and undergrowth all around them.

"Run! Run for cover!" shouted Gumbashuma.

His men scattered. Four comrades ran towards the river. They exited the scrub before bolting along the sand bank hoping to get across the slow moving river where boulders acted as stepping stones. In doing so they unwittingly exposed themselves. The section of Police who were in place as a stop position along the river saw the terrorists running towards them. A volley of bullets cut into them. They fell into the water which turned a crimson colour before dispersing downstream.

The comrade who first saw the Police ran several hundred metres past the camp before he rushed straight into the other section of Police. He stopped and threw up his hands. Several Police officers rushed up forcing him down before handcuffing him.

Six comrades elected to stand and fight. Standing exposed in the clearing of the camp they stood no chance of survival.

Gumbashuma's snap decision to run was taken up by two of his comrades who joined him. They left the camp by running along a gully, using low lying bushes for cover. From the amount of gun fire Gumbashuma knew that there was no option other than flee. To do anything else meant he would be killed or captured. Neither of those two options warmed to him.

"We must run hard now. It is not the time to fight with the Police. That can wait another day," he shared with the two running behind him.

They nodded their agreement. They both wanted to keep living. A volley of gunshots rang out shattering bushes around them. Gumbashuma kept running, lowering his profile by bending forward. The comrade behind him did the same. The third comrade stayed upright and was hit in his left temple in mid stride. Gumbashuma felt a sharp pain in his arm as more shots rang out. He glanced down to see blood seeping into his shirt, but he kept running regardless.

It was late in July when Gambashuma arrived at the guerrilla training camp inside Zambia in poor physical condition. He had been on the run since the encounter with the Rhodesian Police.

"We should call it the Battle of Chinhoyi. It will mark the start of the war of Independence for Zimbabwe," said Vhukile when he met with Gambashuma in the crude infirmary building.

Gambashuma grimaced as Vhikule hugged him. His wound was still infected and had not responded to medication. Vhukile suspected his comrade would not make it.

CHAPTER EIGHT

August 1966

"Mum, where's dad?"

Richard was looking for his father. He was a lanky teenager having recently completed a growth spurt. Carrying two small Elastoplasts on his neck as a consequence of his battle with a razor blade this morning, the novelty of shaving had soon worn off. Fortunately he had ducked the embarrassment of acne having only endured a mild infliction.

"I think he's at the pool," replied his mother. "You know the bother we have had with it recently. He may be trying to fix it. If not, he's somewhere in the garden."

Richard left his mother sitting on the sofa in their large lounge room reading a magazine.

"Sixpence have you seen the boss?"

"Yes my baass." Sixpence humbly offered. "The big baass is there at the pool."

He grinned showing his large front teeth as he pointed towards the direction of the pool, before returning his attention to weeding the garden bed.

"Okay thanks Sixpence."

Richard made his way along the stone pathway and down the steps of the rockery. It was Saturday. The sun was shining. A cool breeze was blowing and the sky was a gorgeous blue with only a few scattered clouds towards the east. He saw his father sitting in a garden chair reading a newspaper under a large Flamboyant tree which was threatening to blossom.

"Dad, can I ask you something?"

"Certainly you can Richard. Is it your homework? This is your last year at school and it's essential you do well so you can get into University."

"I know I have to pass my 'A' Levels dad," he muttered, rolling his eyes, tired of his father on his case these past few months about passing his examinations. "And no it's not homework that I want to talk to you about. I will do my homework tomorrow."

His father had cajoled him to apply for admission to the University of Cape Town and study Law. That was not necessarily what Richard wanted to do.

"You must get a professional education son because the privileged position the Europeans have now with employment will not last. The Africans will swamp the menial jobs," was the message that resonated in the debate. The problem was Richard did not know what career he wanted to pursue and thus was unable to offer up any alternative option to counter his father's obsession.

"What I want to understand is this UDI thing. We had a class debate on Thursday and ... well I was confused by the opinions put by the teacher and some of the boys in class. Why did we break away from Britain and why have Britain and the United Nations applied economic sanctions against us? What did we do that was so wrong?"

"Okay son I can explain this, but it will take a while to understand it so we should get ourselves something to drink. I am thirsty." He looked around and saw Sixpence. "Sixpence!"

Sixpence looked up, dropped the rake and ran over towards where the two were sitting.

"Yes baass."

"Sixpence, tell Finias to come here now."

"Yes baass."

He stood with a wide grin on his face wiping his grubby hands against his trousers.

"Well go on. Move it then."

Sixpence turned and ran off towards the back of the house.

"I sometimes think he's got no bloody brains," offered Richard's father. "The other day I told the fool to sweep the leaves off the front lawn. Your mum told me it was a farce to watch him. He would sweep away, building a pile of leaves. He would then sweep away and build another pile. The wind would blow the first pile all over the lawn again so he would start the whole bloody thing again. Instead of picking up the piles as he went so the wind would not blow them about, he kept building piles of leaves all day. Consequently he did not get onto chopping the fire wood he was supposed to do as well. Bloody useless!"

Perhaps he's smart rather than stupid, thought Richard. *At least he avoided chopping the wood that day.*

"I like him. He seems to work hard with the garden though and he does keep the pool clean ..."

"Don't get me started on that one," interjected his father. "Yes he can clean the pool okay but I can't leave him with the chemicals. Remember the snafu ... oh .... a few weeks back now, when we couldn't swim in it for God knows how long after he put all the pool acid in? I had told him several times exactly how to measure it and what does he do? He bloody well put the whole lot in the pool at once. When I asked him why he did such a bloody stupid thing he offered the excuse that by putting all the chemicals in the pool at once saved him doing it each day for the rest of the damn week."

Finias arrived dressed in a white shirt and brown trousers, tennis shoes and a tea towel folded over his left arm.

"Finias. Get me a Castle Lager and Richard a Fanta. Bring two glasses."

"Yes my bwana."

He hurried off back to the house. Sixpence sauntered back towards where he had been working, picked up the rake and continued to busy himself with the garden bed.

"Okay Richard so you want to know about the Unilateral Declaration of Independence that was declared back in November? To understand it properly we need to go back to the beginning, okay?"

Richard nodded and settled back in the pool deck chair.

"Firstly we have to recognise that the British politicians are a bunch of untrustworthy bastards. Whitehall in London is where the external affairs of Britain are run from. It is full of left wing patsies, socialists, who are scared to their boots by the newly independent African states up north. That's because Britain has this macabre guilt complex about its colonisation of Africa.

Anyway way, back in 1923, Britain gave Southern Rhodesia its own constitution which set us apart from the rest of the British colonies. We were still part of the British colonial structure but here in Southern Rhodesia we have self-government with our own elected parliament. Then back in the early fifties Britain set up the Federation of Rhodesia and Nyasaland, some called it the Central African Federation."

"Why was this Federation set up by the English?"

"Bugger if I know son. In the wisdom of those bastards in the British Foreign Office they figured that if they set up a political union in Central Africa this

71

would sort of be a half way move towards full independence for the three colonies while being a bridge between the balls up of black African ruled countries and the white dominated rule of South Africa, Angola and Mozambique. Blind Freddy could tell you it was never going to work Richard."

"Why is that?"

"Once the Federation was set up the African nationalists in Northern Rhodesia and Nyasaland agitated against the Union and it was essentially doomed from inception. Britain had no will to support the Federation against increasing black African agitation and so they eventually agreed to break the Federation up in 1963. Britain rushed to give Northern Rhodesia and Nyasaland their independence based on the principle of immediate black African majority rule. That's how Zambia and Malawi came to be and as expected, democracy flew out the door in a flash. One-party states were set up, which is in effect a dictatorship."

Finias arrived with the drinks. He put them on the round table between Richard and his father.

"Come back in thirty minutes Finias and bring the same again."

They sipped at their drinks. Sixpence had moved closer to the pool area weeding the flower beds that were at the base of the rockery. Superb dahlias with large red and yellow flowers filled those garden beds. The pool sparkled as its surface began to ripple as the pool pump kicked in.

"What is the one party state dad?"

"It's become the definition for African democracy son. These half-baked newly independent countries hold a general election when they first get independence and the political party that intimidates the most people wins government. Once elected they make sure they get control of their police and army, they tear up the constitution, draw up another one that says only one political party can be registered. The one in power obviously. All other political parties are then banned. They masquerade democracy by holding elections to elect people within their political party to government. That political party will never relinquish power unless the army take over as has happened in some of those Mickey Mouse countries."

"That's like a dictatorship isn't it?" queried Richard.

His father nodded his agreement as he took another sip of his beer.

"As I said, Southern Rhodesia has been a self-governing country since 1923. So after the Federation broke up and Britain gave independence to the other two countries, we rightly expected and believed Britain should give us our own full independence under the Southern Rhodesian Constitution which was introduced by the bloody British Government in the first place.

But what did those lily livered politician bastards in Britain do? They reneged on every promise they made to us about our own destiny. They capitulated to the pressure of those mongrels up north in their one-party states. They played right into what the commies want which is to turn Central Africa into satellite communist states.

When we elected Ian Smith as Prime Minister in 1963 he had the mandate to demand Britain give us what we deserved. Our own independence. It makes me so mad. We've been loyal to Britain and for that those bloody hypocrites in Whitehall and now that half ass Labour Prime Minister of Britain, Harold Wilson, stabbed us in the back. We willingly sent more men in total population percentage terms to fight for Britain than any other colony in both world wars. We stood up when Britain needed us to. Ian Smith flew in the RAF in North Africa and Italy. He was shot down, managed to avoid being captured by the Nazis and went back to fight again for Britain. That's why he has the disfigurement on his face ... it's where he got hurt in the plane crash."

"Why didn't the British give Southern Rhodesia its independence when they gave it to Zambia and Malawi?"

"The British politicians changed the rules to appease the black African countries up north. They said the Constitution they gave us and by which we have effectively run this country for over forty years, was no longer the right one. They said we must have immediate black majority rule before they give independence to Rhodesia. Jesus, Mary and Joseph! We all know what will happen. We would have that buffoon Nkomo or Sithole as the Prime Minister or as bloody President. The place would go down the shute as fast as you could say Jack Robinson."

Finias arrived with two more drinks and departed. Richard father looked agitated.

"Can you imagine him or Sixpence running this place? What a mess it would be. Didn't I say come back in thirty minutes? It's only been ten."

He shook his head in frustration as he leant forward to grab the bottle of beer to pour it into the half empty beer glass.

"Tommy says that the last time any country broke away from England were the colonies in North America and that ended in a war between them and England. He says his parents are packing up and going back to England. Will England invade us?"

"Tommy's parents are born Brits and they can all bugger off back to England, that's what I say.

Okay, you ask will Britain invade us. No I don't think so Richard. There will be more negotiations between Ian Smith and the British government before some compromise will be arrived at. Soon I hope."

"Mr. Wiltshire said that this UDI will only play into the hands of the nationalists and the Eastern Bloc. He said that the UDI makes us an illegal state and those nationalists will get more support now from the Communists, like China and Russia. He said Southern Rhodesia will be the next Vietnam where the West and Communists fight it out. He said he is glad he is not young and have to do National Service and risk being killed. He also said that the recent killing of the white farmer in Hartley and the Police gun fights with communist terrorists is just the start. Is he right dad?"

"Your history teacher perhaps should not speculate like that and put that fear into his class. I am not at all happy to hear he speaks like that to his class Richard. I have a mind to take this up with the headmaster and ..."

"No dad! Please don't. That would be awful and I will get into trouble. Please."

"Okay. I won't then. But he should not say those things. Southern Rhodesia will not be another Vietnam. Ian will sort this out with the Brits. Mark my words. And regarding the recent Police stuff with those gangsters ... well I am sure the Police will be able to deal with them in the future."

"What are the nationalists doing? I mean, what do they want?"

"Nationalists. Fancy name for communist gangsters if you ask me. They are jumped up opportunists who see the chance to grab political power through intimidation with violence and by talking communist mumbo jumbo. Stuff they learn like a parrot from the commies and rattle off to the Africans in the townships who have no clue what it means except it sounds good."

"Like what?"

"Stuff about the Europeans having everything and them having nothing. They tell the Africans that they can have everything for doing nothing. My God! Its cods-wallop. No one gets anything for nothing in this world. We have worked damn hard to build this country up. You and I are born here. We may have white skin, but that does not make us any less African than ... than ... old Sixpence over there."

"How many Africans are there in Southern Rhodesia dad?"

"Let's see. Ah .... it must be around five million now. When your grandfather arrived here in eighteen ninety eight, what's that ... sixty eight years ago .... there was an estimated five hundred thousand. Now it's up at five million. They are breeding like flies."

"That increase seems a lot in a short time. How come?"

"The Europeans brought in medical care which stopped the high mortality rate amongst the Africans. We also stopped them killing each other. The farmers worked the land so we over supply food."

"How many Europeans are in Rhodesia?"

"That's a problem. Not enough. It's around the two hundred and thirty thousand mark. We must increase the immigration of Europeans from UK and Europe, but this political uncertainty will prevent people coming here. They will rather go to Australia or South Africa."

"That's a big gap between the Europeans and Africans dad. It's about twenty to one. Surely the Africans will want to have a greater say in the government?"

"Yes and they will one day when they get better educated. But it's not going to happen overnight. The Africans are not ready yet to run a responsible Westminster type democracy. And that is why we ended up having the Unilateral Declaration of Independence. The Brits insisted on immediate hand over to black majority rule, regardless if they had the capability to run a sophisticated country. The only option then was to break away and declare ourselves separate from the Brits.

I have told you before son that when your grandfather bought his first Model T Ford, one of the first cars to come into Southern Rhodesia, the Africans were petrified of the car. As he drove through the bush on dirt tracks, the Africans would run away frightened. They thought it was evil spirits. Dad used to tell them that he chopped up Africans and fed it to the beast, as a joke of course, but they believed him. That was only sixty years ago. We have brought these Africans along at a fast pace in the short time, one generation really, from spears and animal skin loin cloths to now. It's far too soon to thrust such a sophisticated economy and government administration on them. They would wreck it in a few years."

He paused to take two long draughts from his beer glass.

"Tommy also said that the Europeans have more land then the Africans in Southern Rhodesia. He says the Africans have the worst land and that's why they get upset with us. Why's that dad?"

"Well Richard I don't think Tommy has his facts straight. I know a lot about this stuff. Way back we, the Europeans, realised it was essential that the country needed to produce food. The Ndebele did not really farm and the Shona only farmed to feed their own village. We needed to produce lots of food to feed the Europeans and Africans and then to export food to earn foreign currency. That's what we did. It was not going to be achieved by leaving vast tracks of land vacant or by trying to get the Africans to do what they had never

77

done before in commercial farming. So we had to take decisive action and get Europeans farming the land."

"Was that land just taken because we beat the Africans in the war?"

"No. The government sold unused land to the Europeans who could farm properly. They also allocated large areas of land to be held on trust for the exclusive use of the traditional tribes. These are the Tribal Trust Lands. Other land was reserved to only be sold for the exclusive use of African farmers."

"Did the Africans get paid for the land that was reallocated to the European farmers?"

"Of course not Richard. God no! It did not belong in law to anyone other than the Government. I know that seventy odd years later the Communist terrorists say we stole the land but my God .... who has farmed this land over that time to feed them all and make this country the bread basket or Central Africa? We're the envy of this part of the world because we are efficient in growing the food. Besides, did the Normans pay the Saxons for Britain when they took over the lands in England? Not likely. The Africans can buy farming land if the European farmers sell it. There is no law to prevent that, only economics decides who can afford to buy it."

He drained the glass. He felt his heart rate was racing and needed respite to settle his emotions.

"Now it's time to get ready to go out. You and I had best get ready."

They strolled back towards the house crossing the expance of manicured lawn.

"Sixpence, tell Finias to fetch the glasses," ordered Richard's father as he walked up the steps to the front patio.

"Yes Baas."

Sixpence put down his garden fork then rushed off towards the kitchen to find Finias. Before he entered the house Richard looked around at their front garden. It was a large expanse stretching one hundred and fifty metres from the rockery to the garden beds on the fence line where tall Silky Oak trees lined the one side. A long curved tarmac driveway bordered by substantial flower beds swept up to the house from wrought iron gates.

The next day Richard's father gave him a piece of paper entitled '*The Declaration of Independence*'.

"Read this son. It is an important document with profound words."

"Thanks Dad. I will study it."

He read it several times.

"*Whereas in the course of human affairs history has shown that it may become necessary for a people to resolve the political affiliations which have connected them with another people and to assume amongst other nations the separate and equal status to which they are entitled:*

And whereas in such event a respect for the opinions of mankind requires them to declare to other nations the causes which impel them to assume full responsibility for their own affairs:

Now therefore, we, the Government of Rhodesia, do hereby declare:

That it is an indisputable and accepted historic fact that since 1923 the Government of Rhodesia have exercised the powers of self-government and have been responsible for the progress, development and welfare of their people;

That the people of Rhodesia having demonstrated their loyalty to the Crown and to their kith and kin in the United Kingdom and elsewhere through two world wars, and having been prepared to shed their blood and give of their substance in what they believed to be the mutual interests of freedom-loving people, now see all that they have cherished about to be shattered on the rocks of expediency;

That the people of Rhodesia have witnessed a process which is destructive of those very precepts upon which civilization in a primitive country has been built, they have seen the principles of Western democracy, responsible government and moral standards crumble elsewhere, nevertheless they have remained steadfast;

That the people of Rhodesia fully support the requests of their government for sovereign independence but have witnessed the consistent refusal of the Government of the United Kingdom to accede to their entreaties;

That the government of the United Kingdom have thus demonstrated that they are not prepared to grant sovereign independence to Rhodesia on terms acceptable to the people of Rhodesia, thereby persisting in maintaining an unwarrantable jurisdiction over Rhodesia, obstructing laws and treaties with other states and the conduct of affairs with other nations and refusing assent to laws necessary for the public good, all this to the detriment of the future peace, prosperity and good government of Rhodesia;

That the Government of Rhodesia have for a long period patiently and in good faith negotiated with the Government of the United Kingdom for the removal of the remaining limitations placed upon them and for the grant of sovereign independence;

That in the belief that procrastination and delay strike at and injure the very life of the nation, the Government of Rhodesia consider it essential that Rhodesia should attain, without delay, sovereign independence, the justice of which is beyond question;

Now therefore, we the Government of Rhodesia, in humble submission to Almighty God who controls the destinies of nations, conscious that the people of Rhodesia have always shown unswerving loyalty and devotion to Her Majesty the Queen and earnestly praying that we and the people of Rhodesia will not be hindered in our determination to continue exercising our undoubted right to demonstrate the same loyalty and devotion, and seeking to promote the common good so that the dignity and freedom of all men may be assured, do, by this proclamation, adopt enact and give to the people of Rhodesia the constitution annexed hereto;

God Save The Queen."

CHAPTER NINE

February 1971

The late afternoon storm had brought welcome relief to the heat of the day.

Bhekizizwe was visiting his family's kraal before returning to the University in Salisbury to complete his final year of the Bachelor of Arts degree majoring in political science. The scholarship, funded by the Church, had enabled him to progress his education to tertiary level.

His cousin had told him about a clandestine political meeting that was to take place this evening not far from the mission school he used to attend. He got soaked from the rain storm as curiosity drew him to the meeting.

A small framed man spoke passionately about the *Chimurenga*, or what was being termed the War of Liberation. The man stirred an emotional response with the majority of the crowd when he explained how there had already been two wars fought against the white settlers who came from South Africa to steal their land. The man, in his forties, told the audience that the leader of the white settlers, Rhodes, had tricked the great Ndebele King Lobengula to agree to these white people entering the lands of the Ndebele. When these settlers moved in, the British South Africa Company set up its own government, made its own laws, and seized all the land. He painted a vivid picture of lies and deceit by the settlers that led to the death of their great King.

Letting that picture settle in the minds of his audience, he then turned his oratory talent by drawing on the canvas the second war when in 1896 the Ndebele rose up as one against the British South Africa

Company and its settlers. He skilfully drew the sketch showing how the settlers had tried to starve the Ndebele people by stopping the rains and putting sickness into the cattle herds. The great spiritual leader called Mlimo, who carried with him the spirit of Lobengula, unearthed this plot and rallied 50,000 Ndebele to raid settler farms and their towns while renewing their traditional plunder against the Shona dogs. Hundreds of settlers and Shona were killed before the settlers tricked Mlimo and killed him. He immersed his audience with rich colours in the belief that because of these deceitful events the Ndebele now live under the tyranny of the minority white settler regime. He concluded with a breathtaking plea for the Ndebele to once again rise up and unshackle the chains of oppression and to support the leader of the Zimbabwe African People's Union, Joshua Mqabuko Nyongolo Nkomo.

Bhekizizwe knew about Nkomo. He first heard the name when many years back his father told him that Nkomo was not the right leader for the Ndebele as he did not come from the ancestors of Mzilikazi. He recalled that his father said that Nkomo would bring trouble and sadness to the Ndebele people. Nkomo was the subject of much debate amongst the students at the University, especially amongst those undertaking political science studies. Having risen to lead ZAPU after the split in 1963 with two other prominent nationalists, Sithole and Mugabe, Nkomo was interned in 1964 by the Government of Southern Rhodesia at the Gonakudzingwa Restriction Camp for sedition. He was an emerging hero amongst a growing following of militants attracted to the concept of overthrowing the white minority Government of Southern Rhodesia, a concept that Bhekizizwe himself had warmed to.

Bhekizizwe left the meeting with an uneasy discontent and a growing sense of urgency. He felt time

83

was of the essence to take action, action to rectify the wrongs of the past, action to bring justice back to his tribe.

During the mid-year winter break, Bhekizizwe again returned to his kraal where he began discreetly asking the whereabouts of the man who had given the speech earlier that year. It took a week before he received word from his cousin of a clandestine meeting which Bhekizizwe was given permission to attend. When he arrived at the venue, again close to this old mission school, a different man addressed the gathering and outlined how the Zimbabwe People's Revolutionary Army had been formed to lead the war against the white settlers. The man spoke of many things; a new order where the Ndebele would join with the other people of Zimbabwe to create a nation run by Zimbabweans, not the white settlers and where Zimbabweans would make the business decisions and own all the land, have cattle and possessions, drive expensive cars and live in big houses.

But before all this could happen he explained they must drive out the white settlers. The masses must rise up and kill many white settlers so as to frighten the rest to leave the country. He implored those attending his meeting that the Ndebele must join ZIPRA to fight against the Rhodesian Security Forces and the British South African Police. Disclosing that some of the Ndebele people supported the white settler leader, Ian Smith, because they had been brain washed to do so, he explained that the Zimbabwe People's Revolutionary Army would re-educate these people. But he said it would become necessary for some of the Ndebele people to be killed to teach a harsh lesson to the masses. He saw this process as the sacrifice of some people so as to free the rest of the masses from their

84

misguided beliefs that Ian Smith and his settlers were their friends.

"Our struggle will put the oppressed masses with the liberation movement against the settler bourgeoisie, a conflict between the colonised and the coloniser, between the true owners of the land and the white land-mongers, between the exploited workers and the white capitalists. A liberation war is upon us to free us from the chains of oppression. We have taken up arms and will drive out those who stole our land, oppress and exploit us. We want you to join the armed struggle."

Bhekizizwe felt invigorated and inspired. Surprised at the level of his own emotion where he felt the urge to kill a white Rhodesian there and then, he walked back to his kraal realising that time was upon him to take decisive steps to make a difference and contribute to this noble cause, the new war of liberation.

Bhekizizwe awoke with a clear mind. He would spurn his current course to complete his degree and become a teacher to join ZIPRA and take up the armed struggle. At this fateful moment Bhekizizwe did not imagine what was ahead of him and how his life and the lives of so many others would change as a consequence.

Within a week plans were set for Bhekizizwe to join others at an assembly point. Strict instructions were given to him that he was not to speak of these plans to anyone, not even his family or friends. He was warned that to speak of the plans would bring death to his family. He was to disappear like a sprit into the dawn.

It was pre-dawn on a Wednesday when Bhekizizwe awoke from a disturbed sleep. He tossed and turned for most of the night as his mind raced in anticipation of the adventure he was about to embark on. Cautiously dressing into the green kaki clothes he was given, he put on a brown cap and picked up the water bottle together with a bag of meal and dried meat before quietly leaving his hut and the kraal, merging with the surrounding bush, to make his way towards his destiny.

The sun was up and the air was already hot when he arrived at the designated assembly point. It surprised him to see several young women amongst the people gathered there. After an hour of his arrival the number of people had swelled to twenty eight. They had been told not to speak to each other at this assembly place because the bush had 'ears' and the Police would pounce on them. By midday, an hour after the time they were told to be at the assembly point, there was no sign of the man who had arranged this gathering. A few in the group began to doubt the merits of this arrangement speaking in quiet voices about whether they should retire back to their villages.

Suddenly five men dressed in green jackets and denim trousers appeared surrounding them. Three carried AK 47's. One held a RPG-7 and the fifth held a Czech M52/57. Their sudden presence frightened the group, but they soon calmed when the man holding the Czech M52/57 spoke to them. He explained that they were the freedom fighters to liberate them from the shackles of colonialism. He told everyone to sit down. As they did so the other four freedom fighters blended back into the bush.

"I am Comrade Colonel Vhukile Ncube. I am the *one who has been woken*," he said convincingly in Ndebele. "I will lead you all across the Zambezi River to Zambia where you will be taken to a camp and trained as warriors to return and liberate Zimbabwe."

He set about explaining the ground rules about how they were to proceed so that the Rhodesian Security Forces would not detect them and what they should do if, by chance, they did stumble across the Rhodesian Security Forces, or if a plane or helicopter flew overhead. He told them that they would travel mainly in the late afternoons and pre-dawn and they would rest during the day. Vhukile ended with the instruction that each of them must find a bush to settle under and rest because they would be walking for many hours later that afternoon.

Two young boys arrived mid-afternoon. These *mujibas*, young collaborators who fed the freedom fighters valuable information about the local activities and especially the movements of the Rhodesian Security Forces, spoke with Vhukile for a long time. They relayed disturbing information that the Rhodesian Security Forces had set an ambush along the track that Vhukile planned to use.

The *mujibas* explained to Vhukile that one of the twenty eight was a 'sell out' who had collaborated with the Police about this particular transportation. It was because of this betrayal the Security Forces were preparing the ambush. The 'sell out' was called Lungani. The two boys neglected to tell Vhukile that Lungani was in a romantic relationship with their uncle's daughter, a relationship which displeased the uncle.

The *mujibas* and Vhukile were not to know that his band of five freedom fighters had been spotted early the previous day by the SAS. Fortunately for Vhukile the stick of SAS was tracking another group of terrorist insurgents who were making their way out of the Tribal Trust Land towards farming properties. The SAS had elected not to engage Vhukile at that time preferring to continue their objective to take out the band of terrorists before they attacked white owned farms. The SAS passed the information to the Rhodesian Light Infantry who after further clandestine reconnaissance recognised this band of five was preparing to transport recruits out of the country. The ambush was set to prevent this from occurring.

The news of a 'sell out' and the ambush disturbed Vhukile. Being hyper-vigilant, he acutely knew the dangers of being caught with recruits and how impossible it was to defend them and his own comrades if they were engaged by the Security Forces. This had happened twice before and on both occasions he had lost some comrades and all the recruits. While his men knew to use the recruits as human shields when the initial contact occurred and to shoot through the recruits if necessary to escape the contact, once the bullets started flying there were no guarantees his men would survive. He feared that any ambush could see casualties to his men regardless of whether they could use the recruits as shields.

Squatting under a huge thorn tree pondering the information, Vhukile believed the news about the ambush was a message sent to him by the spirits. He elected to undertake these missions into Rhodesia to gain field experience that would be useful in the future as this bush war unfolded, but as one of the most senior commanders in ZIPRA, his capture or death would mark a body blow to the movement. He decided on an alternative longer route that would add an extra day to their overall trip to get to the Zambezi River before he pondered what to do with the 'sell out'. That was an easy decision.

After a few hours marching and as they all walked in single file in the dim light, Lungani was lured towards the back of the column by a comrade speaking to him in a whisper before a knife was thrust into his right lower back and sharply pulled upwards penetrating his liver. The hand over Lungani's mouth stifled the cry to a muffled groan. Lungani sank to his knees with a startled expression on his face. The comrade lowered him to the ground then bent down to collect his water bottle and bag of food before wiping the knife on Lungani's shirt. The hyenas would soon smell the blood and descend on the corpse, tearing it apart in a feeding frenzy. Then the vultures would pick at what's left in the morning.

Lungani's absence was explained to the recruits the next morning as a lesson not to fall behind the column because leopards and hyenas would attack those who lingered. The twenty seven recruits learned that lesson quickly.

The column of recruits entered the morning of the third day feeling exhausted. The heat and humidity in the Zambezi Valley the day before had sapped their energy and the hike that evening, using the dappled light from a full moon, was arduous through rough terrain. They slowed down to a crawl as Vhukile led them through a gully that was cut from commanding rocks and which was thickly covered by small trees. Once inside the gully the group settled down to eat some of their food just as the sun pierced the horizon.

The sudden sound of the helicopters startled the group. Vhukile reacted quickly telling the recruits to hide by lying down under the canopies of the small trees and to camouflage themselves with dead branches. They all did this with alacrity, lying still in nervous anticipation as the helicopter engines throbbed overhead.

Bhekizizwe had seen many helicopters before when as a boy they flew over his kraal. He waved at the people in the helicopters and they had usually waved back at him. Lying face up looking skywards through the trees as one helicopter flew past he was now fearful. This was the enemy. Soon the noise of the helicopters dissipated until they were hardly audible. Vhukile waited a few minutes before indicating to the group it

89

was safe to emerge from hiding. He ordered the group to quickly finish their meal, instructing them to rest and disclosing to them that early the next morning they would cross into Zambia.

One of the recruits, Gugulethu, named by her mother as *our precious one,* made her way to a small low hanging tree to settle down under it to sleep. She was drained of energy and exhausted from the forced march over the past few days. She had strong muscles, a straight strong back and good child bearing hips, but she lacked stamina. On the second day two comrades who had taken a liking to her spoke about having sex. Overhearing the overtures Vhukile had admonished the comrades sternly. He did not want any distractions on this extraction mission. His last mission, several months before, had been a disaster. He vividly recalled that he had lost two comrades plus all the recruits in a fire fight with the Security Forces. His comrades had been careless, dropping their vigilance by engaging in sex with some female recruits and losing focus. He did not want any repeat performance.

Gugulethu knelt down to clear the undergrowth to make a place to settle down. She felt a sharp pick on her forearm. Instinctively pulling her arm back from the grass, terror shot through her mind as her eyes focused on the two puncture marks each with a drop of blood oozing from them. She let out a blood curdling scream falling backwards to sit heavily on her buttocks.

A comrade immediately leapt to muffle her scream, managing to cut it off by ramming his hand over her mouth. The AK 47 that was slung over his left arm cut deeply into her side tearing her shirt as they both fell heavily to the ground.

The black mamba moved out from the rock crevice that was covered by grass and dead tree branches. It made its way across the ground towards a larger rocky outcrop, the sun catching its olive skin. Three recruits and a comrade in the vicinity scattered when they saw the snake. The black mamba petrified them. It carried evil spirit and besides it was deadly.

Gugulethu had her breath knocked out of her by the comrade jumping on top of her. Managing to catch her breath she once again looked at her forearm and she tried to scream but the comrade held his hand firmly over her mouth.

A tingling sensation spread throughout her arm. The two pin pricks on her forearm started to swell. Lying on her side with the comrade on top of her she saw Vhukile speaking to another comrade who then tightly tied her hands and feet together with a rope that he took out of a back pack before tying a cloth over her mouth. She struggled to no avail, her face etched with terror. Vhukile knew what was going to happen to Gugulethu. He was not sure where any Rhodesian Security Forces were. Noise could attract them to his position. Vhukile dispersed the recruits who had gathered to watch before ordering three comrades to position themselves on look out in case the noise already made had attracted the Rhodesians.

She felt the tingling sensation spread up her arm and then as if water overflowed from a container, it progressively spread quickly throughout her body. She wondered if she was lying on an ant mound. It felt as if a million ants were crawling all over her. She attempted to thrash around but was unable to move much with her hands and feet tied and the comrade holding her down. He readjusted his position to sit astride her and put his large hands on her breasts as he pressed down.

Gugulethu started to salivate. Ten minutes had passed since the bite. Spittle seeped through the cloth that was over her mouth. She felt as if she would drown. Another ten minutes passed and her clothes were soaked from sweat. Then suddenly she felt drowsy, closing her eyes. She became still. Her breasts were soft, a tear in her shirt revealing a large nipple and the comrade moved his hands back and forth as he became sexually aroused, but that was cut short when Gugulethu lost control of her bodily functions discharging her bowels and bladder. He let go as he reeled sidewards to get off her.

Her muscles seized, contorting her in a macabre horizontal dance while continuing to discharge body fluids from all orifices. The dendrotoxins from the snake bite together with the fasciculins and calciseptine, being a protein of low molecular weight, travelled extraordinarily fast to disrupt the exogenous process of her muscle contractions. Her breathing became laboured. Then she died leaving her eyes wide open, her body wet and covered with vomit, urine and faeces. Unemotionally two comrades picked her up and dumped her corpse in a thicket a short distance away.

At four o'clock in the morning the recruits and their comrade escorts crossed into Zambia. They were met one kilometre from the river by other ZIPRA comrades, loaded onto two trucks and driven to a camp near Lusaka.

It was late afternoon when Bhekizizwe stepped off the back of the truck. Surprised to see so many people in this camp, he relished the thought that this was day one of his training to become a freedom fighter.

CHAPTER TEN

June 1977

"Remind me why you joined the Police if you feel this way?" queried Rob.

Time moved slowly on a lazy Sunday afternoon. The sun radiated sufficient warmth to chase the winter chill away. The outside paved section of the Norfolk Hotel in a leafy suburb of Salisbury was yet to fill with patrons.

"Jesus I don't know, but ...."

Richard stopped mid-sentence. He had been melancholy and reflective for the past two weeks. His appetite for conversation was sparce.

"But what?" quizzed Rob.

"My father had me down to go to University and do law after school. I had fuck all idea what I wanted to do except there was something niggling at me Rob. It was hard to fathom at the age of seventeen but deep down I felt that I would be wasting my life poncing around a court room wearing black robes and a wig, or drawing up contracts, or whatever lawyers do. I don't know, but my gut told me that I should look elsewhere."

"I didn't know that. How come we never talked about it?"

"You had already left school and were in the army at that time. If you recall I didn't see you for ages and then only briefly on a few occasions. I guess I felt ... I dunno, maybe awkward because you were going to fight in the bush war and I was going to gap it to South Africa."

93

A waiter dressed in white trousers and an ill-fitting red jacket appeared. He hovered around the courtyard like an eagle searching for prey to feed its young, pouncing on the unsuspecting patrons when he saw their glasses nearly empty.

"Can I introduce you fine gentlemen to more beer," he asked.

"Two Castles thanks."

"That is a very good selection if I say so myself," he happily responded.

Pleased to have secured another order he quickly made his way to the bar inside the hotel to fetch the beers.

"My father had a close friend in the Police and I happened to be at his house before the Christmas after I finished school. I liked his daughter and ..."

"Oh yes. Did you do her?"

"Jesus no, I was bloody naive back then Rob. It was pathetic. Anyway, we got talking, her father and me. One thing lead to another and ... well before I really knew it I found myself joining the Police. I figured that I would have to do my National Service one day and so why not do it in the Police. Three years with the Police and then perhaps I would know what I really wanted to do as a career. You can imagine how that went down with my old man. Jesus he was beside himself."

"Ya I can see him blowing his top. So, it sort of just happened then?"

"Ya sort of. I did my homework and thought I would like to get into Special Branch. Be a spook. MI5. James Bond espionage stuff."

"James Bond was MI6. MI5 is internal affairs in the UK. I guess I am more like MI6," lectured Rob. He was a Captain in 'C' Squadron Rhodesian Special Air Services.

"Okay maybe not James Bond, but I was impressionable enough to think spying was glamorous. Special Branch was an attraction even though back then I certainly did not know much about it. Dad's friend mapped out a possible career path to the SB. I thought it was bloody marvellous."

"Well Ric you got there fast. What it's ten years and you're a Superintendent in SB. One of the top Rhodie spooks. That's impressive."

"Ya I'm lucky I guess. The openings happened at the right time."

The waiter returned with two Castle beers. As Rob was paying him he was already looking around for his next order.

"We make our own luck Ric. I don't believe in pure luck and chance. I can't in what I do. I have to make my own path and make sure I don't get whacked on the way through."

Two young women wearing tightly fitting mini-skirts walked past to settle at a nearby table. The girls noticed them with one making it obvious she was on the prowl by showing off her legs to the absolute maximum effect as she sat down.

"Nice. They seem keen Rob. You should make a move hey?"

"Ya they have great bods. Legs up to their armpits man, but hey I'm trying to make it with Monique."

Richard looked puzzled.

"You know Monique? The air hostess. The one I told you about on the phone."

"Oh yes, that Monique." Richard lied. He could not recall Rob telling him.

"Ya, well I am trying to make it with her and stay one on one. I really like her Ric and we get on well. The sex is bloody terrific I can tell you. I think we'll move in together soon. So there's no one night flings for me now."

Rob drank his beer while flirting with his gaze at the young woman.

"So Ric my buddy, you're in SB which is where you wanted to be. You're involved with ComOps and in the zone with all the top brass. You get to do some James Bond stuff. What's the bloody problem?"

Running his hands over his head and through his hair Richard thought deeply before answering.

"Do you wonder what are we doing here? I mean what is the end game?" he asked.

Rob looked puzzled but said nothing. He hoped Richard was asking a rhetorical question. He was right.

"Remember when we were young boys growing up in this country? It was safe for Christ sake! We had a lovely big home in Highlands with manicured gardens, a house boy, a garden boy, annual holidays to Durban, trips to Vumba, Trout Beck. You had the carefree farm life on that bloody motorbike which you never let me ride, going wherever you wanted to. Remember those hunting expeditions? Hell they were great. We went to good government schools that gave us the best education. Man I used to spend all day on the weekends riding my bike in the bush out by the railway past Eastlea. I never felt threatened or scared of the Africans. Our parents didn't worry about us. Hell most of the time they didn't even know where we were.

When I joined the Police the crime rate was so bloody low it was occasionally a concern to find things to do each day to keep busy."

"And your point is?" queried Rob.

"My point? What has happened? That's my bloody point. In the last decade we have gone from safe to fucking unsafe."

"That's easily answered buddy. You joined the Police and the place went to shit," quipped Rob.

"Very funny. Jesus. You and I know what the security in the country is really like ..."

Richard stopped. He looked around, concerned he may be speaking too loud so others could overhear him. They had chosen a table well away from anyone. No one near them looked at all interested in listening to their conversation.

"... the security situation is seriously screwed. So why has it turned so bad so quickly?"

Rob hoped that was another rhetorical question. He picked up his beer and drank so as to avoid replying.

"So what happened hey?" Richard persisted.

"You know the bloody answer to all this. You've seen it unfold. You see the politics and how it's completely buggered things up. Those politician bastards in Britain who renege on promises and are too chicken to back the internal settlement Smithy made with the Africans within the country. The fact we are caught in the middle of the bloody Cold War shit with the commies having the upper hand because the US is so bloody petrified to get involved to kick the Chinks and Cubans out. All because they got a hiding in Vietnam! The South African Government who we have to depend on are using us as pawns to salvage their own future in Africa.

The problem is that we made Rhodesia prosperous in eighty years and now the terrorists look at us and say to themselves we want what they have. They forget that they had this land before the Brits came along and did diddly squat with it. The Ndebele got here not that long before the Brits and that bloody Nkomo has the gall to claim ownership rights. It's a bloody joke. It's a sick bloody joke because the rest of this screwed up world agree with him. How that bastard Mugabe has the world twirling around his bloody finger amazes me. Jesus! I need a piss."

Rob got up and made his way to the gent's toilet, leaving Richard looking into his half empty beer glass. He drained it, made eye contact with the waiter who rushed over to take the next order.

"Don't look so damn suicidal Richard," said Rob in his usual upbeat tone as he sat down. The waiter arrived with the next round of beers. Richard paid him and he left.

"Thanks for this round Ric. It will have to be my last. I have to get back to barracks to get ready for the next op." He looked closely at his friend. "Jesus man you look really depressed. I hate it when you go this way every time you talk this philosophy shit."

"Don't you ever think how futile all this is? I mean you lie for days on end in foreign countries gathering intel, maybe taking out the odd insurgent or whatever, then you feed the intel back to ComOps and we mount a raid, insurgents are taken out, then you move on to another spot and it all starts over again. It never ends."

"We have been here before Ric. It's my job. I do it for Rhodesia. You do your bit for Rhodesia. Like you I'm trained to do a job and I am good at it. You are good at your job too. But I agree with what you have been saying that this bloody war is not going to be solved in the fighting but by those asshole politicians. But right now the reality of it is that there is no end in sight. So what's the bloody alternative hey Ric if you and I stop doing what we do? Hey? What the fuck will happen? Shit will happen to the whites in this country like what happened to those poor European sods when the Belgium Congo went tits up. Belgium ran away leaving their people to the mercy of the ravaging bastards who raped and murdered them. Look what happened to those poor bloody Portuguese in

Mozambique when Lisbon pulled out. The Portuguese left high and dry got the same treatment that the Belgian's got. I'm not going to let that happen here and nor are you."

Both drained their beer glasses in silence.

"I really believed we could create something special, unique even, here in Rhodesia," said Richard sombrely. "But now I am not at all certain that is possible. I wonder to myself whether it was a naive dream or did we just lose the chance. Either way it's not going to happen is it?"

"I dunno buddy. Look, there is too much hatred flying around. I seriously hate the terrs and what they stand for. I hate what they do in their cowardly way to our farmers and to their own people. Jesus you and I know how brutal they are to their own kind. Yes I know its commie instigated, the Chinks philosophy to totally intimidate the masses through brutality, but that doesn't excuse what these bastards are doing out there. It's got to a point of crystallisation Richard."

"What has?"

"Hatred and distrust. Our African troops hate the terrs more than I do. The Europeans are open targets for the terrs and they hate them. The tribe people distrust the Europeans and African's in the Security Forces and they live in fear of the terrs. My men hate the terrs and can't trust the Africans. It's gone beyond the pale, but regardless we have a job to do to keep the terrs at the bloody gates. It's up to you in SB and those wankers in CIO to get the bloody politicians to sort out the politics of this. Okay?"

"Yes I know. But hey, thanks for the pep talk again Rob. I needed it to refocus on finding the solution to get us all out from under this pile of crap. I am meeting with Smithy again soon to discuss the options for this internal settlement."

"Good to hear that Ric. Oh yes, I meant to tell you that Simon is in hospital."

"Why? Is he alright?"

"Not really, but he's bloody lucky. He took a round in the jaw …"

"Where? When?"

"In a contact. It was one hell of a firefight apparently. His stick was paradropped into the contact. They found themselves outnumbered by four to one. They fought themselves out of it without taking a casualty, but then old Simon caught it in the side of his face. Went right through taking out teeth but not shattering any bones."

"Thank heavens for that. I'll go and see him tomorrow. How's your old man and his farm?" queried Richard.

"Ya look he's okay. No terr activity in his district."

Rob looked at his watch.

"Well it's time to make the move Ric. I am not sure when I'll be back, maybe in a while. We'll catch up then anyway."

"Ya, we'll catch up then okay."

It was a ritualistic goodbye. They were very aware they may never see each other again.

"Hey! You boys are not leaving are you?"

The young woman with reddish hair called out loudly.

"Sadly yes," said Rob.

"Why not stay and have a drink with us then? You may enjoy the experience later on."

She was flirting. Her colleague flushed red in her face and diverted her eyes.

"Duty calls and I am heartbroken. But perhaps my colleague here would take you up for a three some?"

Rob looked for Richard with the intention of pushing him into the fray, but Richard was already well on his way out of the hotel lobby.

"Ah .... seems he's gapped it. Wet blanket, hey? Sorry ladies."

He shrugged his shoulders as he backed away. The young lady looked disappointed. Her friend looked relieved.

CHAPTER ELEVEN

July 1977

Bhekizizwe, together his eight comrades, had laid low for several weeks. The five new recruits on this mission were fresh from the FC training camp north west of Lusaka. They replaced the nine seasoned comrades who had been killed two months before in a running contact over two days with the Security Forces. They were yet to be blooded but the presence of the Rhodesian African Rifles in the district meant it was unwise to engage these new recruits in any contact. The RAR troops were hardened soldiers and Bhekizizwe was respectful that his current band of freedom fighters was no match.

Since becoming a field commander in the Zimbabwe People's Revolutionary Army he had returned many times to the main training camp in Zambia after incursions into Rhodesia. But each time he felt something different within himself. The euphoria he experienced when he killed, that feeling of satisfaction, waned that little bit quicker. He yearned to get back and kill again.

His current mission was to take command of the eighty ZIPRA comrades in the Urungwe Tribal Trust Land and adjacent farming areas. His task was to step up attacks on European owned farms bordering Urungwe, while ambushing the Rhodesian Security Forces as often as was practicable avoiding sustaining heavy losses. Because the people from the Batonka tribe in the Urungwe Tribal area were stubborn and non-compliant to the liberation cause, he was to 'persuade' them to back ZIPRA.

His eighteen months in the USSR five years ago, where he trained in insurgent warfare, including that on how to turn the hearts and minds of the peasant population, was being put to the test. His cunning and bush senses were primarily responsible for his survival over these past six years. His bitterness and hatred for the white settlers, which had grown exponentially over this period, fuelled his resilience to keep fighting against what had at times seemed overwhelming odds.

Bhekizizwe rose up in the ranks of ZIPRA primarily because of his leadership qualities. The rapid attrition rate of guerrillas on the ground from the engagements against the Rhodesian Security Forces also helped his promotion prospects. Excluding the countless dozens of tribe people he and his men had executed, his tally was three white soldiers and seven black soldiers dead, one white farmer dead, several wounded, nine vehicles blown up from land mines injuring many soldiers, plus five schools and four clinics burned. He had lost fifty seven comrades and while in the earlier years of the liberation struggle this loss ratio would have been a concern, ZIPRA's swelling numbers in recent years meant they could afford the casualties knowing the Rhodesians could not. The war of attrition taught him by the Soviets was becoming easier to understand.

Under his leadership his comrades had largely subverted the tribe people so that little collaboration with the Rhodesian Security Forces existed. Many villages now openly supported the ZIPRA comrades. This success was the reason the RAR had been deployed in an attempt to arrest this trend. But the presence of the Rhodesian Security Forces in Urungwe was on the wane. The intelligence he had received was that Mugabe's ZANLA troops were flooding their guerrilla forces into the eastern border of Rhodesia which was drawing the Rhodesian Security Forces attention away from the northwest where ZIPRA operated. He estimated it would possibly be another week before the RAR moved out of the Urungwe Tribal Land. That's when he could resume his subversive activity against the Batonka people and some terrorist attacks. He planned to take his comrades south into the farming districts to lay land mines and kill a white farmer and his family. This would be a soft target giving his new comrades a taste of blood without too much danger to them. They would then retreat back to the Tribal Trust Land and stay low once again until the Security Forces, who would reappear after the attack, were redeployed elsewhere.

It was imperative for their survival that he and his comrades kept on the move to mitigate the chance of detection by the Security Forces. The reputation of the SAS to track down the freedom fighters was well respected. The SAS melted into the bush like spirits who could 'see' deep into the night. To stay in one place was an open invite to these spirits to 'see' them and once seen the helicopters and Rhodesian Light Infantry would swoop. Things got difficult when this happened and that's when he lost men. Bhekizizwe's experience taught him to avoid this. Seldom did he move other than late afternoon, early morning or, when the moon was out at night.

As the sun dropped towards the western horizon, Bhekizizwe stirred from his disrupted sleep. He was in a foul mood. The day had been hot and the bush flies particularly troublesome which had made his attempt to sleep difficult. He had wedged himself deep under a thicket that gave him plenty of cover from the branches and leaves, but still the bush flies found a way in to crawl over his face, up his nose and in his mouth in search of moisture and sweat.

Extracting himself cautiously from his hide he was ever vigilant that this was a high risk time. Had the Security Forces found their resting place and set up an ambush? He half emerged and listened. Were the birds making sound? Was it a different sound? Were they behaving differently to what they would normally do? He squatted on his haunches still half concealed and he listened.

Ah yes. They talk to themselves with no concern. All is well.

Bhekizizwe moved out from under the thicket and stood up. Positioning himself close to a tree he stretched listening to his joints crack as he did so. He bent forward and touched his boots before he knelt down on his left knee, checked his weapon and adjusted his webbing. He whistled. Two short bursts. A pause, then two more. He waited a few seconds and repeated this. His whistle sounded like a bird. It was his signal to his comrades to emerge from their own hides.

Gathering around Bhekizizwe so he could check with each comrade if they were well and rested, he then relayed his plan for this coming evening.

"This night we will again visit the village of Batonka. Those dogs will learn that we, the ZIPRA warriors, are the masters of this land. We will be respected and feared. The Batonka dogs will learn that selling out to the white settlers and their hyenas will bring them death."

"Aye Comrade," was the unanimous reply in hushed tones.

"This night we will visit the Batonka and feast on food and young women."

Bhekizizwe motioned for his comrades to follow him as they moved swiftly away from their resting place. They felt rejuvenated at the thought of securing cooked food, something they had gone without for many days, beer and sex.

***

The night sky started to turn a pale blue which spread quickly westwards. The bush burst into song as birds awoke and rejoiced the start of another day. Dew was thick on the ground, the grass wet and leaves dripped.

Bhekizizwe suddenly opened his eyes. The noise from the birds awoke him. Sitting up with a start he looked around to see his comrades asleep on the ground, scattered around in various stages of undress. Their weapons were resting against the back packs which were twenty metres away.

This is not good. I have slept too long and now we are in danger.

Noticing how quickly the morning light was spreading across the bush, panic stuck. He had a headache and his back hurt. He looked where he had laid and saw the reason. A rock. It would have been pressing into his lower back.

We must move now and quickly.

He whistled two short bursts. Waited a few seconds and then repeated it. Only three of his comrades stirred. The others did not move. He felt angry. Not as much towards his comrades but towards himself for allowing them get into this vulnerable position.

"Get up you dogs!"

The longer they took to re-group and move away the more danger they would be in. He got up, fastened his belt of his trousers, did up his shirt buttons, picked up his cap and methodically kicked each of the comrades hard to wake and motivate them to move.

"Move quickly. We must leave this place now."

Some were near naked so they had to search for their clothes. They all had headaches, the consequence of the beer they had taken from the village that evening. The Batonka beer carried a hefty punch which had been effective in knocking them out.

Bhekizizwe looked down on the naked body lying face down in the grass. She was lying with her legs apart. Her hands were tied together. She had given the comrades many hours of pleasure, squealing as they took turns with her. At some stage during the night she fell silent. She serviced two more comrades before it was determined she had died.

Bhekizizwe looked down at the corpse. He kicked it hard.

"Move!" he commanded as he set off northwards at a jogging pace.

His comrades followed in single file. His objective was to get to the river six kilometres away and then wade in the water for a few hundred metres. In this way he felt they would perhaps be able to lose their trail. He needed to reduce the risk of being tracked by the Security Forces. The prospect that the Batonka villages would make contact with the Rhodesian Security Forces worried him. If they told the Security Forces of their presence then certainly troops would be deployed to search for his men.

His head throbbed with each jar as he ran along the uneven ground. He was on auto pilot and not concentrating. He usually would have kept a keen eye on his comrades to ensure they were all in column formation, but today his mind was fuzzy. He did not notice that two comrades had stopped to vomit, while two others failed to maintain the pace. Therefore his column of men became fractured.

As Bhekizizwe reached a patch of open ground his sixth sense kicked in. He immediately stopped and fell to his haunches. Signalling with his left arm to those men behind him to do the same, he brought his weapon to the ready. He looked around to see two of his men kneeling down behind him ten metres apart. He scanned the bush and listened. Silence. The birds were quiet. He could hear his heart pounding. His temples throbbed. He shifted left to position himself near a tree and signalled the men behind him to do the same. He scanned behind him once again.

Two? Where are the others?

The decision to rise up to search for the other comrades was one not to take lightly. His senses shouted danger. But was this paranoia because of his failure to secure their safety before the dawn broke? He felt angry with the world and himself. Was this causing his overreaction?

Where are the others? The lazy dogs. I need to see where they are. Is it safe to look?

Bhekizizwe cautiously rose up from his squatting position. Through the bushes he spotted one of his comrades bending over as he vomited before he jerked backwards and swivelled sideways as the dreaded unmistakable sound of an FN rifle firing reached Bhekizizwe.

CHAPTER TWELVE

July 1977

Corporal Koch was in his fifth month of National Service when he led his stick into the Urungwe Tribal Trust Land. The orders for this deployment had been received with trepidation. This was a 'hot' area with plenty of gooks running around. The RAR had been in there to deal with the terrorists resulting in many contacts. Dozens of terrorists had been killed as were some Security Force members. Now that the RAR was pulling out on redeployment ComOps had decided to put territorials into to Urungwe to 'maintain a presence'.

The territorials, part of the Rhodesia Regiment, were mostly white National Service men. Boys straight from school, serving two years in National Service, plus other civilians on rotational military service call up. Manpower shortages to defend the country were at a critical tipping point as the insurgency rate escalated and the number of white Rhodesians leaving the country increased.

His initial National Service training at Brady Barracks in Bulawayo had been eventful. A natural larrikin who drank lots of beer whenever he could David often got himself into trouble with the WO. Yet he trained hard, showing that he was a leader of men in the making. The challenge the army trainers had was to channel his impetuous nature to ensure he exercised good military judgement.

He was three or four years older than the other recruits in his National Service call up group. He had gone to university after school, before new regulations came in to ensure National Service was completed straight after leaving school.

His three years at Rhodes University in South Africa were also eventful. He got his Bachelor of Commerce degree because he was intelligent not because he applied himself regularly. He preferred to play and drink hard, never becoming romantically attached essentially because he was a blokes bloke, rather self - centred and awkward in the company of women.

Living in the shadow of his father, a senior pilot with Air Rhodesia, a hard authoritarian man, David struggled to please, never managing to gain the unconditional acceptance and the love he so desperately sought. Kept on a short leash with a basic allowance, that was spartan compared to most of the students, forced David to apply his emerging entrepreneurial skills to earn extra cash. Focusing on his favourite beverage, his initial attempt to become a beer baron to supply fellow students with home brewed beer was a good idea in concept, but poorly executed. It could have worked had he and his colleague, whom he partnered with in the venture, not sampled the brew as they were bottling it. They both became pissed, misjudged the amount of sugar to put into each bottle and the pitfalls of home brewing struck at midnight the following evening when the bottles began to explode. They were stored in his clothes cupboard and aside from giving him the fright of his life, he smelt of beer for weeks afterwards.

But undaunted, David moved on. If making the beer was fraught with difficulties he changed the business model. Negotiating a wholesale price from a liquor outlet based on volume, he sold beer to the students on campus at retail, less ten percent. This unlicensed practice took off, becoming very lucrative albeit the business partner progressively became a nervous wreck contemplating them both being arrested and jailed for illegal trafficking of liquor without a licence. They got away with it in the end and even sold the rights to this business enterprise to a fellow student when they graduated. The fact that someone paid a price to buy essentially nothing was a business revelation to them both.

After graduating, David returned to Rhodesia and joined a firm of Chartered Accountants to begin his career. But within four months he received his National Service call up papers and so he began his next life journey.

As a Corporal in the territorial force he led a stick of five men. The role of those in the territorial force was as foot soldiers to patrol the countryside. A primarily role when on patrol was to establish a contact with the terrorists, then call in the regular army to deal with the fighting.

Five months into his two year stint Corporal Koch and his stick were yet to encounter any action. Their patrols had been in relatively 'cold' operational areas, being deployed after an attack on white Rhodesian farms to give security presence. They had enjoyed lavish hospitality from the farmers who were grateful of their presence after having survived a terrorist attack. Their presence allowed the farmer and his family to at least get some sleep at night rather than being on edge, waking at every sound in case that was the start of another attack. Koch and his stick would keep watch over the homestead and the workers compound in the evenings and present a visual presence to the workers during the day. Their presence would filter by bush telegraph throughout the district and generally the terrorists would keep away.

Corporal Koch was on the front porch of a farmhouse sipping tea and looking out over the manicured lawns towards the rolling hills in the distance when his new orders came through. They had done one short patrol earlier that day before spending the rest of the time lounging around the homestead. The sun was descending changing the colour of the sky to a muddy orange. Clouds in the distance threatened to form into a rain bearing system but it was too early in the season for the traditional afternoon thunder storm. His radio operator brought him the radio and he took the instructions on the redeployment.

"New orders," he said, looking grim. "We are being picked up at oh five hundred tomorrow and will be transported to Urungwe. We will be there for three weeks. The Bedford will pick us up at Tingle Junction to take us to Urungwe."

"Why are we going there? Is there going to be action?"

Michael immediately felt excited at the prospect of seeing some action in the field. He found these deployments on farms tedious and boring. He desperately wanted to shoot his FN at someone rather than at targets. He had not discharged his weapon once over these past few months.

"There could be action. It's a hot area. The RAR boys are being redeployed so we are going in to maintain a presence."

"Yeah but what does that mean? Maintain a presence. Sounds like zip to me."

At seventeen Michael was outspoken, extremely self-assured and impetuous. He often irritated Koch with his incessant bleating about wanting to see action. His round freckled face topped with fair hair made him look more suited to a school uniform rather than the army camouflage kit.

"Maintain a presence is what it says. Show ourselves so the Africans will see the Security Forces

112

are there protecting them and the gooks will piss off. If we see the gooks the orders are to call for the fireforce."

"Does that mean we don't make contact with the gooks if we see them?" asked Rusty.

"Yeah. Looks like we are just going to baby sit a whole bunch of Africans in that Tribal Trust Land and tattle tell on any gooks we see so the RLI guys can come in and get the action," offered Michael.

"That's not the case Michael," retorted Koch. "For Christ sakes. Jesus! Just shut the fuck up will you!"

Recognising that he had pushed the envelope with the Corporal far enough, he kept quiet.

"Okay guys, I'll brief you on what the orders are later," continued Koch. "Now let's get packed up. We do the final patrol here in one hour so let's get moving."

While his instructions were clear about avoiding contact with the gooks, the reason was understandable. The tribal people were in the main subverted. This meant the gooks knew nearly everything that was happening on the ground through the 'bush telegraph' network. Any contact with the ZIPRA gooks would mean a fight that the territorials may not be equipped for, therefore his commander emphasised it was essential to call in the fireforce to deal with the real fighting.

Koch guessed Michael may well get his wish to see action soon.

***

Nine days in and they were feeling the effect of adrenalin overload and the lack of sleep. They were tired of the heat and the bush flies which persisted to annoy with their attraction to moisture around the eyes

113

and mouth. The army ration food was awful in comparison to what they had been used to and they had run short of water soon after arriving in Urungwe.

The initial excitement of being deployed in a 'hot' zone was wearing thin. Keeping the morale up with his men challenged Koch. He was suffering with blisters on his left foot, while chaffing in his groin had caused his skin to become red and irritated. Every step hurt and with it his demeanour progressively worsened. To make matters even worse he was also fighting off a head cold. They had got wet to the skin when a sudden unseasonal storm raced through the bush one late afternoon a week earlier. His throat became inflamed before his nasal passages blocked forcing him to breathe through his mouth most of the time which invited the bush flies in.

Two others were sniffling and one other was inflicted with a skin irritation. Koch was the only one with blisters at this stage. The challenge for him was to motivate his men when he felt like shit.

Yesterday they visited a local village arriving around noon. They approached with caution, fanning out before Koch and one other soldier went ahead to alert the villagers of their presence. The other four knelt in a semi-circle with weapons at the ready in case something kicked off.

When Koch entered the village and his presence was observed, the villagers scattered, most running to their huts and closing the doors, some running off into the bush. Within a minute the village was deserted leaving cooking fires with pots hanging over them unattended. The only life observable were the chickens going about their daily routine of foraging for insects in the dust.

Adrenalin surged through his body as he looked anxiously around hoping that he would not be shot by some gook lying in ambush in one of the huts. It would

114

be so easy to put the barrel of an AK through one of the gaps in the huts and fire at virtually point blank range. There would be no time to react and it would be all over in a flash.

The reaction of these villagers was the same as the five others they had visited these past nine days. The villagers did not want to have any contact with the Security Forces. They were truly frightened. He was frightened. His men were frightened. So it seemed everyone was frightened which led him to think that this was an impossible situation to be in. While their deployment objective was primarily to show the villagers that the Security Forces were in control, he knew most of the villagers sought protection not presence. The Security Forces had proved they were not able to offer the protection the villagers sought. They could not stand guard over every village day and night because there was not enough manpower in the Security Forces to achieve this. Everyone knew that within hours of the Security Force patrol leaving the area the terrorists would be back. The cat and mouse game was being played on and on each day with no end in sight, albeit in Urungwe the game was currently favouring the mouse. The terrorists were largely in control of the population.

Koch had signalled with his left hand for his men to move forward from their holding positions. Cautiously they walked into the village with eyes wide open, searching for any signal that gooks were present, each with his weapon trained on what was the nearest hut as they made their way slowly through the village.

Villagers peered out of cracks in the walls of their huts. Their sad eyes searching for hope where none was on offer. No words were spoken as tension notched up amongst the soldiers.

A dog ran across the clearing in the centre of the village giving off a half-hearted yelp. Koch had seen it first and immediately sunk down on his haunches swinging his FN around to his right as he did so. He lost balance and fell to his side kicking up a shower of dust. Confused the others searched for the cause of their Corporal's action. Had he taken a round? Fortunately they saw the dog bounding off and Koch managed to recover quickly enough to indicate to his men all was okay so no one discharged their weapon. They completed a cursory search of the outside of the nine huts before Koch signalled to his stick to leave. They moved off making their way towards a river that was seven kilometres away. It was where Koch planned to set up his evening camp.

After a few hundred metres they came upon an open cultivated field. This was where the villagers grew their cash crop of cotton. The field, several hundred metres wide was freshly ploughed and ready for the seeding of the next season's crop. There was nobody around.

Koch had directed his stick to move along the one boundary of the field. He had noticed it had a large gully running through the middle of it which could conceal people. It was unwise to walk across the field and be exposed in the open. They had not gone far when Koch raised his left hand to stop the stick. They sank down on their haunches. He had seen a person walking towards them through the bush.

The old woman came hobbling towards the men. She had a weather beaten face with sunken eyes. A face reflecting much hardship. A tattered, stained floral patterned, ill-fitting dress covered most of her skinny legs. She kept her gaze low, wringing her hands. Koch was wary of her approaching him and searched around to see if any danger existed. He felt trepidation.

116

What does she want? He thought. *This is out of the ordinary. They don't approach us out in the open. Shit, is this an ambush? I can't see anything suspicious other than her. Maybe she is a fucking gook? Is she carrying an AK?*

"Look around guys to see if there is anything else out there," he said to his men. "I'm not ... ah ... sure what this old bat wants."

Maybe I should just shoot her and that would be the end of it? I haven't shot anyone, so she'd be the first. She looks harmless enough. She's seen better days. Bugger, what should I do?

"Anything?" he asked.

"Negative Corp," came back the replies.

She had stopped thirty metres from him so he signalled her to approach. He moved forward to meet her keeping his FN pointed at her belly and his finger on the trigger. When they came within metres of each other she had rattled off a string of words which he did not understand. He had looked blankly at her. Realising he had either not heard or understood her, she rattled off another string of words, this time with more emotion.

I don't know what she is saying.

Koch did not speak the dialect of the local people so this attempt at communication was never going to work.

"Gavin," he called out. "Come here. The rest keep a watch out, okay."

"Yes Corp."

"You speak this lingo don't you?"

"I speak some Shona Corp."

"Well interpret what she's saying will you. I can't understand a fucking word."

The old woman jabbered and Gavin replied. They both bumbled along unconvincingly.

117

"Well? What's she want?"

"I can't quite follow what she is saying Corp. She is Botonka. Look at her feet. They speak a different dialect. But what I think she is saying is that there is a gang of gooks, nine I think, near here visiting villages at night. She said these were young gooks who are led by an evil spirit. There was also another gang to the east. She said they were putting metal in the ground where roads were. She asked if we can chase these evil men away from her village. I said we would."

"That's good intel. Thanks for that Gavin. We should radio this in."

Gavin gave her an army ration pack and a dollar note and then he had to fight her off as she shook his hand vigorously with gratitude. She scurried off disappearing into the bush.

David slept badly. Before they had settled for the night he selected a flat spot atop a small hill overlooking the steep valley where a river flowed towards the Zambezi River fifty or so kilometres to the north. His groin irritation itched. Scratching had made some parts raw. He could not breathe easily with his nasal passages partially blocked. He woke very early, before four, and was unable to get back to sleep. His mind bounced between his health problems and the real threat of gooks being close by. Two gangs of gooks close by with one gang laying land mines. He had never had a contact with gooks. Actually he had never even seen one. He lay awake on the hard ground scratching, pondering what a contact with gooks would be like.

What would it be like if I killed a gook? I guess I'd be relieved the fucker had not shot me. These bullets would rip a bloody great hole so it would be a mess.

His commander had acknowledged his intel when he reported in. The intel he got back was that the incursions into north east Rhodesia by ZANLA was taking priority and considerable manpower. It was not possible to deploy regular troops back in the area at this time. His orders were reiterated. Keep a presence, but if contact is made call for fireforce and take orders for the ground action from the fireforce commander when they arrive. The local Police station would be told of the information albeit they would in all probability not be able to do much with it.

He thought of reporting his health issues but had decided against it. It played on his mind what his father may think that, if as a consequence of him reporting in sick, his stick was pulled out. He imagined the lecture he would have to endure. What could anyone do anyway? But he suspected that he would be in more bother with the skin irritation as the days progressed.

The birds started to stir as a light tinge of pale blue crept over the horizon. The light raced across the country side and hit the hill stirring Koch's men to life, each moaning and groaning about their own issues. While the place they selected to rest up was flat, the ground was rocky and this made for an uncomfortable place to lie down. Two of the stick elected to sit with their back to a large boulder which caused stiffness in the lower back and neck. They broke open ration packs and shared the pre-prepared food in it. Their small gas burner had stopped working. A wood fire atop the hill would send a smoke signal for kilometres in a 360 degree circle and with the threat of two gangs of gooks in the vicinity they did not wish to draw attention to their location. No morning coffee, only cold water to drink.

Koch was keen to get down the hill quickly to set up an ambush position near the river. They would settle down in ambush formation for several hours before setting off on a short circular patrol that would take them to the river so they could top up their water bottles and then back to the hill for that evening. He did not want to walk too far or exert too much energy because he felt poorly.

They moved in single file as they made their way towards the river. The sun was now well above the horizon taking the coldness of the morning with it. Koch was third in the line and had inadvertently allowed a large gap to develop between him and the man in front of him. He struggled with the blisters on his foot which slowed him down. It was a battle not to cough given the mucus going down his throat.

What's that?

He thought he saw something move in the bush off to his left. It was a blur. He focused his eyes to search the bush while slowing down his pace even more.

Nothing?

He picked up the pace again momentarily but then froze, immediately sinking down on his haunches and signalling to those behind him to do the same.

Shit! That was a person running. Where are the guys up front?

He could not see the two men ahead of him. They had turned left and were obscured by heavily foliated bushes.

I can't call to them. Shit! What if these are the gooks?

He searched to the left, squinting his eyes as if to make them more bifocal. Nothing, except thick undergrowth. He looked back. His men had all crouched down. He made hand gestures to them indicating that they should look left.

Michael was leading the patrol. He was thinking about nothing in particular. Every now and again he would look down to check his footing as he navigated the rocky ground. He was right handed and held his FN rifle barrel in his left hand. His right hand gripped the handle tighter than he should and his index finger was wrapped around the trigger. If he was in tune with the bush it would have told him what was about to happen. The birds were quiet.

Michael rounded a thicket. He suddenly stopped as his mind assimilated what his eyes were looking at. His adrenal glands immediately pumped cortisol into his blood and his body reacted with increased blood sugar. His fight or flight response kicked in without him knowing it.

The gook was bending over vomiting. A flow of yellow liquid spurted from his mouth onto the ground in front of him. His left hand was pressing into his stomach. The right hand held the AK 47 to one side to prevent the vomit splashing over it. With his eyes closed as another heave thrust more liquid out of his mouth he did not see Michael come around the thicket thirty five metres to his right, nor did he see him stop in his tracks with an astonished look on his face. He did hear the metallic sound and lifting his head up he saw a Rhodesian soldier bringing his rifle to a horizontal level pointing in his direction. The gook tried to do two things at once. He tried to swing his AK 47 around to his right. He also tried to run to his left. Neither worked well.

Fuck! It's a gook. He's got an AK.

Michael saw the distinctive curved ammunition clip hanging below the rifle.

Look at the magazine first. If it's curved shoot! Don't wait to ask questions. Just fucking pull the trigger or you won't see the next day!

The words of the WO at Brady Barracks during his basic training flooded into his mind. This was the message that was drummed into the recruits' brains. Over and over until he wished the WO would drop

121

dead. But now remarkably those simple words were all Michael could think of.

He instinctively levelled his weapon. Their eyes locked as he saw the fleeting terror in the gooks eyes.

I'm going to pull the trigger!

With that thought he pulled hard on the trigger. He felt the recoil, then again and again. The gook spun as the first bullet caught his upper right thigh. Then his lower back took a hit. Blood spurted out of the entry hole. A burst of gunfire erupted from the AK drowning out the scream as the gook went down hitting the earth hard face first and landing on his weapon. The wounded gook tried to get up by pushing upwards with his arms, his head drooped below his shoulders. He kicked ineffectively with his left leg only managing to stir up the sandy soil. A guttural sound came from his mouth before he fell forward. His body twitched and then stopped.

Michael stood motionless holding his FN pointing towards the body lying ahead of him.

I've shot him.

He started to shake.

"What the hell!" said his colleague as he emerged from behind the thicket. "Is it a terr?"

"Yes! Shit, I've slotted a bloody gook."

"Is he dead?"

"I slotted the fucker. And he went down."

"Hey you're shaking. Are you hit?"

"I don't think I'm hit." He felt his chest with his left hand. "I've slotted a gook."

"Get down! Take cover for fuck sakes," yelled Koch as he came running onto the scene. "Get down. There may be more gooks."

The message sunk in quickly. They immediately sank down on their haunches. Koch and the three others fanned out looking for the best defensive vantage points.

Zip! Zip! Zip!

"What the fuuc.....,' shouted Koch as the bark of the tree a few metres in front of him shattered. "Contact! Contact!"

Koch scrambled down a small incline.

"Return fire!" he shouted to his men.

The indiscriminate return fire into the surrounding bush stopped the incoming bullets as quickly as they started. When the gunfire stopped it became eerily quiet. Koch struggled to hear anything other than his heartbeat pounding in his ears. His breathing was fast. His hands were shaking.

Okay what to do now? Call in the contact. I've got to call it in.

He signalled to Gavin, his radio operator, to join him. Gavin crawled across the uneven ground. They positioned themselves behind a smooth rock and to the side of a tree to get the best cover possible before they fired up the radio.

"We are to hold our position until they get back with details of the fireforce deployment. Keep eyes open for the gooks and call in a sighting!" Koch snapped his orders.

He listened. Silence.

"I slotted a gook." said Michael more to himself than to his colleagues.

"Well done you prick now shut up and keep looking for movement," barked Koch.

Waiting anxiously for the information on when the fireforce would arrive, his mind raced to take it all in.

Hell we are in a contact. How many gooks are out there? Is that gook dead? Looks like it.

His first contact had been short and sharp, confusing and not like he imagined it to be.

123

Zip, zip, zip.

The bark of the tree and boulder where Koch and Gavin were positioned were hit by incoming bullets. Gavin who had moved to a kneeling position to access the radio fell backwards onto the ground. Koch pressed himself hard against the rock.

Bloody hell! That came in from those rocks over there.

He made a mental note of the location of a rocky outcrop sixty metres or so off to the right of where the gook lay motionless. That outcrop was lower than where they were and was at a tactical disadvantage. He fired several rounds towards it. Two others also fired off some rounds.

Koch saw that Gavin was not moving.

"I'm hit Corp! Oh Christ I'm hit!"

"Where are you hit?" asked Koch searching for any signs of blood.

Koch shifted over to get a closer look at Gavin while trying to keep low behind the rock and the tree trunk between him and where he thought the gooks were. As he moved incoming bullets struck the rock again, ricocheting in all directions.

"Get in behind this rock," he shouted to his wounded colleague. "Return fire. Return fire!"

The sound of FN fire erupted as the stick opened up in unison firing wildly into the bush not knowing exactly where the gooks were. Koch took the opportunity to lean out and grab the webbing around Gavin's upper body hoping that the FN return fire would keep the gooks heads down and him safe. He yanked hard to get his colleague across to where he was. At the same time Gavin thrust his feet into the dirt and pushed. He let out a scream of pain as the webbing cut into his wound, but Koch did not let go and kept pulling. Having gone this far it was no time to stop.

124

"Okay. Okay. Stop firing. Stop firing."

Koch looked to see where the wound was. All he could see was the blooded jacket around the left shoulder. Gavin grimaced as he adjusted himself to lean against the rock.

"I can't see a thing other than this blood. Where are you hit?"

"My shoulder. Bloody hell, it hurts."

"Medic. Medic!"

"Yes Corp. I'm over here."

"I need you here now. Gavin's taken a hit. Listen up. On the count of three the rest of you return fire to keep the gooks occupied. Then you get over here pronto. Okay?"

"Okay Corp."

The medic positioned himself for the twenty meter dash across the rough ground.

"One. Two. Three!"

FN fire broke the silence, bullets spraying the bush ahead with hot metal. The medic dashed across the ground and crashed down behind the boulder. Dust rose everywhere.

"Cease fire! Hold it."

The medic immediately examined Gavin. This was his first real life casualty.

"I've got to get the jacket and shirt off to see what's happened."

Koch turned his attention to the immediate danger. Gooks.

Where are they? Geeez this is real!

The months of training followed by the months of walking around the bush and farm land had led to what was always going to be inevitable. To be shot at by gooks and to shoot at gooks.

"Anyone seen the gooks?"

He spoke just loud enough for his stick to hear. Feedback was negative.

"Okay. The incoming was from the gomo fifty metres down to the right of the dead gook. You see it? I'll put a few rounds in. So look to see if anything moves. If it does, shoot at it."

Koch raised his weapon and discharged five rounds, the bullets hitting the rocky outcrop.

"Anything?" he asked.

Negative.

"Okay, keep a watch out. I'll check in to find out where the fireforce is."

Koch fired up the radio. He was relieved to see it worked. It had not occurred to him until then that it may have been put out of action when Gavin took the AK round.

Looking sullen it took him a few moments to assimilate the information received.

We're on our own. Damn it. We better get this area secure.

"Okay listen up. We need to sweep the area. Make it secure."

He instructed his men to sweep from left to right. Two of his men would flank the outcrop where Koch thought the AK fire had come from.

The stick cautiously fanned out and swept the surrounding bush. There is a first time for everything and this was it for them. With trepidation they finally moved in on the outcrop. It was clear, but trampled grass, a large amount of empty bullet casings, a discarded water bottle and blood was evidence they had been there. Blood was in two places with significant spots leading off into the bush. It was clear a gook or gooks had been wounded. They were not experts, but the general opinion amongst the stick was that the injury must be substantial for so much blood to be found. Finally they searched the dead gook for any documents. There were none. They took the AK 47 and ammunition.

Gavin's injury was a deep flesh wound to the upper arm which bled profusely. The main artery was not severed. The medic bandaged up the upper arm and shoulder after administering a pain killer injection. The wound prevented the use of the left arm. The injection at least numbed the pain.

They regrouped around Gavin who remained seated leaning his back against the rock. Jibes about his condition flew about which broke the nervous tension amongst them, while the impact of what had just occurred took hold. They held a morbid fascination with the dead gook that lay in the dust. It was the first dead body any of them had seen.

Koch fell silent trying to decipher what they must do next. All this was new to him.

There were two gangs of gooks in the vicinity, or so that old woman said. This must have been one of them. It looks like they have taken off. I have got two guys keeping a look out in case they return.

He looked around to check.

Gavin's injured. Not fatal. But he needs medical attention. He is probably still able to operate the radio. Thank Christ the radio was not taken out. What's the time now?

He lifted the camouflage wrist band to see his wrist watch underneath.

"Right listen up. The news from the JOC is that there is no fireforce coming." The men looked at each other with surprise. "The choppers are all deployed elsewhere on a big op in Mozambique. So we have to make our way to the Police camp … its thirty something clicks away going south west. It's not going to be that flash a trek what with Gavin hurt, but we

127

need to get him to the camp ASAP. We will stop here now to eat rations but we must make it snappy. At dusk we can settle in somewhere for the night and tomorrow make the dash to the camp."

He paused to look at each one before adding.

"You guys did good. Our first contact. What a buzz hey? We zapped a gook and fought the fuckers off."

"Corp what do we do with the gook? Do we bury the bastard?"

"No leave it. The hyenas deserve a free meal."

***

The sun waned, sinking towards the horizon. A light red tinge seeped between the white clouds scattered randomly across the sky.

They had been on the move for near on five hours through difficult terrain taking it in turns to carry the radio so as to relieve their wounded colleague of its burden. He was nursing his damaged shoulder which had started to bleed again after he stumbled and fell hard a few hours ago. New dressings were applied and a second pain killer injection given.

Koch was suffering with the blisters on his foot and the skin rash. The skin on his inner thighs wept liquid. Each step was painful. Two others in the stick complained of blisters forcing them to stop a few times so these blisters could be treated.

In studying his map, Koch had targeted a small hill to spend the evening. It looked like a position they could defend if need be. He wondered if they should get a fire going in the event they were unable to get the gas burner alight to at least have a hot drink. The following day was going to another long march so they really needed to get some sleep and nourishment. However, the delays through attending to Gavin and the others meant his plan to get to the designated hill was becoming unlikely.

A tree thirty metres in front of Koch exploded into a thousand pieces. A yellow flame erupted. He was showered with gravel and bits of bark and leaves.

Zip. Zip. Zip.

The ground popped around him. Koch instinctively dived forward and to his left away from where the bullets were landing.

"Contact! Down. Down. Take cover," he yelled before his face hit the ground and his mouth filled with soil.

The others scrambled for something to hide behind. There were plenty of boulders and trees so it was not difficult for them all to find cover quickly.

Koch put his weapon on automatic and lifting his FN above his head pulled the trigger sweeping the barrel back and forth as he emptied his magazine. As he fumbled with disconnecting his empty clip, he saw flashes coming from several positions on a slight ridge running parallel to the route they were walking. The ridge was about eighty metres away. Soil spat up around him as the bullets hit into the ground. Two of his stick returned fire.

We're exposed here, thought Koch. *Surely it's not our own shooting at us? This must be a gook ambush?*

He looked behind him and to his left in search of a better defensive position.

"What hit the tree Corp?" queried Rusty.

His name was Robert. He had picked up the name 'Rusty' while at training camp. It was his orange red hair that was the trigger for his nickname. He had been walking behind Koch when the contact occurred and now lay next to him behind a large tree that was pocked with bullet holes around its base.

"I guess an RPG by the way it shattered the tree. We need to get better cover Rusty. They may put another rocket in and it would take out this bloody tree and us with it. We are too exposed lying here."

He spotted a granite boulder to his left. It was thirty metres away with open ground between them and the boulder.

"Can we make that boulder?"

Koch gestured with his left hand. Rusty swivelled to look.

Zip. Zip. Zip.

The earth around them popped and the bark of the tree splintered. The decision was made. In unison they both lifted themselves up and ran for their lives towards the boulder.

A bullet whizzed past the back of Rusty's head when he was about fifteen metres into his dash. He was five metres behind Koch. Instinctively he ducked forward. Turning his head to see what caused the noise of bullets hitting the trees to his left he did not see the large rock which caught his right foot. He went down hard. The momentum propelled him so he rolled over his right shoulder onto his back. As he did so he cramped his stomach muscles and pushed down with his legs to lift himself. He was propelled onto his feet again, moving forward flapping his arms to regain balance. Diving forward he skidded into Koch who was already behind the boulder, badly grazing his one hand and forearm.

Michael opened up with a burst of gunfire when he saw Rusty and his Corporal make a dash. Others in the stick followed suit. The gooks stopped firing.

This is fucking serious. I must get a radio message out that we are ambushed.

"Rusty where is Gavin. I need him to radio in about the ambush."

130

Rusty cautiously lifted his head to search for Gavin.

"I can't see him."

"Gavin," shouted Koch. "Gavin."

"Ya Corp."

"Are you okay? Where are you?"

"Bleeding again Corp. Over to your right. I can just see you and Rusty."

He waved is uninjured hand. Both Koch and Rusty saw him. He was twenty metres away.

"Radio in the ambush and coordinates. We need help here. They have RPG."

Gavin fired up the radio. FN fire erupted to the far right, followed by several bursts of AK.

"Gavin. What's up over there?"

Gavin called to the others who were stretched out in an irregular line.

"Michael says the gooks are flanking us."

Michael lay in a ditch surrounded by small rocks eight metres from Gavin.

Oh shit. If they do that we will be screwed. Think David. Think.

A wave of panic swept over Koch as the thought of being out flanked by the gooks gave way to the prospect of being killed. When he was first called up for National Service he had discussed the prospect of being killed in action with his father. Subsequently a couple of light hearted discussions about death with some of the recruits while on training passed a few boring moments. But now? His second contact in a day made the prospect of being killed real. He needed to make decisions upon which his life and the lives of his men depended.

Can we fight it out with these gooks? They must be ZIPRA. They will be better trained for contact than the other ZANLA bastards. Okay David. Think! What's important? Nightfall coming? How long? Ammunition?

131

Oh shit. How much ammo do we have? I need to find out.

"What should we do Corp?" asked Rusty. "If the gooks outflank us we're in deep shit."

"Yes I know! I'm trying to figure it out. How much ammo do you have?"

Rusty took his inventory.

"Two clips plus what's in the rifle now. And ... two grenades."

The realisation of what that meant sank in immediately.

"We need to conserve the ammo. We need help to get out of this. I'm going over to Gavin to radio in for help, so cover me if they open up, okay? Stay here and watch out for movement."

Koch moved backwards into the shallow gully keeping the boulder between him and the ridge. He spotted the gully as he ran to the boulder and thought it may offer a route to get to the others. Once in the gully he ran bent over to where Gavin was. There was no AK fire. The silence was strange.

"Have you made radio contact?" he asked while he surveyed the surrounding bush from the vantage point where Gavin had taken cover.

"I'm getting the connection now."

He passed the telephone receiver to Koch who detailed the predicament they were in and their coordinates. He waited for a while before listening to the reply. He passed back the receiver.

"What?" asked Gavin, but from the expression on Koch's face, he knew the answer.

"Shit! Shit! Bugger and fuck! They can't help us. Same orders as we already have. We have to extricate ourselves from this ambush and get to the Police camp."

Gavin replaced the receiver in to the radio pack. His eyes reflected his sentiment. He knew they were in dire straits.

If they are flanking us to my right and I guess some are remaining on the ridge to keep us pinned down, then what do we do? Ammo?

"Michael."

"Yes Corp."

"Check with the others. How much ammo? We can't run out so we have to watch usage. Keep the voices low so the gooks don't hear."

Okay then. We need to challenge them on the right to see if they retreat. We have about ... oh thirty minutes before the light fades then we must then get the hell out of this mess by moving quietly along this gully and off to the left.

Koch got the ammo inventory. It confirmed they could not engage in any elongated contact with these gooks. He passed on his decision to Michael. Three of the stick would swivel right and move down the gully to pepper the bush with gun fire, ideally killing all the gooks. That result was probably unlikely. But it should halt them in their flanking attack. Then as the sun set they would retreat using the gully for cover and belt it through the bush as fast as they could until finding a suitable place to settle in for the night.

***

Michael was on the two to dawn watch sitting atop a boulder that was surrounded by small bushes and long grass. The others rested as best they could at the base of the boulder. It was dark when they stumbled across this rocky outcrop so it was anyone's guess if it was really suitable. Koch decided to settle for it because to continue to crash through the bush at night was not the best option given he was fairly sure the gooks were not chasing them. They had not heard them since they made their exit along the gully.

 Michael heard a rustle off to his left.

What's that?

It was cold, but thankfully there was no wind. A sliver of light was peeping up over the eastern horizon.

It must be around four thirty. There it is again. Animal? Maybe I should lower my profile.

He lay down on his front. Fortunately the boulder had a relatively flat top. He pointed his weapon towards the direction of the noise.

Definitely something down there? It must be an animal. Shit I hope it's not a bloody Leopard or something.

He squinted his eyes, noticing movement in the bush about fifty metres away. Something was moving quietly through the long grass.

Koch could not sleep having only dozed momentarily throughout the night. His mind was in overdrive attempting to compute how to extricate his stick from the predicament they were in.

Gavin was feverish and lethargic. Obviously an infection was setting in to his wound. The medic had one pain killer injection left in his pack. JOC at Kariba were not going to send a fireforce to assist. This meant they had to get to the Police camp, perhaps 15 klicks away by his estimate, but until it got light he could not really tell where they were. He knew there were two gangs of gooks in the vicinity and now he also knew that they had RPG weapons. They had fired one already. He was not sure why they had not used more. His men had not eaten much the day before. Their water was low. Worse still they had limited ammo which could not support an extended contact. His blisters and his skin rash between his upper thighs were bleeding. He pondered how worse it could get while questioning whether he was making the right decisions.

Jesus. What a screwed up situation we're in. It's dawn so we had better get going.

He grimaced when he stood up, stretched half-heartedly, picked up his FN and made his way to where Michael was supposed to be. He crept up the side of the boulder spotting Michael lying on his belly facing away from him.

The bastard's asleep?

He tapped Michael's boot which was closest to him. Bad move. Startled, Michael pulled the trigger of his weapon as he spun around while lashing out with his legs. One boot caught Koch in the jaw and sent him reeling backwards sliding down the side of the boulder. He clung onto the FN as he fell, landing on solid ground with a heavy thump that expelled the air from his lungs.

The gun shot immediately galvanised the stick. Scrambling they gathered their weapons, searching for the contact in these unfamiliar surroundings. Gavin sat still. He felt bad. He was hot, sweating and nauseous.

Michael looked down the side of the boulder with his weapon ready to shoot what he thought was a leopard, only to see it was his Corporal laying spread eagled on his back.

"It's okay! It's okay. The Corp gave me a bloody fright. Hey, it's okay."

"Jesus man. You prick. What you let off a round for? You scared the shh ….."

Zip. Zip. Zip.

Bullets ricocheted off the rocks around Michael. Struck in the calf by a shard of rock that cut a deep wound he fell forward down the boulder.

"It's the bloody gooks again," yelled Rusty.

Other than Gavin, Michael who was clutching at his calf and Koch who was still trying to catch his breath, the other three moved into a defensive position, urgently searching the bush below them.

Rusty saw them first. Five gooks. They were running for the cover of a clump of trees about fifty metres away. The sun peeped over the horizon and its rays blinded him.

"Shit!" shouted Rusty. "Gooks. I saw five."

Koch scrambled up next to Rusty immediately recognising the problem they faced. The gooks could easily see them if they stuck their heads above the cover, but it was near impossible to see the gooks with the sun shining into their eyes.

"Shit man. Did they track us here?" asked Rusty.

"Guys we have to conserve the ammo, okay? These gooks want a contact. But we must only fire when we have to. Understood! We must defend ourselves, so get behind good cover, okay? The sun will block our vision for about thirty minutes and these gooks will probably come at us."

Koch crawled over to the radio which was lying on the ground next to Gavin. He called in to report they were being attacked, pinned down and low on ammo.

Koch picked it right. The gooks opened up and bullets cracked against the rocks and surrounding trees. They were attacking them using the sun rising over the horizon as a blinding shield.

Rusty found a position where he could place his weapon through two jagged rocks with a shadow that cast across his face. He saw movement. It looked like two people running up the slope zig-zagging left to right. He pulled the trigger.

The bullet hit the gook under his rib cage, ripping through his liver and exiting out his lower back. He recoiled from being hit, his arms spreading out, his AK

136

rifle flying into the air. The other four bullets whizzed harmlessly into the ground forty metres beyond. Several rounds were discharged from another FN but it was drowned out by the clatter of incoming rounds hitting the rocks around them. The other gooks, two of whom had sunk to their knees, while another flopped down on his belly, continued to discharge their weapons until they expelled all the bullets in the clips. Feeling exposed and having made little impact, the three turned and ran. Rusty let off three more rounds. He was not sure if he had hit anything.

The radio crackled to life. Gavin answered it while the exchange of fire was occurring. The JOC informed him that a Trojan aircraft was being dispatched from Kariba to assist. It would be on scene in twenty minutes. Exact coordinates were given. Koch felt enormous relief sweep over him at this news, because without the support of the Air Force the prospect of fighting themselves out of this situation to get to the Police camp looked bleak.

The noise of the explosion was deafening. All the soldiers instinctively ducked down as they were showered with fragments of rock. The RPG grenade had hit the outer rock face. Its noise far exceeded the threat to life.

"That's an RPG," Koch announced.

The RPG was a favoured grenade launcher used by the gooks. ZIPRA had theirs supplied by the USSR. They were easy to carry and very user friendly. The Security Forces feared them because of their destructive force and ease of use.

"If it hits the inner rocks behind us were gone. The sun's up now so it should be out of our eyes. We have to shoot the gook with the RPG. Rusty, get the glasses out and spot the gook, okay? You two, up there to get vantage. Rusty you direct us okay? A Trojan is coming to assist us here. We will have to break for it when the plane takes on the gooks. Gavin's looking in a bad way and with Michael hurt we're goners if we don't get to the camp."

"Incoming!" Rusty yelled. They all dived for cover. Rusty fired his FN towards the spot he saw the flash.

Again the explosion was against the rocks on the outside of where the soldiers were. AK rounds followed sending earth, splinters of trees and shards of rock flying. Return fire was limited. Then silence once again.

"The gooks are moving. They are circling us. See there?"

The soldier who had moved up the rocky outcrop let rip with his rife. The gooks scattered and dropped out of sight.

It was six past seven when the radio came to life again. Gavin answered it and called his Corporal.

"The Trojan is here. ETA three minutes," Koch announced. "Get ready with your kit to move when we get the go ahead. Gavin and Michael need assistance. When I say so to we will lay down fire, say five rounds each, to keep the gooks focused on us and not the Trojan. When he strafes the gooks and if any of them break cover, shoot them, okay? "

Coming in with the sun behind it, the engine of the aircraft could be heard in the distance before they saw it. Koch set off the white flare so as to guide the pilot to where the stick was. No internal casualties were desired through misdirected aircraft fire.

The radio buzzed. Koch answered it. He had put the radio pack on his back so he could more easily keep in radio contact with the pilot as he moved about.

"Okay fire!"

The soldiers discharged their weapons in unison. The pilot turned to his starboard before he laid down a carpet of gun fire across a path where Koch had told him the gooks were. The ground erupted as bullets rammed into the soil while tree branches were shredded.

Koch's men watched. There was movement. Several gooks bolted to get away from the havoc from the Trojan's machine guns. The stick laid down another wave of FN bullets. The plane banked to port and swung back for another run in.

A flash indicated where a RPG grenade was launched skywards. They saw the Trojan dive and twist to its starboard in an attempt to avoid the projectile. AK fire was heard and as no incoming bullets were seen it was clear to the stick that the gooks were shooting at the Trojan. The pilot climbed and banked in a wide turn. He radioed in to Koch saying he would do another strafing run which was the trigger for Koch to move his men to the south west and then on towards the Police camp.

**

It was early afternoon when the stick stumbled across the sandy road. They were physically and mentally spent. Gavin was very ill, pale with a high fever. Michael was being virtually carried. Koch and two others were limping badly with burst blisters. Koch himself was in agony with his raw bleeding rash. They had run out of water several hours ago.

After making a break from their overnight position they went as fast as they possibly could on a south west route across rough ground. The Trojan pilot reported three strafing runs before signing off. Koch figured they needed to put distance between them and the gooks quickly because although it was not the modus operandi of gooks to seek out contact with the Security

Forces he was concerned this gang seemed pretty determined.

Koch thought this was the road to the Police camp but was not entirely sure. He directed his men to stay in cover rather than emerge onto the road. They found a clump of trees with thick scrub to settle in while he studied the map. He felt anxious once again because forty five minutes earlier they had spotted six gooks in a valley. Koch's spirits sank lower when looking through his field glasses he saw these gooks were moving towards them. He wondered if it was coincidental that they seemed to be tracking in the same direction as his stick. He thought it strange they were prepared to be so exposed during the day. That was unusual. It seemed incredulous to him that they were tracking his stick looking for another contact. He radioed it in, but got the same response. No fireforce available.

He calculated that he and his men may still be a few kilometres from the Police camp. He radioed in and JOC patched him through to the camp where he spoke to the Police Sergeant. The Inspector was out of the camp attending an incident. Koch explained his predicament to the Sergeant who, being unsure as to what assistance to offer, hesitated. He said he would have to speak to his officer and that he would call back. Reluctantly Koch had to accept this.

The ten minutes it took for the radio to beep was like an eternity for the exhausted men. Koch answered it and listened in silence acknowledging the message. Looking at the demeanour of their Corporal the men expected that there was no relief and that they must walk the rest of the way to the camp.

The weary soldiers were elated when Koch told them that the Police were sending a vehicle to collect

140

them. They all felt relieved that this ordeal, their first contact, was nearly at an end.

Another twelve minutes past before the Police Land Rover came around the bend. It was an open vehicle with no covered cab or back. Concern swept over Koch when he saw it.

Damn it's a bloody jeep. I hoped it was going to be a Leopard.

The Leopard was the name of an improvised mine and ambush protected vehicle driven by a VW beetle engine. The monocoque hull provided ballistic protection against AK 47 rounds and the sturdy externally mounted roll cage protected the occupants from the inevitable roll-over in a mine incident. The wheels were offset from the hull, a feature designed to minimise the blast around the hull. The vehicle could comfortably seat 5 - 6 people.

Well it's better than nothing, Koch rationalised the risks. *We can't take on another contact, low ammo. No water for hours, Gavin looks like shit. I can't bloody walk another hundred metres. Damn it. What about landmines? Okay ... well if there was a land mine on the road the jeep would have hit it coming for us.*

He directed his stick to get aboard the vehicle. Gavin sat in the front seat next to the constable. The other five squeezed in the back tray with Rusty and David sitting at the two ends over the back wheels.

The constable turned the vehicle around quickly. He was anxious to get back to the perceived safety of the Police camp. It was surrounded by high fences with mortar proof bunkers within the camp. It had been mortared twice in the past few months without anyone being seriously injured. For the constable this meant it was safer than being out in the open. He dreaded the Police patrols which had become very dangerous in recent times.

141

He put his foot to the floor and leaving a cloud of dust behind set off back to the camp. The men collectively gave a cry of appreciation and their spirits lifted dramatically. Even Gavin managed to pull a smile. Rusty gave David the thumbs up sign.

"You did good Corp," he said with genuine sincerity. "You did really good."

"Thanks Rusty. It's been a bloody rough few days but we got through it with only slight injury. My balls hurt like hell."

The men cracked a laugh.

"Ya I slotted a gook," yelled Michael as he punched the air.

"I think I got one today," offered Rusty.

"Bullshit you did."

David opened his mouth to acknowledge that Rusty had hit a gook but no words came out. He felt the Land Rover lurch up under him, saw the shocked look appear on Rusty's face, then a sharp agonising pain spread all over.

Then nothing.

***

The Inspector arrived back at the Police camp five minutes after the constable drove down the other road to fetch the soldiers. After failing to get hold of the Inspector the constable was acting on orders of his Sergeant who made a decision to fetch the soldiers with the remaining vehicle in the camp.

The ungainly Leopard vehicle that the Inspector used was being unloaded of its cargo. A mutilated dead body of a villager killed by a terrorist, or that is what he suspected happened. The other villagers were not speaking.

142

He heard the explosion and immediately turned towards the gates of the camp. Beyond the bend in the gravel road he saw the dreaded plume of dust and smoke. This meant only one thing.

The Land Rover had detonated a land mine.

***

The news reader was Geoffrey Atkins. He was a seasoned professional having read the news on the TV for the Rhodesian Broadcasting Corporation for more than a decade. His expression remained the same. What he was about to say he had said so many times before.

"Combined Operations Headquarters regrets to announce the death of three territorial members of the security force and the critical injury of three others, plus the serious injury to a Police constable.

Corporal David Koch, Rifleman Paul Cunningham and Rifleman Robert Davison were killed in action.

Thirty-three terrorists are reported killed over the past twenty four hours in separate contacts.

Now to other news ....."

CHAPTER THIRTEEN

July 1977

Manquoba knelt down to carefully place the land mine into the shallow sandy hole. It was a cloudless sky and, with only a partial moon, was blazoned with a billion stars.

Manquoba used his considerable experience when selecting this location. The sandy road was two semi parallel tracks with tufts of grass in between them. The 's' bend was over six hundred metres from the fork in the road that led to the Police camp and wound past two large clumps of trees. Manquoba figured that a driver would, in all probability, be concentrating on navigating the bends to avoid the trees rather than scrutinising the road. He dug the hole for the land mine slightly off centre of the one track estimating the driver would manoeuvre towards that part of the track to make the 's' bend less sharp.

He primed the land mine before packing sand in gently around it. It was hard to see in the dark. Manquoba stepped away. Picking up the grass that he had clumped together, he gently swept over the area to remove the traces of any foot prints from the surrounding vicinity.

The enemy had become wary of land mines and many were expert in being able to spot where they were laid. If the land mine was not packed in well then indents could be seen especially if it rained. The soil would sink in around the mine. If the track had a tire marks then it was difficult to put replica tracks back over the soil disturbed by laying the mine. The cut out on tarmac roads was a sure give away. Laying land mines so they were undetected was a skill, one which

144

he learned well when he was in the ZIPRA training camp in Angola.

Manquoba moved back towards his comrades sweeping the ground as he went. The scene was left as if no one had been there.

They blended into the surrounding bush making their way towards their hide. The elevated site was selected so they could overlook a large part of the countryside and in particular several gravel roads including the one they had mined. Surrounded by very large boulders, thickly treed with heavy undergrowth, they planned to stay there for a few days to observe if the land mines they had laid went off, then, depending upon the response from the Security Forces, they would elect to engage in a gun and rocket battle with them or disappear to another sector of this tribal trust land.

The ten comrades arrived at the hide after thirty five minutes just as the tinge of light in the east heralded in the start of another long boring day. Before it became light they ate dried meat and maize biscuits. They would sleep most of the day because tonight would be another busy evening for them.

Manquoba selected his spot under a small stone ledge where he could lie flat facing outwards. He was able to see down the shallow valley towards where the Police camp was situated. The overhanging rock gave protection from the sun and cover from above if a helicopter should come. He pulled some branches near him which gave his exposed side adequate camouflage before he settled down to sleep. But he found sleep did not come to him. His mind was too active as he recalled what brought him to this place.

Manquoba was not his original name. He chose it when he arrived at the training camp. '*The one who conquers.*' The meaning of that name felt right because he was on a crusade to conquer the white settlers and reclaim his country, to deliver to himself and his tribe the justice and equality he and they deserved.

His European name was Samson. He could not recall how he came to inherit that name. He understood that Samson was a strong and powerful man and had wondered if he got that name because he is a big man, with the strength of an ox.

He was born and lived his early years in a remote tribal village. His memories of this time were happy ones where he would play in the dust around the village with other children. As a young boy his mother, who was a devout Methodist, gave him tasks which included fetching water each day from the river. That was hard work because it involved a long walk to the river and back carrying a tin full of water, but that task made him feel important. The women who also went to fetch the water were able to somehow balance the tin on their heads. He never mastered that. When he got older he was promoted to minding the cattle. That was a time he particularly enjoyed. He was able to walk in the bush and explore the rocky outcrops hunting lizards. He felt like a warrior with his small assegai which he would stab unsuspecting lizards with.

Another boy from his kraal who herded cattle was killed by a leopard. The villagers found his half eaten body hanging from an old thorn tree the day after he went missing. There was great sadness in the village and the women wailed for days. He recalled that was the first time he saw a white man other than the priest who visited their village occasionally. This man was the 'District Commissioner', a very important man who came to investigate the killing. He came with several black men in uniform. They spent the day looking around. Then they left.

The next time he saw white men was in the next season when two men arrived at their village to talk

146

with the headman. These men said they were from the Department of Agriculture. The village remained unsettled for months after that visit. He never fully understood why, except it had something to do with the men wanting the villagers to grow different crops. His mother said the villagers were Ndebele and they raised cattle. They were not like the Karanga dogs that ate soil. She said that they were not going to dig the soil and plant the seeds that these men had given them.

He felt abandoned when his two older brothers left the village to seek work in the city. When they returned to the village after a very long time he recalled that they spoke of wonderful things. They wore good clothes, fine shoes and they brought with them different types of food in many bags. Their stories inspired him to think he could share in these things.

In this fifteenth season he left his village to seek work in the city. Bulawayo was daunting for him. The hustle and bustle of a city and the large amount of people there caused him to become anxious. One of his older brothers took him under his wing which was reassuring. His brother worked for a family tending their garden and Samson soon found himself in the same line of work, albeit working for another family.

His work involved doing whatever the owner of the property told him to do each day and for this he received rations of meat, a helping of sadza, tea with sugar and two thick slices of bread. He was allowed to live in a small out-house at the back of the property where he was allocated a room that was attached to an open fire kitchen. There was a shower with cold water. No electricity. He received money at the end of each month as wages which allowed him to buy things he previously never thought was possible.

Samson worked day in day out, six days each week tending the garden. Digging this garden bed, mowing

147

the lawns, chopping down that tree, sweeping up here and then there. Life went from week to week, month to month and then year to year.

The 'madam' of the property was generally pleasant but her moods proved unpredictable. Several servants who worked in the house came and went, each complaining that she was harsh and demanding. She did not get involved in the garden that much and so Samson had little to do with her. The 'boss' was the one who gave him the daily instructions and checked up on the work at the end of the day. The 'boss' was hard to understand because he spoke with a strange accent and could not speak Ndebele. They however established a workable hand gesturing routine between them. His brother told him the 'boss' came from Wales, somewhere very far away and that was why it was hard to understand him.

Years had passed until one day he noticed a young woman working as the housemaid in the adjacent property. He saw her each day when she was hanging the washing out to dry. A young buxom girl with a round face, sparkling eyes and huge wide smile, she stirred a strange emotional and physical reaction within him. She was terribly shy, as was he, so it took quite some time for them to finally talk. He liked her very much. Her name was Thembelihle which meant '*good hope*'. Her European name was Mary. She told him that was the name of the mother of Jesus. They became close, eventually spending every Sunday together. Sunday was their day off work.

It was on a Sunday when they were in bed together in his room when it happened. The door flew open and the 'madam' screamed at them hysterically.

"You bloody filthy bastards!" she shouted over and over.

Sampson leapt off Mary. Both were naked. As he attempted to find his clothes he felt the whip hit his bare buttocks. Mary tried to get off the bed and as she did so she was struck across her bosoms with the whip.

Manquoba lay on the rock recalling this incident with rising bitterness. It was chaos with the 'madam' screaming while thrashing them both with the whip. Mary cried. The humiliation of seeing Mary being chased around the back garden while naked as she tried to avoid the whip and he himself still naked trying to get in between Mary and the white woman was burned into his memory. He had wanted to hit the white woman, but knew if he did that the Police would arrest him and put him in jail. Thinking of it all those years ago caused a surge of anger to rise in Manquoba.

Later that day he was sacked from that employment and did not get his pay for the week before. His brother said that it was pointless going to the Police as they would do nothing about him being hit or not getting his wages.

Samson found another similar job a few weeks later but he found the children of the people he worked for were disrespectful, teasing him for being black and stupid. They did not call him by his name. Rather they called him 'boy'. He was a young man, six feet tall with a large muscled body and these children called him 'boy'. Their parents knew what the children said to him but did nothing. Samson decided to leave after a few months.

He then secured a job as a yard hand at a timber mill. The work was hard with ten hour days, six days a week. The pay was better than that as a 'garden boy', but there were no rations nor was housing provided. After a few weeks he managed to get a room in a block of flats. These flats, situated in a part of the city that was designated as an 'African township', were owned by the municipality and rented to single black men. He shared this room with one other man who worked delivering ice creams. He would take a bicycle attached to a cold box in the front and cycle around the suburbs ringing his bell to attract custom to sell ice creams. Thirty men shared a common kitchen area as well as ablutions that consisted of two toilets and two showers. At least there was hot water supplied.

It was during this time that he was introduced to some Ndebele men who spoke of political matters that stirred up nationalist emotions amongst many men there. They spoke of the white settlers who came from the south and stole the land from their forefathers, brought their own laws, paid low wages to the Ndebele while paying themselves much more money. He learned about how their forefathers had been slaughtered by these settlers. Much of this information was new to Samson and hearing it made him angry and eager to learn more.

These men spoke of how the Ndebele must rise up and take back what is rightfully theirs. To do this he was told that the masses must chase out the settlers. He heard about Joshua Nkomo who was the Ndebele leader that the settlers had imprisoned. He was now in Zambia leading the revolution. He also heard about the future Zimbabwe where he could have the house of that white woman who beat him and Thembelihle, or if he chose, he could have the house where those nasty children lived.

These men explained how all the settler children went to good European only schools and were educated so they could be 'bosses' to earn more money than the Africans. He was told that the settlers restricted the schooling of the blacks so they would remain uneducated and thus stay as slave labour to the settler's business and industry. Samson found this information to be a revelation, facts he had never heard of before. He progressively became inspired the more these people spoke about these matters, eventually finding he was unable to think of anything else. Finally he asked them how he could assist with the struggle to liberate Zimbabwe.

He left Bulawayo one Sunday on the back of a Datsun pickup which took him to the border with Botswana where he discovered a gathering of many other men and women. That evening they all crossed the border and once in Botswana were transported by trucks north to Zambia. After a week spent in a staging camp in Zambia, they were taken by truck in a journey lasting five days to a training camp situated in Angola. It was here he started his training to be a nationalist guerrilla, a fighter who, together with thousands like him, would overthrow the Smith settler regime in Rhodesia and install Joshua Nkomo as its President. It was here that he gave up his European name and adopted his new Ndebele name, Manquoba.

The recollection of the harsh treatment the recruits received from the Cuban instructors came pouring back to him. At the time he felt resentful at the cruel military justice that was arbitrarily metered out, but now the reality of survival in the bush depended on that training. That physical and mental training was what kept him alive.

He proved to be adept with the weapons, learning quickly to use the AK 47 and the RPG rocket launcher. Each afternoon for seven days a week, he was in the class room, a ramshackle corrugated iron building with a leaking roof and no doors or windows, only gaps where they should have been. This is where he was taught about communism. He learned about a man called Marx and how he brought great changes to Russia, where like Rhodesia, the few governed and ruled over the masses who worked hard for nothing. A revolution like what was to occur in Rhodesia had happened in Russia where the masses, led by Marx, had risen up, killing the oppressors taking the land and industry that was rightfully theirs. Communal farms and factories were established benefiting all the masses with a better life, better schools, health and happiness. They explained that this system of Government called 'Communism' was sweeping the world freeing all the oppressed people. It did not take much encouragement for Manquoba to believe that Communism was a good system for governing a country.

Manquoba looked out over the valley without seeing.

He remembered how sad he was leaving Thembelihle behind in Bulawayo. He promised her he would return triumphant and take her as his woman, have ten children and live in the house of the white woman who beat her. She had been sad to see him leave on that Sunday, crying as he was driven off.

He adjusted himself on the rock wondering where Thembelihle was. It had been nearly three years ago since he left to become a liberation fighter.

When we have won this liberation struggle I will go to Bulawayo a hero and find her, he told himself.

Manquoba drifted into a light sleep resting his face on his hands. His AK 47 lay next to him. The dull thud awoke him with a start but he did not move. His training and instinct told him not to make any sudden movements that would alert the Security Forces who may be nearby. He looked downwards and scanned the valley.

There! Smoke.

He saw a plume of smoke rising over the trees. He calibrated where this was in context of the dirt road and the Police camp.

Aw, it's the land mine I laid this night.

He felt exuberant, wanting to get out from under the ledge and dance around shouting. This was the feeling he always got when he found out one of his land mines had been detonated. But he restrained himself. It was unsafe to let his guard down. He lay still until he noticed that some of his comrades were stirring. Two stood on a rock looking towards where the smoke was now disbursing.

Fools. The Rhodesians will see them.

He crawled out of his hide taking his weapon with him and skulked around the rocks to where these two were.

"Get down you fools," he ordered in Ndebele. "The Rhodesians may be looking. Do it now."

The two men cowered, immediately obeying him. He was their field commander. The others who were contemplating breaking their cover decided against it. Manquoba dished out rough military justice with his fists. He once shot a comrade dead for not obeying him. The dead comrade was a burden as he was a sickly one, slowing them down, so his demise was no great loss, but nonetheless seeing their comrade being shot in the head was enough to convince them never to cross Manquoba.

He looked back down the valley to see the smoke had already disbursed in the breeze.

I will wait and see what the Rhodesians do before I make a decision on what we will do.

With that he settled back down and watched. It was not long before he saw a truck moving slowly along the road from the Police camp. He saw it was one of the trucks built to withstand the land mine explosion. It had a 'v' shaped belly and its wheels were on the outside of the chassis. He hated these vehicles because his mines

153

didn't kill the Rhodesians in them. He despised the Rhodesians for inventing such things.

The truck disappeared behind trees near where the smoke was. It did not emerge.

That is where I put the mine. I have a kill.

He noticed some black men with weapons fan out in a circle. He saw they were Police. Manquoba continued to scan the scene carefully calculating that if the army were to come they would already be on the scene. They would have arrived in their helicopters by now. He considered his options and decided that his men could take on the Police. He estimated it would take fifteen minutes to get to the site, then a few minutes to position themselves before engaging the enemy.

He paused briefly to reconsider but finally decided that it had been long enough to be certain the Rhodesians were not sending in the fireforce. Summoning his men and briefly explaining to them his battle plan they set off in single file at a trot down the hill. As they jogged Manquoba psyched himself up for the forthcoming battle. He always went through a routine in his mind ahead of a gun battle, deliberately making himself angry. The anger chased away the fear.

Manquoba and his men were close to the site of the explosion when they heard the helicopter. Manquoba could not see it, but knew from past experience that it would be coming in low at treetop level and there would be more than one. He stopped immediately as did his men.

"We must go away from here now," he barked to his men. "We are in danger. We must not go back to the place we came from but further away. Stay under tree cover so you are not seen. Move now."

Manquoba sped past the others at a sprint. The others followed.

The two helicopters arrived at the scene of the explosion and circled before one descended. The scene confronting the medics debussing was one of destruction. What was left of the Police Land Rover was ten metres from a crater in the dirt road. Its back end was missing having been blown away by the blast. The blast flipped what was left of the vehicle high in the air. All around the blast area was debris. Bits of army kit and the vehicle all tangled together. Bodies of dead and injured soldiers lay around the ground.

The second helicopter veered off circling in ever increasing circles from the scene. The pilot, gunner and the RLI troops in the helicopter searched for signs of terrorists. They had a low expectation of locating any but nonetheless an aerial search was mandatory.

Later that afternoon Manquoba and his men arrived at a village situated many kilometres from the blast site. They were exhausted having run nonstop. The villagers welcomed them wholeheartedly, offering them food and drink. They spent the night resting in the huts of the village before leaving in the early dawn to find a secure place to spend the day. Manquoba would lay two more land mines that coming evening.

CHAPTER FOURTEEN

February 1978

The insect slowly crawled along the rifle barrel breaking the monotony of the past six hours. Rob wondered what he would do if the insect progressed all the way along to his face. He was not certain what type of insect it was or if it would be inclined to bite him. His face was coloured with green and black dye with tree branches attached to his webbing to assist his camouflage. Not wishing to make any unnecessary movement he decided to blow at it when it came within range hoping that his bad breath would be enough for it to retreat back the way it came.

He had carefully selected this observation post which gave him the best vantage of the whole camp. He chose a kopje to the south of the camp to avoid early morning and evening sun blind spots and to mitigate any reflections.

The camp consisted of what looked like a disused general store building with a dilapidated veranda at the front. The door at the rear of the building hung open by one hinge. There were two windows in the front, two windows at the back, one smaller than the other and one window on the side. A chimney poked out the corrugated iron roof near to the back door and a steady stream of smoke oozed out of it. Rob figured that was where the kitchen would be. There was an outside 'long drop' toilet about thirty metres from the back door. It was a square tin hut with a sloping tin roof.

To the west of this building were two parallel lines of ten large canvas tents. They were painted with shades of brown markings that merged in with the earth around the camp. Camouflage netting was also erected at various locations. Rob suspected the tents and netting were ex USSR given this was a ZIPRA terrorist camp.

A cleared patch of scrub revealing a stony uneven surface to the east of the building was being used as a parade ground where training was haphazardly conducted during the day. Several trucks were parked off to one side. Rob was unable to determine their make. There appeared to be a bunker on the other side of the parade ground as men disappeared when they were near that part of the camp. Rob thought that must be where their weapons and ammunition are being stored.

While there was no perimeter fencing, Rob observed there was some semblance of defensive security being deployed with five guards usually walking the perimeter of the bush clearing. They were not vigilant, often falling asleep under a thorn tree around noon each day.

The insect came within range and Rob blew at it. It stopped with its antennae moving frantically. He blew again. The insect turned and rushed back down the rifle. Rob smiled to himself as he watched it leave.

He felt stiff. Having been in one position now for several hours made his muscles sore and his one elbow ached from how he leant on it. It was time to readjust his position. Being on covert surveillance was a lonely task. To be on top of a rock in the middle of the bush for days on end, in a foreign country with hostile people only too willing to kill, being unable to move around freely and only eating dry rations, gave a sense of complete isolation. But that's what SAS troopers did and Rob was expert at his job. Once the sun set he would be able to move about, eat and drink some water before reporting back to his commander via radio. He expected to be recalled back to base camp soon. He had seen enough to confirm what the Special Branch had suspected and what ComOps wanted validated.

Rob reflected on how he got to be on this kopje while he watched a group of terrorists start up a game of soccer on the parade ground. He was pleased to have been briefed by his close friend Richard as it had given them time to catch up once again.

"One of our SB informers in Botswana has reported ZIPRA presence near his village close to the Botswana Rhodesia border. By his description the camp looks like its set up as a transit camp to ferry insurgents across the border and may also act as a rest and recreation stop off point for exiting insurgents," Richard had said as he addressed a joint SAS and Police briefing.

"Why would the Botswana Government allow this camp to be established? They are supposed to be neutral," asked the Police Commissioner.

"While they outwardly state neutrality Sir, they continue to be sympathetic to the insurgency and thus allow ZIPRA to operate, albeit within a limited unofficial mandate. It's something CIO is working on at the Botswana government level," Richard had replied. "What we require is close reconnaissance of where our informant says this activity is occurring and the commander of SAS 'B' Troop has agreed to deploy his men for that purpose. We also suspect that a key ZIPRA commander, Vhukile Ncube, may be located at this camp. We have been after him for some time now and if we can confirm that he's at this camp and we take him out, or capture him, it would be a coup for us."

Richard had run through the specifics of the intel and they had reviewed the maps of the area before the SAS commander outlined what course of action he was going to adopt.

"I will deploy Rob to undertake close in surveillance and based on his intel we can develop the attack plans. I will also deploy a unit of men to trawl along here and through here." He pointed to the map to identify the area he was referring to. "This will be so they can gather intel on the wider extent of any terr activity and be in close proximity in case Rob needs assistance."

Rob noticed the clouds building up overhead. He hoped it would not rain. It was miserable to get wet and while his wet weather gear was of some help, it really did not prevent water seeping in when the rain was heavy.

A car arrived at the camp. It had a single truck escort with several armed terrorists in the back. Rob peered through his field glasses to examine who the passengers of the car were. He observed frantic activity erupted as terrs rushed around to form two imperfect lines. Standing to attention they were inspected by one of the men who had got out of the car. By the way all the others behaved it was obvious this person was important.

This must be Ncube, he thought as the group disbursed and those who arrived in the car went into the building.

Night fell casting the landscape into darkness. He moved slowly backwards down the rock until he was out of the sight line of the camp. He removed his webbing to which the foliage was attached and relieved his bladder before fetching his water bottle. He drank feeling satisfied as the warm water passed through his parched mouth and down his dry throat.

He fired up his radio to make contact with his base. His prediction was correct. He was instructed to pull out, so he cautiously packed up his gear ensuring he left nothing to indicate his presence before he left the kopje to merge into the night.

159

His rendezvous point was five kilometres away. It took him most of the night to cover that distance. The cloud cover occasionally blocked out the half-moon which made his transit through the bush more difficult. At one point, as he traversed a gully, he stumbled and fell heavily. Hoping he had not sprained his ankle Rob felt relief that apart from a graze on his forearm all was okay.

He was confident he was close to the rendezvous point where his SAS colleagues would collect him for the return leg of this mission back to Rhodesia when the first signs of dawn appeared. He looked at his watch. Five ten. His pickup time was at five thirty. He recalibrated his position and figured that he was not that far off the mark but needed to move at a pace to find the right spot. He broke into a steady trot to make up the ground.

A Land Rover with two men in it bounced along the sandy track. Rob hid himself from view watching its slow progress towards him.

Is that them? Looks like it. But let's be certain.

He stayed hidden with his weapon at the ready. When the Land Rover was forty metres away Rob could see it was his colleagues. He stepped out showing himself clearly. The Land Rover stopped and Rob got into the back. Laconic greetings were exchanged before the vehicle moved on travelling down a rough narrow track. It looked like it was hardly used. They soon found themselves driving parallel to the four strand barbed wire fence that separated Rhodesia from Botswana. The risk of land mines was ever present which made them anxious as they made their way slowly along the track. Their experienced eyes were trained on the track ahead. None of them spoke.

A loud explosion shattered the still morning followed by the zipping sound of bullets.

160

"What the fuck!" shouted the driver, the steering wheel and bonnet of the vehicle offering him no real cover.

"There at one o'clock," shouted Rob, "Terrs! Standing in the grass."

He lifted his weapon and together with the other SAS trooper in the passenger seat, they fired. The driver, with no option but to carry on along the track, put the accelerator flat to the metal. The Land Rover reacted, jerking forward as it gained speed.

Seven ZIPRA terrorists standing in waist high grass off to the one side of the track fired their weapons at the Land Rover as it sped past them. One terrorist was kneeling out of sight trying to reload his RPG-7 rocket launcher. When the Land Rover appeared from nowhere he was startled and, in the rush to discharge the weapon, he misaimed.

The Land Rover belted past the terrorists, the two SAS men returning fire, emptying their magazines on the way through.

"I'm hit! In the foot. Jeeees."

The driver's left foot was shattered. Bleeding profusely, he had the presence of mind to keep his other foot flat on the accelerator.

"I'm hit too. Bloody hell!" shouted the other SAS sitting next to him.

The Land Rover lurched along sending a cloud of dust up all around them offering some camouflage as they sped away from the ambush. Rob fired his weapon, aiming at the flashes of light he saw through the dust that came from the terrorist weapons as they discharged them. A terrorist recoiled backwards when a bullet hit him in his upper chest just below his neck. His AK flew into the air. He was dead before he hit the ground. Another terrorist spun around and fell after a bullet hit him in his right abdomen.

161

"How bad?" queried Rob. "How bad are you?"

"In the foot. Shit it hurts."

"Both of you hit in the feet?"

"Looks that way."

"I'm not feeling that flash," announced the driver and the vehicle began to slow down.

"No! Don't stop for fucksakes. Carry on. Keep going," yelled Rob.

The driver summoned more reserve and once again accelerated. Although his vision was blurred he managed to keep the vehicle within the track until hitting a rock, one of the front tyres burst and the vehicle lurched awkwardly. It took the last of his reserve strength to struggle with the steering wheel to prevent the vehicle from tipping over.

"Keep going," shouted Rob. "Just keep going. We need distance between us and the terrs."

The vehicle came to a grinding halt when the driver slumped forward on the steering wheel.

"Okay let's get him out. I'll get the kit," instructed Rob.

Fetching the medical kit from behind the driver's seat Rob ran around to the front driver's door and opened it. He grabbed his colleague roughly by his webbing lifting him out of the vehicle and laid him on the grass by the side of the track. The foot was nearly severed from the leg.

"Fit the drip and give him the shot. Patch him up as best you can okay? I'm going to radio this in then do a recce to check the terrs are not on our tail," said Rob.

If they come after us they may try to outflank us? My guess though is they will turn tail and gap it. Fucking bastards.

When Rob returned to where the others were, the soldier on the ground looked deathly pale. He noticed the other colleague's shoe was red with blood.

162

"How's it looking? Will he make it?"

"Should do, but probably not his foot. It's pretty shot up. How long?"

"Casavac chopper is thirty minutes."

"Good. This drip will be okay for that time."

"How's your foot?"

"Bloody sore. I think the bullet went straight through and I suspect no bone contact. I'll dress it when I'm done here."

"Okay. Look I'm going out to do another recce. If the terrs come we'll have a tonk on our hands. Keep your eyes beaded. Get more cover. I'll give the signal before I appear so don't slot me hey? "

Rob gave a reassuring smile before moving quickly into the bush. Time passed slowly. He felt vulnerable as he tracked along the side of the road for a short distance then circled back to the Land Rover. Nothing. Then he repeated it, searching for any signs to indicate the terrorists were following up their ambush.

When he neared the location of the Land Rover for the second time he looked at his watch. Thirty five minutes. He sank to his haunches when he heard talking. English. He moved closer to the vehicle very cautiously. Parting the long grass he saw that two other SAS soldiers had arrived on the scene. Relief flooded over him. This had been a close call, the closest yet. But he had survived uninjured. He lay down on his back and closed his eyes.

In the distance he heard the sound of the chopper.

***

When the chopper landed at Victoria Falls airport the SAS commander rushed up to it.

"What the hell happened?" he barked. "How the hell did you allow yourselves to be ambushed?"

163

The medics immediately started attending to the injured driver. They replaced his drip before moving him onto a stretcher to take him to the plane that waited to ferry him to the hospital in Bulawayo.

Rob was cut off in his explanation of what had occurred.

"Get your kit. We're moving out to get those bastards," ordered the commander.

An army truck with twenty seven men in the back, five of which were SAS, the rest territorial troops who were stationed at Victoria Falls rumbled onto the scene.

"We are still waiting on ComOps Sir," informed the radio operator when the commander approached the truck.

It was a 'Crocodile.' The distinctive 'v' shaped undercarriage and sides both with armour plated steel had proved these trucks offered excellent protection from either a land mine explosion or a rocket attack.

"Damn. Those terrs will be long gone if they don't hurry up with the go ahead. Ask them again for hot pursuit clearance. I want to go across the border and get those bloody bastards now!"

Ten minutes passed before ComOps approved the hot pursuit into Botswana. The commander in the meantime reconsidered his options.

"It is likely that the terrs who ambushed you are from the group located at that camp Rob. They did not follow up the ambush and in all probability they are making their way back to the camp. Once there it is likely those bastards will abandon the camp."

"Agreed," said Rob.

"Okay then we go straight to the camp rather than attempt to track the terrs from the ambush point."

It was coming up to five hours since the ambush and time was pressing on the Rhodesians to initiate their attack before the terrorists at the camp could be alerted.

164

The commander continued his debriefing with Rob in the back of the lead truck as they sped to the border in a two army truck convoy.

They arrived at the designated drop off point in the early afternoon and the soldiers split into three groups each with an SAS soldier commanding them. They quickly disbursed to make their way to predetermined points in preparation for the ground attack on the camp. Meanwhile Rob and his commander made their way to the look out where Rob had spent the past few days to set up their command post for this op.

Looking through their field glasses they saw plenty of activity in the camp. Men ran back and forth with boxes from the bunker to the five trucks parked nearby.

"Bugger! They've been alerted. The bastards are pulling out," observed the commander.

"Look," whispered Rob, "BDF. They were not there yesterday."

"What the hell? What's the bloody Botswana Defence Force doing here? Is this a BDF camp instead of a terr camp Rob?"

"No it's a ZIPRA camp. The ZIPRA terrs are there as well. See them? In those green uniforms and those over towards the tents, between the tents and the building. They're in the East German fleck kit. Those are not BDF. They're terrs."

The presence of BDF troops suddenly made the situation a whole lot more complicated.

"I know exactly what's going down. The BDF are helping the terrs clear out the camp so when we hit it we won't find evidence of ZIPRA. The Botswana Government keep bleating on that they only have refugee camps. They don't want us to find the evidence of ZIPRA." Rob summed up the situation for the commander.

165

"Yes I agree. To hell with it. I'm not going to let these bastards get away. If the bloody BDF want to sleep with dogs they can get the bloody fleas. They have chosen to get involved with ZIPRA and they can now take the consequence. We're going for it. Tell the sections to move."

Rob passed on the instructions via radio to the three groups who moved forward in unison in their sweep lines towards the camp.

"We should have laid mines on the road," muttered the commander.

This op was put together so quickly he had not managed to think through all the permutations.

"The terrs may gap it by that road," he added.

Rob scanned the scene below with his field glasses.

"Bugger it."

"What?"

"Looks like Ncube has gapped it. His car is not there, nor is the truck that arrived with it yesterday."

Then with dismay they watched as three trucks began to leave the camp each with a full load of terrorists and piles of boxes.

"They're on the move. Tell the section commanders to get a move on. We must strike these bastards now. I don't want those bloody trucks leaving."

Rob passed on the order. While being wary not to break cover too soon nor allow any one group to get too far ahead so that they would cop any cross fire when this contact went off, the three sweep line groups immediately sped up their advance.

"Can we sweep around quick enough to cut off those bloody trucks?" asked the commander.

Rob looked through his field glasses to survey the position of the men closest to the road.

"Nope. Those trucks will get away." He thought for a moment. "Unless .... unless we call in the Air Force?"

"Yes. Great idea. I really want to take those bastards out. Call it in and see what we can do."

Rob radioed the JOC ops room at Victoria Falls requesting Air Force support. He gave the coordinates and detail of what was going down on the ground.

"So? Are we getting air support?" queried the commander when Rob finished.

"JOC have referred it to ComOps. They need to make the call on this request seeing it would be an air strike inside Botswana. They will let us know."

Gun fire broke out as a sweep line engaged with terrorists near the bunker. BDF troops also engaged in the contact. Rob watched as the second sweep line engaged with a torrent of fire that was intense and devastating, sending terrorists and BDF troops scattering amongst the tents. The gun fire ripped through the canvas. The third sweep line arrived at the road but the trucks had already passed by. They turned right and started to make their way towards the camp.

"The boys are slotting the terrs," observed the commander excitedly.

The radio buzzed to life and Rob answered it.

"Okay thanks for that," he said into the receiver. "ComOps have okayed the air strike. A Hunter. They are arming it with frantan. It will be twenty minutes though."

"Great! Pity about the time delay. I should have had mines laid. Damn it. We had better tell JOC where the Hunter will find those bloody trucks. Let's see the map."

Unfolding the map they calculated the possible location of where the trucks would be in twenty minutes. Rob passed the information to JOC before resuming his observation of the contact unfolding below.

"The contact is all but over," said the commander.

The firing was now only sporadic. The third sweep line that was moving down the road arrived at the camp without firing a shot.

"Let's get down there pronto."

The commander and Rob scrambled down the kopje and jogged towards the camp.

"You realise Sir that this will cause a stir" said Rob as they ran side by side. "The BDF involvement complicates this."

"Noted. We must gather evidence of their complicity with ZIPRA and take it back for CIO and Foreign Affairs to deal with."

"Do we dispose of the BDF bodies or leave them?"

"Good point. Let's see what the body count is first before we make a call on that."

Something moved in the clump of trees off to their left. It moved quickly.

"What's that?" exclaimed the commander.

He flung himself to the ground. Rob stumbled before steadying, then sank to his knees. His heart pounding. His eyes searched for danger.

A large Warthog broke cover and ran passed at breakneck speed.

"Bloody hell. It's a fucking Warthog."

Relief swept over both men.

They heard the sound of a fighter jet in the distance.

***

While the pilot scrambled into his cockpit, the Hunter was fitted with two frantan and two Golf bombs. Once he buckled himself in the engine was fired up. The engineer gave him the thumbs up after he took the wheel stops away. The pilot spooled up and when he released the wheel brake the Hunter lurched forward. Within a minute the plane was airborne and streaking at

168

full throttle towards the Rhodesian border with Botswana.

"Red Leader. This is the tower. Over."

"Tower, this is Red Leader. Go ahead."

"Red Leader. You will take ops guidance from the SAS Commander on the ground. He will direct you to the target using this frequency. Over."

"Roger that. I'll stay on this frequency."

The target was going to be difficult to find given there was no one on the ground observing it. The three trucks were on the move and the SAS commander was guessing where they would be. Looking down, the ground below whizzed past. It would be tough for Red Leader to pick up the land marks to find the area and then identify the target.

"Red Leader, this is the SAS Commander. Do you read?"

"I read. What's your call sign?"

"Call me B Squadron."

"Okay B Squadron. My ETA is three minutes. Do you have the landmarks for me?"

"Ya, I will get this to you just now."

He scanned the map to relocate the landmarks Rob had identified as the best ones to guide the Hunter pilot to where they thought the target would be when he heard the plane. He looked skywards to see the Hunter in the distance.

"Fire the flare," he ordered to one of his men.

The flare sent white smoke skywards.

"Okay Red Leader. We have you visual now."

"Roger that B Squadron. I have the smoke visual. Give me the lead."

"Can you see the track leading north, northwest?"

"Roger that."

"Okay. Then follow that. It will turn west after a river. A large kopje will be on the right at the bend.

After ten klicks it turns sharp north. Another river, a depression, large one, then the road turns west again. The target will ... or should be about there."

"Roger that."

The Hunter flew over the camp leaving behind the distinctive roar of its engine. The troops on the ground waved enthusiastically, some throwing their caps into the air.

Red Leader throttled back to reduce his speed to assist him with the search for the land marks. It was mid-afternoon and as he swung west the sun poured into the cockpit. Then he turned north. There was no vehicle traffic on the road. He saw many people walking along it and a cart being pulled by a donkey. He saw the river and then the depression. His heart rate increased as he anticipated the target getting closer.

"Red Leader, this is B Squadron. How you doing?"

"B Squadron. Red Lead. Okay. No target yet. I can see the depression. Turning west again now. The road winds a bit .... still no target."

"Damn," said the commander.

"What's up?" asked Rob who anxiously awaited the news of the Hunter strike.

"The bloody trucks are not where we thought. Damn it. Could they have diverted? If so, where?"

They both searched the map once again looking for any possible options where the trucks would have gone.

"Sighted!" came the enthusiastic call from the pilot. "Three trucks. Ya?"

The commander picked up the receiver to respond.

"Ya. Its three trucks with ...."

"I have them," said Red Leader. "On the road. Three trucks. With troops. Do I have your okay to strike?"

Thank heavens. We've got the bastards. Okay let's get this over with.

"B Squadron. Do I have your okay? Quickly!"

170

"Yes. Yes! Take them out," instructed the commander.

"Roger that. Steadying. They've seen me. I've got them! Bombs away."

Two frantan bombs left the wings of the Hunter and sped earthwards. They hit the ground between the second and third vehicle exploding into huge fireballs that engulfed the two leading vehicles. The third and last vehicle swerved in an attempt to avoid the fire ball but its momentum took it into the flames.

Red Leader turned his aircraft in a long sweeping circle. Black smoke rose from the carcasses of the three trucks. He could see burning patches that looked like bodies lying around the last vehicle. His job done, with no need to deliver the golf bombs, he turned his aircraft for home.

"Red Leader this is B Squadron. What's the status over?" queried the commander anxiously.

"Beautiful! The target is taken out. Looks like a complete kill. I'm going home. Good luck on the ground."

"Thanks for that. Good news. Fly well." He put the receiver back in its cradle. "He's taken out the target. All three trucks with all the bastards. Bloody well done hey?" he said to Rob who nodded in agreement. "Let's clean up here and get the hell back home."

***

March 1978

"The ballistic evidence, the weapons brought back, the photo evidence ... they all clearly show BDF involvement with ZIPRA and insurgency action against Rhodesia."

Richard presented his briefing to the military commanders in the ComOps headquarters deep in the guts of Milton Buildings. Two Government Ministers were present, plus the head of the CIO. As suspected, the political fallout from the raid into Botswana had hit the fan.

"We will be able to demonstrate to the UN envoy when he arrives in Salisbury tomorrow that the Botswana Government was complicit in the insurgency activities by ZIPRA against Rhodesia. We will be able to absolve our action which took out BDF forces as appropriate defence when they attacked our troops who were in legitimate hot pursuit against ZIPRA insurgents."

Richard, being a key instigator of the actions that lead to the attack on the ZIPRA camp, had taken considerable criticism for his involvement in the cross border actions that now embroiled Rhodesia in a diplomatic crisis. Following the attack on the ZIPRA camp and the air strike against the fleeing vehicles, the Botswana Government closed the Kazangula border between the two countries cutting off the vital trade link at a point where four countries met on the Zambezi River. It had been the last remaining land trade link between Rhodesia and South Africa with the rest of Central Africa.

The Botswana Government took their complaint to the United Nations where Rhodesia was not represented. Surprisingly for the Rhodesians, rather than blanket criticism of the Rhodesian action, the UN had resolved to send an envoy to Rhodesia to examine the evidence that purported to implicate the BDF in supporting the insurgency activity against Rhodesia.

Other than those in the SAS and Air Force, not many others seemed pleased with the outcome. Militarily the operation was a success, with only three Rhodesians wounded and scores of terrorists eliminated. It was somewhat unfortunate then that the

172

unintended consequence involving BDF troops resulted in such a diplomatic stink.

The South African Government had formally lodged its displeasure to both the Rhodesian and Botswana Governments that the border was closed which was disrupting their trade. Pik Botha, the outspoken Foreign Affairs Minister for South Africa, admonished his counterpart in Rhodesia reminding him in no uncertain terms who exactly was supporting Rhodesia in its war against terror. The Ministry of Foreign Affairs in Rhodesia were put out by having to defend the avalanche of complaints and criticisms without pre-warning that the raid had occurred. The Prime Minister, Ian Smith, was unhappy the Botswana Government was now embroiled in the whole complex problem. He had hoped the Government of Botswana would play a part in moderating the escalation of violence and assist him in his current initiative to bring Nkomo to the negotiation table.

"Rhodesia should be vindicated diplomatically once the evidence is analysed," continued Richard. "But Gentlemen, let us not overlook the main objective here. That is the seeking out and destruction of insurgent forces who threaten this country each day. We must keep the insurgents at bay to allow the diplomatic solution to this conflict to be found, to negotiate a political settlement to this conflict, otherwise we run the real risk of having a military solution imposed on us."

This message was one that some of his military colleagues did not want to hear repeated. They baulked at the prospect they would lose this conflict in the field. Richard and the Special Branch hierarchy however were of the view that a loss on the battlefield could become a real prospect if this war dragged on. They had the intel from both inside the country and externally to support their belief. Their conclusion in looking at all the intel was that the medium term outlook was not pretty and it was with this knowledge that they had briefed Ian Smith that a political solution was the only option to stop the war.

Ian Smith had heard this message loud and clear.

CHAPTER FIFTEEN

April 1978

Richard drank the strong coffee whilst in deep thought. The past two weeks had given him plenty to think about.

Wearing a new light blue and grey chequered short-sleeve shirt, tan slacks and brown leather shoes he had been surprised how expensive the clothes were in Libreville compared to Rhodesia.

Although still early, he could feel it was going to be another humid day, but thankfully with a forecast mild maximum temperature. Several days earlier it was a very hot day with extremely high humidity. He spent most of that day soaked from his sweat and had hardly slept that night. The ceiling fan in his hotel room was ineffective as it attempted to move hot air around in a meagre offering of some relief to the stifling evening weather.

The coffee was nice. A different blend and flavour to what he was used to back home. He sipped at the cup between looking at his watch and scanning the passing parade of humanity from the small café that was situated on Felix Eboube Avenue near Rue du Gouvernear Balley.

Everything written and spoken was in French in the République Gabonaise. Fortunately he had taken French when he was at school and was therefore able to read the menus. English plus one other language was compulsory for the first four years in the European high schools in Rhodesia. On reflection he found it perplexing that Afrikaans, Latin and French were offered as the second language, rather than any of the local African languages. That in itself was perhaps an

175

indication of the cultural problem his country had experienced and clearly one the politicians had not resolved over the past eight decades. It was pressure from his mother that made him take up French after he totally failed his first exam in Latin. At thirteen his father thought he may like to be a lawyer and therefore persuaded him that Latin was the way to go. '*Amo Amas Amat*' was about as far as he got before he lost complete interest. He could not recall the fourth word in that First Conjugation.

In a few hours he would be flying to Salisbury and back to the harshness of the civil war. He would be debriefing his superiors tomorrow.

Celine arrived late, emerging suddenly. She had observed the café for the past fifteen minutes from a vantage point across Felix Eboube Avenue ensuring there were no unwanted or suspicious people lurking. Espionage was a secretive business where trust was a scarce commodity, always being on the lookout, surveying everything. She was experienced in the clandestine and secretive requirements of espionage having been with Direction Générale de la Sécurité for the past eight years.

"Hey," she pouted sporting a smile that revealed perfect white teeth.

They spoke English when they met. Richard's French was not that fluent and she wanted to practice her English.

"Hello." He stood up without thinking making an unsuccessful attempt at helping her to her seat. "Do you want a coffee?"

She nodded and Richard clicked his fingers to attract the waiter. He strolled over to their table. Richard ordered two coffees. The waiter sauntered off towards the kitchens. Richard and Celine both looked around trying to avoid each other's eyes. The memories of last evening were still vivid in both their minds.

"So?" Richard broke the emerging difficult pause. "You look lovely Celine. I ... I want to say that last night ... it was ..."

She leant over the table and placed her right index finger on his lips. His eyes looked into hers and he drowned. Her big brown eyes captured him and drew him in. He was mesmerised.

"There is no need to say anything my darling," she purred as she withdrew her finger and leant back into her chair.

His eyes surveyed her face, followed a drop of sweat down her neck and his gaze settled on her cleavage.

She's gorgeous.

'You want more, yes?"

She saw where he was looking and she lifted her foot into his crotch.

"Yes please."

"Well you can't. There is no time and you have a plane to catch."

She withdrew her foot and straightened up. The waiter brought the coffees and deposited them on the table without cracking a smile. He turned and shuffled off once again. Richard lingered with the memory of them in his hotel room the night before. However, time was pressing and he needed to get the business of the meeting out of the way.

"Have you received any more intel on what the Cubans and East Germans are planning regarding the Congo insurgents in Angola? Will they invade Zaire?" queried Richard.

"We expect the invasion to be .... how do you say? ... now ... no ... imminent. Weeks if not days away. My French Government is currently making diplomatic initiatives with all parties to try and stop this from happening. The Angolan Government is not responding."

"If it goes ahead then what of the plans for the Cuban assisted invasion by Nkomo's forces into Rhodesia that you outlined? Would the invasion into Zaire slow down or speed up their plan to invade Rhodesia?"

"That plan with Nkomo's forces to invade your country is well advanced according to our intelligence. The Soviet Ambassador and his staff in Lusaka are co-ordinating that plan. The educating of Nkomo's ground forces is continuing and ... how do you say ... re-equipment is to happen fast. There are six MIG's ready for them in Angola. More military equipment is being delivered. Details are in the folder."

They both looked down at the folder she had put up against the table leg.

"You also have the information in there on the spy," she added.

"Thank you. It will help tie up the loose ends."

"Tell me how this is so?"

"Ah."

Herein lay the dilemma of one spook having a personal relationship with another spook. It was hard to differentiate what information should be passed over and what should not. He hesitated momentarily but then decided to explain what the 'loose ends' were while she sipped her coffee and listened.

"The Air Force raids in Mozambique against ZANLA in …"

"ZANLA?"

"That's the bunch behind Mugabe. ZANLA is the military wing of Mugabe."

"Ah yes. They are supported with military from the Chinese yes?"

178

"Yes that's right. Well the raids against his bunch recently have generally been less than perfect. On a few occasions the planes have dropped bombs on empty parade grounds and the army have attacked virtually empty camps. The question has been whether this is bad luck, poor planning or timing or something else? Or had they been tipped off and if so how?"

"You suspected a spy, yes?"

"We don't plan these military operations badly and don't believe in bad luck. Maybe a raid could go belly up once, but a few times in a row? That is not at all likely. So the thinking is there is a leak. If there was a leak it would have to be in ComOps, Combined Operations Headquarters. The nerve centre of the Rhodesian Military."

"Why is that?"

"The Air Force and army units don't get that much advance notice of when the raid is to take place. Our intel from SAS who watch the camps is that the camps start to empty out four to five hours ahead of the raid. The raid is only notified to the Air Force and army three hours in advance. So there is around one hour gap between the two times."

"You say the Air Force and army only get told three hours to plan the raid? That's incredible."

"No, no. The commanders are briefed a long time ahead of that and they have the maps and battle plans drawn up and studied. But the actual timing of the raid or attack is held back from them until three hours. Three hours so that they have that time to muster the troops, arm the planes and so on."

He sipped his coffee. It was warm, not hot, so he drank it all.

"Only ComOps would know the timing of any raid beyond that three hour period ... so the leak has to be coming from there."

179

"Yes I can see how that is a conclusion."

"Our Central Intelligence Agency has been looking into it, but there is suspicion with the Army that CIO may not want to find the leak. So this …"

"Why would that be? Your intelligence agency should find this traitor for national security, no?"

"Yes they should Celine but we have a lot of problems right now as you know. Trust is not something high up on the list of ... of ... well ... trust is faltering with some top military officers right now. The Army chiefs don't want to consider a leak in ComOps and suspect the leak could be in CIO. So anyway, that's one reason why I am here in Libreville, as well as getting the intel on the ZIPRA plans and ... how I was lucky enough to meet you."

His emotion welled up. He looked at her with sad eyes.

I don't want to leave.

She saw the sadness in his eyes but knew within herself she must not show her feelings towards him. So she looked at her watch.

"I have to go now. No sad goodbyes, please."

Standing up they awkwardly embraced before she turned and left the café melting into the throng of humanity on the street. Richard sat back down, feeling as if his guts had just been ripped out of his body. He fought the urge to rush after Celine. It was a struggle. He had not felt such loving emotion towards anyone for many years. After a short while he picked up the leather folder that she had left. He did not open it to see what was in it. He knew it contained the name of the spy in ComOps or CIO. He did not need to know who it was right now. When he was on the plane he would look.

Richard pulled out his wallet from his trouser pocket taking out some paper money. He put a ten CFA franc note on the table placing the sugar bowl on it to prevent it blowing away. He left the café.

I had better convert these Communaute Financiere Africaine francs to pounds before I leave. I saw a currency exchange place somewhere. Where? Hmmm ..... oh yes, it was down this way.

His mind wandered back to last night and the passion. It was exciting and fulfilling. Celine had let herself go and she did things that he had never thought about before. He reflected on their first meeting.

His arranged meeting with a French agent was to be at a nightclub in Quartier Louis. The place was dingy, full of smoke and filled with dodgy characters. Hookers grabbed at him as he entered, persisting in offering their services until he found her sitting at a table in one corner. Looking into her eyes he fell in love with her instantly. When she spoke with her heavy French accent, he melted. They quickly agreed that he should abandon his attempts to speak French. He recalled that the meeting was rather strange because they both parried and skirted around the real reason they were meeting. He was not a skilled spook, but wanted to give the impression he was. In the end, the main topic was not raised and a further meeting was scheduled for two days hence.

The subsequent meetings each several days apart were held at Mont-Bouët and Nombakélé, both busy commercial centres in the city. Richard longed for these meetings so he could see Celine again. He had nothing really to do in between the meetings other than think about her. He spent his days walking around Libreville taking pictures with a Nikon camera of what he thought to be interesting logistical and strategic features, not that Rhodesia was ever likely to attack the city. The industrial area at Oloumi interested him as did the port, albeit it was nothing to write home about. He liked

181

ships and the coming and going of a port fascinated him. In the evenings he would go out to find a decent place to have a meal as the dining room at his hotel was not that inviting. He went back to the Quartier Louis several times to get his evening meal and in the hope of seeing Celine. Having to fend off prostitutes became boring.

Then a few days ago, after their meeting at Mont-Bouët, she kissed him on the cheek suggesting they meet for dinner. He floated through the afternoon and rushed to the restaurant she had selected. She arrived late. Richard did not taste the meal. He was lost in her brown eyes. She left him that evening with a kiss on the mouth, an erection that he had to relieve himself of later in his hotel room and an invitation to have dinner again the next evening.

The next night after dinner she came back to his hotel room and they made love over and over until from exhaustion they both fell asleep. She was gone before he woke up. That ritual was repeated for a further two nights.

The car hooted and swerved to avoid hitting him. He unconsciously had stepped into the road.

Hell! That was close. Being run down in Libreville would be hard to explain. I wonder where I would be buried. British passport means UK, but who would know?

He looked at his Seiko watch.

Twenty to twelve. I had better get back to the hotel to collect my bags and head off to the airport. Don't want to cut it fine.

The taxi was parked a short distance down the road from his hotel. He instructed the driver to take him to the airport before the driver set off at breakneck speed. Richard noticed they were travelling along Cours Pasteur towards the coast. He looked out of the back seat window to see they were passing the Presidential Palace.

Bongo did to Gabon what the rest of Africa does and that's what will happen to us in Rhodesia if we let it. The inaugural Prime Minister or President never leaves. It is simple enough to do. Declare a one-party state and that party stays in power forever. It's a democratic dictatorship African style. And the West accepts it as democracy. What bloody hypocrites they all are. Bongo will never leave unless they shoot him. But then the West doesn't understand Africa. Perhaps the one-party state concept is the solution that works given that the Colonial powers divided the place up based on geography and not tribes or races.

The driver of the Taxi turned right onto the coast road and belted along the road hitting every pothole there was. The driver recklessly weaved in and around the other vehicles. The road veered inland and Richard saw the runway off to his right. He leant forward to instruct the driver to take him past the main terminal entrance and further north to where some hangers could be accessed via a secondary road. The driver grunted his acknowledgement. He stopped fifty metres before the gate. Showing no intention to assist Richard retrieve his baggage from the car trunk he popped the truck open while remaining seated in the Taxi. Richard paid the driver who took the money without any acknowledgement before spinning the car around to speed off back south. Richard stood on the road side with his two luggage bags on the ground watching the maniac leave. He looked around somehow hoping to see Celine. That was never going to happen. With a sigh he picked up the bags and walked towards the entrance.

A boom gate blocked the road and on either side was an eight foot wire fence with razor wire rolls along the top. To the right of the boom gate stood a small hut and inside it Richard found two guards. They were both seated. One was listening to the radio, the other reading a magazine. Richard observed both had holsters with hand guns. He recognised them as MAB PA15 French pistols.

The guard listening to the radio saw Richard standing at the door and lazily got up asking him what he wanted. Richard took out a plastic folder from the smaller of his two bags, removed a paper from it and passed it to the guard. The guard looked at it briefly before he showed it to the other guard who had put down the magazine to stare at Richard. They talked between them before Richard was told he could go through. The boom was lifted half way to allow Richard access. Once past the gate he made his way towards the row of hangars. He searched for the one that had 'Tango Romeo' on the side.

A door on the side of the hangar was open. Richard adjusted his sight to the light as he entered the dimly lit building. In front of him was a plane with tail markings TR-LNY. He recognised the plane as a DC7C, a stylish looking plane, although this particular one was rather drab, reflective of its extensive use.

"Richard. Glad you could make it man."

Richard tuned to his left to see Jack Malloch striding towards him.

"Hello Jack. Yes, I'm glad to be here as well."

He lied. He wanted to be lying in bed with Celine.

"Lovely plane."

They shook hands after Richard put his bags down.

"Yes she is. I came in on this one from Salisbury early this morning. The one we will be going back on is in the next hangar. It's being loaded up now."

"How long have you had this one Jack?" queried Richard.

184

"Oh … a while. This one was used to ferry arms into Biafra in nineteen sixty seven through to nineteen sixty nine or thereabouts. It's certainly seen interesting times has this old girl. The one we are going back on, TR-LNZ, was used a few times for the long range para drops of the Rhodie SAS into Zambia and Mozambique. These are C's fitted with long range fuel tanks originally to allow trips across the Atlantic nonstop. It's also stretched by ten feet and has more powerful engines that the 'B' series."

Jack indicated that they should move on by walking away and signalling to Richard who picked up his bags and followed. They walked out the front of the hangar onto the hardstand where three 'Affretair' planes were parked.

"These are the planes that link north and south for our arrangement Richard. You probably have not seen these before."

"No I haven't Jack. I am aware Affretair is owned by you to carry freight to Europe and other places. What are these aircraft?"

"Those two are Douglas DC-8-50F's. Really lovely to fly and that one with TR-LVO on the tail is a CL-44. They freight Rhodesian beef to Europe and the ammo for the Rhodie army back. The beef we brought in this morning on TR-LNY, the one we saw in there," he pointed back to the hangar they had come from, "has now been loaded on this one and will be in Europe by tomorrow. It will load up with ammo and other goodies and be back here the day after that. Very sharp operation if I say so myself."

"The trading of the weapons, is that still okay?"

This was a touchy subject that was very secret. They both looked around instinctively to see that no one was in ear shot.

"Look it's tricky Richard. I understand the war is costing Rhodesia six hundred thousand pounds a day and that it is heating up. More ammo and equipment is required to fight this thing out. The beef is not enough to pay for the extra ammo required and that other 'goodies' are required to help fund the purchase of your ammo and equipment. I get all that, but it guts me to think that I am ferrying captured communist weapons out of Rhodesia to Gabon so they can be sold back to those commie bastards. I get it that its part of the ruddy game. But jeees man it pisses me off big time I have to tell you."

"Hmmm …. It's a primed hand grenade alright." Richard paused to consider what he was about to say. "Our Police, who as you know record everything so meticulously … they record the serial numbers of all captured insurgent weapons. Well some of the serial numbers of previously captured weapons have turned up again."

Jack's eyes opened wide and his mouth opened involuntarily. He scratched his head, looking worried.

"Fuck man that's bad."

"Yes Jack I know it's a bitch. The bloody weapons that we captured and which have been exchanged here are being recycled and returning to Rhodesia with the insurgents and being recaptured."

"Has this been clocked yet?" asked Jack looking distressed.

"It's bound to be reported on Jack. If a few have returned and been logged then more will follow. Bound to hey? When more are tagged as duplicated then shit will hit the bloody fan."

"Jeeees this worries me Richard. I don't like it at all. I brought another load of commie weapons in the plane today which will be traded within the week. I don't want to get my business caught up in any emotional

186

shit that kicks off back there. There can be a nasty backlash you know."

Richard thought it best to divert the conversation away from what was clearly going to become an increasing contentious matter. He was aware that Special Branch was working on mitigating any fall out that may arise if, or rather when, this matter hit the fan.

"Okay. I know the issue. We're working on it." Then to change the subject he asked. "Any more grief from the UN snooping around your operation?"

Jack and his air freight operation were on the hit list of the United Nations for Rhodesian sanction busting violations. UN agents had snooped around his hangars in Libreville regularly and occasionally they would pop up at the collection points at some airports in Europe. This attention from the UN only arose after Britain made a formal complaint with the UN about Jack and Affretair breaking the trade embargos against Rhodesia. Jack was not fazed by the UN attention. He had been gun running around Africa for a long time, arrested for landing in Togo with nine tons of illegal Nigerian bank notes and chased out of several African states just saving his skin and plane, albeit with some bullet holes in the fuselage. A few UN officials poking around would not pose a problem for him.

Having his planes and business registered in Gabon was opportunistic. It offered him the excuse of legitimacy and legal protection. A friendly nation that was able to close its eyes, ears and its mouth encouraged with an appropriate monetary donation system. Politics in Africa was generally corrupt, business in Africa was corrupt and so corruption was an integral part of the Jack's business plan.

"They poke around Richard. Useless pricks. As long as they can report process and activity they get paid their travel quotas, lavish salaries and allowances. They

187

don't want to find anything that will shut the greasy pole down, I can tell you that for nothing."

They entered the second hangar where the DC7 was being loaded by teams of black workers lifting wooden crates through a large door on the port side.

"She's fuelled up and once those last creates are loaded we can think about heading off. The exit formality stuff is sorted. Did you get what you wanted from the French?"

Jack was on the payroll of the Direction Générale de la Sécurité, the French Secret Service. He also got regular pay cheques from the CIA for various assignments. His connection with the Direction Générale de la Sécurité was what brought Richard to Libreville and it was Jack who set up the contacts here that led Richard to meet Celine. Richard felt he 'owed' Jack an awful lot.

"I believe so. Thank you Jack," he said sincerely. "Time will tell with these sorts of things. I suspect you already know that, hey?"

"Ya, I sure do." He noticed something going on near the rear of the plane. "Hang on. I have to sort something out over there." Then in French he yelled out. "Hey you. Yes you, you prick!"

Jack dashed off shouting abuse to some poor fellow who apparently had done something he shouldn't have. Richard watched as the last crate was loaded on the plane and the side door closed. Standing under the port wing he looked up to study the two large engines above him marvelling at how these large chunks of metal lifted off and flew through the air. He understood the science of flight but still it seemed incredulous when standing under the plane.

It's like radio, he thought, *I use it all the time and understand the theory of how it works but I don't know how it actually works.*

188

"Richard." Jack's call snapped Richard out of his pondering theories. "It's time to make a move."

Richard looked around to search for Jack, but could not see him.

"Up here." Jack was leaning out of the cockpit window. "Get up those stairs."

Richard quickly ascended the metal stairs, ducking down to enter the plane.

"Where do you want me Jack?"

"Turn right. You'll see a row of seats. Take one and buckle up."

Richard stashed his two bags on a rack overhead. He selected a seat on the starboard side by a window. Behind him was a curtain stretching across the width of the plane. He peered through a gap to see boxes and crates stacked high and seeing that they were strapped in, he felt relieved. His initial thought being that he may be crushed by them falling on top of him in the case of any turbulence dissipated.

The co-pilot entered the plane shutting the door and locking it before going into the cockpit without any acknowledgement. He looked to be in his late fifties, weather beaten face, moustache, bald on top with longish grey hair on the sides of his head. He wore a brown leather jacket with a red embossed logo on the back. '*To hell and back.*'

I hope that's not a reflection of this flight, thought Richard. *Unfriendly sod. Then again I guess in his job its best not to know who your passengers are.*

Richard overheard Jack talking to the co-pilot as they ran through a pre-flight check. Below them a tractor was being hooked up to the plane's front wheel to pull it out of the hangar. He stood up to get his smaller bag, opened it and pulled out a leather folder before he sat down again and strapped himself tightly in to his seat. Looking out the window he saw the plane had cleared the hangar. The first of the four engines fired up, smoke bellowing from its exhausts.

His mind focused on the leather folder that had two bundles of papers and a single sheet in it. Putting the folder on the chair beside him and the papers on his lap, he scanned the top sheet of the first bundle.

This is interesting. The inventory of armaments being supplied to ZIPRA. Hell! This stuff has grunt. T-34/85mm and T-54/100mm tanks plus 3 MIG-17 and 3 MIG-21 planes. This is bad news. And this? He turned the pages over. *The political strategy plans for ZIPRA's to invasion of Rhodesia.*

He put that bundle on top of the leather folder. He scanned the second bundle of papers.

This intel on the Nigerian involvement with Nkomo and Sithole to broker a settlement with Smithy with Kaunda's blessing is interesting. They are keen to get this war over which is exactly what we want.

He moved on.

Pretty detailed intel here on Smith's visit to Lusaka with Tiny Rowland of Lonrho involvement. So much for it being kept secret.

Hell there is a fair bit of stuff in this batch. I'll have some detailed reading to do on the flight.

He flipped through the wad of papers stopping every now and again to read something.

But who's the bloody spy?

The single page had two words on it. It was a name. He stared at it and a cold chill went down his spine.

The fucking bastard!

Jack pushed the engine throttles forward. He released the brake and Richard was pushed into his seat as it sped down the short runway. Closing his eyes Richard counted slowly. For some reason he believed that if a plane did not lift off after fourteen seconds it either had to break hard and stop or it was all over. He hated flying.

Thirteen, fourteen, fifteen....oh hell ... six ... no seventeen....

He felt the wheels lift. Opening his eyes to peer out the window and feeling slightly more relaxed, the DC7 was up he could see the coastal road racing past below them, the beach and then the sea.

Goodbye Celine. God I hope we meet again.

CHAPTER SIXTEEN

July 1978

A cold wind swept across the Zambezi valley.

Conditions were harsh as winter left a parched brown land in its wake. A scarcity of water and food for both the wild animals and people alike took its inexorable toll.

It was at this time of the year that the guerrillas relied on the local tribes for food and water to survive. The guerrillas were restrained in their insurgency activities because the vegetation had thinned, restricting natural cover, making it vulnerable for them to move about. Once the rains came in November and the vegetation leaped back to life creating thick undergrowth with flowing streams and abundant wildlife, the insurgency activities would recommence in earnest.

It was in the early 70's that the Rhodesians started building protected compounds in the tribal areas to achieve two objectives. It was a concept based on the experiences in other parts of the globe, Malaya and Vietnam, where insurgents were re-supplied by the local population either willingly or from coercion and where the protected villages could offer sanctuary to the locals from intimidation and murder. Whole villages were erected surrounded by high wire fencing and a 'keep' in the middle. The 'keep' was a small barrack for Security Force personnel who guarded the village. The barrack building was itself protected with sand bags against shrapnel or bullets. Several tall fortified lookouts were built within the village.

However cutting off the food re-supply of insurgents by the locals increased the attacks by the guerrillas on local stores. The army initially deployed territorial troops to protect stores but this was not that effective. There was not enough manpower to give this blanket protection across the country side. As part of counter insurgency operations, Special Branch initiated a clandestine scheme where they left sacks of maize meal, a staple African food source, in certain stores that were then left unprotected. Special Branch leaked information of the whereabouts of these unprotected stores to locals knowing this would be passed through the 'bush telegraph' to the terrorists. These stores were easy targets for terrorists to break in and steal the maize meal. At first Special Branch laced the maize meal with strychnine. This achieved some initial success, but the initiative failed when the terrorists got local villages to eat samples of the meal first. Strychnine killed too quickly so the Special Branch hatched another plan. They laced the maize meal with ground up fibre glass. It would not kill the conscripted food sampler instantly thereby giving the 'go ahead' to the terrorists to eat the maize meal. But once ingested it was fatal, albeit taking many agonising hours or even days to take effect. Many dead terrorists were found rotting in the bush, their intestines shredded as the fibre glass clumped and cut the gut tissue like razor blades.

The introduction of the Protected Village concept into the Urungwe Tribal Trust land came late in the bush war. The first few did not really disrupt the activities of guerrillas. Nonetheless it had been a lean and dangerous winter for Bhekizizwe and his guerrillas. The Rhodesian African Rifles and some Selous Scouts had again been deployed into the Urungwe resulting in many contacts. Bhekizizwe lost good experienced men to the dogged RAR. He still was unable to fathom why these black soldiers persisted to fight against the Freedom Fighters. It did not make sense to him why they supported and upheld the settler regime. He was even more perplexed why the black Selous Scout soldiers were able to betray their own kind. Made up of mostly 'turned' ex-guerrillas, the Selous Scouts were becoming a force to be reckoned with as they continually managed to infiltrate the guerrilla forces.

As this winter draw to a close, Bhekizizwe had few experienced men left and worried once again that the new recruits recently sent from Zambia were not equipped in stamina or courage to take on the RAR or the Scouts. He had therefore decided to hold them back from contacts with the Security Forces as far as he was able. Given that the Rhodesians were pressing hard to seek out and destroy, this was proving a difficult objective.

The day ended as it usually did in the Zambezi Valley with a flush of colour splashed across the sky. Crimson with light blue patches flooded the western sky as the red ball sank towards the horizon. Bhekizizwe positioned himself on a low lying flat bolder before speaking quietly to the group of comrades assembled around him. He arranged this gathering by sending mijubas out into the bush carrying his messages. The comrades who gathered at this place listened intently to what he was saying.

"It is our duty that we undertake this important task. It is a most significant task we have to do to bring the settlers to their knees and bring victory to our liberation cause," said Bhekizizwe punching his right fist into his left hand to make the point. "My comrades we are destined to perform a heroic thing for Zimbabwe."

His comrades nodded their agreement. They thrust for action and especially to use the new weapon they had recently received.

"That dog, Mugabe," he spat on the ground with disgust, "said we, the mighty Ndebele, are cowards.

That dog says it is only his puppies, those ZANLA swine, who carry the fight against the Rhodesians. That dog," he spat once again, "says ZIPRA is frightened to fight. He lies and now it is time to show that dog and his ZANLA swine, those who suckle from the tits of pigs ... we will show them all who the real warriors are."

The comrades raised their fists into the air in unison and shouted defamatory remarks against ZANLA and their leaders.

"Quiet!" shouted Bhekizizwe. "Quiet. Do you want the Rhodesians to hear us?" It was a rhetorical question.

He stepped down from the rock to walk amongst his comrades. They cowered, none making eye contact with him, each expecting a sharp clout across the head or kick in the ribs.

"Our mission is to use this powerful weapon to shoot down the Rhodesian planes when they leave Kariba. We will shoot them down as that sun goes down when it will be too late for the Rhodesians to find the plane. This will show the ZANLA swine who the true warriors are in Zimbabwe."

None of the comrades showed enthusiasm to applaud this sign of strength for fear of being kicked. Bhekizizwe picked up the weapon that lay on the ground and held it as if he was to fire it. He grinned.

"This weapon will bring the fear of our ancient spirits to the Rhodesians. Comrades this weapon will win us liberation from the white settlers, those maningi, and deliver us Zimbabwe."

He continued to pretend to deploy the weapon by kneeling on the ground and pointing it skywards.

He held a Russian 9К32 "стрела-2" - arrow, with a NATO reporting name SA7 Grail or SAM7. It was a shoulder-fired, low-altitude surface-to-air missile, with a high explosive warhead and passive infrared homing guidance supplied by the Soviets to ZIPRA essentially for the defence of their main camps in Zambia from strikes by the Rhodesian Air Force. ZIPRA high command however had decided to deploy these weapons with their insurgency guerrillas with the intention of downing a plane inside Rhodesia, believing such an action would curtail the use of aircraft against their ground forces, while striking a devastating blow against the morale of the white Rhodesians.

Bhekizizwe was selected to receive one of the SAM's to use in the Urungwe TTL to target the Kariba airport. The other weapon was sent to a ZIPRA guerrilla group operating near Victoria Falls in the far west of Rhodesia. The five comrades who had brought the weapon into Urungwe from Zambia were those trained to use it. Bhekizizwe, being the district field commander, was responsible to direct all the guerrillas, including the new arrivals, on insurgency operations within the Urungwe area was now responsible to down a Rhodesian plane.

It was dark by the time he finished giving his detailed instructions to the men on what the mission plans were. All the time he spoke he stroked the muddy green weapon.

CHAPTER SEVENTEEN

August 1978

The group of men had spent the past forty five minutes inspecting the new fleet of armoured transport vehicles and Eland MK7 armoured cars. They were by far the most substantial pieces of hardware to be acquired by the Rhodesian army and their presence on this sports field culminated a long period of procurement from South Africa.

With the inspection over they walked along a tarmac road before entering one of the buildings in the barrack complex. Once inside they helped themselves to refreshments before sitting down on two rows of steel chairs facing a wall covered with a curtain. A weather-beaten wooden lectern stood off to the one side of the drab room. Behind that was a table with rolled up maps scattered on it.

The top brass of the Security Forces had flown to Inkomo Barracks that morning for the purpose of inspecting the newly acquired military equipment and to receive an intelligence briefing. Some of them would fly onto the Mount Darwin Forward Airfield to receive the briefing on the progress in dealing with the influx of ZANLA terrorists from Mozambique before partaking in a meal with the troops stationed there.

Inkomo Barracks had become the home base for the infamous Selous Scouts. This army unit formed in 1973 established its raison d'entre as a regiment of pseudo operator teams that infiltrated the enemy ranks both inside the country and externally. Their clandestine operations utilised manpower from all branches of the Rhodesian Security Forces but its numbers were mainly swelled by captured and 'turned' terrorists. Because of the nature of its operations and the unusual make up of its ranks, the Selous Scouts received its orders from a co-ordinating committee made up of senior military and intelligence agency personnel. That was not a perfect chain of command. The genesis of this clandestine unit came from the Special Branch who believed it essential to have 'eyes and ears' on the ground in the tribal areas, where men posing as terrorists could glean vital intelligence from the local tribe people and from the terrorists themselves.

"Gentleman. Shall we begin?"

Standing behind the lectern Richard waited a moment while the audience became silent. The bush war had been going badly for the Rhodesian Security Forces for some time. It was always going to progressively go badly as this conflict dragged on purely because of the combined effect of international sanctions that the United Nations had imposed on Rhodesia back in 1966, the arms and oil embargo that was associated with those sanctions and the imbalance in numbers between the two terrorist armies, now estimated at over 40,000, compared to the significantly smaller size of the Rhodesian Security Forces. The rolling national military call up of civilians, mostly white Rhodesians, was draining the economy at the same time as the morale amongst those white Rhodesians fell. They were packing their bags and leaving the country in increasing numbers. More black Rhodesians were joining the ranks of ZANLA and ZIPRA as the civil conflict entered its fifteenth year. A deteriorating security situation was an understatement.

"Thank you gentlemen. My briefing today will focus on ZIPRA and its strategy. Our recent combined intel confirms our earlier suspicion that the ZIPRA strategy has shifted significantly and this will explain

198

why we have been experiencing progressively less ZIPRA insurgents internally over the past few months."

"Confirmed by whom?" queried Lieutenant General Walls who sat in the middle of the front row of seats.

"Intel from the French, Sir that suggests the ZIPRA strategy is to launch a conventional invasion to secure Matabeleland. They are presently building up troop strength in three camps. We now know heavy armament and troop carriers ex the Cuban army stationed in Angola are being moved to Zambia."

Richard pulled on a rope and the curtains opened revealing a large map of Zambia, and the northern part of Rhodesia.

"Here at FC camp, here and here."

He used a metal rod to point on the wall map.

"From this recent French intel we now believe the timing for the launch of their major offensive is going to be in November this year."

"That's around the timing of the proposed election for the acceptance of the internal settlement. I guess that's no coincidence?" queried one officer.

"There is no coincidence here. It is also to coincide with the start of the rains. Mugabe and ZANLA plan to push thousands of insurgents across our border with Mozambique, the current spike in border crossings in the north east and eastern regions is the start of this .... ZANLA's plan is to infiltrate the tribal lands, saturate them to stop the rural African voting at the election. A low election turnout will nullify the credibility of that election so the West will not recognise it.

ZIPRA's strategy on the other hand is based on the premise that we will redeploy more of our forces to the north and east to fend off this large insurgency by ZANLA and thus less of our Security Force will be deployed in Matabeleland. The withdrawal of ZIPRA insurgents in recent months from Matabeleland is

199

tactically designed to lull us to make this redeployment decision easier. At that point ZIPRA will invade. Our back will be toward the north west as we front up against ZANLA in the east."

The audience nodded. This interpretation put all the other intel they had received in context. Richard continued.

"We glean that the invasion point will be at Msuna, west of Devil's Gorge at the tail end of Lake Kariba. Once across en masse they would push west to take Wankie."

"It will be far easier to wipe ZIPRA out if they do get across the Zambezi in numbers. They will be concentrated and the boys in blue can take them out with the RLI mopping up what's left. It will be a rout." ventured General Hammond.

"That is an option, Sir. Once ZIPRA are over the border and having established a bridge head we possibly could deal with them when we have finished with ZANLA in the east. However our intel from the French leads us to believe we will face a serious complication. They have ground to air missiles that will pose a huge problem for the Air Force. But that's the least of it. We understand that Nkomo will declare Matabeleland independent of Rhodesia at that point. Wankie will be declared the interim capital. They will get immediate recognition by the Eastern Bloc and most of the African states, thereby giving him legitimacy. Any action by us moving against Nkomo's forces in Matabeleland from that point would be seen by those countries as an invasion giving them the excuse to intervene. We could well have USSR, the Cubans and a whole host of African states to contend with. Our Israeli friends tell us that scenario causes the US CIA great concern."

Richard paused while the hierarchy considered the ramifications. He wondered if he was about to state the bleeding obvious.

"It's SB view that it is imperative that we prevent ZIPRA from gaining a foothold on Rhodesian soil as a consequence of a conventional invasion. SB and the CIO believe therefore that the current political initiative by the Prime Minister to create a detente with Nkomo and ZIPRA and to bring Kaunda into the political solution is the most urgent priority and our military initiatives must support this. This political solution initiative is well advanced. As most of you are aware I accompanied the PM to Lusaka recently where he met with Kaunda and Nkomo. Indications are that it's on track for Nkomo to throw his support behind the current internal settlement process. That said, SB believes ComOps should not rule out a pre-emptive strike to smash ZIPRA's capacity to invade in the event that this political solution is not achieved.

That concludes my briefing. I'll answer any questions then Lieutenant Colonel Reid, Director of Military Intelligence, will brief you on the ZANLA offensive we are currently experiencing."

The briefing session lasted a further 90 minutes as further military intelligence data was disclosed. The broad framework of an external raid on ZIPRA was tabled for comment. There was plenty to think about, much to worry over as the realisation that many hard decisions were going to be required relatively soon sank home.

The Dak lumbered down the runway eventually lifting off before turning to port to disappear into the haze. Richard waited to see the plane take off before he planned to set off by road in his Government issue Peugeot 404 to return to Salisbury. He took every opportunity to linger when he visited the operational sites often picking up useful titbits of information from the troops.

Looking to see if there were any Selous Scouts around whom he could engage in conversation he heard the helicopter. The distinctive engine noise announcing it was a Bell. The acquisition of the ex-Israeli Bell's by the Rhodesian Air Force were a triumph in sanction busting. Richard searched the sky to see where the helicopter was. It came in low and fast landing on the designated hard stand. He strolled towards where the Bell landed curious to see what cargo it brought.

Several black troops exited the chopper. Two people, blindfolded and bound, where thrown out the aircraft, both landing hard on the tarmac. The remaining three troops exited. They roughly manhandled the two who were lying on the tarmac, dragging them towards the buildings.

The chopper lifted, swivelled on its axis and left, flying low over the tree tops.

"Hey you!"

Someone yelled out to Richard's right. He turned to see a stocky man walking determinedly towards him.

"Yes you. What the fuck you doing. You lost or something?"

Clearly aggressive. I see he's a WO in the Scouts. At least he's trying to do the right thing. I am in civvies.

"Who me?" queried Richard.

Turning to face the man, he observed the WO was short, well built with a thick neck and bulging muscles in his upper arms. He had a reddish face with a dusty coloured moustache.

"Yes you! What the fuck you doing wandering around here?"

Spittle flew out of his mouth and Richard involuntarily stepped back to avoid being showered by it. Then as an afterthought, the WO asked.

"Who the fuck are you anyway?"

Richard extracted his identification badge and showed it to the WO without offering any response.

"Sir." The WO stood to attention and saluted. He looked admonished. "Apologies, Sir."

"Stand down Warrant Officer, no offence taken."

The WO relaxed, putting his hands behind his back and spreading his legs apart.

"Tell me …?" Richard searched for his name.

"McIntosh Sir."

"Thanks. Tell me McIntosh I am curious to know what the Bell brought in. The two Africans who were blind folded and bound. Terrs?"

"Yes Sir. Fucking terrs. Our boys captured them today. They took out four others. These two are here for interrogation. One is a field commander so we need to extract intel from him quick smart so our boys can clean up the rest."

"Our boys being?"

"Scouts Sir. We have an op going in the TTL east of Salisbury. The Scouts went in eight days back to find ZANLA terrs trying to get to Salisbury. They have explosives. There are two gangs. We took out the one lot and we need to get intel on the other bunch."

"I see. And these two are from the gang your boys engaged?"

"Yes Sir. Now if you'll excuse me Sir I have to assist in the interrogation." He hesitated for a moment looking at Richard with a quizzical expression. "You wouldn't like to observe would you Sir?"

"Yes McIntosh, I would like to see how the Scouts do the interrogation. Thank you."

They set off together, walking quickly past several buildings until they came to open ground. On the western fence some hundred metres away was a line of blue gum trees. A solitary small windowless tin hut with a flat roof was situated in the middle of the open space. Richard looked at the scene puzzled before being distracted by the sound of shouting coming from the building a short distance ahead.

"The interrogation has started Sir," informed McIntosh. "It starts with some physical stuff, brings out a bit of the red cherry and speeds up the pulse. The terr thinks he is going to be beaten to death. They usually are agreeable to talk at this stage having been in the chopper and threatened with being thrown out. We don't of course."

"Don't what?"

"Throw them out of the choppers Sir. The Porks in Mozambique did. They often threw terrs out of the chopper. They would take two up, thrown one out and the second would blab like a baby. We aren't allowed to. Mores' the pity."

"Glad to hear that McIntosh. What was the complement of the Scout stick that had the contact?"

"Six Scouts Sir. Four turned terrs and two regulars. They infiltrated the area as terrs and … well did what terrs do. This linked them up with the two gangs. These two gangs kept apart, quite canny actually. Our boys found out these two groups were tasked to get to Salisbury and to blow stuff up in the city. Our boys were working on finding out what the targets for the bombings were. Anyways it went tits up last night when our boys cover was blown so they took out the one group of terrs. What we need to find out from those two in there is what the target in Salisbury is. The other gang of terrs had moved off yesterday evening with the explosives and it's bloody important we find them."

The door of the building swung open and a body was flung out. It hit the ground short of the four stairs that led down to the ground, bounced and then rolled down the stairs. It spluttered as it rolled onto its back.

Richard saw it was a woman. Her shirt top had been torn open, her mouth blooded and one of her eyes was swollen closed. Two Scouts came rushing out holding the other insurgent between them, trouser less, his bloodied legs dragging along the ground. He was yelling something that was inaudible to Richard. Another Scout came out of the building carrying a sack. Two Scouts grabbed the woman insurgent and dragged her behind the others who were walking towards the shed.

"The one in front, Sir. He's the section commander. It's him who we need to get talking fast. Obviously the helicopter and beating have not worked. So now it's Matilda's turn."

"Matilda? Who's she?"

Richard noticed the wry smile on McIntosh's face. He seemed to have a twinkle in his eye.

"With respect, Sir, if you can wait and see?"

The woman insurgent began to struggle, pushing her feet in all directions attempting to prevent her forward motion towards the hut. She screamed, spitting blood out of her mouth. Throwing her on the ground the two soldiers bent over her exerting considerable strength to hold her down as she trashed about.

Jesus they are not going to rape her are they?

Richard moved forward. McIntosh put his arm out to stop him.

"It's okay Sir. They are binding the bitch's legs to her arms. It will restrict her from moving."

Richard saw that her legs were bent at the knees and she was bent backwards with her arms fixed to her feet. The door of the shed was opened and she was flung in. The Scout holding the sack stood at the door speaking to her before showing her what was in the bag. She wailed. Her one uninjured eye was as large as a saucer as she shook her head from side to side. The Scout knelt down to release Matilda into the shed before he closed the door. The woman screamed hysterically.

The Scouts holding the other insurgent took him back to the building shutting the door behind them.

"What did he put into the shed," asked Richard.

"Matilda Sir. She's a female black mamba. One bite and …well its curtains. The Africans are petrified of the black mamba as you probably know Sir."

"So the snake will bite her and then she will die an agonising death. How does that help get the intel?"

"Ah. Well, Sir, as you can hear by her reaction, the screaming, the bitch is absolutely terrified. She will talk. The boys will open the door shortly, gag her and take her to another building, the one over there." He pointed to a smaller building off to their left. "She will be asked to spill the beans and I bet you a dollar that she will."

"And what about the other insurgent? You said he's the one who needs to talk. What's going to happen to him?"

"Well Sir, he saw the goings on with his comrade and he saw Matilda. Right now he is having his future explained to him by the boys. It's his turn next in the hut unless he talks. In fact it's his turn with Matilda either way."

"So if he talks he will go in the shed anyway?"

"Certainly. He may lie first time. Matilda will see if he did."

"And what if the snake … this Matilda … what if it bites them. The window between the bite and severe spasms is quite short. If it bites, doesn't that defeat the whole objective?"

"Well Sir, the thing is Matilda is defanged. She can't really do much damage. They don't know that though. It's totally dark in that hut." He smiled and winked. "If you will excuse me Sir, I have some information to gather from the bitch."

The WO walked to the shed and together with his men they pulled the woman out. She was screaming. She was unable to move because of the way she was bound. They quickly gagged her before dragging her off to the smaller building. Another soldier went into the hut to fetch Matilda.

Richard looked at his watch.

How long I wonder?

The door of the small building opened and the WO emerged with a huge grin. He raised his right hand with his thumb pointing up.

She's talked! Well I never. He looked at his watch. *Six minutes!*

CHAPTER EIGHTEEN

September 1978

"V1 speed …. Rotate," said Garth Bythell, the first officer.

Captain Howlett nodded his acknowledgement and pulled back on the yoke. The nose of the Viscount lifted. Garth looked out of the side window of the cockpit and waved to the troops in the sandbagged bunker situated fifty metres from the end of the runway. The Ferret Scout Car that started its patrol along the runway six minutes earlier had veered off and was travelling along the dirt track running parallel to the tarmac giving rise to a dust cloud. The four soldiers in the bunker waved back as the Viscount carrying its fifty six passengers lifted off.

Howlett pulled on the yoke to bring the aircraft hard to starboard. The four 1,576 horse power Dart 510 engines screamed as the intense pressure of the sharp turn pulled on the fuselage.

It was eight minutes past five in the afternoon. The sun dropped towards the horizon turning the sky crimson to herald in another stunning Rhodesian sunset.

At 36 John Howlett was already a veteran pilot having served with Air Rhodesia for the past eight years. He used to fly the Viscount from Salisbury to Durban, but that route was now the domain of the new arrivals to the Air Rhodesia fleet. The sanction busting Boeing 720. Three second hand jet aircraft acquired from the defunct Eastern Airlines of Miami were the pride of Air Rhodesia and their unexpected arrival was shrouded in secrecy. Sanctions had been spectacularly broken. With the Boeing 720's taking the longer haul

208

routes to Johannesburg and Durban, the Viscounts had been relegated to the domestic routes and for the past year Howlett's route was Salisbury to Victoria Falls and to Kariba.

"Wheels up and locked," informed Bythell.

"Okay check. Leave the seat belt warning on for another minute or so Garth while I get her steady."

The Air Rhodesia pilots were all cognisant of recent terrorist security warnings that required a steep assent in a spiral motion so as to avoid lower level flying outside of a ten kilometre radius of the airport. Although Kariba was less tricky than the other airports because it had the lake on one side it was surrounded by tribal trust land which was infiltrated with terrorists. The route to Salisbury took them over the Urungwe Tribal Trust Land soon after takeoff. The plane would have had to reach its flight ceiling by the time they flew over it.

"One sixty knots. Seat belt lights off now. We'll level off at fifteen thousand feet."

The passengers of the Viscount, called 'The Hunyani', were mostly people returning to Salisbury from holidaying at Kariba. There were only four men and two women returning from doing business there. After winter and before the oppressive heat, September was a good time to holiday at Kariba with its clear skies, warm days and cool nights. The lake, built to provide hydro-electric power to Northern and Southern Rhodesia, especially the power hungry mines of the Copper Belt, occupies five and a half thousand square kilometres between Rhodesia and neighbouring Zambia. The dam wall, 128 metres tall and over 570 metres long, tamed the mighty Zambezi River to create the lake that stretches 220 kilometres long with a maximum width of 40 kilometres.

Howlett brought the plane out of its sharp starboard turn over the lake.

"Do we do another circle to get the height?" queried Garth.

"We should be okay. Do you know if the Group Captain got on board?" Howlett asked.

"No he missed us but he will be going back on the next one."

An Air Force Group Captain had spent a few days on leave with his family on a house boat on Lake Kariba. They were booked to fly back on Air Rhodesia Flight RH 825 but were delayed due to engine trouble with one of the outboard motors of the house boat which left them wallowing off the Kariba town site for over two hours while the engine was repaired. A call was made to the army JOC commander at Kariba who then notified the Air Rhodesia booking staff at the airport informing them that the Group Captain and his family would not make the five o'clock flight. The airline reallocated the four seats to a mother and her young daughter and a newlywed couple who were scheduled to leave Kariba for Salisbury later that evening.

"Okay I will level off now. Cancel the no smoking sign and you had better tell the tower."

Bythell turned off the 'no smoking' sign, adjusted his headset and moved forward to turn on the radio.

He also served in the Rhodesian Air Force on national service call ups in No 4 Squadron flying Trojan aircraft. No 4 Squadron's motto was "Seek and Strike" and it existed to supply light transport, reconnaissance, forward air control, casevac and light ground attack. He was relieved to have completed his last six week call up a few weeks ago in which he had to casevac several badly wounded soldiers who were injured in action against the terrorist bases situated in

210

western Mozambique. Two had died en-route to the hospital which saddened him deeply.

The Viscount suddenly shook violently. Warning lights flashed in front of the two pilots.

"What the hell's that," shouted Bythell.

'Dunno! Something's up!" exclaimed Howlett as he frantically searched the control panel."Jeeeesus it's pulling down."

"Fire alarm?" Bythell looked out his side window towards the wing. "Oh Christ John, we're on fire."

"What?" Howlett fought with the yoke which shook violently.

"We're on fire! The damn wing is on fire," exclaimed Garth. He searched the dials in front of him in dismay. "Both starboard engines are out?"

"She's going down Garth! Engage engine fire procedure."

"Oh Christ no! What the hell happened?"

"We're going to go in. Where can we land?"

"Can we get back?"

"No option we won't make the airport. Look for a place down there. Do it now. Engaged engine fire procedure?"

The yoke continued to shake violently making it extremely difficult for Howlett to hold it.

"Okay. Okay. Shut down systems on engines three and four ... ah ... close off high pressure cocks and fuel lines .... to ... to contain the fire."

Howlett feathered both props and set off the first fire extinguisher. He set his wrist stop watch. He had to wait 45 seconds before he could then shoot the second fire bottle.

Christ I hope that stops the bloody fire. The fuel tanks may explode?

"Help with the yoke Garth. Adjust the flaps. We have to slow down."

"There! There's a field. It's too bloody small," shouted Garth.

"Where? I can't see it. Only damn bush."

"There. Starboard. Two o'clock."

Howlett squinted his eyes to focus. He saw a patch of cleared agricultural land surrounded by the bush.

"Okay that's it. It will have to do." Howlett used his full strength to turn the stricken aircraft. "She's responding." he said with relief. "Landing gear down."

He set off the second fire extinguisher.

"Should we lower the gear?" queried Garth.

"What? We have to slow this bitch. Wheels down may help? Help with the yoke here? I must call the tower."

John switched on the radio.

"Okay. Okay. Oh Christ. I'll tell the cabin crew to prepare."

Sweat poured down Garth's forehead and he wiped it with his forearm, desperately trying not to panic.

"Kariba tower this is RH eight two five. Copy."

"RH eight two five, this is Kariba tower. Over."

"Mayday! Mayday. Rhodesia eight two five. I have lost both starboard engines. We are going in."

"Ah? …. RH eight two five … both Starboard engines out? Are you returning to Kariba? Over."

"Level off. Level off!" Garth shouted at the plane realising they were on a far too steep incline to attempt any landing.

"I can't ... bugger ... the engines are going …like ... help me here Garth ..... Negative tower. Negative. Both starboard engines out. We are going in."

"Monique!" shouted Garth into his headset attempting to make contact with the head airhostess. That was never going to happen.

"Leave it. Help me here. Flaps?"

The plane's rate of descent escalated. The earth came towards them fast.

"Help me level this thing off. Adjust the bloody flaps!"

The starboard wing began to disintegrate. The intense heat from the flames, the damage from the explosion and the severe stress on the plane as it fell earthwards proved too much for the wing's integrity.

Both pilots pulled as hard as they physically could on their yokes in an attempt to level off the rate of descent. The nose lifted slightly.

"There's the field. Straight ahead. Can we make it?" queried Garth.

Trees that seemed to stretch up towards them to grab the aircraft stood as a barrier to their survival.

"Please Jesus get us over those trees."

Garth's muscles of his arms were straining with the yoke. Every sinew in his body was at breaking point. He pulled back on the throttles of the two port engines.

"RH eight two five. This is Kariba tower. Over."

"Should I answer that?" queried Garth.

"RH eight two five. This is Kariba Tower. Over."

"Leave it!" John's voice shrill as his neck muscles tightened. "No time. Look. This is it. Oh Lord! I need to tell the cabin."

John switched on the intercom to the cabin. He took a deep breath.

"Fasten seat belts. Stay calm. Prepare to brace. Place your heads between your legs. We are going to have an emergency landing."

Then as the ground raced up towards them John said "Brace! Brace yourselves for impact!"

The tops of trees hit the plane. Instinctively Garth ducked as the branches swept across the windshield. The branches were not large enough to smash the glass. The two engines on the port side screeched as they collected branches. Then suddenly there was the clearing in front of them.

"There it is. Okay let's put it down. Now!" yelled John.

The Viscount hit the ground with an almighty thud. The undercarriage had not been lowered. The plane belly flopped and skidded. The noise of metal scraping along on the ground reverberated throughout the cockpit.

"We're down!" Garth involuntary shouted with relief.

John and Garth continued to hold their yokes tightly, albeit they were now of no use at all. Both were instinctively pushing their feet forwards in a vain attempt to push through the floor to help the plane stop.

John saw it first. Garth was not far behind him in observing it.

"Oh Lord help us."

That was the last thing John said.

The Viscount's nose was pulled into the ditch through gravity and its forward momentum. It slammed into the other side of the ditch with tremendous force. The front of the plane disintegrated into a thousand pieces as the force and weight of the body of the plane propelled it forward. The two pilots were crushed and then ripped apart. The front crumbled in on itself before the plane snapped in two. The back of the plane with the tail intact leap frogged over the front section and cart wheeled along the field beyond the ditch. The wings exploded into flames to immediately engulf the front and mid-section of the stricken plane. A reddish yellow plume of flames erupted like a mushroom incinerating all the passengers in that part of the fuselage. Thick black smoke poured out of the wreckage that was strewn around the ditch for a hundred metres in all directions.

Grass fires started.

***

Seated with another air hostess at the rear of the plane Monique unbuckled her seat belt and helped her colleague get the drinks trolley ready. She made her way towards the front of the plane to take drinks orders. The flight time to Salisbury was under an hour so they needed to get a move on with the hospitality part of the flight.

She was in her second year with Air Rhodesia. After leaving school she began her training to be a teacher but soon realised that was not going to work for her. She had no trouble getting accepted into Air Rhodesia. Her figure swayed the all-male interview panel. She looked gorgeous in the air hostess uniform which was designed to accentuate the curvature of the women's hips and breasts.

Monique was hoping to get engaged to a man she had met at a game of tennis a year ago. She was immediately attracted to him and had manoeuvred herself to be paired up in a game of mixed doubles. He was a strong man physically, mentally agile and considerate towards her. The only impediment was that he was a career army man in the Special Air Services. He often disappeared for weeks at a time and recently for two months. Before she knew what his job was, she suspected that he was playing the field and these absences were when he was with other women. But now she worried endlessly about his safety when he went away. He was good in bed and certainly had stamina especially after the long periods away. She thought that was a significant compensating factor that should be considered when deciding on her future with him.

Monique was less than half way down the aisle when the plane shook and she grabbed onto a seat to steady herself. She twisted her ankle as she stumbled forward thinking she may have seriously hurt herself as a sharp pain shot up her leg from her ankle. She bent over and felt her ankle with her hand through the stockings. As she looked up she caught the eye of a passenger. The woman's expression was one of horror.

Shame, thought Monique, *I only stumbled. I must have really frightened this poor person.*

She was about to say something to reassure the distraught passenger when he saw a flash of red.

What's that? That's not right.

She leant over the seat to look out the window. At the same time she heard the rising commotion going on around her.

Oh my God! The engine is on fire.

She reeled back from the window.

"Please remain calm," Monique shouted to be heard above the rising chatter around her. "Be calm and fasten your seat belts please. Now please!"

Her colleague saw the flames sweeping past the windows and gasped. Terrified she froze in the aisle. The plane lurched downwards as its starboard wing tipped lower making it difficult to stand up without support.

"We have to get everyone calm and seated," instructed Monique, surprising herself at how calm she felt.

"The engine is on fire. Oh my God! Oh my God," shrieked the other airhostess.

Grabbing her colleague by both shoulders Monique shook her.

"We have to get everyone seated and buckled up and we must do that now. Do you hear me? Now! John will get us back to the airport. Let's do our job."

It worked to snap her colleague out of panicking. But panic spread throughout the cabin as the passengers grasped the situation.

"Get a fire extinguisher! Get the extinguisher," shouted a male passenger who ran down the aisle towards the back of the plane. He bumped into another passenger who fell down on the floor. "We need the extinguisher. Get the fire extinguisher."

Monique saw him coming and stood steadfastly in his way.

"Sit down in your seat now!" she said firmly.

The man's speed along the aisle was impeded by the nose dive of the plane. He did not have the momentum to push past Monique. He stopped a meter from her before falling backwards to slide down the aisle towards the front of the plane hitting his head several times on the metal of the seats. Blood spurted from the cuts on his head.

Turning her attention to those passengers close by, Monique tried to ensure they were buckled in their seats. Sheer terror was etched in the faces of these passengers some of whom were children. Above the pandemonium which had broken out all around her she heard John's announcement. Then the warning.

"Brace! Brace yourselves for impact."

I'm not going to get back to my seat. Sweet Jesus we are going to crash!

"Lean forward and hold the chair in front of you."

Her shout was drowned out by the screams all around her. She grabbed the seat next to her with both hands and clung to it with all her strength when she heard the plane hitting the trees and the high pitch of the engines. The plane hit the ground with a horrible thud. It seemed to bounce before skidding.

John's got us down? We've made it. Thank heavens.

The whole aircraft juddered. An awful ripping sound cracked though the cabin. Monique saw sky. She was thrown upwards. Her arm caught the seatbelt and she was suspended in mid-air as the cabin rolled over. She felt her arm break as it was wrenched from its shoulder joint. Then she hit the floor hard. Searing pain tore through her arm and down her side. She let out an anguished scream before being hurled upwards once again.

Then blackness.

CHAPTER NINETEEN

September 1978

"RH eight two five. This is Kariba Tower. Come in. Over."

Silence.

"RH eight two five. This is Kariba Tower. Over."

"No luck?" asked the one other person in the unspectacular air traffic control tower at Kariba airport. "It's been five minutes now."

"Nope," said the air traffic controller. "They must have gone in."

The expression on his face mirrored what he thought. He feared that something terrible had happened to the Air Rhodesia Viscount named after a river in Rhodesia that flows past the capital Salisbury as it makes it way south eastwards towards Mozambique.

"How? I mean, why? What the hell happened?"

"Howlett said both starboard engines were out and they were going in."

"The plane can fly with two port engines so maybe he's coming back. He was only ... what less than ten minutes out? Let's keep a look out."

They searched once again towards the south with the field glasses.

"But .... why no radio contact then?" queried the air traffic controller on reflection.

"Maybe it's knocked out. Who the hell knows? But ... hold on. What's that?"

He pointed towards the south eastern sky. The red and orange that splashed across the evening sky had spread fast. It melted with the wisps of white cloud scattered intermittently across the horizon. Spirits lifted

219

momentarily as they both searched the sky with the binoculars.

"It's nothing. Bugger it. What would cause two engines to fail at once?"

"I had better tell Salisbury that we have a problem," said the air traffic controller.

He hesitated noticing his legs felt rubbery. He made it to a chair just in time.

"You okay?"

"No not really. We've lost a plane on my watch with fifty something people on board somewhere out there. Those poor people."

"It's awful. But we have to hope for the best. He still may make it back."

"No they ruddy well wont. They would be back here by now. They have crashed out there in the bush."

"Okay, then we must tell the Salisbury Tower and alert authorities now so a rescue effort can get underway."

"What in the dark? In the bush with ruddy terrs running around? We need choppers for this and the army. The choppers will have to come in from Salisbury or the nearest FAF. They can't fly in the dark. They need to get army guys organised. So it's going to be tomorrow before anyone searches for them. Those poor people."

"Okay, but we have to do something and that means informing Salisbury."

The dreadful news spread like wildfire from the Salisbury Air Traffic Control tower to ComOps and then to the Air Force control at the New Sarum Air Force base.

The telephone ring sliced the silence at the home of Major Barnett. His wife answered. It was ComOps. She summoned her husband to take the call. He was relaxing in the lounge of their home with a gin and tonic preparing to watch the television.

"Can you please mobilise paramedics, place them on standby and ready for immediate deployment Sir," said the ComOps Sergeant tasked with contacting all the relevant personnel. He rang Major Barnett first. He was SAS.

"What's the op Sergeant?" queried Barnett.

"We have a situation Sir where there may be several civilian casualties. They may be situated in a hot area. An extraction is being arranged Sir."

"Not good enough of an explanation Sergeant. I want details if I am to mobilise my men. What are the details?"

"Sir, I am limited in the information I can pass on at this time. The situ is fluid. More information is yet to come in. My orders are to arrange the casevac, the hot extraction detail and ...."

"Fuck all that Sergeant! What's the detail you have in front of you? Tell me now or piss off the phone."

"Sir? Ah ... A Viscount is missing at this time."

"Where?"

"At this time we are not certain Sir. It left Kariba at seventeen hundred and went missing soon after that Sir."

"Has it been downed by terrs? Shot down? Blown up?"

"Sir, at this time the details are unknown. If it has gone down then we need the paramedics ready to deploy."

"If it has gone down? Has it crashed or not?"

"Sir, we don't know at this time but we think it probably has."

"How many on board?"

"We think its fifty six, Sir."

The Major agreed to supply a small tracker and medical team. After terminating the call with the Sergeant he immediately made the telephone calls to his men to get this squad assembled. Within half an hour he had twenty men, including two doctors, a SAS medic and a skilled tracker making their way to the designated assembly point. They met at the SAS HQ and packed five panniers of kit to support the rescue mission.

At the same time the army mobilised to divert troops near Kariba to assembly points to be picked up for deployment at the crash site once it was located. The central hospital in Salisbury was alerted to prepare for casevac casualties.

Those at ComOps suspected that the Viscount had in all probability gone down somewhere in the Urungwe Tribal Trust Land. That was particularly bad news as that region was currently infested with aggressive terrorist gangs.

A concern considered by the ComOps commanders was that the terrorists may ambush the recue parties. The site of the crash would be obvious and could well attract the terrorists to it, therefore care to protect the searchers in the rescue operation was required. This could slow down the process of a rescue and thus put any survivors at greater risk if they had sustained life threatening injuries which required urgent attention. Plans to deal with this and other contingencies would be made overnight.

By seven thirty in the evening the order went out to commence the search for the crash site. At eight fifteen an Air Force Dak took off from New Sarum to do an aerial grid pattern search of the suspected crash area. This search was to be carried out throughout the night if required with the Dak refuelling at Kariba airport.

The crew aboard the Dak searched throughout the night but found it very difficult to identify any crash site fire because there were so many open village fires in the area. They returned to New Sarum at 0500. A ParaDak filled with the SAS paratroopers set off at 0515 to continue the grid pattern search and to drop the troops at the crash site when it was found. Helicopters were redeployed to Kariba airport. Army sticks operating in the Urungwe Tribal Trust Land were redeployed to search for the wreckage on the ground and render any support required if terrorists were found to be in the vicinity. They knew it was going to be a grim day as this drama unfolded.

CHAPTER TWENTY

September 1978

The old man looked to the sky with his tired eyes, his weather beaten face etched with deep furrows telling a story of the hard life he had lived.

He sat on a tin can near the open fire where his second wife was cooking the evening meal. His large flat feet had the three middle toes missing. He is of the Doma tribe. Sometimes referred to as the lobster-claw syndrome, this affliction is an autosomal dominant condition resulting from a single mutation on chromosome number seven.

His large forehead outlined with curly grey hair carried a gash which was well on the way to healing. His distinctive large flat nose had recently been broken. He was lucky to still have some good molars in his mouth. He had long since lost many of his teeth including his front teeth mostly from decay, some from ritual removal, but two teeth had been knocked out quite recently. His hands were battered and two of his fingers were absent of finger nails. His left hand was wrapped in a dirty strip of material, stained with dried blood hiding a crushed index finger. His faded blue chequered short sleeve shirt, with several buttons missing, had dried blood stains down the front.

He was in deep thought about his troubles when he heard the sound of plane engines in the distance. He had gotten used to the sound of the engines as the plane flew over his kraal each day, although in recent times he noticed that the noise was louder and the planes seemed to be at different angles as they climbed into the sky, or so it seemed to him anyway. He wondered why?

These were troubled times and they were getting worse. In his seven decades he had witnessed many things, but none as troubling as this. He had lived a carefree life in his village as a young boy. His father had three wives, eleven cattle, several goats and many chickens. He was the fifth child of the third wife. His family grew millet along with the five other related families that lived in their village which consisted of round mud walled huts built off the ground on stilts, all with grass thatched pitched rooves. His father, being wise and highly respected, had risen to be the headman of their village.

As was the case in his youth many of the children died at early ages, but enough had survived to keep the community supplied with workers to tend the livestock and the fields. Their community had been successful and prosperous.

It had been a long time since the village had been attacked by the marauding amaNdebele. It last occurred months before he was born. His family spoke about it regularly when they recalled their history usually when sitting around the cooking fires after a meal had been consumed and the night sky was pitch black.

He learned from his father that the amaNdebele, scum dogs, had come to the village one day without warning. Arriving with their distinctive cattle hide shields and short stabbing spears, they killed the men and boys in the village, raped the younger women many times, preferring to kill the older women and those bearing child. Woman bearing child were treated especially brutally as their gut was sliced open and the unborn child taken out to be swung around before being slammed to the ground. The women were then left on the ground to bleed to death. The scum dogs burned the village stealing all the livestock and the young women whom they had not killed.

225

That day some men and boys were away from the village on a fishing expedition while a few women, including his mother, had gone to a nearby river to wash clothes and fetch water. They survived to tell the tale and to rebuild their fractured lives. But the horror of that day left a lasting fear of the scum dogs with the survivors and the story was relayed to each generation that followed. The scum dog, amaNdebele, who had stolen their lands to the west many seasons ago and who raided the lands to the east to steal livestock and kill their people, would never be forgiven.

The old man remembered vividly when on one morning a strange occurrence happened, something that was to forever change his life and which now seemed to be causing him and his village much trouble. He was in his eighth season when he saw a white person for the first time. He remembered the fright that his father, mother, aunts and uncles experienced when six pale men on horses came into their village. They were the spirits of their ancestors who had come alive to haunt them all. They wondered what had they done to deserve such a terrible fate?

His father had ordered his people to flee into the bush to hide from these pale spirits. The villagers stayed away for two nights and then only returning when his father said it was safe to do so. The spirits had vanished as quickly as they had come leaving several bags on the ground in the centre of the village which, after many days, his mother, being the third wife of the headman, was cajoled by the villagers to inspect. She was more expendable than the first two wives who had more authority over her, so his father had agreed for her to be sacrificed if need be.

She had opened the bag with terrible trepidation, fearing that evil spirits would leap out of the bag and seize her in a terrible death. All the others in the village kept a good distance away from her and the bags, some even electing to stay in their huts. With relief, his mother found no evil spirits but rather seeds in one bag and some white powder in the other. The spirits had brought the village good tidings. The village was introduced to maize.

The spirits did not return for many seasons. His father had in the meantime heard more about these strange pale skinned people from other villagers in the district. They were not spirits. They had come from far away to take this land for themselves. This news was deeply disturbing, causing much anxiety within the village as they recalled the amaNdebele who, many seasons before, had arrived to take their land from them and had killed his forefathers in the process. But what was to be done to stop this? But over time it became clear that the pale skinned people were not going to kill them and happily they even stopped the amaNdebele, scum dogs, from stealing.

These white people brought their laws to these lands that were hard to understand. They said the land north of the great river, Zambezi, was a separate land. They also said that their tribe in that land were no longer part of the tribe to the south as it had always been. The white people called this land north of the great river, Northern Rhodesia and that to the south, Southern Rhodesia after a white man, Cecil Rhodes.

White people came to their villages to teach new beliefs. They spoke of a great man called Jesus who spoke for the only God of everything. This white God was more powerful than all of their own spirits. He was able to heal sickness. These people, wearing white collars around their necks, told the villagers that they must believe in this God from now on and if they did this they would be saved. The old man still wondered what this white God was going to save him from because, given where he found himself today, he did not feel like he was being saved.

Something the white people called money was introduced. Money seemed to be all powerful. It made people behave differently. They also brought medicines to the village that stopped many people dying. They brought seeds for growing better crops, including crops that were not for eating but which could be exchanged for money, like cotton.

The white people dissected the land. Some of the land was taken by the white people and some was set aside for the villagers. This was called the Urungwe Tribal Trust Land and was only for the tribe people to use. But now they were not able to take their livestock onto land that was outside the designated Tribal Trust Land.

The white men then challenged the spirits of the great river by building a big wall that made a huge lake which ate up a large part of the Doma tribe's land. This changed how the villagers lived forever.

After all this upheaval life had then settled into a comfortable safe routine in his village. It seemed the white man had brought stability and order to things, as well as certainty of food. The money earned from the crops they grew was most beneficial in getting new products that made life easier overall. The clinic that was built close to his village meant illness could be fixed with white man's magic. This made the n'anga very angry, but the white man's magic was stronger than that of the n'anga and so most people went to the clinic when they got ill.

When his father died, his uncle became the headman. By the time he became the headman on his uncle's death the village had grown rapidly over many seasons. He took three wives himself. The first wife bore him six children. His second only three before she

228

died and his third had so far produced five. She may be pregnant with his sixth. Of the thirteen children only three had died which was both good and bad news for him. The white man magic helped to prevent most of his children from dying when they became sick. Therefore he lost less than half of his offspring as his father had experienced. But of the ten left, he had only 3 daughters and this was bad news. The three children who had died were female which presented him with a huge dilemma. Daughters were needed to work the field and then to bring him, as their father, a fortune in dowry payments when they were taken as a bride. His sons, of which he had seven, were more of a liability. They would need to pay over dowry payments which he would have to find when they took a bride. They were not as useful workers as the daughters were in his farming endeavours. His family had cost him dearly and he was less prosperous now in his old age as he hoped he would have been.

But all this was incidental to the troubles that he faced today.

When seven people dressed in green uniforms and carrying guns, which they called AK 47, arrived in his village a few seasons ago he suspected they meant trouble. When they told the villagers that they were going to kill all the white people and take back the land these white people had stolen he knew trouble was not far away. They said that they were Zimbabweans and not Rhodesians and that all Zimbabweans must rise up and take back what was stolen. They spoke of the Chimurenga, the war to liberate Zimbabwe of the white settlers. They called themselves comrades and freedom fighters.

Their arrival and presence in the district caused widespread anxiety with the villagers. These armed men were young and enthusiastic about what they believed in. They spoke with conviction about matters that resonated with many in the village. But they were amaNdebele, scum dogs. The collective memory of the villagers for the amaNdebele, that story told at night while sitting around the cooking fires throughout the ages, meant the villagers did not trust these freedom fighters.

The old man called a meeting of village elders after these scum dogs had left. The elders discussed the matter at length each morning for three days before they came to their collective decision. They would tell the Police about these freedom fighters.

Not long after the Police were told about the visit from the freedom fighters, many soldiers arrived in the Tribal Trust Land. Helicopters flew overhead scaring the livestock. Then late one day as the clouds were building up for a thunderstorm, the stillness of that afternoon was shattered by the sound of gun fire. Explosions followed more gunfire before silence settled in once again. Later that evening the news came to the village that the soldiers had shot and killed five freedom fighters, the ones that had visited the village several weeks earlier.

Life seemed to have gone back to normal until suddenly some armed men arrived at the village again. They were un-kept in appearance and far less friendly towards the villagers than those who came before. They ominously gathered all the villagers together before one of the men spoke to them. He was in charge and his presence made the villagers feel frightened. He made the old man sit down on the dirt in front of him showing disrespect to the headman of the village.

Things turned nasty when the villagers hesitated in their response to the freedom fighters request for assurance of the village support. The freedom fighter in charge became agitated and aggressive. He set about kicking some of the villagers with this heavy set steel capped boots. The old man tried to stand up to protest but got a rifle butt to his mid-section and a clenched fist to his right temple. He fell breathless crumpled to the ground.

The freedom fighter in charge called for food and drink to be served to the eight comrades. He allowed some older women to leave the assembled group to prepare the food. While they waited he selected four young girls of puberty age and took them into one of the huts. For the next two hours as the eight freedom fighters were served food and drink they took turns with the young girls, some of the freedom fighters going back for a third time. During this period several villagers suffered severe beatings when they protested. The enthusiasm for objection soon dwindled.

The eight freedom fighters took food supplies and one of the young girls who had yet to be introduced to their sexual advances leaving the villagers in confusion and turmoil. They were told that the freedom fighters had 'eyes' in the bush, 'eyes' in the dark and that if anyone told the Security Forces of their presence they would return and kill that person.

Two days later one of the young girls died from her injuries she had sustained from the repeated attention of the freedom fighters. She seemed to have been favoured more than the other two girls because of her voluptuous buttocks and bosom.

Ten Rhodesian soldiers arrived a week later. They were members of the Rhodesian African Rifles. Their presence also made the villagers anxious. The way they acted towards the villagers was different to many of their previous visits. They approached the huts with extreme caution. Two soldiers would point their rifles at the hut while two of their colleagues ascended the steps. Then one soldier would burst into the hut with

231

the other close behind. This process went on for a long time as each hut was searched.

The soldier in charge was tall well-built man. He was Shona and could speak to the villagers in their own language. He instructed that the villagers all assemble. The headman was allowed to sit on his upturned tin can. The atmosphere was sombre. The soldier in charge, introducing himself as Sergeant Major Simon Mutambara, asked the headman if any terrorists had been to the village. The headman not prepared to say anything, diverted his eyes downwards and kept his mouth shut. That was not good for him. He caught a fist from the Sergeant Major that put him down on the ground bleeding from his mouth.

The question was asked of other villagers. Silence was the response. Some villagers were beaten, but still nothing.

"These terrorist rats are not your friends. They will not give you freedom. They are thugs, rapists and murderers. They must be hunted down and killed like rats. We are here to do that and you must tell me where these terrorist rats are so I can take my men to go and kill them now," said Mutambara.

The headman with his lip swelling and blood in his mouth remained confused and bewildered. The rest of his villagers were fearful. Fear has a strange effect sometimes. It makes people impervious to listening to any message. That applied to most of the simple minded villagers that day. The message from the soldier was meaningless to those villagers who were more afraid of the freedom fighters than the Rhodesian soldiers.

To the relief of the villagers the soldiers soon left. At least they did not take food nor did they take any young girls. The headman rationalised that the beatings they had been subjected to from the Rhodesian soldiers

232

were worth it. No information was revealed to the soldiers about the freedom fighters and therefore the 'eyes' in the bush would not have seen any disclosure to the Security Forces. His village was therefore safe from any reprisal from the freedom fighters.

It was a few weeks after the soldiers visit to the village when late in the afternoon, as the evening meal was being served and the villagers were assembling around their cooking fires, the eight freedom fighters returned. They came skulking out of the growing shadows. Their presence was immediately felt as ominous as they surrounded the village, herding all the villagers into a central place.

The older freedom fighter, clearly the one who was in charge, looked tired. Without provocation he grabbed the headman and gave him one hell of a whack with his fist. It broke his nose. Blood gushed from it. He then punched the old man in the mouth dislodging two teeth before he hit the old man in his forehead with the butt of his weapon. The headman went down like a stone. Regaining consciousness he discovered that he was bent over in the middle in a foetus position bound by a rope with his feet and his arms altogether. He felt a sharp pain in his hand. Opening his eyes he saw with horror a freedom fighter holding his index finger in what looked to be pliers. He yelped and struggled to get away only to get a hard kick in his back which stunned him.

The headman was told by the older freedom fighter that the 'eyes' in the bush saw the Security Forces visiting the village and that someone in the village had spoken to the Rhodesians. The headman vigorously denied this only to receive yet another heavy kick to his rib cage. Then his finger was crushed. Screaming in agony, the pain caused him to pass out which was just as well so he did not have to witness what followed.

The older freedom fighter informed the assembled villagers that his 'eyes' knew who the informant was and that person was a traitor, a sell out to the white settlers, and who was now going to be killed. Terror swept through the villagers while they attempted to assimilate what was actually happening to them. One elder protested that none of them had spoken to the Rhodesian soldiers only to get a fatal blow to his head from a log wielded by a short stocky freedom fighter. The impact sounded as a dull crack as the log shattered the right temple. He fell forward into the ground. Screams erupting from the other villagers were silenced when a freedom fighter let off a burst from his AK 47 into the early evening sky. The villagers cringed in absolute fear anticipating what horrors lay ahead of them.

The freedom fighter in charge let off another verbal assault against the evils of the white settlers and the determination of the liberation movement to eradicate their land of these thieves. The cooking fires cast dancing shadows that sent macabre silhouettes across the ground. Then suddenly, turning his attention to the villagers sitting directly in front of him, he scanned the crowd with his deep penetrating stare. Shouting out hysterically that his 'eyes' knows the person who had spoken to the Rhodesians, the villages all bowed their heads with their eyes diverted to the ground hoping to become invisible.

Springing forward like a leopard he grabbed a man by his arms at random, dragging him out of the crowd. The middle aged man let out a yelp, thrashing about to get away, but to no avail. The freedom fighter threw him on the ground, lifted his AK 47 and pumped a burst of bullets into his chest. His body bounced as the bullets went into him. Blood spurted out drenching his torn shirt. The villages gave a collective scream

234

huddling closer together. Then the freedom fighter fired another burst of bullets into the dead man's face totally shattering his skull and disfiguring him beyond recognition.

Looking back at the petrified villagers he screamed hysterically at them that this man was the 'sell out' to the Rhodesians. He shouted out that this would be the fate of anyone else who spoke to the Rhodesians and next time, not only would that person be killed, but his whole family would be killed as well.

He ordered two women sitting in the front of him to fetch food and beer for his men. They quickly scurried off in fear of losing their lives. Telling his men to choose a young girl who they would take with them, two freedom fighters rushed into the seated crowd and salivating, they searched for the most suitable girl who they dragged out kicking and screaming. They bound her hands behind her back.

After the food and drink, which included many containers of beer, was packaged up and after a burst of machine gun fire was sent over the heads of the assembled villagers, the freedom fighters disappeared into the night.

***

The old man sat on his upturned tin can feeling sad while in deep thought as he searched for the plane in the early evening sky. He heard a muffled bang. Then the pitch of the engine noise sounded different.

He wondered what that meant.

CHAPTER TWENTY ONE

September 1978

The smell was the first sense that came to Terry. It was a pungent burning smell. Not something he could recall smelling before.

Am I alive? he wondered. *Or am I dead? I can't hear a bloody thing. I must be dead ...... What's that smell?*

Feeling disorientated, covered in dirt and dried grass, his mouth full of soil, he rubbed his eyes. He spat out to clear the soil, but he did not have enough saliva to get it all out. The seat belt cut into his side. It hurt. When his ears popped he heard noises. Anguished sounds that seemed to come from all around him. Someone screamed behind him. It was a woman. She sounded hysterical.

Am I still in the plane? Where's the bloke who was sitting beside me? The seat's empty.

He tried to look around.

Jesus that's sore.

He felt his neck with his right hand. It was wet. Looking at his hand, he reeled at the sight of it covered in blood. Impulsively he tied to stand up. He couldn't. His seat belt cut into his waist. Any movement was very painful.

Where the hell am I?

He again turned his head to look around, grimacing at the pain in doing so. As he lifted himself with his left hand to alleviate the discomfort of the seat strap cutting into him, he saw something over his right shoulder.

What's that?

He focused his eyes on a body hanging limply from its seat. A piece of metal from the side of the plane just below the window had virtually severed the head from the shoulders.

Oh Jesus!

Overwhelmed with a surge of panic Terry flayed around disregarding the sharp pain in his neck as he unfastened his seat belt. When he did unclip the buckle he fell forward towards the ground hitting his shoulder on the other seats. Stunned, he found himself wedged between the two rows of seats on the opposite side of the plane looking at the blooded legs of a woman. She was still strapped in her seat; her blouse was covered in blood from a deep gash to her head and shoulder. She stared at Terry in stunned disbelief. She was alive.

"Help me," she said weakly. "Please help me."

Terry stood up and still confused he searched around the confined space. He was standing on the side of the plane and saw the whole fuselage in front of him was open to the outside. He noticed movement as people crawled over seats to get out of the wreckage.

"Please help," she pleaded.

"Ummm .... yes I will. Let me unbuckle you. Okay?"

She nodded. When the buckle was unfastened she slumped forward. Wetness from her blood seeped into his shirt as he caught her.

"Am I going to die?"

The question shook him momentarily.

"What? No. No. It's going to be alright," he said without conviction. "Let's get you out of the plane hey."

Terry was an insurance broker. He had been on business to review insurance cover for the Cutty Sark Hotel. Named after a clipper ship that was built in 1869 and which is now preserved in a dry dock in Greenwich, London, the hotel was built on the shores of Lake Kariba. It had become a prime holiday

237

destination offering spectacular views of the lake, some of its islands, and the Matusadona Mountains. His stay at the hotel was to be his last. He had decided to migrate to South Africa. He saw no future in Rhodesia for his family given the increasing terrorist activity and the imminent hand over of Government to the Africans with the political settlement that had been arranged.

Terry struggled to get the injured woman out of the fuselage. She was stoic as he hauled her over two rows of seats. He could see her injuries were severe and she was bleeding profusely.

"I'm cold," she mumbled.

"Okay. Once we're out of the plane I will get you a blanket hey."

When he got out into the open the smell hit him once again. He gagged as the stench hit the back of his throat. Recovering and settling the injured woman on the ground he searched for something to cover her with.

Oh hell. What the ....?

The scene presenting itself to him was one of utter devastation. In the distance, a hundred metres away, fire bellowed out of what was the front and mid-section of the Viscount. Black smoke rose skyward. Grass fires were spreading outwards from the wreckage.

What's that?

Squinting to focus on two mounds that were smouldering twenty yards from where he stood, he took a few uncertain steps towards them as his curiosity took hold. Someone screamed in anguish and he turned sharply to his left to look. The sharp movement of his neck caused pain to shoot up to his forehead and down his left arm. He saw a woman in anguish as she held her child. Terry suspected the child was dead. When he turned back to face forward he was less than ten metres from the smouldering mounds.

Ah hell no. Jesus.

238

He reeled backwards and fell over a rock scuffing the palm of his right hand as he hit the earth. Transfixed on the charred bodies, he knew where that smell was coming from. Quickly standing up he stumbled in an attempt to get away before doubling over to vomit.

"Terry? Is that you? Thank goodness. Am I glad to see you?"

Terry looked up to see a tall man wearing a badly scorched cream coloured safari suit rushing towards him. Most of his hair on his right side of his head was missing.

"It's me Cormack."

"Cormack. Hell, am I glad to see you."

The two embraced briefly but Cormack let go quickly when Terry grimaced.

"How badly injured are you? Let me take a look," Cormack said with concern.

"I think I am okay. Just banged up. But hell man what happened to the plane? I saw flames out of the window and then it just fell out of the sky."

"I don't know what happened to the plane. But there are survivors and we have to get those still alive away from this wreckage. It may blow up. Can you help me with this?"

"Sure. How many are alive? There can't be many."

"A dozen? Maybe more but let's get them moved?"

"What about the bush fire? Where can we go?"

"Look if we stay in this vicinity, see its ploughed field. Dirt. See? That won't catch fire."

Terry nodded agreement, dismissing his fear of being caught by the grass fire. He remembered the woman he had pulled from the plane and went to her.

"I think we should move away from this part of the plane in case it blows up. Can you stand at all?"

He bent down to help her up. She did not move. Her glassy stare told the reality.

Oh no. Ah hell man.

He slumped down on his haunches and closed his eyes. Opening them after a few moments he put his hands over her face to close her eyelids. Taking a deep breath he stood up to notice a woman passenger, who also was remarkably uninjured, take off her dress to begin tearing it into strips to use as bandages. The dress was made from a bright coloured cotton fabric. The pattern soon disappeared when the bandages were applied and blood saturated the cloth.

"Terry I think we need water," yelled Cormack in his Celtic accent.

"What?"

"Water. We need water. I will take a few people who are fit enough to fetch it. Will you stay here and keep attending to the injured?"

You are the doctor, why don't you stay and I'll go to fetch the water? Oh this is terrible.

Cormack did not wait for Terry's acknowledgement. He already had assembled a small group of four people and they were walking towards the bush. A gravel track led off from the ploughed field. It made sense to follow the track as it should lead to a village.

It was then that two things struck Terry. Firstly, scanning the scene, there seemed to be several young children who had survived the crash. They were amazingly calm. Probably stunned, but nonetheless they were not hysterical. The second was that terrorists may be in the area. This thought chilled him. Recognising the danger he decided to go to the fuselage to see if there was perhaps a gun in the luggage just in case terrorists pitched up.

"Please give me some water."

He looked over his shoulder to see an air hostess leaning up against a log. By the angle her arm was to her body he could see that it was fractured. He carried on his mission to find a weapon in the tail section of the plane.

**

Cormack's group of five, each carrying cuts and bruises, hurried along the track before coming upon a village blanketed in shadow as the sun sunk behind the granite kopjes in the distance.

Cormack immediately noticed that the village was disserted.

Strange? There is no one around. They must have heard the plane crash. Where have the people gone?

He stopped. The others behind him did the same.

"What's wrong?" asked the mother.

"I am not entirely sure," said Cormack in a quiet voice. His suspicions aroused and his senses alert. "There's nobody around and that's rather strange."

"They all probably had the crap knocked out of them, what with the crash and the explosion," Michael, the newly wedded groom, ventured his opinion. "They probably took off into the bush."

He sat down as his lower back ached. The young girl held her mother's hand in a vice like grip, her eyes as wide as saucers.

"Stay here. I will go on ahead from here. If anything bad happens, get going into the bush. Okay?" said Cormack as he moved tentatively forward.

"What bad things can happen?" asked the young girl, tears welling up in her eyes as she looked up at her mother, searching her face for reassurance.

241

"Nothing sweetie. It's all going to be okay. Just keep holding my hand tightly. But if I say run then you must run with me into the bush."

Cormack approached the closest hut. The door made from several thick branches tied together with twine was closed. Speaking in fluent Shona he spoke out loud.

"Greetings. I come with no malice towards you. I come in search of water. There has been an accident and we need water for the injured people. Please offer help."

His mouth was still gritty from the soil he had swallowed during the crash.

The door opened slightly. The face of an old woman peered through the small gap. She looked terrified and quickly shut the door.

Cormack looked about repeating his plea. No one was prepared to leave their hut to greet these visitors into the village. Making the plea for water a third time, the door of the hut opened again and the old woman passed him a large tin can that contained water. She shot back into the hut closing the flimsy door before he could thank her.

"The villagers are petrified and we won't get much help from them," he informed the others.

"Why not?" queried Michael's wife.

Cormack shrugged his shoulders as he cupped some water into his two hands and splashed his face to try and remove the soil that was around his eyes.

"They're frightened that if they offer help to us the terrs will kill them. Anyway.... let's get this water back to the others now and I will come back later to see if I can get more."

They each had a sip of water before the sad group of five turned and headed back along the track to the crash site. The sun had descended below the horizon. The glow of the fires ahead guided them back to the crash site.

***

Where are they with the water?

Terry was thirsty. His throat was sore as the saliva had dried up.

It's getting dark quickly. I can hardly see a bloody thing.

Terry stumbled around the inside of the fuselage looking for clothes he could tear to use as bandages and blankets. He still hoped to find a weapon just in case terrs pitched up. He was pretty certain they had come down in an African tribal area and so the odds were on that terrs would be in the vicinity.

Two others, an older couple, who were not badly injured and who had joined him in the search for blankets, were looking around the outside of the wreckage. It was not easy to give assistance to the injured without any medical supplies, fading light and the smoke in the air from the raging fires.

What's that? He stopped and listened. *That's Ndebele?* His sprits soared. *The RAR have arrived.*

He started to make his way out of the wreckage when he froze.

Hold on? He listened to two men talking on the outside of the wreckage. *Shit they say these people are white settlers. They're terrs. Oh hell. What am I going to do now? Will they take the injured as prisoners? Bloody hell I'm not being taken captive by those bastards.*

He edged further forward to cautiously peer around the torn metal of the cabin. Men silhouetted against the light coming off the fires were standing in a semi-circle, their backs to where he was hiding.

Those are AK's. Shit! How many of them are there? Eight ... nine. Quite a few anyways. Oh hell where are the other two?

He scanned to see if he could see the other two passengers who had been looking for blankets. He could not see them.

I hope they don't blow their cover and bring these terrs over here. What are these terrs doing anyways?

He strained to hear one terrorist say in English.

"We bring you help and water."

Then he heard another say.

"You all move over there. Now! Move over there."

Terry looked around the metal edge of the wreckage once again to see two terrorists pushing some passengers towards where the air hostess was sitting.

Monique stared at the terrorists standing in front of her. The fires were behind them so their faces were in shadow. She was petrified.

Are they going to help us? she wondered.

She felt numb.

"You. Pick up that person now and put them there. Do it now!" ordered one of the terrorist's aggressively.

The female passenger bent over and gave a helping hand to another woman who had a broken leg. They struggled across the fifteen metres to where the others were. The light from the fires continued to cast grotesque shadows.

Terry crawled out of the wreckage to kneel behind another piece of the plane's fuselage. The terrorists were in a tight semi-circle around the ten injured passengers. Two young girls in the group of survivors sobbed while a woman tried to comfort them.

Monique did not understand what the terrorist said, but it did not sound friendly. Her heart rate soared as panic gripped her when she saw the terrorist lift the barrel of his weapon. It looked like he was grinning.

244

Oh no they are going to kill us. Sweet Mother of Mary. No.

"What do you bastards want now?" came a shout from a male passenger.

"You have taken our land!" yelled a terrorist.

He pulled the trigger of his AK 47. His comrades did the same and the hail of gun fire cut into the sad group of injured passengers. Those standing fell to the ground. The terrorists carried on firing and the bodies twitched as the bullets hit them over and over.

Oh God, they're shooting them.

Terry stared in disbelief. A wave of sheer terror swept over him.

Bloody hell I have to make a run for it or I'm next. Right .... Oh shit. I must take my white shirt off. It's a target. Oh shit.

Terry lifted his shirt off over his head and tossed it aside then he ran.

One hundred metres to that clump of trees. Run. Run. Don't look back.

One of the terrorists turned away from the carnage to replace the clip of his weapon. He saw a flash of white. Alerting the others, three terrorists levelled their AK's and fired. The firing kicked the barrels upwards sending the bullets high. They shot over the man's head as he ran bent forward, ducking to avoid being hit.

Keep going. Run. Twenty metres to go. Don't look. Oh shit!

Bullets tore into the trees. He searched for more cover than the few trees that were ahead of him.

They are shooting high. Where's more cover? Okay. There's a ridge thing over there.

Turning sharply to his left he bounded to a ridge line. The terrorists stopped firing at Terry when he disappeared from sight. The others stopped firing into the clump of bodies lying on the ground when their magazines emptied.

"White settler pigs!" said one of the assassins before he moved closer and undid his trousers. He took out his penis and urinated on a dead woman clutching a young girl whose torso was riddled with holes.

"There," shouted one on the comrades. "Come here!"

He pointed towards the gravel track where there were some people standing on the path. They were a long distance away and only their outlines were visible.

"Come here," he yelled in English.

The comrade to his left lifted his weapon and pulled the trigger of his AK. Four of his comrades followed his lead. The others were still replacing their clips. The bullets ripped into the trees as the people on the path scattered into the darkness.

"They may be the Rhodesians. We must leave now," shouted the leader, the one who first started shooting the survivors. Speaking in Ndebele he rallied his men and together they vanished into the bush leaving a pathetic scene behind, piles of dead bodies illuminated by dancing light from the fires. While some of the grass fires had burned out, the tail section was now alight. Smoke sat heavily in the air holding the stench of burnt bodies in its grasp.

Two solitary people emerged from under a panel of wreckage. The husband and his wife were both bloodied and filthy. On spotting men approaching and sensing danger the husband had lifted a panel of fuselage for his wife to hide under it. They huddled together in fear of two things. Being burned if a fire swept their way, or being discovered and brutalised by the terrorists. He had to cover her mouth with his hands when the firing began to stop her sobbing being audible. Both were traumatised, numb from what they saw and frightened of what horrors lay ahead for them. They staggered off towards the bush to find somewhere to hide.

Terry lay flat on his back in the depression he found on the ridge. He had cuts all over his body sustained when he dove into a thicket of bushes to escape the bullets that shot past him. Whilst in pain he lay still and listened.

Are those bastards coming to look for me? What'll I do if they are? Well it's dark now. I'll stand a better chance running for it if they are looking for me. The Security Forces should be here soon enough. But what if they don't know we went down or where we are? They must know surely? How long will it take them to find us? If it gets light those bloody terrs will be back? So what should I do? Think man. Think.

He listened. There were no sounds other than from the fires.

I will stay put for now, he decided.

***

The little girl squeezed her mother's hand. She looked down at her daughter. She looked so tiny, vulnerable and scared.

Thank you God for saving my little girl in the crash. Now help us get to safety. Bring the Security Forces here quickly to save us please God, she prayed to herself.

The five shuffled along the trail, Cormack carrying the tin can trying not to spill the water, Michael's back caused him more acute pain so he walked bent over and his wife limped having stood on a sharp rock that cut her bare foot.

That sounds like gunfire? Hold on. There's a bunch of people in the silhouette there. Are they our soldiers? thought Cormack as he stained to see ahead.

"Come here!"

Cormack shivered as he heard the shout from the wreckage.

Oh no, they're terrs.

A burst of gun fire sent tracer bullets shooting overhead ripping into the trees behind them.

"Run. Run for cover," shouted Cormack.

The five survivors darted in amongst the trees lining the track to their right. They ran through the scrub until the shooting stopped. Cormack led the way. The undergrowth took its toll. Their arms and legs bled from being cut by the bushes. The little girl sobbed.

"Those were terrs. I hoped they were the army. We had better find a place to hide. It looks like we may be on our own for now," said Cormack anxiously.

The fading light made it difficult for them as they looked around searching desperately for a suitable place to hide.

"Okay. Look over there ... there see? It's a dry ... a river bed. Let's make our way into that and find somewhere," said Cormack.

They quickly made their way down the slope to the soft sandy dry river bed and walked purposefully along it until they came across a spot where dead trees and logs had been snagged against some rocks. Cormack suggested it as the place they should hide. The men moved a pile of debris to find an opening for them to crawl into.

"Mommy is here with you sweetie. But you have to stay very quiet, okay. We don't want those nasty men to hear us. Okay sweetie?"

The little girl nodded and hugged her mother, trying to be brave.

"She can lie on me," offered Cormack. "It may help her stay calm and get some sleep."

The girl crept along the ground and over a log to lie on Cormack's lap. He leant up against a solid tree trunk with his legs stretched out in front of him. Michael and his wife found a gap where they both fitted next to each other.

"I suggest we don't talk now," said Cormack. "It's best we stay very quiet. We don't know where those bloody terrs are."

It was less than thirty minutes when they heard the noise. Twigs breaking. The muffled voices. Ndebele. Cormack put his arm around the little girl holding her tight. His other hand was positioned ready to smother her mouth if she gave out a scream in panic.

I'm scared, thought Cormack. *Trapped like a rat by these bastards. What should I do? If I'm going to be killed I certainly will not show those bastards that I am scared. I have to stay stoic. They must not get their filthy hands on this little girl. Do I snap her neck if it's all over and the terrs come to get her? Yes. I will have to do that as I can't let those filthy bastards get their fucking hands on her.* That thought sunk home. *Oh God.*

The terrorists moved on along the river bank and soon all fell quiet once again. After a while Cormack nodded off to sleep only to be startled by a baboon crying out.

Thank God I didn't startle her. My leg has gone to sleep. This is terrible. The waiting. What's the time?

He lifted his left arm to try and see the time.

Bloody impossible! I wonder if Terry made it. It's cold. There will be frost tonight.

The terrorists came back along the river bank. Their steps were audible, as was their muffled conversation. They made their way back towards the plane crash.

249

They are searching for us. Bloody bastards. I wish I had a gun. I would try and take some out. I wonder if the army will get here first light. I hope they can locate the crash site though. By morning the fires may have burned out. There may not be any smoke to signal where the plane went down. What the hell happened to the plane to bring it down anyway? Was it mechanical or perhaps it was shot down? At first light we must move to higher ground. Find somewhere with more cover.

With his mind racing, no more sleep came to him.

***

Terry heard the excited voices off in the distance. While faint he could tell that they were not the voices of the Security Forces. He decided to edge his way along the rocky ground towards a big tree trunk that was lying on its side. Once there he cautiously lifted his head over the top.

He was higher up than the flat ground where the wreckage of the Viscount was scattered. Fires still burned in several places. He noticed that the tail section was still alight.

Terry saw terrorists emerge from the bush. They were eighty metres to his left. Moving towards the wreckage they spread out. Terry watched with morbid fascination wondering what they were planning to do.

They're bloody well looting the plane.

The comrades searched the area for the luggage. They opened luggage emptying the contents out on the ground. Some comrades searched bodies taking watches and jewellery off the corpses.

Oh my God no.

Terry watched in horror as two comrades attached bayonets to their weapons. Then standing with their legs apart over the bodies and with their AK's lifted above their heads they shouted out something before ramming the sharp end into the corpses. He stared transfixed by the brutality unfolding once again as the bayonets sank into flesh. His stomach churned as panic swept over him. Concerned they may do a sweep of the area he decided to look for better cover.

Creeping backwards away from the log and crouching low, he moved into the scrub. He stumbled upon a dry river bed tumbling head over heels down the sandy bank. Recovering and thankful that no limbs were broken from the fall, he walked along the river bed finding it hard to see in the dark. After a few minutes he came across some rocks butting out of a steep earth bank. Feeling with his hands he found a gap and squeezed himself in behind a rock. With his back up against the earth bank he settled down for the night.

Sleep did not come easily but eventually the emotional stress and physical exhaustion took its toll. He drifted off into an unsettled slumber.

CHAPTER TWENTY TWO

September 1978

Staffing was at full complement in ComOps at eight in the evening.

As soon as the news filtered in from Kariba that Air Rhodesia flight RH825 was missing the duty officer, Major Woods, decided to assemble staff. Even those who were rostered off trickled in as they heard the news either from colleagues or on the radio and television broadcast by the Rhodesia Broadcasting Corporation.

"Air Rhodesia announced that the scheduled flight RH eight two five from Kariba to Salisbury with fifty two passengers and four crew has gone missing. There is no information at this time as to the cause. Every effort is being made to ...."

The ComOps team gathered intel on the missing plane especially on where it may have gone down so that the rescue operation could be planned overnight and executed at dawn. Time would be of the essence for many obvious reasons. This was going to be an all-night effort that would continue until the operation was over when the plane and any survivors were found.

"In all probability the plane's gone down in the Urungwe, Sir."

Major Woods was on the telephone with the chief of ComOps, Lieutenant General Walls.

"That is bad news Major. Urungwe is a hot spot. We must get our boys in there at first light. Throw everything we have at it."

"Understood Sir. We have the Dak grid searching now but no sightings as yet. It will continue through the night to locate the crash site. We'll have the ParaDak

ready to drop men at first light. We have four choppers
..."

"What type?"

"G-Cars Sir. To extract any injured, if there are any
that is."

"Unlikely."

"Agreed Sir, but we will ferry in troops who are
assembling at Kariba on the G-Cars and casevac out
any injured."

"Air cover?"

"The Hunters are on standby sir. We have two at
New Sarum. Also there are two Lynx on standby at the
FAF. They will go in if the guys get resistance."

"Do we have any idea what happened yet Major?"
"We are tracking the general flight path of the plane
Sir. The weather is clear so the likelihood of a lightning
strike is ruled out. According to air traffic, Kariba
Tower got the distress call somewhere between five
and six minutes after take-off. We assume the pilot
called it in within say a minute max of experiencing
problems so that makes somewhere between six to
eight minutes out. Depending on what aversion route he
took on take-off we can get an approximate area Sir.
We also have to factor in if he went straight in after the
Mayday or whether he turned around to try and get
back. All unknowns at this time."

"What that tells me is that we have a hell of a big
possible area to search. We need more choppers
Major."

"Agreed that it is a big area to search Sir. We may
get lucky. The Dak is on grid search, but intel already
suggests difficulty."

"How so?"

"Kraal fires all over the area make it hard to
distinguish what would be the plane fire Sir."

253

"The Dak that's up there now should see the fire where it went in. It would be larger than any kraal cooking fire surely? That will pin point the site for us?"

"The pilot reports there are village fires all over the place. He has not seen any large concentrated fire as yet."

"If we cannot locate the site tonight can we estimate how long it could be to find it after first light?" queried Walls.

"If we're lucky Sir it should be before eight, but it could take until noon."

Walls paused to think before responding.

"You know what Urungwe is like. If there are survivors and if we don't get to them first the terrs will. So ... as yet do we know why it went down?"

"No Sir. Air Rhodesia is unable to say at this stage. They say the plane was in good nick Sir. The pilot told Kariba Tower his two engines were on fire and he was going in. It's probable the wing broke off and well ...."

"Yes Major, I know. Fifty something on board."

Woods hesitated before venturing the next comment. He was well aware of the sensitivity of what he was going to say.

"Sir, we are leaning towards the conclusion the plane was shot down. A site inspection will confirm what actually happened to the plane, but given the intel on the Strelas ZIPRA have it's a pretty good assumption to draw. Two engines on fire at the same time."

"I sense you're on the right track. ZIPRA have already fired off the Strela at the SAA plane at Vic Falls. Damn lucky it failed. But Kariba is a hell of a way from Vic Falls. Did we have intel that the terrs have Strela capability near Kariba? Because if they do it poses a big threat to the ops out of there."

254

"There is no intel they have Strela capability at Kariba, Sir. If this attack is a Strela then we have an issue to deal with in mopping up the TTL Sir."

"Okay, keep me informed of progress Major."

Woods hung up the receiver, leant back in his chair and putting his hands behind his head, he looked at the ceiling before closing his eyes.

When we find the site it won't be pretty.

CHAPTER TWENTY THREE

September 1978

Dawn crept in painfully slowly. The early morning air was bitterly cold with thick frost covering the ground.

Cormack stirred when the light first pierced through the gaps in the logs. He had dosed in and out of sleep without any real rest coming. The young girl was lying asleep on his legs. He gently woke her whispering 'shhhh'. No one spoke for fear of being overheard by the terrorists. They had not heard any noises for many hours other than that of the occasional wild animal. Each screech from an owl or laugh from a hyena sent shivers down their spines.

Slowly they crawled out from under the pile of logs and wearily they surveyed the surroundings.

"We should stay clear of the wreckage in case the terrs are still lurking around," ventured Cormack once he felt it was safe to say something.

"Should we not stay near the plane? That's where the Security Forces will be coming too surely?"

Michael's wife recalled she had read that it was best to stay at the scene of an accident because the emergency response teams would find the scene but it was harder to find an individual wondering around in the bush.

"Good point. But I'm concerned that the terrs are still lurking and we don't want to be spotted by them. I think we need to find a better place to hide close by until the troops arrive. They'll come in by chopper soon so we will be able to hear them."

It did not take long for them to find a small rocky outcrop which offered them shade. They settled down, hidden by the trees and bushes to wait for the rescue teams to arrive.

It was well past ten and the sun was high in the sky when thirst finally overtook the small group of survivors. The little girl was parched and her lips cracked. There was no sign of any rescue. No sound of any aircraft. No sign of movement by any one.

"Look its ten thirty now," said Cormack. "We need water. I cannot understand why the army have not arrived yet. Surely it's not that hard to locate the crash site. But we have not even heard a plane yet."

"They must know we've crashed surely? We need medical help," said Michael.

Michael's wife had a broken arm. Swelling caused her considerable pain. Michael's back was aching and both their feet were torn and bleeding. Cormack fashioned some soles from bark and tied them to their feet with thin twisted twigs. It was a crude attempt to assist them in walking over the rocky ground.

"I think we must find water and … well ... to get ourselves out of here," ventured Cormack.

After an inconclusive debate they set off towards a gravel road Cormack had seen from atop the rocky outcrop. He suggested to them it was a way that could take them to the main Kariba road. They reached the gravel road just as the bark soles broke apart. Rob and his wife shuffled behind the others. Cormack took the little girl off his back and she walked hand in hand with her mother.

I hope there are no land mines on this road. The thought shot across Cormack's mind. *Okay. If there were mines they would be for vehicles not anti-personnel mines so if I stood on one it probably would not go off. If it did, well that's it all over red rover.*

They had not ventured far when they came across some Africans walking in the opposite direction.

257

Worried they may be terrorists, Cormack searched to see if they carried weapons. He could not see any. When they got close Cormack spoke to them in their native language asking them for help and for water. They refused to render any assistance and scurried off past them.

After a further few hundred metres they came upon a small village. These villages were hostile, chasing the five survivors away.

"Why are they so mean to us?" queried Michael's wife.

"They are petrified. If they help us then they fear they will be killed by the terrs," offered Cormack as a feeble explanation.

"What's the matter with these people? Can't they see we need water and are injured? They should help us and stand up against those nasty brutal terrs."

She started crying.

"It's complicated," ventured Cormack.

But he knew this was not the time or the place to debate the merits and right or wrongs of the situation. He looked around searching for the mother and her child.

"Where are the others?"

"They went down the road. Around that bend," said Michael pointing. "Don't worry about them. We must still try get some water from this village."

"I can't leave them to wander off. This situation is dangerous."

He set off at a pace down the road towards where Michael had pointed.

What's that noise? It's a plane.

He scanned the sky for it. The Dak was painted a green and brown camouflage colour making it hard to see at a distance.

There. It's circling. That's where the crash site is. Oh lord we should have stayed there, Cormack admonished himself.

"Look the plane is dropping paratroopers," shouted Michael.

Cormack ran out to a clearing and started waving his hands above his head in a vain attempt to attract attention. He yelled but it was futile. The Dak having discharged its cargo of paratroopers had banked left and was already heading back to base.

Feeling disheartened he looked around to see mother and daughter sitting on the side of the road under a large tree.

Oh God what can we do now? Hold on what's that?

To his delight he saw a vehicle driving towards them, a swirl of dust rising behind it.

"A vehicle! There's a vehicle coming," he shouted at Michael.

The Police Land Rover came to an abrupt halt then reversed to where the two were sitting under the tree. Cormack ran along the road towards the Land Rover. Michael and his wife hobbled along as best they could.

After drinking the water offered them by the two black Police officers, the five survivors clambered aboard the Land Rover. They drove along the road for five minutes before coming to a junction where several army trucks were parked each carrying territorial soldiers, who were being taken to the crash site. None of these young soldiers had ever seen anything like what they were about to see. In all probability they were unlikely ever see such things again.

The five ragged survivors were taken to a clearing not far from the junction where an Allouette helicopter came in low over the trees to land. The pilot kept the rotors running while the survivors were escorted aboard. They flew tree top level before landing on a field to the one side of the Karoi District Hospital. Medical staff rushed to assist them off the chopper, taking them to the emergency entrance of the hospital.

Two Special Branch officers arrived in the late afternoon to interrogate the survivors.

***

Although the sun was high in the sky Terry elected to stay hidden between the rocks and the river bank. He heard the terrorists laughing at one point during the early morning. He assumed they were jovial having looted the wreckage. He worried that the terrorists may set up an ambush for the rescuers and he certainly did not wish to be caught in any cross fire.

He needed a drink. His throat was raw. He ached all over. The multitude of scratches were sore, some festering. And as the day wore on and he did not hear any planes or helicopters his sprits sagged.

He awoke with a jolt having drifted into an exhausted sleep when he heard the Dak pass overhead. The throbbing sound of the engines soon faded.

Am I dreaming? Was that a plane I heard? Surely they must have seen the crash site? Why have they left? Should I get out and look?

He felt delirious and feint. Caution prevailed and he waited.

The Dak came back circling again before it departed. Soon after that he heard helicopters. Slowly extracting himself from his hideout and looking at it in the light of day he felt it was quite remarkable that he had found it in the dark.

It's just as well there were no snakes in it, he thought to himself. *Being killed from a snake bite after surviving a plane crash and those bloody terrorists would have really been a bad joke. Nobody would have*

260

found my body and they would have suspected I was one of those poor sods burned up in the plane.

With difficulty he scrambled up the bank of the dry river and foregoing any caution he rushed towards the crash site. Anxious to get to safety, he began jogging, bursting out of the undergrowth onto the ploughed field to be confronted by the wreckage and carnage.

He staggered forward putting foot ahead of foot, his hands over his nose and mouth to shield the stench. He did not see the two soldiers rushing up to him. When they reached him they asked him if he was injured. He stared at them with blank eyes, then sank to his knees and wept, his whole body shaking.

CHAPTER TWENTY FOUR

September 1978

The helicopter landed gently on the edge of the field. Richard unbuckled his safety belt and jumped down from the helicopter. He leant in to get his bag from the floor while thanking the pilot. The short flight from Karoi was uneventful as they flew treetop level to the crash site. The gunner, a young man, kept a sharp eye out the open side looking for any potential threat from terrorists on the ground.

Richard moved away from the aircraft instinctively bending down to avoid the rotor blades which posed no threat to him. Looking around he began taking in the scene for himself. He saw the tail of the Viscount first. It was off to his left about one hundred and fifty metres. He could see the scorched Air Rhodesia markings on it.

Okay, so the plane came down over there. The soil has been churned up. It must have come in at a slight angle to have skidded so far, which means it must have been intact when it hit the ground. If a wing had come off it would have gone straight in, nose first. The bulk of the plane is on the right where that gully is. But the tail is over there on the left. Hmmm .... why is that I wonder?

He walked towards the tail.

There's a prop. And another. So the wings stayed attached to the bulk of the plane. It's totally burned out. I guess that's right given it had a full tank of avgas. There's baggage all over the place.

He stepped away from the tail to follow the trail of wreckage.

Christ the stench!

Covering his nose with his left hand he put his bag down to pull out a handkerchief from his trouser pocket. He folded it into a triangle and then tied it around his face, the handkerchief covering his nose. It helped to stem the smell only marginally. He noticed the charred remains lined up to his right. The soldiers had been salvaging the bodies and putting them in a line on the ground ready for the police to try and identify them.

Richard decided to avoid the rows of charred bodies and moved back towards the tail.

There are eight survivors taken to Karoi. They were all in the tail section. Some ordeal they went through. He stopped to look around to orientate what the survivors had described. *Well wooded. Some rocky outcrops over there. Oh Jeeees!*

He saw the line of bodies off to his left. Some of the bodies were partially covered with blankets so he could see they were not burned.

These are the poor souls who were murdered. Those bastards who murdered them! A surge of intense anger and hatred came over him as he stared at the legs of two small children. *How many children were shot? I can see two sets of small feet.*

Wrestling to get his emotions under control he turned away and walked towards the gully. Two men, Wing Commander Pointon and Captain Long, were inspecting the remnants of the plane in the gully.

"Glad you could make it Superintendent," said Long. "It's a mess isn't it?"

"I presume it's too early to say what brought the plane down," queried Richard.

"It's not certain yet," said Pointon. "But by the looks of it, the pilot brought it down. The grounding appears to have been relatively soft which meant he must have had some control over the plane. After hitting the ground it skidded, losing props and bits of wing, but then it hit this gully and broke up. Damn unfortunate. The tail split off and went over there taken by the forward momentum. The bulk of the plane would have stopped here, crumpled and as the fuel tanks ruptured, it exploded.

The fuselage is badly burned out, as are the wings and engines as we would expect. The fire was ferocious. We will have to take a very close look at the starboard engines .... what's left of them that is, when we get them back to New Sarum. The pilot radioed in that they were non-operational before he went in. But from what I can see the one starboard engine must have exploded."

"How long will that take? I mean, how long until we know for certain what happened?" queried Richard.

"Can't say. A few days perhaps. Look, we all know that the probability of this being a missile strike is high, but we can't jump to conclusions," said Pointon.

"ZIPRA has Strela's but intel was that they were near Vic Falls targeting SAA. There was no intel the insurgents had Strela's here," said Richard. "I suppose it couldn't have been RPG fire?"

"Not RPG. The plane was too high up. If it's a missile then it's the SAM. In that case it will tell us some unpleasant news. They have spread the infiltration of the SAM's further than we hoped or thought," concluded Pointon.

"The dissemination of information about this must be kept tight. Special Branch and CIO are dealing with how the info is sent out. The potential for general morale damage here is huge so we have to be very careful on how this story is told. I need to be the first to know what caused this crash."

The two officers nodded. They both knew the score on how Special Branch and CIO would run the media and public perception spin.

"Captain John Heap from Air Rhodesia and Phil Palmer, he's the chief security advisor to the Department of Aviation, will arrive soon. They will run the crash investigation from the civilian perspective given this is a civilian plane, but they will liaise with both of you, okay? CIO have arranged for the Vultures to be flown in first light tomorrow. Chief Inspector Farrell from SB will accompany them and guide them in the right direction. I hope your blokes get those who did this Captain. Kill the bastards. I'm going to have a look around a bit more gentlemen then I'll head back to Salisbury."

Richard stood at a distance watching the soldiers putting bodies on canvas mats while several Police officers collected forensic evidence so that the terrorist atrocity could be validated.

How they can manage to do that? he thought as he saw two soldiers pick up bits of charred bodies. *The image of this will haunt us all for a very long time.*

"Sir, there's a message for you from ComOps," said a corporal.

Richard made his way to where the radio receiver was located.

"Intel received from overseas indicates that ZIPRA are preparing to claim responsibility for the downing of the aircraft," was the message.

"That's bad news indeed," he replied before pausing.

Damn! Why would he do such a stupid thing? This one act of inhumanity means the end to a year of pre-planning to bring Nkomo into the political settlement, he thought. *The plan is going down the toilet.*

"Okay. It's pretty terrible here on the ground. I'm going to catch the next chopper back to Karoi and drive back to Salisbury. I'll be back there in the early evening. Find out where Nkomo is. He was in Salisbury yesterday to finalise the political detente initiative."

Richard boarded the chopper knowing with increasing foreboding that without neutralising ZIPRA within the political solution, the Rhodesian Security Forces were unable to hold the thin line of a semblance of security within Rhodesia. He feared the country would spiral into chaos for years, if not decades.

Smithy will be shattered when ZIPRA claim the responsibility for this horrific act of barbarism.

Ian Smith was not a willing participant to the Special Branch plan for a detente between Rhodesia, Zambia and ZIPRA. It took a lot of convincing before he saw the imperative to undertake this course of action in absolute secrecy. Richard saw it as the mark of a true leader that Smith had shown bravery to venture unsupported to a hostile nation to talk with vowed enemies about a peaceful settlement. The Zambians could easily have arrested him, tried him, shot him or even handed him over to the British who wanted Smith arrested for treason. Smith could easily have been shot or blown up by ZIPRA when he was driven unprotected, except for the two Zambian police on motorbikes, from the airport in Lusaka to Kaunda's residence and back. Remembering the occasion vividly, because he was there accompanying Smith, sent shivers down his spine.

Richard realised that he should start thinking about how to mitigate the damage and what a diplomatic Plan B was. The problem was there was no Plan B. Plan A had to work and it was going down the drain.

He could not think of any other option than to attack and destroy ZIPRA's military capability quickly.

266

The evening news broadcasts carried the ComOps communiqué as the lead story over the Rhodesian Broadcast Corporation.

"Combined Operations Headquarters regret to confirm that on Sunday evening the third of September, an Air Rhodesia Viscount, flight RH eight five two, carrying fifty two passengers and four crew crashed forty kilometres south east of Kariba dam.

The wreckage was found this morning by Security Forces who reported that the starboard engine appeared to have exploded and the starboard external side of the plane was heavily scorched.

The pilot was able to bring the plane down to land in a field but it broke up on impact. Eighteen people survived the crash.

Of those who survived, five left through thick bush to seek help from local tribe people and thirteen remained close to the aircraft. Terrorists later approached the scene and ordered the shocked and numbed survivors to their feet.

The terrorists then opened fire with Communist-made Kalashnikov assault rifles and ten of the passengers - as yet unnamed, but six known to be women - died in a hail of fire.

The terrorists then looted the plane.

The names of the terror victims are yet to be released."

***

Later that evening, Air Rhodesia Chief Pilot, Captain Travers, released a statement confirming the loss of the aircraft from engine failure.

The London Press rushed the story to the street.

"Rhodesian terrorist leader Mr. Joshua Nkomo said yesterday his men brought down the Rhodesian airliner near Kariba at the weekend, but denied that his men killed 10 survivors on the ground.

Mr. Nkomo, co-leader of the Patriotic Front alliance with Mr. Robert Mugabe, said the Air Rhodesia Viscount aircraft was brought down because the planes flying to Kariba on ostensibly civilian flights were being used for ferrying troops and military supplies to the Kariba lakeside area, on the border with Zambia where Mr. Nkomo is based, Iana-Reuter reports.

Mr. Nkomo declined to say how the aircraft had been brought down. Only eight of the 56 people aboard survived.

"We brought that plane down, but it is not true that we killed any survivors," Mr. Nkomo said. "The Rhodesians have been ferrying military personnel and equipment in Viscounts and we had no reason to believe that this was anything different," he said.

He said his ZIPRA (Zimbabwe People's Revolutionary Army) was "not interested in killing civilians, but when people start using civilian aircraft how do you know when the plane is up there? The Rhodesians should know this is a military zone," he said.

Mr. Nkomo said it was tragic that there had been a massive outcry in the West because white civilians had been killed.

"You forget that the regime kills 30 of our people a day. So the life of a black person is different from a white person? Is any European child supposed to be worth a million blacks," Mr. Nkomo said. "As far as we are concerned we were bringing down an aircraft

268

that's being used to ferry military personnel and equipment," he continued.

Asked if the reported downing of the plane marked a turning-point in the fourteen-year-old war he said: "We have said that it is going to be intensified every day, we will make it much more bitter."

"This is a downright lie," Captain Travers said. "The airline is not engaged in any military operations neither does it carry troops, arms, ammunition or supplies for this purpose. It never has been. No words of mine could adequately portray the sense of complete horror and deep rooted revulsion which is felt by the whole of the Air Rhodesia Corporation at the wanton, brutal and bloody massacre of ten innocent and unarmed survivors, mostly women and children, who were bludgeoned, shot and bayoneted to death by a gang of unspeakable thugs."

In the Rhodesian House of Assembly, Wing Commander Rob Gaunt, MP, called for martial law, the banning of ZAPU, and a postponement of the planned white Rhodesian referendum on the internal settlement that was to lead to black majority government.

Donald Goddard, the virulent young MP for Matobo District, interjected:

"Hang them publicly." Gaunt then warned that "Africa was now going to witness the wrath of really angry white men."

The British Foreign Office expressed its shock at the incident, but said it had no independent evidence of what had happened or who was responsible.

"Yet again there has been a horrible and tragic incident in Rhodesia involving innocent civilians. We deplore the whole incident which, once more, underlines the need to bring this disastrous war to an end by negotiation and achieve independence and majority rule for Zimbabwe."

269

The killing of the crash survivors was condemned by Bishop Desmond Tutu, General Secretary of the South African Council of Churches in a statement in Johannesburg. The statement said,

"No condemnation could be strong enough for such a heartless act of slaying defenceless and helpless people, and heartfelt sympathy went to their relatives and friends."

The South African Foreign Minister, 'Pik' Botha said in the parliament in Cape Town "...that the murderous monsters who committed such a heinous act must be hunted down and killed like the rabid dogs they are." He later went on to state that ".... Nkomo was an international terrorist who has committed crimes against humanity and must be brought to justice in the international courts."

***

Richard anxiously sipped at his tea in his small office in ComOps awaiting receipt of a document.

It doesn't really matter what caused the plane to come down, he rationalised to himself. *The killing of the survivors has finished off any hope of détente with ZIPRA completely. That bloody fuckwit Nkomo. What was he thinking? The door on the detente plan has well and truly shut and we're in the pig's poo up to our necks .... what a stuff up.*

A soldier knocked on his door.

"Come."

"Here's the sitrep Sir."

Richard took the brown cardboard folder from the soldier who left his office closing the door behind him. Richard drained his tea cup and then opened the folder. He read the contents.

270

A single Strela to the inside starboard engine. Fire spread to the outer engine. Fire extinguishers deployed. No hope of extinguishing the fire. Wing crippled. A matter of minutes before it broke off. The pilot brought it down. Brilliant effort under extreme circumstances. Commended for his ability. Hit gully, broke in two.....

He closed the folder and placed it on his desk. Closing his eyes he rested his head in the palm of his right hand while reflecting what it must have been like for all those on the plane. He had a vivid idea from the interview transcripts from the eight survivors. Disbelief, chaos, abject fear, sheer panic, resolve to fate ... all the emotions mixed up in a metal tube hurtling to the ground.

He lifted himself up from his wooden chair and left his office. He got to a door that had a sign on it. '*Lt. Gen. Walls.*'

He knocked and waited.

"Come," said Walls.

Richard entered the large office closing the door behind him. The high ceilings were framed with ornate cornices, resplendent from the type of period finishing when the building was constructed in the mid 1920's. There were two windows that overlooked the inside paved courtyard. They were open allowing a slight breeze into the room. The wooden flooring was well worn as was a carpet that covered a part of the floor where two settees were at right angles to each other. A long table covered with maps stretched along a wall covered in pictures in mismatched frames, all of military scenes. Behind a wooden desk was a picture of the President of Rhodesia. Either side of it hung flags, one being that of the national flag of Rhodesia and one representing the Rhodesian Army.

"Sir, we now have the definitive confirmation of the cause for the Viscount crash. It's as we suspected. A

271

single Strela to the inside starboard engine. ZIPRA initiated."

"Sit down Richard."

Walls did not get up from his seat behind his desk. He pointed to one of the three chairs on the opposite side of the desk.

"So what's the next step here?"

Richard ran through the scenario outlining that, realistically the initiative to neutralise ZIPRA through a political initiative was now dead in the water. He briefed Walls on the PR and other media initiatives that CIO were pursuing to garnish maximum international condemnation against ZIPRA in an attempt to get international support for the settlement between Smith and the three internal black Rhodesian leaders.

"I remain pessimistic that we will achieve any momentum for recognition from the West for the internal settlement primarily because I am now very concerned that we will not be able to get the voter turnout that will give the process to elect the new Government any credibility."

"Why's that Richard?

"We have to face the prospect of ZANLA pouring in masses of insurgents to intimidate the poor sods in the TTL's who won't turn out to vote, while ZIPRA initiates their plans to invade Matabeleland. It's a done deal that the internal settlement is tits up before it gets off the bloody ground Sir."

"That's a very bleak outlook Richard. Is it the view of SB or just you?"

"SB has serious concerns which we briefed you on a few weeks ago."

"Alright then, go on."

"The intel we have on ZIPRA capability and their strategy to invade Matabeleland is a real and present threat. Now that the political option with Nkomo is out the window we only have a military option left. Therefore we must neutralise the ZIPRA threat sooner than later, before Mugabe sends the bulk of his insurgents in. So I think ...."

"Why do you suggest we focus on ZIPRA when the main threat is Mugabe and ZANLA?"

"We have already managed to push the ZIPRA camps away from the border for fear of Air Force attack. Our intel suggests their guard is down because ZIPRA think we won't attack them because they are deep in Zambia. Their view is that they enjoy the protection of the Zambian Air Force.

Mugabe on the other hand has his insurgents in dozens of camps that are spread over large areas. They are not massed together. When we go in to whack them our kill rate is low because of the way the Chinks have taught them to set up their camps.

ZIPRA has eight to nine thousand conventionally trained insurgents massed and when they do invade in November, as our intel suggests they plan to, we could be screwed. The massing of their troops is perfect for the Air Force and SAS to deal with. In and out, to knock the wind right out of Nkomo. After this quick decisive strike, we can focus on ZANLA as planned, but obviously with a re-think on keeping some troops deployed in the west and northwest to deal with residual insurgents on the ground Sir."

"Makes tactical sense. But what about the Zambian Air Force and the ground to air defence missiles?"

"That remains the main stumbling block to us getting to the targeted camps in Zambia, Sir. CIO intel is that the Zambians don't have the appetite to engage us in the air or on the ground. The AF guys are working with SAS on neutralising the missile threats."

"Is the intel solid?"

"Yes it is Sir."

"What about the MiG's the Soviets have supplied ZIPRA?"

"They are in Angola and don't pose an immediate threat."

"Right then. I'll activate ComOps to finalise the plans ASAP. As we suspected time is of the essence, so let's get this ball rolling shall we?"

Richard left the General's office and headed off to brief the Minister of Transport regarding the status of the investigation of the plane crash. Five days after the Viscount disaster the Minister of Transport confirmed that the plane had been shot down by a 9M32 'Strela' missile, commonly known as a Sam 7.

A sombre mood sat heavily on a demoralised society and an anxious military.

CHAPTER TWENTY FIVE

September 1978

The Cathedral bells rang out summoning attendance. The pigeons took flight from Jacaranda trees in Cecil Square which were showing the first signs of their blossoms threatening to explode in colour before laying down a purple carpet.

The media assembled across the road from the Cathedral and mourners began to assemble. A motorcade of dignitaries arrived at eleven. The President of Rhodesia's ceremonial vehicle arrived behind a dozen Police on horseback, followed by Ian Smith and his wife Janet and then the Tribal Chiefs. The precession of families of the victims was long.

The Cathedral bells fell silent.

The Anglican Dean of Salisbury, The Very Reverend John da Costa stepped up to the pulpit. A tall, bearded, white-robed man with a flamboyant personality he was trained by the Society of the Sacred Mission. Prior to taking up the post in Salisbury, da Costa had worked in West Africa and then among the Coloureds of Cape Town where he served as adviser on missionary work to the Archbishop. He looked around the majestic building holding two thousand people. He allowed an eerie silence to descend before he inhaled a deep breath and spoke.

"Clergymen, I am frequently told, should keep out of politics. I thoroughly agree. For this reason, I will not allow politics to be preached in this Cathedral.

Clergy have to be reconcilers. That is no easy job. A Minister of religion who has well known political views, and allows them to come to the fore, cannot reconcile, but will alienate others and fail in the chief part of his ministry. For this reason I personally am surprised at there being two clergymen in the Executive Council. It is my sincere prayer that they can act as Christ's ambassadors of reconciliation.

My own ministry began in Ghana, where Kwame Nkrumah preached: '*Seek ye first the political kingdom, and all these things will be added to you.*' We know what became of him. We are not to preach a political kingdom, but the kingdom of God.

Clergy are usually in the middle, shot at from both sides. It is not an enviable role. Yet times come when it is necessary to speak out, and in direct and forthright terms, like trumpets with unmistakable notes. I believe that this is one such time.

Nobody who holds sacred the dignity of human life can be anything but sickened at the events attending the crash of the Viscount 'Hunyani'. Survivors have the greatest call on the sympathy and assistance of every other human being. The horror of the crash was bad enough but that this should have been compounded by murder of the most savage and treacherous sort leaves us stunned with disbelief and brings revulsion in the minds of anyone deserving the name 'Human'. This bestiality, worse than anything in recent history, stinks in the nostrils of heaven.

But are we deafened with the voice of protest from nations which call themselves 'civilised'? We are not! Like men, in the story of the Good Samaritan, they 'pass by on the other side'. One listens for loud condemnation by Dr. David Owen, himself a medical doctor, trained to extend mercy and help to all in need. One listens and the silence is deafening.

One listens for loud condemnation by the President of the United States, himself a man from the Bible Baptist belt and again the silence is deafening.

276

One listens for loud condemnation by the Pope, by the Chief Rabbi, by the Archbishop of Canterbury, by all who love the name of God. Again the silence is deafening.

I do not believe in white supremacy. I do not believe in black supremacy either. I do not believe that anyone is better than another, until he has proved himself to be so. I believe that those who govern or who seek to govern must prove themselves worthy of the trust that will be placed in them. One looks for real leadership; one finds little in the Western world; how much less in Africa!

Who is to be blamed for this ghastly episode?

Like Pontius Pilate, the world may ask 'What is truth'? What is to be believed? That depends on what your prejudices will allow you to believe, for then no evidence will convince you otherwise.

So who is to be blamed?

First, those who fired the guns. Who were they? Youths and men who, as likely as not, were until recently in Church Schools. This is the first terrible fact. Men who went over to the other side and in a few months were so indoctrinated that all they had previously learned was obliterated. How could this happen if they had been given a truly Christian education?

Secondly, it is common knowledge that in large parts of the world violence is paraded on T.V. and Cinema Screens as entertainment. Films about war, murder, violence, rape, devil possession, and the like are 'good box office'. Peak viewing time is set aside for murderers from Belfast, Palestine, Europe, Africa and the rest, to speak before an audience of tens of millions. Thugs are given full treatment, as if deserving of respect. Not so their victims' relations.

Who else is to be blamed?

I am sure that the United Nations and their Church equivalent, the World Council of Churches, both bear blame in this. Each parades a pseudo morality which, like all half-truths, is more dangerous than the lie direct. From the safety and comfort of New York and Geneva, high moral attitudes can safely be struck. For us in the sweat, the blood, the suffering, it is somewhat different.

Who else?

The Churches? Oh yes, I fear so!

For too long, too many people have been allowed to call themselves 'believers' when they have been nothing of the kind.

Those who believe must act. If you believe the car is going to crash, you attempt to get out. If you believe the house is on fire, you try to get help and move things quickly. If you believe a child has drunk poison, you rush him to the doctor. Belief must bring about action. If you believe in God you must do something about it! Yet churches, even in our own dangerous times are more than half empty all the time. We are surrounded by respectable heathens who equate belief in God with the Western way of life.

In many war areas, Africans are told to 'burn their Bibles'. If this call was made to us, what sort of Bibles would be handed in? Would they be dog eared from constant use, well-thumbed and marked? Or would they be pristine in their virgin loveliness in the same box in which they were first received?

There are tens of millions of all races who call themselves believers who never enter any house of prayer and praise. Many are folk who scream loudest against Communism, yet do not themselves help to defeat these Satanic forces, by means of prayer, and praise, and religious witness. For make no mistake, if our witness were as it ought to be, men would flock to

278

join our ranks. As it is, we are by passed by the world as if irrelevant.

Is anyone else to be blamed for this ghastly episode near Kariba?

I think so. Politicians throughout the world have made opportunistic speeches from time to time. These add to the heap of blameworthiness for a speech can cause wounds which may take years to heal.

The ghastliness of this ill-fated flight from Kariba will be burned upon our memories for years to come. For others, far from our borders it is an intellectual matter, not one which affects them deeply. Here is the tragedy! The especial danger of Marxism is its teaching that human life is cheap, expendable, of less importance than the well-being of the State.

But there are men who call themselves Christians who have the same contempt for other human beings, and who treat them as being 'expendable'. Had we who claim to love God shown more real love and understanding in the past, more patience, more trust of others, the Churches would not be vilified as they are today.

I have nothing but sympathy with those who are here today, and whose grief we share. I have nothing but revulsion for the less than human act of murder which has so horrified us all. I have nothing but amazement at the silence of so many of the political leaders of the world. I have nothing but sadness that our Churches have failed so badly to practise what we preach. May God forgive us all and may He bring all those who died so suddenly and unprepared, into the light of his glorious Presence,

AMEN."*

The hierarchy in the Church moved swiftly. The Very Reverend John da Costa received a letter to inform him

279

that his tenure as Anglican Dean of Salisbury was at an end.

* Sermon extract from original given by The Very Reverend John Da Costa at the Cathedral of St. Mary and All Saints in Salisbury in September 1978.

CHAPTER TWENTY SIX

September 1978

"If we worried about what the West says, we would have had our necks wrung a long time ago."

Lieutenant General Walls slapped his hand down on the table, upon which maps and aerial photographs were scattered, to emphasise his point to all those in the room. The atmosphere was tense. The men in that room fully understood that the decisions being made today would have a profound effect on the course of the bush war that was raging fiercer than ever before. Unintended consequences that may arise from these decisions were not easy to derive, nor were they easy to calculate in any meaningful manner. Yet decisions had to be made based on the best available intelligence information at their disposal. Aerial surveillance, SAS intel from their clandestine ops deep in Zambia, the 'spy' network within Zambia which extended to several senior Government officials and data from Special Branch and Central Intelligence Organisation all pointed to the same conclusion. A real and present escalation of the threat to Rhodesia's security now existed.

"We have to stop ZIPRA from launching any major offensive," said the head of CIO addressing the assembled commanders.

Ken Fletcher looked tired and gaunt. He spoke quietly but with authority. As Rhodesia's top 'spook' and one of a handful of people in the whole country who knew the true status of the war, the personal pressure to make the correct call on the emerging situation was mounting on him. Like any 'spook' network anywhere in the world, gathering intelligence was not a precise science, but rather it relied upon piecing together desperate bits of information from many sources, analysing it and then forming a view.

Fletcher had focused his CIO operatives on gathering the information about ZIPRA activities over many months and in the past few weeks he had been engrossed in looking at the data with his analysis teams to make sense of it. He had not slept much nor eaten well, hence his appearance.

"ZIPRA have built up the troop numbers considerably and their field commanders who we have been tracking, are now back from Moscow. Equipment has been pouring in, air freighted to Lusaka from USSR, while the heavy transport vehicles have arrived via Angola."

Scanning the faces of his audience, looking closely at each person to assess their reactions so he could decide how to pitch the rest of what he needed to say, he was politically savvy to realise that putting facts on the table was not enough. The right emotion, inflection and inference of fear were essential to arrive at the correct decision today.

"ZIPRA have trained hard on conventional warfare and this means we are facing …."

"Ja but ZIPRA are still coming over the border with insurgency objectives," interjected Major van Heerden.

He was a liaison officer in the South African Defence Force seconded to ComOps so that the SADF were kept informed on what the Rhodesians were up to. This was an uneasy arrangement that the Rhodesians begrudgingly were forced to accept given that the SADF was supplying more and more of the military hardware for them to execute the bush war. South Africa remained the sole supplier of oil and aviation fuel to Rhodesia.

"This indicates to us no change to past practices. They will just push more terrorists over the border to do what they have always done. Subvert the kaffirs in the bush and attack the farmers. We in SADF don't believe that Rhodesia has to commit to a cross border attack on any big scale that will draw in international attention on us all and bring Cubans in to this fight."

Fletcher looked hard at van Heerden with his light blue eyes, a stare to drop a person at fifty paces. His lips thinned as his jaw tensed.

This fool is not listening to the bloody message. How many times must I tell him before it sinks in to his brain! After the hammering they got in Angola he and his South African Boers are shit scared of the bloody Cubans entering this bush war. All they are concerned with is their self-interest. They care bugger all that we are carrying the fight and keeping the terrorists away from their borders.

"If I may finish, thank you," he said purposefully after a long pause. "Okay then. ZIPRA are conducting two separate tactics. Yes they are still infiltrating, but as we have seen these past months, less communist terrorists are coming across and those CT's inside the country are generally limiting themselves to the TTL's. Few, if any, venture outside of the TTL. Inside the TTL they focus on subverting the population. In some districts they have political commissars teaching entire villages.

But as I have said before, their troop numbers on the ground are lower now than what it was twelve months ago. They have pulled many men back to Zambia to retrain them. The fact some CT's are still coming across the border is tactically designed to give us the exact impression you have formed Major and to entice us to draw the exact conclusion that you have come to. That is the incorrect conclusion to draw. They want us

283

to think that we can expect the same old terror and subversive approach and therefore not prepare ourselves for the en masse invasion we know they have planned and gearing up to execute."

He paused again to gather his thoughts and drink from the glass of water that was on the table near him.

"We must remember that nine to twelve months back they focused on rounding up hundreds and hundreds of recruits either voluntary or by the threat of force. This swelled their numbers as they took these recruits out of Rhodesia into Botswana and Zambia. These are the thousands of bastards we now see on the parade grounds in the aerial pictures before you. Four thousand at FC camp outside Lusaka and several thousand more in the other three camps.

Before now their training was around two months from raw recruit to infiltrate back into the country as cannon fodder in their tactic of attrition. Now they have had six to nine months training in conventional warfare. Why is that? To subvert the population, ambush farmers, lay some mines? No man! They plan to invade north west Matabeleland."

"Ja but we know you can take the terrorists out if they come over the border in columns of trucks. It will be pigs to the slaughter house for them. Your Air Force will belt them," said van Heerden.

Ken knew this theme still resonated with some of the Rhodesian army officers around the table.

"Not if our forces are all occupied dealing with ZANLA on the north east and eastern borders as is presently the case. We have explained this before." Fletcher felt exasperated. "We know ZIPRA plan to make their move when they see Mugabe push the thousands of CT's in Mozambique across the border ahead of the planned general election. It's already escalating and by year end it will be in full swing. They want to screw the election up so that the West don't recognise the new African PM and the black dominated government. That's when Nkomo will make his move to occupy the north west of the country. ZIPRA don't have the same modus operandi as Mugabe. They don't care about the election because they see themselves occupying the country. If they achieve this objective, the bloody election is meaningless."

He paused to again look closely at the men in the room. They were still assimilating this prediction, recognising the myriad of potential consequences.

"Why else do they have the heavy equipment, the armoured transports, the SAM's and thousands of well-trained soldiers?

We already know that their political motives will bring the Eastern Bloc and Cuba into the conflict."

"Okay." Wall stepped in. "I believe gentlemen that enough factual information has been relayed and we have enough visual information in front of us to reaffirm the threat is the most credible explanation for this build up. What we have to decide now is the response."

Seldom did Walls and Fletcher see eye to eye, exchanging progressively divergent views on how the war should be conducted over recent years. Fletcher was a staunch advocate of a rapid increase of the black Rhodesians into all facets of the Security Forces and their promotion well up into the commissioned ranks along with political reform to transition towards black majority government. This was a radical proposition at a time of grave political and national security uncertainty with the civil war raging. Fletcher saw this as the only practical solution to winning this war. Walls and his fellow senior officers worried at the potential for a Trojan horse scenario within the Security Forces if such a concept was enacted.

Walls was unable to decide if Fletcher was a true patriot to the country regardless of what government regime it had, or a very clever MI6 spy with loyalties to the United Kingdom, the country of his birth, or something else. Walls had ordered the Director of Military Intelligence to conduct covert surveillance on Fletcher and the CIO, but nothing untoward was found yet.

"The decision to be made gentlemen is whether we attack the ZIPRA bases as set out in the earlier briefing. I have listened to the concerns regards this ... Op Gatling? Is that what's it called?"

He looked around for confirmation. He got the nod from the officer who gave the earlier briefing to them.

"Right. Op Gatling. Who comes up with these names?"

He gestured with his hands and smiles broke out around the table. It relieved the tension momentarily.

"One of the concerns raised was that if we strike the ZIPRA camps at FC near Lusaka, and Mkshhaha?"

"Mkushi," offered the briefing officer.

"Mkushi? Okay Mkushi to the east of Lusaka and CGT Two, all of which are deep inside Zambia, we run several big risks. Firstly, the Zambian Government may see this as a hostile act against Zambia and declare war on us. We can knock the Zambian army flat. Their Air Force has better planes, but terrible pilots, unless they get the Cubans in to fly the MiG's. Either way to take on the Zambian army while dealing with ZIPRA and Mugabe's ZANLA will strain us. The Eastern Bloc and the Commonwealth will rally support for Zambia. We cannot rely on South Africa to come to our support in that scenario."

Walls paused and looked at van Heerden

"Ja we have built the new airfield at Fielde near Hartley so that the SADF Mirage planes can operate

286

from there. But we cannot be seen to be supporting this military action," ventured van Heerden.

"Acknowledged. Secondly, it opens the door for Zambia to call in the Cubans from Angola and with Soviet support this could become a huge issue. Overall we can all agree this would be a bad scenario. But we also have intel that Kaunda does not want Zambia embroiled in a war scenario and that their military chiefs are adverse to that concept as well.

Thirdly, there is a risk the West will condemn these raids as an act of aggression and you know my view about what the West think. Are they the risks in summary?"

There was unanimous nodding of heads by the military officers. Ken Fletcher stood motionless.

"Okay. Then we have the risk of doing nothing about these camps and the troop and armament build up. Can we deal with an invasion?"

This was a rhetorical question. They had debated this earlier. Walls went on quickly so as not to allow that debate to reignite. It had divided opinions.

"In summary, my assessment, although not necessarily all of you agree, is that we won't be able to deal effectively with a ZIPRA invasion of the north west which we now expect is imminent. Our manpower will be stretched far too thin and in this situation we will have to forego one part of the country. An unacceptable scenario.

The SB boys have credible intel that Nkomo would declare Matabeleland independent of Rhodesia and thereby get recognition by the Eastern Bloc and the African states, giving him legitimacy. That will totally complicate the whole situation with the USSR, the Cubans and a whole host of African states to contend with."

He stopped to look around the room. He made eye contact with Fletcher who nodded. Fletcher knew Walls was going to make the 'correct' decision.

"The final risk is one we face each day. Casualties. Deep penetration into Zambia by the Air Force, with choppers on the ground in hostile territory, the planes exposed to the air defence supplied to ZIPRA by the Soviets and to Zambia by the Poms, and our troops going in. Serious risks of casualties arise. But are we afraid of the risks? No! Because we are the best at what we do with what we have. So gentleman ...... my decision is that we adopt Op Gatling."

Most of the officers looked instantly relieved that a decision had been made. They now had a firm objective to focus on which was what they were good at. The decision process on how to deal with the emerging ZIPRA threat to Rhodesia was now ended. The action phase was to commence.

"Gentlemen, to date we have dealt with whatever is thrown at us with professionalism and courage. I am confident we will be able to deal with this challenge in the same way. Okay, let's get to it then."

CHAPTER TWENTY SEVEN

October 1978

"Green Section. That's a go," announced the air traffic controller.

"Roger that. Thanks," replied the squadron leader.

Dixon spooled up the Canberra before releasing the brakes that sent it rumbling forward. Three other Canberra bombers followed in sequence down the runway at Salisbury Airport, the longest civil aviation runway in the world, before lifting off and turning north on their way to Zambia.

"Red Section. Taxi out and hold."

Looking out of his glass enclosed control tower situated across the tarmac from the civilian airport buildings, the Air Force air traffic controller felt a surge of pride sweep over him as the reality of the situation sunk home.

The Hawker Hunter fighters, painted in their drab green and brown camouflage, their wings heavy with bombs, rolled out from the hard stand. They emerged from behind the barricades surrounding the Air Force apron moving purposefully in line along the taxiway towards the main runway.

The sun was yet to break the horizon. A light easterly breeze swept over the airport. The weather forecast at the target sites was for scattered clouds, moderate wind, but no rain. The pilots were warned to expect smoke haze that could cause target acquisition issues. The cool morning meant smoke from the cooking fires would be more prevalent as it clung close to the ground.

The navigators in the Canberra bombers and the pilots of the Hunters were armed with photographs taken by a Canberra from a high altitude flight over the targets the day before. These were blown up to magnify the picture causing the resolution to be poor. Navigation was essentially to be by sighting key landmarks on the ground.

Looking down to the apron in front of him the air traffic controller noticed two engineers working on an engine of a Dak. Its cowling was off. One engineer was half way in the open engine, his feet sticking out horizontally. The other man was standing on a transportable steel ladder holding a torch. Other Air Force personnel fussed around the back of the Dak checking equipment. The six Daks on the hard stand were being prepared to ferry SAS paratroopers to Mkushi camp later in the morning. Men from the SAS had started to arrive, gathering in a large hanger to get kitted up for the op.

Air Force personnel wheeled out armaments for the Vampire fighters and Lynx aircraft that were on the apron to the west of the Daks. These aircraft would be attacking CGT II terrorist camp later in the morning.

Much further north, at a forward airfield at Mana Pools on the Zambezi River, 45 SAS were anxiously getting themselves psyched for their transport by helicopters to Mkushi. Their G-Cars were standing by. Final checks by engineers were being made to a few of the helicopters. These G-Cars had flown in from other operational activities yesterday afternoon. One carried damage from ground fire which the engineers were attempting to repair in time for that G-Car to be used for this mission.

Soldiers from the Rhodesian Light Infantry were having breakfast further down the gravel runway. Later that morning they expected to be going by helicopter to CGT II. That target was not going to get a warm up treatment by the Canberra bombers although it would

290

get hammered by rockets and bombs delivered from Vampire jet fighters. These soldiers anticipated immediate contact with the enemy on arrival at the target. Arriving at a firefight by helicopter was both exhilarating and dangerous. The G-Car helicopter pilots were experts in being able to deliver their cargo right into the middle of the action with its twin machine guns blazing away.

At the same time, paratroopers from the Rhodesian Light Infantry were having their breakfast alongside the Kariba airport apron. Their transport Daks were flying in from the Thornhill Air Force base and where expected to arrive soon enough. These soldiers had time to kill before they would have to get kitted up.

Late yesterday afternoon, an area well within Zambia had been secured by the SAS. This 'administration' area was where the helicopters would refuel and rearm during their mission in attacking the targets and while ferrying troops back to Rhodesia once the mission was completed. Drums of fuel and boxes of armaments would be para-dropped to this site by a Dak.

The air traffic controller at New Sarum lifted his field glasses to look down the far end of the long runway.

One, two, three and ... yes four. The Canberra's are all up.

"Red Section. You are go for take-off. White and Blue Sections you are now clear to taxi to the runway and hold."

The first Hunter thrust forward and sped down the runway. This led the procession of Hunters.

"Green Section. Climb to four thousand five hundred feet and hold until you are twenty clicks from the Zambezi then descend to one thousand six hundred feet through to the target. You copy?"

"New Sarum Tower this is Green Leader. Copied."

291

"God speed and good targeting. Over."

Chris Dixon was the pilot of the lead Canberra with the call sign 'Green Leader'. A seasoned combat pilot, now holding the rank of a Squadron Leader he was well respected by his superiors, peers and those he commanded for his leadership qualities, tactical capabilities under extreme pressure and his bravery under attack. Air Force Command did not hesitate to nominate Squadron Leader Dixon to be the lead pilot of Green Section on this mission.

He was elated when he was told of his role with this mission. He guessed that this was to be a historical and defining event for the Rhodesian Air Force, one that hopefully would bring retribution to those who had brought so much misery over the years with their savage terror attacks on the civilian population of his beloved country, those who maimed and killed in the name of liberation, but who in his mind were nothing but barbarians and murderers acting as puppets for their politically inspired leaders. He had seen firsthand what these barbarians were capable of doing to their own white and black countrymen. He felt it was a black farce that those leaders they fought for were not prepared to engage in the peaceful political transition to black majority rule, a process which had already started to occur with Ian Smith offering the olive branch to those black Rhodesian leaders who were prepared for a peaceful political transition.

In response to the initiative of US Secretary of State Henry Kissinger, in September 1976 and blunt pressure from the Government of South Africa, Ian Smith had accepted the principle of black majority rule within two years. That had been a huge paradigm shift in Rhodesian politics. The concession took the nation by surprise. The realisation that political transition was inevitable was adopted and consequently Dixon along with most of the white minority began to engage the concept of imminent black majority rule. But Dixon was appalled that rather than participate in an orderly and peaceful transition, these terrorist thugs still wanted to gain power by the barrel of the gun. Their leadership were not prepared to test their acceptability by all Rhodesians in a democratic election free from intimidation. These Guerrilla leaders wanted unfettered power by doing what was common place in the rest of Africa. That was to become a dictator ruling with an iron fist under the guise of the infamous one party rule mantra.

As he reached the flight ceiling he felt good about himself, what his purpose was and what must be achieved this day.

"Levelling off at four thousand five hundred."

The other Canberra pilots each acknowledged their flight levels.

The Canberra's were part of the Rhodesian Air Force 5 Squadron that sported its motto 'Find and Destroy." The squadron operated the English Electric Canberra B2 and T4's. They were aging. Maintenance was becoming an ever increasing problem. The fleet were under close monitoring with x –ray and electronic testing, plus frequent visual inspections.

There was always a niggle with the pilots of the Canberra's that the metal fatigue which caused one to crash a year before was symptomatic of what may occur to all the others at some stage. That Canberra had gone in near Salisbury airport after taking off in rainy weather carrying a heavy bomb load. As it banked its wing sheared off and it dived earthward, exploding on impact. The subsequent investigation of what was left of the aircraft indicated metal fatigue. This particular aircraft was one of the early models built soon after WWII when the science of metallurgy was at its infant stage. The alloys used then weakened with the flexing and changes in temperatures resulting in fine metal cracking.

The aircraft acquired by 5 Squadron from the South African Air Force, being later models, did not suffer the same metal problems. Nonetheless the pilots knew not to put extra stresses on the aircraft and thus were restricted in flying very fast at low levels and to avoid bumpy conditions. This meant progressively restrictive use of the most formidable weapon in the Rhodesian Security Force arsenal.

The four Green Section Canberra's streaking northwards carried a full payload of bombs tucked away in the bomb bays. For this mission they had bombs designed to deliver the maximum damage to those on the ground. These were innovative weapons developed by the Rhodesian Air Force because they were unable to acquire weapons due to the United Nations sanctions imposed on the country.

Peter Bowerman was the innovative officer of the Air Force who thrived in weapon development technology. Had he been in a different place and different time he perhaps would have developed some truly awesome weapons for the USA or UK, but his time was spent in make shift labs in Rhodesia working with make do equipment and hard to acquire materials. Given that range of impediments, he developed weapons that were highly effective for the bush war Rhodesia was engaged in.

The Canberra's each carried three hundred of the improvised 'Alpha' bouncing bomb. These bombs would hit the ground thereby activating the fusing mechanism and then bounce back up into the air before exploding. The effect was devastating, showering all those below with shrapnel.

The Hunters carried 'golf bombs' that Bowerman had invented. The 450kg version was designed for use by the Hawker Hunter FGA9. The 'golf bomb' detonated above the ground in a manner that limited the energy losses to the ground and upper air mass. Simultaneous initiation at front and rear of the explosive charge provided a 'squeeze' effect that concentrated energy low and flat across the target ground. The 'golf bomb' had double steel plating that contained thousands of pieces of chopped 10mm steel rod. The double skin and chopped rod driven by the high-volume gas generating explosive, Anfo, proved the 'golf bomb' to be a truly devastating weapon. It would pulverise the ground to a fine powder with all vegetation including large trees being flattened for a circular distance of forty five metres. Those victims who were not hit by shrapnel were killed by over-pressure destroying lungs and other vital organs without any damage to outer skin.

The Hunters also carried frantam bombs. This was a derivative of napalm, an incendiary device that set alight the entire area of the target. Everything the thick gelling agent touched would burn without capability to be extinguished.

"I'll get into position," informed Gary Bates, the navigator.

He unbuckled himself from his seat situated below and behind the pilot and settled in his horizontal position facing out towards the glass nose of the aircraft.

"Start descending from this road, Sir," said Bates.

"Okay. Do you want me to maintain the same speed or do you want me to reduce it to two fifty?" Dixon checked his air speed dial.

"No, maintain the speed. We'll have to increase it soon enough to maintain three hundred."

"Okay. Green Section descending. Follow my lead on speed and directions."

The formation of Canberra's began their descent as the Zambezi River emerged in the distance.

"Go right four degrees ...," said the navigator.

"One zero one nine is set now, four thousand five hundred feet, descending and three ten knots," Dixon confirmed.

"Zero, zero five," corrected the navigator.

"Right Green Section, let's tighten it up a bit now."

"Coming up to one minute out. We're on track and we're on time. Get your speed up," informed the navigator.

The sun cracked the horizon in the east sending shards of light racing across the vast country below. The sun suddenly flashed into the cockpit as it emerged from clouds. Dixon involuntarily raised his right hand to cover his eyes. Then he lowered his helmet visor which dimmed the bright light.

"Green, what' your level?" queried Brian Gordon.

Flight Lieutenant Brian Gordon was flying a Hawker Hunter in Blue Section. The Hawkers were gaining ground on the Canberra's, the plan being that they would catch up at the Zambezi then fly in formation until they got nearer to the target. The Hunters would defend the flight if the Zambian Air Force engaged their MiG's.

"Roger, Blue Leader, we're at one thousand six hundred feet."

Dixon looked at his ground speed indicator.

"Two ninety knots coming up."

"Two ninety knots," acknowledged the navigator.

"Got you visual Green," informed Gordon. "Red, White and Blue Sections descend to one thousand six hundred feet. Close in formation with Green Section."

The Hunters descended to settle into formation with the Canberra's as the Zambezi River rapidly approached, its water volume substantially reduced, held back by the dam wall at Kariba. The lush green vegetation near the river was in stark contrast to the rest of the bush which was brown and dry. The summer seasonal rains were yet to arrive.

"Okay. We're coming up to the stream below," observed Dixon.

"Zero, zero six." said Bates.

"Zero, zero, six we've got. We're crossing the stream now."

"Check," reported Blue Leader.

"Well done BG," responded Dixon as he looked to his right to see the Blue Leader Hunter come up alongside him.

"You're looking good Green," said Gordon.

The ground marker flashed past taking Bates by surprise.

"Turn left now!"

"Onto?" queried Dixon.

"Now! Three zero four."

"Three zero four," confirmed Dixon.

The formation turned port in unison. They were now in Zambian airspace. Bates looked ahead to orientate himself with the landscape below. He saw rolling hills stretching across their flight path.

"We're going to have to climb a bit," he announced.

"Ya. Three, zero, four. Rolling out now. How's our speed? We're holding about two ninety," informed Blue Leader.

"Follow my lead. Nudge up a bit then to get over these hills," said Dixon.

Hmmm .... I hope we don't ping their radar.

The prospect of the planes pinging the Zambian radar as the formation lifted their altitude to get over the range of hills was a concern. Flying at 1,600 feet was designed to keep the formation below the Zambian radar. An initial plan to knock out the Zambian radar facilities using the SAS on the ground was shelved. The timing to do this would have to be spot on so as not alert the Zambian army and perhaps the guerrillas in the camps. The risks of alerting the guerrillas of an impending attack when the radar installations were knocked out was assessed as too high. CIO insisted it would be a provocative act against Zambia and result in unintended consequences.

The terrain below shot past in a blur making it visually difficult to track the landmarks especially with several rivers descending from the hills.

"Just checking on these rivers?" he muttered. "Go left. About two degrees."

"Three, zero, two. Roger."

The Canberra accepted the change. Dixon swivelled his head around to see if the formation were still holding a tight grouping.

Good, nice and tight. Hell it looks terrific. I hope the SAS guys are right about the bloody missiles. We're sitting ducks if they are still at the ruddy target.

The SAS observing the terrorist camps radioed in yesterday afternoon to confirm that the two ground to air missile batteries that had been on the perimeters of the FC camp were gone. Activity the day before indicated to the SAS that the two installations were being moved. The batteries were loaded on large trucks and driven off towards Livingstone. This was the news that triggered the frantic action to initiate Operation Gatling. The plans for this operation had been drawn up, training done, more plans considered, more training, all options considered and re-considered. The impediment stopping ComOps giving the go-ahead was the ground to air missiles at the camp and the unacceptably high risk they posed to the planes. ComOps could not risk losing any of its valuable aircraft to a missile attack, especially as these aircraft would be deep inside Zambia. Politically and militarily this was too risky. But when the news that the installations were gone, Operation Gatling was on.

ComOps suspected that the ground to air installations were being relocated to the Zambezi near the tail of Kariba dam in advance of ZIPRA launching its anticipated conventional invasion into north west Matabeleland. Timing seemed right for the anticipated invasion to occur before the rains started in November.

Okay Westland Farm roll out the red carpet. Dixon smiled to himself.

"We're a bit starboard off track," informed Bates.

"Roger. We didn't get round that turn as fast as I wanted," Dixon replied apologetically.

He adjusted the setting.

"Speed back fifteen knots. We're...... on time ...."

"Dead right," Dixon cut in. Looking to his right again to view the Hunters he added. "These Hunters with the bloody golf bombs here .... it's all painted red. Quite fucking weird."

"Go two degrees left."

"Roger, that makes us three, zero, zero. I was on three, zero, two."

"We're on three zero two," informed Green Two, the pilot of the Canberra on Dixon's tail.

Then, without warning, the Canberra started to shake. Dixon grabbed the yoke with both hands and searched his instrument panel to check if something was wrong.

Instruments all okay. This must be turbulence? It's these bloody rolling hills below us kicking up the warm air.

Each time they hit a bump the air was forced out of their lungs from the jarring.

"Oh shit I hope the fucking wings don't fall off!" he remarked.

"Jeeees don't say that Green Lead, I'm flying the oldest bird," said one of the pilots in the Green section.

So do I, thought Bates. *I'll be the first at the accident site.* He mused to himself. *Hell I can't see the map with this bouncing about. I need to gauge the speed to recalibrate.*

"What's your speed?" he asked Dixon.

"Two seven five which is the fifteen you wanted off. Do you want me to get it down?"

"We've got hell of turbulence," informed Pienkie, the pilot of Green Three. "Prefer it if we reduced speed a bit."

This ruddy turbulence is severe. Look at those wings flapping about. Its best we slow the pace a bit here, thought Dixon.

"Yes. You can go down a bit," said Bates as he continued his recalibration. "We're still on track and on time."

"Dead right," offered Dixon with a sense of relief. "It's about a minute and a half before the Hunters leave us."

"Two starboard onto three, zero four," said the navigator. "Make it three ... zero six."

We have not heard from the tower. Let me check if their frequency is set right. Dixon leant forward and looked at the radio. *Ya. It's set for the Lusaka tower frequency. Not a peep?*

"There's not a peep out of the tower so that's going to be superb. We won't have to talk to them."

"The Hunters will be going in fifty seconds," said the navigator.

"Roger."

Dixon took a last look around at the Hunters off to his right.

They are superb aircraft. Go for it boys.

"Go right another two degrees."

The radio crackled.

"That's the bloody tower ....," announced Dixon. "Are they directing civvy traffic in?"

"Just stand by Sir," Bates interjected. "We need to turn ..... we're coming up to ..."

"I think we passed it," offered the pilot of Green Two. "I think that rise on the right, is the one ... that should have been our turning point."

"Oh shut up man!" Dixon admonished the other pilot, irritated with too many things happening at once. "We're onto it okay! Just take direction as it's given."

What do I do about the tower?

"Okay. Go Hunters go," said Bates.

"Roger that. Blue, Red and White Sections break formation," instructed Blue Leader.

"Okay. They are spot on time," informed Bates.

"Roger." Dixon looked at his dials then towards the Hunters. "Two seventy knots. Shit, they only accelerated bloody quickly."

Bates looked up but could not see them.

Those gooks should be on the parade ground now. What a fucking surprise they will get when the Hunters drop the golf bombs on them, he mused to himself.

"Heading now two eight one, Sir."

"Two eight one. Roger."

"When I give you 'doors' can you switch on at the same time?"

"Will do." replied Dixon.

His hands were sweaty. He felt wet under his arm pits. His mouth was dry.

"Okay. We're coming up to forty seconds to turn, Sir."

Where's the bloody river. Bates fumbled with his maps. *There it is.*

"We passed a river on our left here. We'll see the bridge fairly shortly."

Bates shifted his prostrate position as he had cut off his circulation to his left leg, which had pins and needles in it. This was an unnecessary distraction at this very critical time. No mistakes could be made. There was no coming back for a second chance at this mission.

"We've passed two eight one. Shall I turn back on it now?" queried Dixon.

"Yes! Back to two eight one."

"Two eight one we've got," he confirmed.

Dixon's eyes darted between his instrument panel and the horizon. He was anxious to see the target that he anticipated was going to come into view soon.

Things are going to speed up now. I must concentrate man.

"Can you bring the speed back .... two four zero?"

"Roger that. Steering two eight one," confirmed Dixon.

"No. Two eight zero!" said the navigator sharply.

"Everything is set up and ready?" Dixon asked, more to reassure himself.

"There's the school coming up Sir."

Children in the playground waved at the four planes as they streaked overhead. Seeing the school reassured Dixon that they were on track, not that he doubted the capability of his navigator.

"Roger. I have three one zero knots, two eight zero, QNH one zero one nine."

No response? That's okay. It means we're okay. Tower? No response from them also. Am I supposed to call them now or later?

302

"There's nothing from the tower and I am not going to call them. Okay?"

"Okay dokey," replied Bates.

The Lusaka tower was the least of his concern. The terrain below seemed to be speeding past faster than ever and he worried he may miss something.

"Green lead. Red lead here. Confirming MiG's grounded."

"Roger that. It's going to be perfect," replied Dixon with relief.

Red Section's mission objective was to ensure the Zambian Air Force stayed grounded. Their MIG's could bring the whole mission to a sorry end if they were allowed to take off.

"Little dam coming up. We're drifting port. Go to the right. Two eight three. No.... two eight four," informed Bates.

Dixon was puzzled by the instruction. One degree this close to the target could mean missing it.

"Two eight four? Or two eight five?" he queried.

"I want to do a kink Sir to get it spot on."

"Tell me when to roll out," asked Dixon.

"Go left now. Two eight two."

"Roger. Coming up to two minutes to run. Two eight two. Green Section. Got two minutes to run. Perfect," said Dixon.

Yes! It's bloody well going to happen.

"Go left a bit. Steady," exclaimed Bates as his heart rate sped up.

"I'm on two seven eight?" queried Dixon.

"Go to two eight two! Quickly!" shouted Bates.

Two seven eight would take them off the target. Dixon adjusted and the Canberra's behind him followed.

"A school coming up. Acceleration point?" queried Dixon. "Two eight two is the heading."

Dixon did not bother to look down at the children in the playing field.

"Okay. We should start accelerating soon," informed the navigator.

The maximum effect of destruction would be achieved if the bombs bounced higher than four metres before exploding and the aircraft speed was critical in achieving this effect.

"Roger. Shall I accelerate?" Dixon queried.

"Just leave it in case the Hunters are a bit late ... to the minute."

The minute passed very fast.

"Accelerate!"

Dixon pushed his right hand down and immediately felt the plane surge forward. Dixon's back and his hair felt wet. Bates wiped the sweat from his face.

"Target sighted. Jeeesus look at the bloody fuckers ... shit there's hundreds of them," exclaimed Gordon as he guided his Hunter towards the parade ground.

"Blue, it's looking good," reaffirmed White Leader.

"I'm going to get them! Yes! ... just about there ... bombs rolling."

"Bloody beautiful Sir. Your golf's hit the fuckers!" said Blue Two.

"White two. White Leader. Follow my lead in to the right after Blue Two."

Smoke ahead? Observed Dixon. *Okay that must be the target being hammered by the Hunters. Bloody wonderful. Missiles? No report of missiles from the Hunters.*

"You want to get the doors open," queried Bates.

"Yes as soon as I've got my speed up," said Dixon realising he had to get his speed up ahead of opening the bomb bay doors.

"Go left a bit. Go left. Now!"

"More?"

"No! Okay now. Flatten out on two eight two. Quickly! Carry on. Flatten out! Carry on."

"Roger that."

"Up there! Target ahead," shouted Bates.

Looking up from his instruments Dixon clearly saw it.

We're there.

"Ah beautiful! Yes," he exclaimed with excitement. "Speed's up or is it okay?"

"Target ahead. Brilliant!" exclaimed the pilot of Green Two.

"Got it visual. Bloody lovely." The pilot in the third bomber could see the parade ground racing towards them.

"Speed's fine. Go left. Steady! ....Steady! Two seven eight," exclaimed Bates.

Dixon checked that he was on 278 then he looked forward out of his canopy. The parade ground of the Chikumbi terrorist camp situated at Westlands Farm fifteen kilometres from the centre of Lusaka, the capital city of Zambia, was right in front of him. Plumes of smoke and dust rose from the ground from the Hunter strikes.

"Steady.... Steady. Left a touch."

"Beautiful!" exclaimed Dixon.

Dixon stared at the hordes of people running in all directions on the large parade ground. It was a perfect scenario to reap maximum damage, casualties and death.

Thank Christ no missiles. The SAS boys got it right. We're going to get them, thought Dixon.

"Steady ..... Steady. Left a touch."

Bates's voice went to a high pitch as his neck muscles tightened.

"Steady.... Steady.... Steady. Can I switch the doors open?"

Fuck. I forgot the bomb bay doors.

The bomb bay doors were still closed and the target was rushing towards them very fast. What a dog's breakfast it would have been to pass over the target with closed bomb bay doors.

"Yes. Switch your doors!" shouted Dixon.

Bates flicked the switches and they heard the grinding sound of the bomb bay doors opening.

No AA fire? Brilliant, observed Dixon to himself. *The Hunters have blasted the shit out of those bastards.*

The tell-tale signs of the after effects of the golf bombs was evident. There was abject confusion below on the parade ground and the scene was to get a whole lot worse very soon as 1,200 alpha bombs discharged from the four Canberra's.

"Right. I'm going to put them into the field!" shouted Bates.

"Yes!" shouted Dixon as he guided the Canberra straight down the centre of the parade ground.

"Steady! I'm going to get them! Steady! ..... Steady! Hold it."

"Yes! Fucking beautiful!"

"Steady. Steady!... Steady!... Steady. I'm going to get them. Now! Bombs gone ..... they're running ..."

300 bombs left the bomb bay and fell earthwards. The circular shaped anti-personnel bombs dispersed laterally and vertically due to the air pressure that built up between them forcing them apart. As they hit the ground at less than 17 degrees from the horizontal each one activated the fusing mechanism with a three second delay before they bounced high off the parade ground. Each alpha bomb exploded dispersing lethal fragments of metal and 240 rock hard 15 millimetre rubber balls.

"Beautiful! Jeeeez. You want to see all those bastards. The fucking bombs are beautiful," observed Dixon.

Bates slumped forward exhausted relieved that he had done his job.

CHAPTER TWENTY EIGHT

October 1978

The 300 alpha bombs discharged from Green Leader pounded the parade ground unleashing hell on earth.

Minutes before, thousands of ZIPRA troops had commenced their morning muster. Lined up in neat rows, they were about to go through the daily routine. Standing at attention, then at ease. Marching up and then down the parade ground.

Today was no different to the days and weeks and months before.

The officers overseeing the training regimen made their presence known. They barked instructions, haranguing the troops and metering out rough discipline. At the end of the morning parade there was always time allocated for some poor sod to be disciplined. It was a ritual to instil unconditional loyalty to the cause. A few had died from the injuries they sustained.

Twelve men, each with AK assault rifles, manned six of the eighteen perimeter guard posts. Nothing had happened for months to give any indication to the ZIPRA commanders that all the guard posts needed to be operational. The six Anti-Aircraft gun emplacements were unmanned.

ZIPRA HQ, a brick walled oblong building with windows that overlooked the parade ground, was staffed with forty four troops. The insurgency operations against the Rhodesians was being controlled from this building. A hundred metres to the west of the HQ building was a soccer field that was being used to store the newly acquired military equipment. Here the armoured troop transport vehicles, DSHK artillery pieces, SG 43', 82 mm Recoilless and ZPU4 AAA weapons were more closely guarded.

Local Zambians knew to stay far away from the ZIPRA camps. History told them that it was fatal to wander near or inadvertently stumble into any of these camps. It nearly always ended badly. Even the Zambian military steered clear of the ZIPRA troops. Several clashes had resulted in deaths on both sides.

The ZIPRA high command felt secure in the belief that being fifteen kilometres outside Lusaka and well away from the border with Rhodesia it was unlikely the Rhodesians would come close to this camp. The Zambians had newly acquired a squadron of MiG's from the USSR to defend their airspace and the radar recently supplied to Zambia by the United Kingdom to monitor aircraft movements gave an added sense of security.

With eight thousand troops trained in conventional warfare billeted in several camps within Zambia and hundreds more in Angola undergoing training the ZIPRA commanders believed their plans were falling into place. The arrival of the new military hardware and the political support required to win the day once they got their foothold across the border encouraged them further. Their own intelligence indicating deteriorating morale within the country amongst the white settler minority buoyed their confidence which was high at the Westlands Farm guerrilla camp.

Bhekizizwe woke early. The sun was not yet over the eastern horizon.

He quickly got out of his narrow steel framed bed. Once dressed, he started his morning ritual to run around the perimeter of the camp twice. The crisp morning air initially stung his lungs but he warmed up quickly as he picked up his pace.

His torso was strongly muscled, supported by big thighs and well-rounded calf muscles. His arms were powerfully muscled. For such a big man he ran like a gazelle, hardly touching the ground with his feet. His style of running with his straight back was unusual yet effective in propelling him forward at speed. His stamina had been built up over years so he could run at a pace for long periods without stopping to catch his breath.

On order from the ZIPRA high commander, Lookout Masuku, he had returned from his insurgency operations in the Urungwe Tribal Trust Land after being the field commander there for nearly nine months. Nkomo had instructed Masuku to arrange his return from the insurgency operations so he could personally thank Bhekizizwe for his leadership role in bringing down the Air Rhodesia Viscount and to promote him. Nkomo felt vulnerable after his loyal military chief, General Vhukile Ncube, was killed as he opened a parcel bomb in his office in Lusaka which unbeknown to him had been sent with love by the Rhodesian Special Branch. His death sparked political intrigue which caused Nkomo to consider shoring up his support within the military wing of his Liberation movement. Masuku had ascended to the top military job after some infighting, but was yet to convince Nkomo of his total loyalty. Nkomo wished to surround himself with other options. Bhekizizwe was going to be one of those options.

Bhekizizwe was promoted to the fourth in command within ZIPRA and one of two commanders who was designated to lead the troops across the border into Matabeleland to seize their nation back. He eagerly pledged his loyalty to Nkomo and to ZIPRA in that order of priority.

Keeping physically fit and strong was the only way Bhekizizwe believed a leader in Africa could survive. The great kings of the Ndebele were strong men. There was no place for weakness. Nor was there any space for compassion. When he ran each morning he cleared his mind before methodically filling it with the same information. He filled it with the will to reclaim his forefather's land from the Rhodesian settlers, to achieve his objectives through force and to lead his tribe to the victory that destiny had mapped out for him.

He finished his run as the general rally was sounded. He looked at his watch to check it was exactly six. Filling a basin with cold water and splashing some on his face before wiping himself down with a towel that hung on a nail in the wall, he dressed in his camouflage officer uniform, put his holster around his waist then checked the hand gun was loaded. He picked up his AKS 7.62 and slinging it across his shoulder, he set off for the officer's mess hall.

His morning meal was eaten quickly before making his way to the HQ block where he had scheduled to meet the Cuban instructor to discuss the week's training regime for his men. Bhekizizwe was irritated that the instructor did not arrive at the time they had set. This was not the first time this Cuban had not turned up. He often smelt of alcohol. Bhekizizwe knew he was a drunk.

"If that dog instructor comes tell him I will be on the parade ground," said Bhekizizwe to the comrade sitting at a steel desk at the entrance of the HQ. His role was to check and record in a register those who came and went from the HQ, primarily to prevent unauthorised people entering.

"Yes Sir," he said as he stood to attention and saluted as Bhekizizwe left the building.

Bhekizizwe heard the barking of the commanders to the massed troops on the parade ground as he walked along the cement path. When he neared the corner of the building to turn towards the parade ground he suddenly stopped. The hair on the back of his neck rose. His senses came alive instantly.

That noise? Is it Rhodesian planes?

He knew the sound of incoming Hunters well. Being on the receiving end of their air strikes several times, that sound was burned into the inner recesses of his brain. The last time he and the Hunters had crossed paths was in the Urungwe TTL not long before he was recalled. He had led some of his comrades to ambush a Rhodesian patrol, inflicting injuries in the initial contact before pinning them down. When the fireforce arrived his comrades managed to pin down the troops alighting from the G-Car as well. The Rhodesians had a dozen troops. He had twenty three. He went in for the kill ordering two flanks of seven comrades each to encircle the Rhodesians. This was his preferred battle tactic which he drew from the infamous bull's horn pincer movement that his Ndebele ancestors had perfected. He knew there were wounded Rhodesian soldiers perhaps even dead ones so their extraction from the contact with his men was going to be difficult for them. He had shot at least one himself when he sprayed a volley of fire into the oncoming line of Rhodesians. The soldier in front flipped backwards and Bhekizizwe saw red splash outwards from the mid-section. Although two of his own men were seriously injured, he felt confident that this day was going to be theirs through force of numbers and that the Rhodesians would all die.

The fire fight had ranged for just over fifty minutes from the first shot being fired when his left flank closed in on the Rhodesians. Then the tide dramatically turned. The unmistakable sound of the Hunter was audible over the gun fire. He saw it circle overhead in a wide arc. He knew the pilot would be taking instruction from a Rhodesian on the ground. The white smoke rose from the Rhodesian position so that the pilot could pin point where the Rhodesians were so as not to attack them in error. Bhekizizwe quickly calculated that other than his comrades on his left flank, the rest of his men were all exposed to the air strike which was imminent. Only his left flank was close enough to the Rhodesians to prohibit an air strike without the pilot potentially killing his own.

Bhekizizwe made the instantaneous decision to call off the attack and to disburse his men. Better to live and fight another day than to stay and be cannon fodder for the Hunter pilot. But before he could get the orders out to his men some of them engaged the Rhodesians in another gun fight. His order only got a little way along the line before he saw the Hunter swoop in for its attack.

Bhekizizwe bolted away followed by a few of his comrades who had received the order. He ran through the bush at full speed until his ears were filled by the jet screaming overhead. He flung himself prostrate on the ground. He heard the Hunter accelerate and looking upwards over his shoulder he saw it climbing away before the explosion and red ball of fire engulfed his field of vision. The Hunter had dropped its frantan. It incinerated the bush and eleven comrades in its path. He quickly got to his feet to continue running at full pace. He heard the plane come in once again and this time its cannons fired. He lost a lot of men that day.

Bhekizizwe knew the sound of the Hawker jet very well indeed. This was the distinctive sound he heard as he turned the corner of the HQ building.

313

How can this be? The Rhodesians would not dare attack so close to Lusaka. The Zambian Air Force would intercept them. But that sound is the Rhodesian plane. He looked towards the horizon on the far side of the parade ground. *Au! There it is.*

His eyes widened and every muscle in his body tensed as he stared transfixed watching the Hunter coming in towards the parade ground low and fast.

Au! There are many of them.

Bhekizizwe ran forward towards the parade ground. The nearest group of comrades were fifty metres away. Those at the other end were more than two hundred metres away.

"To the fox holes!" he yelled. "Comrades. Disburse, to the fox holes. Disburse. We are under attack."

The nearest group turned to their left in unison on the order of their parade commander who had his back to Bhekizizwe. Hearing shouting he turned to face Bhekizizwe who was running towards him, then he felt the ground shake.

Bhekizizwe saw the bombs leave the wing, followed by the explosion at the outer edge of the parade ground. He fell forward and hit the gravel hard, taking the skin off the palms of both hands. He was too far away to be effected by the exploding bombs. It was instinct that took over to force him down. He scrambled to his feet.

The golf bombs from the Hunter hit the parade ground landing between two blocks of ZIPRA troops. They exploded felling the guerrillas within a hundred metres of the line of attack and in a width of fifty metres. Those close to where the bombs exploded were blown apart.

"Get them off the field!" he shouted. "Do this now." He swung his arms gesticulating towards the buildings. "Get them off!"

314

Time seemed to stop. Those not felled seemed to move in slow motion. Disbelief and an inability to comprehend what was happening engulfed them. The air filled with smoke and dust, masking the full horror of mutilated corpses strewn on the ground. The dead and wounded had horrific wounds from shrapnel. Screams of agony became audible after the sound of the explosions died down.

Kaboom! Kaboom!

The second Hunter dropped its golf bombs again targeting the comrades on the outer edges of the parade ground. These explosions created wild panic as the comrades scattered away from the blasts with the bulk of them now becoming compressed in the centre of the ground. Open and exposed.

Bhekizizwe saw that the situation was chaotic. Dust and smoke filled the air as visibility closed in.

They will come back for a second strike. These comrades must get off this field. But ...

He grabbed a comrade by the arm as he tried to run past him.

"Come with me comrade."

Reluctantly the solder followed Bhekizizwe to the anti-aircraft gun emplacement. They clambered over the sand bags. Bhekizizwe got behind the heavy gun and swivelled it to point the barrels upwards. He immediately saw the problem.

Au! There is no bullet belt loaded.

He bent down and opened the rectangular tin box where the ammunition belts would be stored. Nothing.

"Agggggggh!" he yelled. "Go find ammunition," he told his comrade. "Go to the armoury now to get ammunition for this gun. And then find someone to work this gun. Do it now and don't fail or I will find you and shoot you."

315

The comrade scrambled out of the emplacement before running off towards the building complex. Bhekizizwe decided he should leave the gun emplacement to go back and rally the comrades when through the smoke he saw the plane. It was coming in fast and low. It was not a Hunter. It had an engine on each wing, was painted in green and brown. There was no noise coming from it.

How can that be? No noise? Its belly is opening.

Bombs poured out of the belly of the plane. As it passed he heard the roar of its engines. The earth ahead of him erupted as hundreds of explosions occurred simultaneously. Shrapnel hit the sandbags. Bhekizizwe was knocked backwards into the gun emplacement hitting his head on the gun stand and splitting the skin on the back of his head. Blood gushed out. He lay on the ground dazed. He could not hear anything but felt the earth shake many times as the four Canberra bombers delivered their lethal payloads.

Something fell on top of Bhekizizwe. Lifting his head he looked across his chest.

What is that?

Scrambling to get the thing off him he kicked with his feet. The bloody torso of a comrade rolled off him. Most of its head was missing, one arm gone, the other was in strips and raw meat below the waist. He stared at it. It was horrible.

Bhekizizwe's breathing was fast as he fought off the urge to vomit. An unfamiliar surge of panic flooded over him. Positioning himself to sit with his back up against the sand bags within the gun emplacement he fought hard to compose himself. His head hurt. He put his left hand on his scalp to feel why. When he brought his hand back he saw it was covered in blood.

Lifting himself cautiously to peer over the sandbags which were pitted and torn he could only see thirty or so metres. He saw enough to tell him there had been a massacre. The ground was strewn with dead comrades and many of them were in bits.

With his ears ringing, he could only hear muffled sounds. He checked that he still had his weapon across his shoulder. He did.

I must get back to the HQ to see what can be done. We must disburse the comrades, man the AA guns and protect the equipment. Where is the Zambian Air Force? They should be here to shoot these dogs out of the sky.

He staggered from the gun emplacement finding it problematic to stand up straight. Turning the corner of the HQ building he was knocked down by several comrades running along the path. None stopped to assist him. He felt dizzy. Disorientated. Standing up he tried to regain his balance. He didn't and fell heavily. Positioning himself on his hands and knees he crawled along the path. His ears popped and sounds became more distinguishable.

That is not our guns. That is helicopter sound. How can they have helicopters so far inside Zambia?

He had fought the helicopter gunships many times in Rhodesia. He knew the sounds of their machine guns well. He had once shot a Rhodesian soldier manning the machine gun in a helicopter. That gave him great satisfaction and much kudos with his men. It was even reported back to ZIPRA high command.

He lifted himself up by grabbing on to a wooden pole supporting a veranda. He tried to orientate himself. The smoke that filled the air was getting thicker. Breathing it in burned his lungs which set off a coughing fit. He staggered towards a building that was a short distance ahead of him. When he reached it he felt exhausted so he slumped down with his back against the wall. He was dizzy again and nauseous. His breathing was laboured.

The gunfire, which was relentless, seemed to be all around him. He tried to stand up, but failed. He swung his weapon off his shoulder and cocked it before he leant over and vomited.

There was an almighty bang and a whoosh as flames shot past the corner of the building he was leaning up against. The searing heat singed him as it raced past and on reflex he scrambled away from the fire on all fours. The roar of a Hunter's engine filled the air. He heard a crashing sound as the roof of the HQ collapsed before three comrades ran past him. They were on fire, screaming, trying purposefully yet unsuccessfully to extinguish the flames.

Au! Those poor comrades. The fire that does not go out.

Bhekizizwe had seen the use of this weapon when he was in Rhodesia. Everything the fire touched burned to nothing. It was a horrific weapon the Rhodesians used. The three comrades fell down as the flames engulfed them. There was nothing anyone could do to assist them.

They will put the fire bombs on these buildings. I must get away and into the bush. The bush will be safer than in the camp.

Looking up he noticed that the building he was leaning against was also on fire. He resolved to make his move and staggered across the narrow gap between two rows of buildings which he recognised as the officers' mess and the library hall. Bhekizizwe pushed himself up against the wall of the officers' mess building to catch his breath. He was surprised how little exertion made him tire so quickly.

The whirring sound of the helicopter rotor blades startled him. A helicopter circled overhead, its machine

318

gun firing at will. He lifted his automatic weapon, aimed and pulled the trigger. The bullets missed. But the gunner observed him and Bhekizizwe heard the sound of the rotor blades change. He suspected it was turning to come back to get him. Instinctively knowing he would be killed if he was caught in between the two buildings, he ran towards the corner of the building anticipating the helicopter would come around that side. It did and gathering all his energy he bolted towards it firing his weapon as he ran. His action caught the helicopter gunner off guard. He expected the terrorist to run away and so had his machine gun trained higher. With Bhekizizwe running towards him he had no time to adjust the weapon before Bhekizizwe was under the helicopter. By the time they had swung around, he was nowhere to be seen. They moved off to find other easier targets.

Bhekizizwe heart sank when he got to the field where the heavy equipment was stored. Everything was ablaze. Surveying the scene his emotions erupted as the realisation of the catastrophe struck home. He screamed out abuse.

The ground twenty metres ahead of him popped up in a straight line into a group of his comrades who were running away from where he stood. The Hunter roared overhead.

The spirits are with me. I was saved.

Knowing how lucky he had been to not get blown to shreds by the Hunter cannon rounds, he paused briefly to survey the five dead comrades who lay ahead of him, their life juices seeping into the soil. Immediately refocusing, he moved quickly along the edge of the field, using the trees as cover, before diverting into thick bush at the far end. He made his way under the cover of the trees to a gravel road that circled the perimeter of the camp. On the other side of the road was open bushland. He knew that to survive he must go there. All was lost at the camp. The only tactic now was to survive to be able to fight again.

When he came to the road he stopped. He noticed several dead comrades scattered along the road and suspected they were foolish and naive enough to think the best way to escape is along an open road. Kneeling he waited and listened. He could still hear the gunfire from the Rhodesian helicopters behind him and occasionally the chilling sound of the Hunter engines. He scanned the bush around him. When he felt it safe he crossed the road quickly and blended into the bush on the other side.

After a few minutes had past and feeling less threatened, he lowered his weapon to carry it in his right hand beside him. His ears were still ringing. He used his left hand to tap the side of his head to see if that would stop the ringing. It didn't. He realised he was very thirsty and wondered where he could go to get water.

The sound of a twig breaking off to his left alerted him to danger. Turning his head and body simultaneously towards the sound while lifting the SKS to horizontal at waste height, his instinct kicked in. He did not move as quickly as he usually did and he recognised this. His mind raced, his eyes searching for the danger.

He caught a fleeting glimpse of something 30 metres in the bush.

What is that?

Continuing to turn to his left, he saw the flash and immediately felt something slam into his right side, inches above his hip bone. He winced as he was pushed forcefully backwards. Bhekizizwe involuntarily squeezed the trigger of his weapon as he went down sending bullets into the bark of the trees around him.

He hit the ground hard with his right shoulder. Tumbling down the slight incline he smashed through several bushes before coming to rest against a small tree. Winded he gasped to get his breath back.

I am shot. Bright red blood oozed from below his trouser belt. *There is no pain? Was that a comrade who shot me? Or was it the dog Zambian soldiers?*

The tree trunk above his head split as bullets ripped into it.

"I am ZIPRA. Do not shoot. I am ZIPRA." he shouted.

More incoming bullets shot past him. Bhekizizwe returned fire spraying aimlessly before crawling towards an ant hill to get better cover for himself. Once behind the ant hill he waited and listened. His heart pounded as the unfamiliar sense of fear gripped him. Conscious that he was losing a lot of blood and that he needed medical help sooner rather than later he shouted out.

"I am ZIPRA. Don't shoot. I am injured."

Hearing movement to his right he lifted himself in order to bring his weapon around to face that direction.

The first bullet hit him in the upper right chest shattering his shoulder bones as it passed through. His right arm went limp and he dropped his SKS. The second hit him in his chest. Bhekizizwe looked down in disbelief. He rolled over onto his back and closed his eyes.

When he opened his eyes he looked up through the canopy of the trees to the blue sky. His mouth felt wet and he coughed out blood. It ran down the side of his cheek and soaked into the soil. He tried to move but only his left leg twitched. He felt numb and cold.

He watched, fascinated, as clouds moved across the sky before a face appeared in his vision. Bhekizizwe saw it was a white face with black and green paint on it. He lost focus and the picture became blurry.

"Who? ...Who are you?" Bhekizizwe said faintly. He coughed up more blood.

The person standing over him replied in Ndebele.

"Rhodesian SAS."

Bhekizizwe's body jumped as the bullet went into his chest, piercing his heart, which was already in cardiac arrest, severing his thoracic spine before exiting.

CHAPTER TWENTY NINE

October 1978

Dixon's heart pounded so fast he thought it may leap out of his chest. The enemy were taken by surprise. The devastation concentrated in such a limited space on the parade ground caused maximum casualties. The plan was executed perfectly.

"Green Lead. Bombs gone," was the laconic information feed from the pilot of the second Canberra.

His navigator placed their bombs one hundred metres further along the parade ground.

"Green Leader. This is Green Three. Payload gone. Fucking brilliant!"

"Green Section. Green Four. It's like bloody ants running everywhere being shredded by the Alpha's. Ready ... Okay .... Steadying .... Holding it. Jeeeez it's brilliant! Bombs gone."

Okay. We're clear of the target. Bloody fantastic. No sign of MiG's. Bloody brilliant, thought Dixon. *What's next? Oh yes ... the tower. I have to contact the tower.*

He searched for the piece of paper with the script that CIO and ComOps had authored him to transmit to the air traffic control tower at Lusaka International airport.

"Bomb bay doors closed," informed Bates.

"Roger. Just let me get onto the tower and give them our bloody message."

He put his hand down the side of his seat in search of the paper. The plane bounced again due to turbulence, requiring his two hands to hold the yoke.

"Jeeeees ... where is this fucking piece of shit?"

"Things will be better when you've climbed up Sir," offered Bates.

"Green Lead. Can we gain altitude? We're bouncing around here," queried Green Three.

"Yes. I know. I'm just trying to get the thing .... the ... spiel for the tower ready," exclaimed Dixon. "That was lovely! Hundreds of the bastards. It worked out better than we could have .... ah ..." The plane hit an air pocket knocking the wind out of him. "...ah ... aaah Jesus! A bit rough ..... they ran straight into the bombs. Those fucking bastards. Where the fuck is that piece of shit?"

"Look out for aircraft Sir," informed Bates noticing a light aircraft off to port.

Dixon looked up from searching around his feet. He saw the single engine plane and beyond it the City of Lusaka off to his left.

"There's the bloody city. Got it!"

The paper with the authorised statement was folded in one of his flight jacket pockets.

The radio crackled. Douf. Douf. Douf. The sound of cannon fire filled the cockpit.

"Are we putting in K-Cars here?" queried Bates.

"Yes, they have choppers there. They'll have beautiful time. They are like fucking ants running around there. Jeeez. That was marvellous."

"Blue Section this is K-Lead. K-Car section on target now. So watch out for us okay?"

"K-Leader. Blue Leader here. We have delivered the first strike and Green Section has finished. Let me know what you want us to do. Also White Section is on standby."

"Can we gain altitude?" asked Green Four. "Turbulence is rattling us like ..."

"We should gain altitude. Straight ahead for one more minute," informed Bates.

"Okay, but I've got this spiel to get off," Dixon said as he unfolded the paper.

"Green Lead. This is Red Leader. Confirmed no Zambian AF activity."

No MiG's. Bloody fantastic. The boys must be keeping those fuckers on the ground. It would be beautiful if one tried to get up and they slotted it.

"Keep an eye open Sir!" informed Bates.

"Yes. I was going to say .... a big pylon ... ahead."

"Seen the pylon?" commented Green Two.

Lying straight ahead was a power line taking electricity from the Kariba Dam to Lusaka. Dixon adjusted his altitude to go over the power lines and the other three planes followed suit.

"Just check the tape recorder while you're there will you so we have the record. Otherwise just leave it."

"Okay. It's still running," confirmed Bates.

"Roger. Let me try and get this spiel off. Lusaka Tower. This is Green Leader. How do you read?"

Nothing.

"Lusaka Tower. This is Green Leader."

"Station calling tower?" came the startled reply.

The air traffic controller at Lusaka International airport had seen smoke rising in the distance to the west of the city. He was confused. Looking through his field glasses he saw plumes of black smoke rising from orange flashes. When he spotted what looked like planes heading away from the smoke he called the radar operator to ask if any aircraft were in the vicinity of where the smoke was. The thought flashed across his mind that perhaps he had allowed two planes to collide mid-air without knowing about it. A surge of panic came over him while he waited for his radar operator to get back to him. He had just put the receiver down from the radar operator who told him that there was no sign of aircraft in that vicinity on the radar when the radio cracked with '*Green Leader.*'

Who is Green Leader? pondered the controller.

Okay. Let's get this message delivered, thought Dixon.

"Lusaka tower this is Green Leader. This is a message for the station commander at Mumbwa from the Rhodesian Air Force. We are attacking the terrorist base at Westlands Farm. This attack is against Rhodesian dissidents and not against Zambia. Rhodesia has no quarrel, repeat no quarrel with Zambia or her Security Forces. We therefore ask you not to intervene or oppose our attack. However, we are orbiting your airfield now and are under orders to shoot down any Zambian Air Force aircraft which does not comply with this request and attempts to take off. Did you copy all that?"

"Copied," came the reply swiftly.

"Roger thanks. Cheers."

The telephone rang in the control tower. The controller picked it up. It was the radar operator who was near to hysterical. Unidentified aircraft had suddenly appeared. The controller remained confused. Through his field glasses he saw four jet aircraft in the distance. Putting the glasses down, he radioed the tower at Mumbwa to give them the message from this Green Leader. The message was received by the air traffic controller at the Zambian Air Force base with the knowledge that a Rhodesian Hawker Hunter was buzzing overhead. Frantic calls were being made to locate the Commander of the Zambian Air Force and to notify the President.

As the adrenalin rush subsided Dixon turned his attention to getting back to New Sarum. Once there they would refresh themselves while his plane was

326

refuelled and rearmed for the second sortie later that morning.

Bates gave Dixon their course and altitude to get the Green Section home. Dixon took Green Section up to four thousand five hundred feet. It was a routine matter now for the Canberra's to return to New Sarum base. They settled back to listen to the action as more cannon fire was heard over the radio. The K-Cars were living up to their namesake, *Kill Cars*. The chatter of the K-Car pilots could be heard over the radio as they co-ordinated their attacks on the terrorists fleeing the killing ground.

"White Section now on target."

The White Section Hunters were tasked to mop up and give the K-Cars support. Two Hunters remained over the Zambian airfield.

"What about Dolphin three. Do we need to brief them?" queried Bates.

Dolphin 3? I totally forgot about them.

The Dak carrying the commander of the Rhodesian Security Forces and other officers had left Salisbury soon after the Hunters departed. Its call sign was Dolphin 3. Dolphin 3 was to take over from Green Leader to coordinate the attack as soon as the Green Section dropped their bombs. Dolphin 3 would also co-ordinate the attack by the Air Force on the other two camps later in the morning.

The radio crackled. It was Lusaka tower.

"Rhodesian Air Force one, one, eight point one?"

I suppose I need to deal with this.

"Go ahead," said Dixon sternly, not knowing what to expect from the controller, but anticipating problems.

"Can you confirm we can let our civil aircraft take off from here?"

His voice was pensive.

"Roger. We have no objection there, but I advise you for the moment to stand by on that. I request that you hang fire on that for a short while .... half an hour or so."

"I copy. Can you please keep a listening watch on this frequency so we can ask you what we want to ask?"

"Roger will do."

"What do I call you?" queried the controller.

"My call sign is Green Leader," informed Dixon.

Sound of cannon fire rebounded in the cockpit as two K-Cars engaged terrorists on the ground with their machine guns.

"How does it look K One?" asked the K-Car leader.

"Beautiful!" came the response.

"The bombs have created havoc. These fuckers are running around the joint. Can you bring another K-Car around the back of the barracks ... those at the west side? There are a bunch of terrs there that need sorting out."

"Okay K-One. K-Three, this is K-Lead. Can you assist K-One towards the west?"

"Will do. K-One I'll be there in a jiffy."

"K-Lead. This is White Lead. What would you like us to take out?"

"White Section. This is K-Car Leader. I think that building you are going for was taken out completely but you might like to have a re-go at it just to make absolutely certain."

The lead K-Car tracked around the camp in search of key targets for the Hunters to take out and to direct the other K-Cars in mopping up pockets of terrorists.

"Roger. White Leader. This is White two. Sir if you would like to watch my strikes and then re-strike after that."

"Roger will do."

The pilot of the second Hunter manoeuvred in front of the lead Hunter by turning sharp to his right.

"White Two. I think if you could take out the radio shack down there if you know which one it is?" asked White Leader.

"Affirmative."

With that the Hunter dropped down to run in for the attack on the radio shack.

"If you take out that one White Two I'll put my frans on the headquarters. I'll be attacking from south to north. K-Lead is it clear?"

"Clear," came the laconic reply. "K-Section stand aside from the building complex at this time."

The Hunter fired a short burst from its cannons completely obliterating the radio shack. Having spent endless hours studying the aerial photographs the pilots knew what they were looking at on the ground even while flying in circles and at these high speeds.

"Got it! That radio shack is history."

He lifted his nose and the aircraft soared upwards before he banked left in a wide arc. White Leader banked and turned starboard so he was nearly upside down. He then flipped back and dropped his nose heading straight for the set of brick buildings with rusted corrugated iron roofing. He saw two K-Cars hovering off to his left. No K-Cars were in his line of approach. His pulse quickened as he moved his thumb to the button that would release fiery hell on earth. His frantan bombs would hit the ground with an innocuous thud only to explode into a fire ball that would engulf and incinerate everything within a hundred and fifty metres of where it landed. The splatter that spread many more metres on the sides would burn through anything it touched.

He adjusted his air speed as he swooped down like a graceful fish eagle. He saw some people running from

329

the ZIPRA HQ building at the same time he saw others running into it.

"I'm on my run in. Okay .... its beautiful!"

Got ya. For the Viscount you fuckers.

He pushed the button and the bombs fell from the wings of the Hunter. He pulled back on the yoke and accelerated. The Hunter shot upwards then banked left.

The buildings were ablaze. People who were on fire ran away from the building. Gas cylinders ignited blowing out a large section of the wall. The roof caved in.

"K-Three. K-Four. This is K-Leader. Move in to mop up around the buildings."

The Hunter pilot closed his eyes for a moment savouring the retribution against those who downed the Air Rhodesian Viscount.

"Beautiful White Leader. Direct hit. The frans could not be better placed. I'm going in to strafe. Watch me and follow."

"Roger that White Two," confirmed White Leader. "Watch out for those K-Cars coming in there!"

Two choppers broke away from the target area and cut across the flight path of White Section Two who was coming in low to strafe a group of terrorists running towards a ditch to the west side of the parade ground.

K-Two reported a blockage with its gun. Hydraulically operated the 4x.303 machine guns fitted to the K-Cars had a fantastic saturation killing ability, spitting out hot metal that sliced open anything it hit. But they often jammed and while most times the gunners could un-jam them it sucked up valuable time, often requiring the K-Car to leave the contact.

"K-Car Lead. This is White Lead. Your Cars are cutting across where we are operating. Clear the area."

"White Leader. This is K-Car Leader. We have blockage problems. Those two are clearing the area."

The Hunters pulled out of their run in, circled and then seeing the K-Cars were out of the vicinity they strafed the camp at will, wrecking the vehicles that had not been engulfed by the fires. The Hunters were armed with four 30 mm (1.18 in) ADEN cannon, with 150 rounds of ammunition per gun. When the cannon shell hit a person it would either sever that person in two or blow a hole big enough for a soccer ball to pass through. The Hunters finished off their attack by strafing terrorists who were foolish enough to run in groups which made the killing process that much more economical.

"K-Three. K-One here. There to your left. Terrs in that fox hole. Quickly. Take them out."

The Alouette helicopter banked to starboard so its gunner could have a clear shot at the five ZIPRA cowering in a bunker surrounded by a row of sand bags. A burst of fire was enough to kill them all.

"K-Two. K-Leader. Have you fixed that blockage yet? I need you back here. There's AA gun active. We have to take it out."

"Not yet. The bloody thing is jammed tight. Working on it."

K-Leader's chopper banked around, keeping a distance from the AA placement.

"K-Four. K-Leader. Are you clear to sweep the south perimeter yet? There's a whack of terrs bolting down the access road that need taking out."

"Okay. Just clearing up now."

"Left! Left!"

K-Four's gunner saw movement to his left. His pilot responded quickly. He opened up with two short bursts decapitating a ZIPRA soldier and disembowelling his two companions.

"K-Three. How you doing?"

"Ya, we're doing fine over here, but nearly out of ammo."

"K-Four. K-One. This is K-Leader. You'll see terrs have taken off down towards the south east corner of the camp. I'm setting off down that way now. You want to join us?"

"Roger that. Confirm you have left the area. I'm now at the southern side of the orbit .... Spotted them. Okay going down now. I've got you visual."

The two K-Car's descended on a group of terrified ZIPRA soldiers trying to make their escape from the fiery hell that was around them. They ran as a group down a track at the boundary of the camp hoping to get to the bush where they could seek cover. The bursts of machine gun fire from K-Four cut into them, sending several flailing about. Others veered right only to run into the killing zone of the other K-Car that bore down on them.

"I'm out of ammo. Leaving now."

Having strafed the terrorists attempting to escape and now out of ammo the K-Car banked left. The pilot immediately saw the danger he had put himself in.

"Shit we've got trouble here! AA gun! They've got it firing at us."

"K-Section. This is White Two. I can see it. I will have to bank around to come back and take it out. A minute."

The AA placement spelt danger for the helicopters. They were vulnerable to such a weapon. It had to be neutralised. The red hot shells from the anti-aircraft gun shot past the K-car.

Whack! Whack!

"I've taken a hit!" shouted the pilot. "Instruments out."

He felt a sharp pain then numbness in his leg. He looked down to see blood oozing out of his thigh.

"I've taken something in my leg. Shrapnel?"

Diverting the chopper away from the AA gun emplacement the pilot headed towards a carpet of trees. The gunner lost balance falling forward towards the opening where his machine guns pointed outwards. His harness stopped him from falling out the aircraft. Then the helicopter's tail started to swing sideways. The pilot struggled to keep it going in the direction he wanted it to.

"Visual required. What's the damage?" he asked the second K-Car which had followed him in exiting the scene.

"Your tail rotor is slowing ..... Bugger it. It's stopped."

The reply was bad news. The wounded pilot already knew they were going to crash as he fought a losing battle to keep the aircraft from spinning. Decelerating to sixty knots the helicopter spun violently. It rotated once every three seconds before disappearing into the trees.

"We're going in," he announced moments before the helicopter crashed through the canopy of a tree.

"White Two ...White Lead. Sounds like the K-Cars have trouble with that bloody AA placement. Can you see it? Take it out quick smart!"

"Roger White Lead. I am on it. Will you follow to mop up?"

"K-Three. This is K-One. We have a Car down. A Car down. Going in to recover. Stay overhead to cover, okay."

"Okay, will do K-One."

White Two continued to turn his aircraft sharply to port then he levelled out heading straight to where the AA gun emplacement was. White Lead was a kilometre to his starboard and turning to follow him in. He noted a K-Car hovering off to the right of the AA placement.

Those bastards with the AA haven't seen me yet. Too busy firing at the chopper. Okay you bastards.

The burst of fire from the Hunter was short. It was enough to obliterate the gun emplacement.

"K-Five. Out of ammo. Leaving."

"K-Six. Got a bloody jam."

K-One manoeuvred around the clumps of trees and finally went down into a clearing about fifty metres from the wreckage. Time was of the essence to get to the two men in the downed K-Car.

"We're down. Wreckage sighted. No fire, thank God."

The pilot of the downed K-Car recovered quickly from being winded from the impact when his helicopter hit the ground. The helicopter was upright. The impact had crunched it, twisting metal and the tail had snapped off. He had the presence of mind to retard the fuel flow moments before impact. The fuel tanks had not been punctured. He unbuckled himself. His leg was very painful. He winced when he moved out of his seat falling heavily to the ground before crawling away from the stricken aircraft.

The crew from K-One rushed to the downed helicopter. K-Three remained overhead ready to take on any ZIPRA soldiers who may venture onto the scene.

The gunner of the downed chopper lay motionless twenty metres from the helicopter. He was alive but unable to move. His back was injured after he was punched through the side door when the chopper impacted the ground.

Both wounded men were hauled unceremoniously aboard the stationary K-Car. Once he had assisted his wounded pilot colleague on board, the pilot rushed around to his seat, buckled in and started lifting off before the second injured colleague was fully aboard. The gunner and the wounded pilot heaved their injured colleague in as the chopper lifted above the tree line and immediately banked for a heading south to Mana Pools and the medics.

"K-Leader. K-One here. We've recovered the crew. Both injured. Wrapping up. Leaving for home now."

"White Leader this is K-Leader. We're done here now. We're all out of ammo. Heading back."

"Okay K-Lead. White Section will linger in the vicinity and mop up then follow you boys back in fifteen. Great work lads."

Progressively all the helicopters moved away leaving the two Hunters circling over a devastated scene below. Later that night an SAS soldier set explosives and blew up the downed Alouette III helicopter.

***

"Speed has to go to three ten," instructed Bates.

Dixon accelerated. The radio crackled.

"K-Car Leader, this is Dolphin Three. We've heard nothing from Green Section. Confirm they did go through? What's the status?" queried Air Commodore Watson. He sat anxiously on the metal bench along the one side of the command Dak. Dolphin 3 was in a wide circle fifty kilometres to the south east of Lusaka.

"Affirmative Dolphin Three. Green Section was right on target," responded K-Car Leader. "We have mopped up and heading back."

The relief on hearing that response was infectious throughout those on board Dolphin 3. Not knowing what had happened was agonising and as time dragged on Walls and the other commanders onboard began to envisage all sorts of negative scenarios.

"Okay, Thanks very much. What about Blue and White Section status?"

"All good. Blue Section delivered okay. White Section mopping up."

"And the Zambian AF? What of them?"

"Red Lead said all good there," responded K-Car Leader.

Bugger it. I totally forgot about Dolphin 3, thought Dixon.

"I think you were to hand over to Dolphin Three Sir," informed Bates stating the bleeding obvious.

"Yes I forgot to ...."

"Lusaka tower this is inbound Kenya four three two."

Who the hell is that now? thought Dixon staring at the radio

"Four three two stand by. We have an incident here," replied the Lusaka air traffic controller.

It must be a plane coming into Lusaka. That's a problem. I better get hold of Dolphin 3.

"It must be a civilian plane coming into Lusaka," guessed Bates.

"Dolphin 3 from Green Leader."

"Green Leader, this is Dolphin Three. Go ahead."

"Roger. Shortly I am going to ask you to take over ....."

The Lusaka tower cut in.

"Green Leader. Lusaka."

"Go ahead," said Dixon abruptly.

"How much longer is this operation?" asked the air traffic controller anxiously.

He had watched with morbid fascination as the Rhodesian jets swooped down followed by flashes of orange and red. Through his field glasses he saw

336

helicopters like dragon flies circling and weaving in and out of the smoke.

"Roger. If you'll hang fire. I'll advise you shortly."

The controller's throat tightened when he heard the words '*hang fire*'. He was in a vulnerable situation atop the control tower surrounded by glass. He wondered if he may receive incoming fire for having disturbed Green Leader.

"Ah ... I have one to take off to the north," he quickly offered this information to appease Green Leader. ".... and if you have no objection, one to take off to the south." Then as an afterthought he added, '.... Civilian, you know."

It's too risky to have civilian aircraft up while we're still exiting from FC. He will have to hold them.

"Tell him no, Sir," said Bates who had the same thought.

"Request you hold them for another ten minutes."

"Roger. Will do."

The controller felt relieved. He still wondered what '*hang fire*' meant.

It's better if Dolphin 3 deals with the tower now. I'll be out of range soon enough and we can't afford a snafu here with comms with the tower and air traffic.

"Lusaka, this is Green Leader. Would you now contact Dolphin Three. He'll be taking over my transmissions."

"Roger. Dofin Three? Lusaka."

The controller lifted his field glasses to scan the scene where the attack was taking place. He saw two jets streak off towards the south.

"Lusaka. This is Dolphin Three. Do you read me?"

The controller put down the field glasses and lifted his microphone.

Shit I had better brief Dolphin 3 on the status with the tower and the spiel, thought Dixon before he interjected.

"Dolphin Three, this is Green Leader. Are you listening out on one, one, eight, one?"

"Negative Green Lead. I've been listening out on .... on … the other one."

"Roger. You'll need to transfer over to that frequency to pass on messages which I'll advise you about. Ah .... I have advised Lusaka to hold their civilian traffic for another ten minutes. We're going out of range shortly."

"Have you given them the spiel yet?"

"Roger. Yes I gave the spiel."

"Dofin Three. Lusaka tower. I have two aircraft coming in to land. Civilian you know. Can I give them permission to land?"

"Lusaka, this is Dolphin Three. This is just a message that you are to keep your air traffic on the ground for another ten, TEN, minutes. Did you copy, over?"

"Copied, thank you. I have the civilian aircraft coming in from the north to land in about one zero minutes. Any objection to him coming into land?"

"Roger, there is no problem with that. You can let him come in and land. The main thing is that if there is any air force, repeat air force traffic, they are to remain on the ground. You can let that civilian traffic land. There is no hassle on that."

"Thank you. The civilian aircraft will land," confirmed the air traffic controller with great relief.

The Kenyan Airlines Boeing 707 was on final approach with landing gear down and almost on the tarmac.

The Hunters streaked past the Canberra's on their way back to refuel and rearm. The helicopters headed back to Kariba airport.

"Dolphin Three. This is Red Section. We are still at Mumbwa."

"Red Section. Dolphin Three here. Okay, all objectives met and ops concluded. What's the situ on the ground there?"

"All quiet. No activity."

"Red Section. Dolphin Three here. We are heading to the next objective. Phase Two will initiate. Hang there for another ten minutes then back to NS for refuel and rearm."

Dolphin 3 banked left and headed towards the next target at Mkushi 125 kilometres north east of Lusaka.

"Lusaka, this is Dolphin Three. Our task here is now complete. We are leaving the area. I repeat we have no quarrel with Zambia or security forces or civilian traffic. You must however keep your Air Force on the ground. We will attack any Air Force aircraft that takes off. I would like to thank you very much for your co-operation. Thank you."

"Copied"

The controller sat down with exhausted relief. Who was going to believe him when he reported what had occurred?

**

"We'll be approaching New Sarum shortly Sir."

"Roger that."

Bates moved from the nose cone of the Canberra to his seat and buckled himself in.

Dixon adjusted his radio dials.

339

"Green Section. Ready for approach. Salisbury radar, this is Green Section. Green Alpha section, go radar. Green check."

The three other Canberra's checked in. They began staggering themselves behind him for landing.

"Flight level two five zero. We'll be top of descent at fifty eight, the field at zero eight and request priority landing for all our aircraft."

"Roger, Green Section," responded the air traffic controller at Salisbury airport. "Cleared for landing. One zero, six zero, one eight zero knots, temperature twenty two. Report at topography."

Dixon manoeuvred the Canberra readying it for landing as they approached the runway. There was no turbulence nor was there any cross wind.

"Greens reporting at topography," said Dixon. He lowered his undercarriage, adjusted his flaps and air speed.

The Canberra's landed one after the other and taxied to the Air Force hard stand. The Hunters from Blue and White Sections were already there, being refuelled. The armaments were being driven out to be fitted under their wings. Their nose canopies were open and the cannons where being reloaded with long strips of lethal bullets.

The Vampire's had left for Zambia two minutes earlier.

CHAPTER THIRTY

October 1978

Peering out of the Dak, with call sign Dolphin Three, to scan the brown and dry land below that was speckled with sparse patches of cultivation Air Commodore Watson confirmed "Phase two is a go."

The elation of those at ComOps and New Sarum in hearing the news of a successful attack against Westland Farm terror camp was short lived as they prioritised their minds to the second phase of Operation Gatling.

Upon receiving the news, Rob, a SAS squadron commander for this op against the Mkushi terrorist camp, rushed down from the New Sarum control tower and ran across the apron to the hanger where his troops were anxiously waiting to learn if they were going to board the ParaDaks or not.

"It's on!" he shouted. "Phase One is a complete success, so now it's up to us to make this op an equally successful one. Let's get this show on the road."

He along with the other Section Commanders and their troops had been briefed on the specific details of this op earlier this morning. The Daks would fly into the contact zone at between 400 to 500 feet. This was normal for this type of operation, so as to minimise the time in the air where the troops would be vulnerable to enemy fire. The objective was to discharge the troops as close to the flanks of the contact zone without putting them into the camp. Once on the ground the troops would firstly form into four man sticks and then into 24 men stop groups. Their aim would be to eliminate terrorists fleeing the camp. Then once the air strikes from the K-Car sections were complete, the

341

troops were to move into the camp to mop up and take control of the area.

They were ordered not to blacken their faces with camouflage cream. All white soldiers were selected for this mission to ensure they could be recognisable and not mistaken for the enemy on the ground when the confusion of this contact took place.

Wearing the regulation Rhodesian webbing and camouflage uniforms, with their caps inside out to show a patch of orange sewn on, so as to distinguish them from the air when the choppers attacked, each soldier had 260 rounds, plus the magazine in the rifle, a 100 round MAG or RPD belt, flares and four grenades. The soldiers burdened with the MAG carried ten 50 round belts, a considerable weight to haul. Each soldier wore a 9mm calibre pistol for close combat protection. This also offered protection if they were snagged in trees, where they may not be able to free their rifle as it was strapped to them for the descent. Some troops would also carry landmines and claymores.

The standard operating procedure had been reinforced with all the men. On landing they were to rid themselves of their parachute harness, make contact with the nearest soldier, take cover, orientate themselves and then seek out and shoot the enemy in the vicinity. Once the immediate area was secured they were to form their sticks before forming the larger stop groups. The stop group commanders would position themselves in the middle of his 24 man section in the plane. The man at either end of the stop group would set off white phosphorous grenades to mark the end line of troops so that the choppers and other aircraft would be able to discern their locations.

Boarding onto the ParaDaks was completed quickly and before long the six planes were taxing away from the New Sarum apron and onto the main Salisbury Airport runway.

Similar messages were transmitted by ComOps to the section commanders stationed at Kariba airport and Mana Pools Forward Air Field. Troops boarded the helicopters that were lined up on the runway ready to ferry them to Mkushi and the Communist Guerrilla Training Camp II.

Once all the ParaDaks were airborne they flew in a loose formation descending to near treetop height once they crossed the Zambezi River and entered into Zambian air space. While the cat was out of the bag that the Rhodesians were attacking FC camp near Lusaka, the Security Forces did not wish to send any pre-emptive signals via radar to the Zambians that another raid was commencing. The plan for the second phase of Operation Gatling was based on a complete surprise attack at the other two camps. While news of the attack on FC was bound to have reached the ZIPRA forces at these two camps, ComOps was banking on ZIPRA believing it was not the modus operandi for the Rhodesians to attack several camps at once and particularly not later in the day.

Low level flying resulted in significant turbulence that reinforced the 'Vomit Comet' nick name of the Daks. Soon most of the SAS troops filled their air sickness bags. The smell inside the cramped aircraft became putrid.

Having been refuelled and rearmed, the Canberra's and Hunter aircraft were soon on their way to Mkushi to repeat the attack sequence they used at FC camp earlier that morning. In close formation the aircraft passed the ParaDaks 10 minutes out from Mkushi. Vampire fighter jets and Lynx aircraft had earlier set off from Salisbury for Kariba airport. They refuelled and when summoned by Dolphin 3, they would be commissioned into the attack. The Rhodesian Air Force was totally committed to Phase 2. There was no going back.

The men of the SAS who had set up the fuelling depot, called the 'Administration Camp', in the bush near Mkuski, began pulling the camouflage netting off the piles of barrels containing aviation fuel and the boxes full of machine gun ammo. This clearing in the middle of the bush was where the helicopters would be refuelled and rearmed over the next twenty four hours.

Once in Zambian airspace the ParaDak pilots soon realised the difficulty they were facing. Navigation was problematic once they descended to tree top height. Navigating by looking at ground features and cross referencing these to maps and aerial photographs would be hard enough under normal conditions but they were flying very low and everything shot past far quicker than they would have liked. This difficulty was compounded as they ventured deeper into Zambia where the dust haze from a long dry winter and smoke from cooking fires flooded the sky.

"Dolphin Three this is Pink Leader, over," said the pilot of the ParaDak leading the formation.

"Pink Lead. This is Dolphin Three. What's up?"

"Ya. We are ... ah ... four minutes out from the drop zone. The bloody smoke haze is bad. We have two distinct smoke stacks several klicks apart. I'm unsure which one is the target. Need a clue here."

"Okay Pink Lead, roger that. Blue and White Sections hit the target but Green Section had a snafu. Two of Green missed target. That must be why you see two smoke stacks. We can't be definite which is which at this time."

"Roger that Dolphin Three. We have to choose which one to go for ...."

"Pink Lead. This is Green Leader. You should go for the one to the west," cut in Dixon. "The camp is at the west. The bomb drop towards the east was the snafu."

"Roger that Green Lead. We were tracking to the one to the East," replied Pink Leader.

Dolphin 3 was not in the immediate vicinity. It was circling fifty kilometres south so the commanders on board were unable to give definitive direction. The Canberra's had already vacated the target area, while the Hunters had moved away to give the Daks a clear run in.

"Pink Section. Break formation. Break formation. Quickly! Track to the western smoke site and go to drop altitude," announced Pink Leader.

The Daks broke their tail to nose formation in unison while decreasing their altitude. Soon thereafter the green lights inside the planes turned on to herald the discharge process. Troops poured out the side of each plane.

The navigational confusion meant some troops were dropped 1,200 metres out from the camp, while others found themselves landing far too close to the enemy positions.

Rob landed on the ground with a thud, having crashed through a canopy of trees. He was winded and grazed along his left leg and arm from the branches. Recovering quickly he undid his parachute and roughly rolled it into an untidy bundle. Unclipping his weapon, he checked to see if it was damaged. It wasn't and with relief he slipped the safety off before looking around in search of his men. To his left and right soldiers were in various stages of readiness. Rob was relieved to see they were forming into their four man sticks. The white phosphorous grenades were set off.

The clatter of rifle fire erupted to his front and right, a mixture of FN and AK.

Contact already?

His radio crackled into life.

"Contact! Contact. Section Bravo in contact."

"Ya we've also got contact at Section Charlie. I think we've been dropped in the damn camp. It's a shit fight here. We have terrs running all around us."

Rob swung around hearing gunfire to his right to see several terrorists running through the scrub. His adrenal glands pumped and his muscles tightened. They were firing their weapons indiscriminately as they ran.

"Contact! Contact," he shouted to his right and left, then into his radio, "Alpha Section in Contact."

The soldiers to his right engaged the fleeing terrorists cutting them down quickly. The first contact was short and sharp. Rob then gave orders to his men to form the stop group which they did, each positioning themselves with adequate cover for the expected onslaught of fleeing terrorists.

The initial contacts remained chaotic for all the sections close in to the camp. The ZIPRA troops were mostly confused and terrified as a result of the bombing. They bolted away from the camp threatening to overrun the stop groups by force of numbers. The situation suddenly became even more confused when the wind direction shifted fanning a grass fire that had started. Seeing that his troops could be caught by this fire, the Charlie Section stop group commander marshalled them away from the blaze. They made it with seconds to spare as the fire swept past them.

A land mine that had been laid minutes before on a gravel road leading to the camp exploded as a truck with eight ZIPRA soldiers made a dash to get away.

Despite the initial chaos of this early contact, the SAS commanders managed to get their troops co-ordinated to form four stop groups in a semi-circle around the one perimeter section of the camp. Two K-Cars arrived to patrol the Mkushi River that formed the eastern boundary of the camp, having deposited a stick of SAS to set up an 81 mm mortar position on the opposite bank.

The sound of more helicopters broke the monotony of the sporadic gunfire as more Rhodesian troops arrived at the target. The choppers came in low at tree top level landing behind the stop groups to debus their cargo. But the pilots in the second wave of 7 helicopters carrying 45 SAS troops became disorientated due to the smoke that filled the sky. They circled a wide area to locate their landing zones then, running short of fuel, they were forced to land in a clearing. The troops debussed and moved into their defensive positions in the surrounding bush. The choppers hurriedly departed towards the 'admin area' to be refuelled. It took the SAS commander of Foxtrot Section several minutes to discover that they were three kilometres from the camp. He radioed the lead chopper explaining the error but they were too low on fuel to return. The 45 SAS would have to wait for the choppers to refuel to be collected.

"Section Foxtrot. This is Alpha. Where the hell are you guys? I can't see your marker smoke," asked Rob.

"Foxtrot here. We are screwed. I think we were dropped way out. Trying to get our possie sorted," came the crackled reply.

Damn that means our left flank doesn't have a stop group in place.

"Alpha to Command. The terrs are gapping it to our left. We're missing Foxtrot. Where the hell are they?"

"They got dropped too far out Alpha. They are on the way. ETA twenty."

347

"Ya, but in that time we will lose a whole bunch of the bastards along the river sector."

"See if you can spread your Section out a bit to fill the hole?"

The Major in charge of the ground forces attempted to assimilate and recover the situation caused by the way his troops had been deployed by the ParaDaks and choppers.

"Man down!"

The section commanders' radios heralded the sad news.

"Which Section?" queried the Major.

"Charlie Section. He's gone."

"Has anyone else noticed these fuckers are bloody women?" asked the Commander of Delta Section.

"Man down. Delta Section. Need medic pronto."

Nigel Treadgold, was down. Part of his lower jaw was gone and his shoulder badly shattered. The medic on the scene was soon under fire from the ZIPRA soldier who had shot Treadgold. Bullets zipped past him as he tried to put the drip into Treadgold's arm. The medic was not moving from his patient. Two SAS soldiers charged at the ZIPRA terrorists. When the corpses were examined three of the four were woman.

"Casavac required for Nigel. He's bad," requested the Delta Section commander.

"Okay. I'll request. Get him to the extraction point ASAP. Right let's get the mortars in," ordered the Major.

The mortar party began feeding shells into the tubes. The ensuing dull Doof! Doof! Doof! sound filled the air.

The sporadic gun fire around the camp as ZIPRA combatants fought back was drowned out by the explosions from the mortars. Receiving radio intel from SAS observers positioned on a low ridge overlooking the camp, the mortar group adjusted their settings to zero in on where the terrorists were observed to be sheltering.

"Okay. Stop the mortars. K-Car Leader it's over to you," instructed the Major.

The K-Cars that had been standing off until the mortar attack concluded moved in. They spat out their high calibre bullets from the 20 millimetre cannons while terrorists discharged their AK's at the choppers. Explosions erupted. The sound of the helicopter rotors filled the air. Screams and shouting were audible.

The main part of the camp was surrounded in a semi-circle with fox holes and trenches that the Soviet instructors believed would offer good defence against any possible ground or air attack. Most of these fox holes were occupied with ZIPRA combatants who either were cowering to survive or who were prepared to fight it out. The K-Cars acting in tandem methodically attacked each fox hole, their occupants standing little chance. These fox holes had to be cleared before the SAS ground forces ventured into the camp. If not, too many Rhodesian casualties would result.

Having endured the high explosive bombs delivered by the Air Force Canberra bombers and Hunters, mortars and cannon fire from K-Cars, most of the ZIPRA who were left alive focused on escape rather than fighting. A few groups however again rallied. They attempted to take on the K-Cars scoring several non-fatal hits to the aircraft before being obliterated. After 20 minutes, the K-Cars withdrew to rearm and refuel.

The SAS troops who had been deployed in the wrong place now arrived in the choppers that had refuelled and once on the ground they quickly formed their stop sections.

"Sections Alpha, Charlie, Echo move in. Sections Bravo, Delta, Foxtrot hold as stop groups."

Charlie Section arrived at the perimeter of the camp first and immediately running gun fights broke out as some female ZIPRA soldiers fought for their lives.

Rob signalled to his soldiers on either side of him to move in towards the camp. The message was passed along the line. Spreading themselves twenty metres apart, the twenty four soldiers slowly edged forward through the scrub. Rob felt his pulse rate increase. His senses were on full alert. He and his men were exposed as they walked towards the camp through the brown knee high grass. He held his rifle with its butt in his right shoulder, his trigger finger poised to quickly move to action, sweeping the barrel in a ninety degree ark. Beads of sweat formed on his brow. He decided not to wipe it because in doing so he would expose himself to acute danger through the distraction no matter how momentary it may be. His eyes darted left and right but not too far out of his forward vision so as to blur the view. He strained to listen for any metallic sound or that of twigs being broken, anything to alert him to danger. The noise from the firefight that was already taking place off to his right was making it hard to hear for signs of imminent danger.

He stepped over a decaying branch from a nearby tree to see a slight depression ahead with scattered low lying bushes. A few mature trees were spread across the depression. Forty metres ahead, as the depression levelled off, Rob noticed a fallen tree surrounded by boulders. His instincts kicked in.

That's potentially danger, he thought and signalled with his left hand to his men on either side of him to observe it.

He methodically moved forward putting one foot ahead of the other. He heard the metallic click a moment before he saw movement.

"Contact!" he shouted out, sinking to his one knee and discharging his weapon.

His rounds ripped into the bark and ricocheted off the boulders. He saw movement between the tree trunk and the boulders and sent several rounds into the gap.

Three terrorists burst out from behind the boulders. They ran towards the camp, two discharging their AK 47s into the air. The third had no weapon. They stood no chance and fell in a volley of bullets. Two more terrorists suddenly emerged from behind the tree trunk. Rob put a bullet into the head of one dropping her like a stone. The other, startled, swung around to get back behind the tree trunk but a bullet caught her under her rib cage, tearing through her vital organs.

The section moved ahead once again. When Rob came to the tree trunk he took the liberty to look where the terrorists had been seeking sanctuary. He saw a terrorist lying on her back. Her jacket was blood stained where a bullet had penetrated her upper right lung. She was alive but struggling to breath, blood oozing from her mouth and nose. A gurgling sound was audible. They made eye contact. She moved her right arm towards where her AK lay beside her.

So I slotted the bloody terr. Good shot Rob, he congratulated himself.

He raised his weapon pointing it at her. She continued with her attempt to grab her weapon.

Strange she doesn't look fearful. Rather she looks relieved.

He pulled the trigger twice.

Sentimentality and compassion have no place in battle, particularly in a terrorist conflict and this was the case at Mkushi. ZIPRA terrorists that were not fatally injured were to be shot dead. There were no medical supplies to be wasted on the ZIPRA injured and there was no need for many prisoners. It was brutal anti-terrorist warfare being played out in the bush of Central Africa.

Alpha section entered the camp from the north west. The fox holes and trenches they encountered were filled with bodies.

The K- Car guys have done a great job here, thought Rob.

"Check the fox holes. We don't want to leave anything alive behind us," he instructed.

The message went down the line to his men.

"They are all bitches," said the soldier to Rob's right as he put a bullet into the chest of a wounded terrorist.

Once past the line of fox holes and trenches they moved into an area where accommodation tents had been.

The Alpha bombs have shredded the shit out of the tents. Looking at the bodies scattered around he thought, *bloody hell these bastards are torn to pieces.*

When Rob's Alpha Section arrived at the parade ground they were met by Charlie Section who was already there.

The smell of burned flesh hit them first then the sight of what the Air Force had done struck home. A soldier to Rob's left gagged before spewing the contents of his stomach. Several others followed his lead.

"It's brutal, Sir," observed Rob's Sergeant. "These bastards are pulverised."

"Ya it's the Golf Bombs from the Hunters that did this. Those close in where the bomb went off are torn to shreds, but those over there," Rob pointed to where several dozen terrorists lay, ".... they got their insides

352

scrambled to mush. That's why they look uninjured until you open them up."

"I didn't know we had this stuff, Sir. It's awesome."

Cannon fire to the east was clearly audible. Visibility was limited due to the smoke pouring into the sky from the burning buildings.

"The K-Cars are giving it stick Rob," observed the commander Charlie Section.

"Ya man, they must be cleaning up the bastards who are gapping it across the river," said Rob.

By early afternoon the camp was in the control of the SAS. The Special Branch men were ferried in by chopper arriving before dusk so they could search for documents to extract vital intelligence information. Signals equipment and ciphers were secured intact which was a bonus for them.

A building that had a red hammer and sickle painted on its one side wall was situated near the centre of the camp. It was built from clay bricks and topped with a corrugated iron roof. Remarkably it was mostly in one piece. A corner of the building had taken a mortar round and was caved in with the tin roof pealed back. Inside the building the SAS found two white men. They were both dead. They were Russians. A ceremonial Russian army uniform plus flak jackets were found in a cupboard. The Special Branch boys spent a long time searching that particular building gathering evidence of Soviet involvement with ZIPRA.

Most of the camp's many buildings were in ruins having taken the bulk of the bombs from the Hunters and Canberra's. The officers' quarters were severely damaged. However the library somehow had survived. It was found to be full of Communist propaganda. A large kitchen, while damaged, was still able to reveal that it had been well equipped. It was well stocked with food aid from the Anglican and Catholic Churches.

The armoury off to the far end of the parade ground was stocked with an array of weapons. Hundreds of AK 47 assault rifles, Dragonuv rifles, RPK and DP 7.62 machine guns, 75 millimetre recoilless cannons, thousands of rounds of ammunition, RPG 7 rocket launchers, and wooden crates containing land mines. Many of these weapons were loaded up into large nets which were airlifted out by helicopter before any equipment that could not be extracted was blown up.

It was late afternoon when an engine of a jet aircraft was heard. It was not the engine noise of any of the planes flown by the Rhodesian Air Force. A MiG was sighted coming in towards them at great speed sending the soldiers scattering for cover.

Urgent assistance was called by the SAS Major.

"Red Leader to Red Two. We have company over Mkushi. A MiG. Let's take a look pronto."

The two Hunters turned northwards, accelerating to full speed back to the camp. The pilots had been making their way for a final fly over the CTG II camp south west of Mkushi camp before heading back home. The Zambian Air Force MiG banked high to circle the camp for a third time in a wide arc. The soldiers in the camp remained wary and hidden.

"There at three o'clock Sir," said Red Two seeing a flash of silver as the plane disappeared between two large clouds.

"Okay, I see it. Hold back, but let him see us. Stay high and behind him. Prepare to engage if he makes a move."

The MiG pilot elected to stay close to the clouds when he spotted the Hunters. He then banked sharply and left the area. The Hunters followed a short distance before heading back to Rhodesia.

***

The news came in that the raid at CTG-2 was a flop. It seemed that the ZIPRA soldiers there had got wind of the raids and bolted. The RLI troops that were flown in by chopper encountered only minor resistance and accounted for 54 guerrillas killed in a brief firefight.

It was twenty to seven in the morning when the two choppers carrying the 'Vultures' arrived. This was the fond name given by the troops to the public relations and media folk because they arrived after the battle to pick over the bones. On this occasion CIO were keen for the 'Vultures' to get a good eye full of what had happened at Mkushi. It had come as a shock to CIO and ComOps that Mkushi was mainly occupied by female insurgents. SAS ground surveillance of that camp had been cursory and while female terrs had been sighted, there was no hint that the majority there were women. Upon hearing this news CIO determined that it was essential for photographic and eye witness evidence to be obtained to counter what they believed ZIPRA and the Zambian Government would put out to the global media; that Mkushi was a refugee camp of women and children which had been attacked by the Rhodesians who had slaughtered these defenceless refugees. CIO wanted evidence that it was in fact a communist guerrilla insurgency training camp, armed with an array of Soviet supplied weapons, Church supplied food provisions and with Soviet trainers.

The choppers landed on the dusty parade ground disturbing the actual vultures and kites that were feeding on the dead bodies scattered all around the camp. The journalists soon saw the brutality of the battle scene, the weapons used by the insurgents and their facilities. They were also introduced to three female prisoners.

The 'Vultures' departed after two hours, relieved to be heading back to Rhodesia and away from what was perceived to be a vulnerable situation deep inside a hostile country. The real vultures continued to drop down to pick at the corpses, going for the eyes and tongues first, before attacking the gut.

Soon thereafter the Special Branch officers left with seven prisoners and their booty of documents. A procession of choppers then began ferrying SAS troopers back to Rhodesia. Alpha Section was the last scheduled to leave. They set about arming the explosives that had been laid the night before.

"Sir, we have a problem," informed a sentry on the north east of the camp via radio.

"What's up?" said Rob.

"We have visitors. Looks like terrs coming in to have a look see."

"How many and what's their ETA?"

"Plenty … maybe fifty plus. Fifteen, twenty minutes tops."

"Damn it. We have a way to go to set these bloody explosives and the G-cars are a way out yet. I'll check in to JOC."

Rob radioed his commander who was now at Kariba airport to inform him of the emerging situation. The message was relayed to ComOps. The Major queried if air strike support was an option.

"No go. Hunters or Vamps can't make it for ninety minutes. They are not armed. The choppers taking 'B' Section home are twenty minutes out of Kariba. K-Cars are fifty minutes out," informed the JOC commander. "Take the terrs out and hold ground until the choppers can get back for extraction."

Looking through the field glasses from a vantage point Rob saw that there was an assortment of uniforms being worn and weapons carried by those approaching.

"Damn! They are Zambian Army," he reported to his Sergeant. "Zambian Police and ... also ZIPRA. Counting .... fifteen, or ... no ... seventeen Police. Sixty .... sixty five Army and .... looks like twenty ZIPRA. Okay we have our work cut out for us. We'll take them on east of the river when they come through that heavy wooded part."

Rob and his soldiers set about preparing themselves to engage this group through setting an ambush.

"We wait until they are ten metres out and then we give them a welcome. Claymores set?"

"Claymores set, Sir."

"Okay, then let the party begin."

Having observed many helicopters leaving the camp site hours before, the advancing men were unaware the Rhodesians were still in the vicinity. Wary of bobby traps that the Rhodesians may have set and with trepidation as to what casualties they would find, they moved slowly forward. There were plenty of vultures and kites circling the camp which indicated corpses.

"Fire," said Rob enthusiastically.

The soldiers pulled on the cords which triggered the claymore mines.

Vup! Vup! Vup! .... Vup!Vup!Vup!

The six claymores exploded sending hundreds of ball bearings at bullet speed into the approaching men.

Eight soldiers laying in ambush stood up and fired their weapons into the cloud of dust that the claymores had thrown up. Two soldiers with MAG's opened up with a torrent of gunfire. The bullets and the ball bearings had an immediate and devastating effect. Most of the advancing men went down, cut to pieces.

As the dust cleared Rob, together with seven soldiers who were not part of the initial ambush, rushed towards the killing zone. It was brutal. The claymores had caused terrible injuries.

The first enemy to be encountered were two ZIPRA comrades staggering around in a daze with horrific wounds to their faces and upper torsos. Two bullets each dropped them to the ground before incoming AK 47 rounds sent Rob and his men scurrying for cover. A bullet clipped the left side of one soldier. It was a flesh wound. Three SAS returned fire and the Sergeant threw a grenade which had a terminal effect on the source of the incoming rounds.

Rob indicated to his men with his left hand to advance which they did in unison. Two figures appeared briefly before falling in a hail of bullets. Then three people bolted from behind an ant hill. Rob and his Sergeant gave chase firing at them as they ran. A round caught a Zambian soldier in his right shoulder blade, the force of the impact spinning him around. He collided with the other two who were running close to his left and all three went down.

It took five seconds before Rob and the Sergeant descended on the three, like rabid hyenas. The Zambian soldier was squirming in pain. The two ZIPRA comrades tried to get up but seeing the soldiers were upon them they stayed down on the ground.

"Pleeese no shoot me," yelped the female ZIPRA comrade trying to catch her breath.

Terror swept over her face. She was injured from the claymore blast, her combat jacket torn open revealing her blooded shoulder. Her comrade appeared uninjured.

Rob shot the Zambian soldier in the head.

"Nooo. Nooo. Pleeeese no shoot me," she squealed as she lost control of her bladder.

The Sergeant put two rounds into her chest. Her comrade who said nothing tried to get up before she too received two rounds.

Sporadic gun fire behind Rob alerted him to some resistance but that soon stopped. Signalling to his Sergeant to follow him, he set off on a circular route back to the killing field.

He had only gone a short distance when he came across a terrorist lying face down in a shallow ditch. He raised his weapon pointing it at the man before he kicked him hard in the side below the rib cage. The man rolled over.

Has he got a weapon? Rob's immediate concern. *No. Okay that's good. He's a big bastard.*

He wrapped his figure around the trigger, readying to pull, while watching the man's face.

Wait! His uniform? He's carrying senior officer insignia?

"I am surrendering," announced the ZIPRA officer in English and he put both his hands in the air. "I am an officer of ZIPRA. I have no weapon. I surrender to you."

Perhaps we take this bastard back then kill him? Thought Rob as he released the tension of his trigger finger. *He may have intel the Special Branch boys would like to extract?*

"Don't shoot this bastard," said Rob when his Sergeant came up next to him ready to dispatch the terrorist. "I want him taken back for the SB boys. Bring him and let's clear up here and go home. I have had enough of this shit for one day."

CHAPTER THIRTY ONE

October 1978

"All troops and aircraft are back. Op Gatling is ended," informed Major Harding to the personnel in ComOps.

Cheers went up around the ops room in celebration of the end of the 48 hours treble raid against ZIPRA in Zambia. Castle Lagers and Black Label beers were uncapped as the tension and anxiety melted away.

"This operation had the potential to have gone so wrong. It didn't." said Walls. "But have we neutralised ZIPRA and stopped them in their tracks? Can we now afford to focus the military effort in dealing with ZANLA in the north east, east and south east ahead of the elections on the internal settlement? Gentlemen these are the questions I want the answers to. Get them to me."

While the devastation on ZIPRA was guessed to be substantial, actual numbers were never going to be known, but an informed estimate would give some feedback on whether the purpose of the operation had actually been achieved effectively.

"Several CIO and SAS personnel remain active in Zambia to get post op intel," confirmed Harding.

***

Intel dribbled in almost immediately after the raids ended. Following the attacks, Zambia went on state of high alert. The Zambian army mobilised and poured armed soldiers onto the streets of the main towns around the southern part of the country.

The follow up bombing raids within a few days on other ZIPRA camps nearer the Zambian border served to ratchet up the fear, suspicion and panic. Spies were seen behind every tree. The white folk living in Zambia became the obvious targets in the racially charged environment. Suspected as Rhodesian spies or sympathisers, many were harassed and beaten, some even murdered by gangs who roamed the streets. Two Zambian Air Force planes were shot down by the ZIPRA ground to air batteries which they recalled from the border region. The Zambian Army ambushed two ZIPRA convoys thinking they were Rhodesians. Cars backfiring in the streets of Lusaka sent people diving for cover.

Diplomacy was frantic. The Zambian Foreign Ministry sent official complaints to the United Nations demanding urgent action to be taken against the illegal government in Rhodesia. Threats of open war between Zambia and Rhodesia were mooted by several Zambian Government Ministers. Fearing that Cuba would soon be drawn into the front line, the United States exerted acute pressure on the South African Government to bring the Rhodesians to heel. The President of Zambia however kept remarkably quiet.

**

The ComOps briefing set for eleven on Wednesday morning included the top brass of the Rhodesian military and the senior officers of CIO and Special Branch.

"Gentlemen Gatling was a successful, well planned and executed operation. For the total loss of one K-Car, and the death of one and injury to seven Security Force members, two being serious, we delivered a telling blow to ZIPRA. It is not possible to ascertain exactly what the casualties on ZIPRA were, but our informants on the ground indicate the following estimates which we believe are conservative.

ZIPRA dead were twelve hundred at FC camp with an estimated six to eight hundred wounded. Most wounded sustained severe injuries. Eight hundred killed at Mkushi camp, including some Zambian army personnel. Fifty dead at CTG II camp. This camp had an estimated one thousand insurgents, but most had evacuated before the attack, hence the low casualty count.

Gentlemen, we may have proven our military capability with Gatling, however, we still face formidable odds. While we have mitigated the immediate threat from ZIPRA we certainly have not eliminated it. The intel from captured documents validate that they still have a large manpower capacity which is capable to be mobilised. We have bought ourselves six months, nine months at the extreme, before ZIPRA regroup to pose another serious threat.

Our intel is that the Soviets will re-equip them quickly as they believe that the West have already written Rhodesia off and are prepared to see it consigned to Soviet influence with the East West line in Africa as being the Limpopo River, the South African border, and no longer the Zambezi.

Mugabe's ZANLA force in Mozambique now poses the immediate threat to the security of this country. The military raids we are presently conducting into Mozambique will soften their impact but will not totally mitigate it. Our manpower capacity is at its maximum.

The ZANLA threat will be covered in detail later in the briefing.

Gentlemen, it remains the assessment of Special Branch that a political settlement continues to remain the only viable option to conclude this conflict and the best the Rhodesian Security Forces can achieve is to continue to hold the line. But the timeline for this capacity to hold the line and retain a semblance of internal security in this country is shortening. Our political leaders have less than twelve months to achieve a resolution that will remove either ZIPRA, ZANLA, or both from the conflict. The question remains whether this internal political settlement and the forthcoming elections will yield us the international recognition sufficient for this resolution to be achieved."

Richard looked out at his audience. On the brink of such a huge military success he had succeeded to bring down a very solemn cloud. This was deliberate. He decided to take this approach at this briefing because he sensed that unless those who were charged with the responsibility of conducting the affairs that determined the life and death of so many are kept focused on the reality of the situation, then the risk was they would relax and bask in a false glory.

This civil war is far from over. Thousands more will die, untold misery will yet be unleashed on innocent simple souls as a few continue to manipulate the many so they could achieve their own political ambition, thought Richard as he stepped down from the lectern.

CHAPTER THIRTY TWO

December 1978

Manquoba was in a small room with a tiny barred window high up on the one wall. The room was originally painted white, but the walls were filthy, so looked grey. The floor was cement. Two dirty flea infested blankets were all he had to sleep with. A thin rubber rectangle, five by three feet, was used as a mattress. He received one meal a day at noon and four cups of water during the day. A bucket was provided for his toilet. It had not been emptied for three days so the room smelled putrid.

After being taken captive by the Rhodesians at Mkushi camp, Manquoba was flown by helicopter back to Rhodesia. At one stage he feared the soldiers in the helicopter may throw him out. He saw hatred in the eyes of the young soldiers. They suggested this several times amongst themselves and it seemed to him that they were seriously considering it.

The ambush by the Rhodesian SAS on the group of Zambian Army and ZIPRA took Manquoba by surprise. Along with the Zambian Army district commander he believed the Rhodesians had left Mkushi. The soldiers from the Zambian Army had assembled at a Police station during the morning not that far from the camp and together with a collection of ZIPRA guerrillas who were in the vicinity they made their way to Mkushi first by army trucks, then fearing land mines on the access roads, they debussed and went the last kilometre on foot.

Manquoba had heard of the attack the day before. He was in Lusaka enjoying some R&R. He had booked

364

into a hostel on Manda Hill Road which was close to the University and opposite the National Assembly. He was still asleep when the raid on FC camp took place, but by the time he had woken, the news was on the radio. Upon hearing the broadcast that the Rhodesians had attacked the ZIPRA headquarters he rushed to meet with the ZIPRA commanding officer who he knew was staying at the Protea Hotel. By the time he got to meet General Masuku the news had filtered through that the Rhodesians were attacking other ZIPRA camps. Initial information about the casualties sustained by ZIPRA at FC camp indicated a disaster had occurred. Later that day he was ordered to go to Mkushi to assess the situation.

He had left Lusaka by car that afternoon. When he arrived at the Police Station, the Zambian Police Inspector told him that the Rhodesians were still at the camp. This news shocked him as it meant the Rhodesians were occupying the camp deep inside Zambia and the Zambians were doing nothing about it. The Zambian Police Inspector refused to discuss the situation with Manquoba, informing him to wait and he would revert to him once he himself had received further orders from Police HQ in Lusaka.

When other ZIPRA comrades arrived at the Police Station, Manquoba briefed them on what little information he knew. Later the next day news was received indicating that the Rhodesians were leaving and soon after that troops from the Zambian Army arrived. The Zambian Army Lieutenant assumed control and assembled a mixture of Army, Police and ZIPRA personnel before setting off to the camp.

The ambush by the Rhodesians was sudden and quickly over. Manquoba had dived into a ditch to his left when the claymores went off. He was well behind the main group. Once the initial shock of the detonation

365

had passed he was relieved to see he was uninjured. He searched around but could not find his AK. He had dropped it when he went for the ditch. The gun fire helped him decide to keep his head down until the shooting stopped. But when he decided to lift himself up to look for his weapon he felt a sharp kick to his side. When he rolled over he came face to face with a Rhodesian soldier pointing his FN's at him.

It had been quickly obvious to him that one of two things was about to happen. The soldier would either shoot him or he was going to be taken as captive. He knew there was absolutely zero chance he could scramble to his AK 47 and shoot his way out of this predicament. As he was not ready to die, he diverted his eyes to the ground and lifted his hands above his head to surrender hoping the Rhodesian would accept this. The soldier hesitated. That was a good sign for Manquoba. He kept both his hands on the top of his head. Suddenly he was grabbed by his shirt, pulled out of the ditch and pushed hard to the ground face down. Skin was torn from his left cheek and forehead which bled profusely.

The soldiers in the helicopter did not throw him out. The fact they didn't was of huge relief to Manuqoba. Being a veteran of this bush war, he lived from day to day knowing each one could be his last. So far it seemed to him that perhaps this was not to be his last.

When the chopper landed at Mana Pools he was pulled out by two black Rhodesian soldiers. They roughly manhandled him to a tent without speaking to him, throwing him onto the ground before kicking him hard. He was told not to move and to keep his mouth shut. Gradually recovering from the kicks, he lifted himself to sit cross legged on the ground with his hands tied behind his back. He wondered what the next act of this drama would be. A black Rhodesian soldier sat on a box near the entrance flap of the tent. He looked menacing. Manquoba diverted his eyes so as not to encourage any reaction from him, especially wishing to avoid any beating. He had decided that he should be very savvy on how he played his predicament out with the Rhodesians if he wanted to remain alive. And he wanted to keep living.

A white man dressed in a brown safari suit came into the tent and sat on a fold-out chair. He stared at Manquoba saying nothing. After six minutes he broke the silence.

"I am a Rhodesian Intelligence Officer and will talk to you now about information I know you have in your head that I want to have in my head."

Manquoba studied this man who he assessed as his immediate threat. He looked young. His build was slim indicating he was in good shape. His hands indicated that he did not do manual work. He searched his eyes.

This man has piercing eyes and he can look into my soul. He commands the spirits.

Manquoba had decided to say nothing.

"I am the one who will decide if you die. The process for me to decide this has started. I want you to understand that."

I am not ready to join my ancestors. It is not time for me to be killed this day, thought Manquoba.

"I want you to tell me if you understand what I am saying. I want you to tell me that you understand I am the one who decides if you live."

"I understand," said Manquoba laconically.

"Good."

"You speak good Ndebele."

"I am still learning."

"Are you Zimbabwean?"

"Rhodesian."

"So we are brothers then."

"Perhaps. The first step in establishing our friendship is that we agree on this matter. I decide if you live or die. Is that understood?"

Manquoba nodded his agreement.

"What do I call you?" asked Manquoba.

"My Ndebele name is Londisizwe."

Manquoba thought before replying.

"Ah ... you chose well. To protect this nation. What is your English name?"

"Not important. But now the next step is that you tell me something that is useful to me. If we get past that step then I will know you want to stay alive. But if we do not get past this step you die."

Manquoba weighed up the options. He decided to explore the staying alive option further. After an hour of discussion he had explained what his rank and role was in ZIPRA. Manquoba readily explained what range of weapons ZIPRA had, thinking that the Rhodesians probably knew this information already having spent many hours at the ZIPRA camp where those weapons were stored.

Londisizwe wanted to know information about other guerrilla staging camps along the border. Manquoba hesitated trying to deflect the conversation several times, but all the while he considered carefully the consequence of not divulging the information. Death was not the option he sought to achieve that day and he felt confident that Londisizwe was the type of man who would end his life if he had to. He felt a momentary pang of guilt and betrayal as he relayed information on the whereabouts of a few minor ZIPRA camps close to the Rhodesian / Zambian border. However he felt that by disclosing this information it should cement this stay alive option.

"This news is good," said Londisizwe quietly. "But I worry why you tell me this. This news means your

368

comrades in those camps will be dead by tomorrow. I have not beaten you to tell me this news. You have not been hurt, yet you tell me this news quickly. This puzzles me very much."

"I am not a fool," retorted Manquoba. "I understand the rules you Rhodesians use. You say to me I stay alive if we become friends. To be your friend you ask me for news. News to betray my comrades. I want to stay alive. So to be your friend I have to give you this news and if that means others die then so it will be. Many are dying each day. You can beat me and break my bones, spill my blood to get the news you want but if I do not give this news to you then you will kill me. I will die after being beaten. But I have determined that I wish to be your friend and live. It seems no use for me to be beaten to arrive at this place anyway."

Londisizwe could not fault this clear logic so he moved on.

"ZIPRA has many Rhodesians they took across the river to Zambia. These are Rhodesians who do not want to be taken and are being held in a prison. I must know where this place is and I want you to tell me exactly where we can find this place."

The location of where captive Rhodesians including several soldiers were being held had been elusive. The SAS had searched for this place for months without any outcome.

Manquoba and Londisizwe spoke for many hours that evening.

Within three days of the cessation of Operation Gatling, the Rhodesian Air Force were back in Zambia bombing other ZIPRA camps which Manquoba had disclosed, while the Selous Scouts launched a raid to rescue several dozen black Rhodesians who were held captive in an underground prison by ZIPRA one hundred and ninety kilometres inside Zambia.

Manquoba was put in solitary confinement for six weeks at Inkomo Barracks. His cell was twelve feet long by ten feet wide. He exercised by doing push ups and stomach curls and he engaged in a conversation with himself for two hours each day.

The door opened sending a shard of bright daylight into his cell that made him close his eyes. He was told to turn around and place his hands together which were then chained before he was taken to the quadrangle. He was sprayed with disinfectant and then with cold water from a hose before being unchained. He was given some fresh khaki clothes and a pair of sandals and when dressed, he was led by two soldiers to another part of the camp. They put him into a rectangular room that had two windows on either side. Both were open letting in a relieving breeze. There was a small wooden table with two chairs. A glass and a jug of barley flavoured water were on the table. He drank three glasses.

They leave me without binding. That is indeed interesting.

After a few minutes Richard came into the room. Manquoba had not seen him since they spoke in the tent at Mana Pools. Manquoba stared at him intently. He was in his camouflaged Police uniform.

It's Longisizwe. Why has he has kept me like a dog for a long time? Ah I can see he is unarmed. I could break his neck here. But that would be foolish. I would die as well. What is it he wants of me? If he did not want something then he would have had me killed long ago.

"Are we friends Longisizwe?" asked Manquoba in Ndebele. "You keep me locked up like a dog for so long. Why?"

"Sorry that you have been kept alone for so long," said Richard in English. "Yes we are becoming friends."

Richard's blue eyes searched the face of Manquoba. Manquoba felt as if they were burning into his soul just as he had felt back in the tent the day of his capture. This man's eyes unnerved him.

"Becoming? Huh!" said Manquoba in Ndebele. He was taken by surprise that Richard spoke in English.

"Yes, becoming. Not yet true friends. The next step is the biggest we have to take. You and I together," said Richard pointing to Manquoba and himself. "And I wonder if you have the courage to take this next step?"

"What is this next step?" queried Manquoba, persisting to speak in Ndebele.

"The next step is whether you will join the fight against those people who remain enemies of the new Zimbabwe – Rhodesia. Those people who have not accepted that there is change happening in this land and that change is delivering the power to the people."

He searched Manquoba's eyes.

This man wants to stay alive. He will turn to stay alive but that will not be from any loyalty or conviction. It will be for self-centred preservation.

"You ask me to join you to fight against those whom I have fought with against you?"

"I think you have already made that choice. You gave up your comrades and we attacked the camps you told us about. The people in those camps are now dead. We have found the place holding our people captive based on the directions you gave us. The captors are dead and our people are freed and back here in Zimbabwe - Rhodesia."

"Is this Zimbabwe – Rhodesia giving true power to the people or is it to be a puppet regime controlled by apartheid South Africa with that monkey Muzorewa dancing to their music?"

"Zimbabwe - Rhodesia will give political power to the majority elected by the people who want the war to stop. Yet we still have ZIPRA and ZANLA continuing to fight for what has already been promised, a black African government. Too many people are still dying for no good reason and is it not ZIPRA and ZANLA who are the puppets to their corrupt leaders?"

"You ask me to fight for this Zimbabwe – Rhodesia and support that monkey? I ask you the question. How do you support such a buffoon?"

"My adopted name tells you why."

"Ah, so now you speak to me in Ndebele Londisizwe. You ask the *one who conquers* to join you as *one who protects the nation* and together we, as friends, fight those who seek to destroy this Zimbabwe – Rhodesia?

"Yes. But if you say no then you must tell me now, today. I ask you to decide to join us against the enemies of this new nation Zimbabwe – Rhodesia."

The two men stared at each other, each searching the eyes of the other for the true meaning and answer to this question.

***

February 1979
The sun bore down heating the earth quickly making it yet another hot dry morning. Manquoba stood on a grassy field surrounded by his recruits wearing the uniform of a Selous Scout officer. The beret with the Osprey bird emblem sat squarely on his bald head. He preferred to have his hair shaved off his head. His skin shone a deep black from the oil he applied to it each day.

As the chief firearms instructor for a new para-military initiative he was in command of turned ZIPRA terrorists, which were part of the new Umkonto waBantu auxiliaries. The '*spear of the nation*' was the initiative that the CIO had long pushed for to counter balance the presence of the terrorists in the tribal areas. The army chiefs had resisted this concept for years believing that to arm blacks outside of the regular military regime would in effect give rise to arming another potential threat. But with the new black dominated Government soon to be place and its leaders bringing their separate guerrilla armies with them, the arming of ex- terrorists was up and running in full force. The plan was for these men to flood the tribal areas and counter the rapidly increasing subversive activities of the ZIPRA and ZANLA terrorists now fighting to bring down the soon to be elected black Zimbabwe – Rhodesian government.

Surveying the recruits as they practiced pulling their AK rifles apart and putting them back together again, he thought about the recent events that brought him to where he was today. He avoided death by not being at the FC camp when the Rhodesians attacked it and then again the next day by being taken captive. His subsequent internment that involved many discussions with Londisizwe, whom he now respected and admired, placed him as an officer in command of many soldiers. He grinned to himself.

I now have my own private army. I am powerful, commanding much respect. I will have the influence with these men to make the people vote for Nkomo when the next change comes and the new true Zimbabwe is born.

CHAPTER THIRTY THREE

February 1979

The news had come as a mortal blow to many, none more so than to Richard. It made him feel physically sick.

That was several days ago when he was at New Sarum Air Force Base. He was attending a briefing given by senior Air Force officers on yet another cross border bombing raid in its final stages of preparation. This was to be a daring top secret joint raid by the Rhodesian and South African Air Forces, this time without ground support, on a terrorist camp at Boma near Va Luso deep inside Angola. The SAS who weeks earlier put two men into that region to observe the camp had reported that it held around 3,000 ZIPRA and 2,000 South African ANC terrorists in training. The raid was to be a 2,000 kilometre circular route from Rhodesia through Zambian airspace and into central Angola. The major risk was that the Canberra and Hunter planes may be attacked by the Angolan Air Force MiG's flown by Cubans. Intel was scarce but Special Branch had people working with the French to see what more could be gleaned.

Richard's demur had progressively worsened since he received the bad news. By the time he attended the briefing at ComOps he was in a foul depressed mood.

The briefing officer addressing the senior ranks at ComOps delivered his message in a very frank factual manner.

"As previously briefed, Air Rhodesia Flight 827, the *Umniati*, was shot down on twelve February by ZIPRA terrorists using a SAM missile soon after take-off from

Kariba airport. The circumstances were very similar to that of Flight Eight Five Two last year."

Richard found it surreal to be sitting virtually in the same seat he had sat in five months ago to receive the briefing on the Viscount Hunyani. Yet after all that followed another Air Rhodesia civilian aircraft was downed.

"We can confirm that a Strela Two missile hit the inner port engine severing the wing from the aircraft. It disintegrated on impact. No comms came from the plane to Air Traffic Control. All fifty nine passengers and crew would have died on impact. The plane came down in very rough country in the Vuti African Purchase Area east of Lake Kariba. Debris was scattered over a wide area."

"Do we know why the plane was flying below the missile ceiling?" queried Walls.

"We can only speculate without certainty what the circumstances were Sir."

ComOps didn't listen to the intel SB fed in. We told them that ZIPRA had the Strela missiles back inside the country targeting Air Rhodesia once again as retribution for the damage we did to them with Op Gatling. They chose to disregard that intel, thought Richard.

He was angry and disillusioned.

Did we tell Air Rhodesia about the threat? No! Did we deploy troops to mitigate the risk? No! Did we do anything to warn those poor souls getting on the plane that the insurgents had missiles? No!

Richard listened but did not hear the officer rattle on about details of the number of reported terrorist attacks over the past 24 hours, specifying dozens of incursion sightings, scores of black civilian deaths resulting from intimidation and subversion actions and two attacks on farmers. The officer moved onto outlining the results of

375

the Air Force raids against ZIPRA camps across the Zambian border in retaliation for the downing of the second Viscount and the air raid on ZANLA buildings within the confines of the Mozambique FRELIMO army camp at Mutarara near Chimoio. The air raid with Security Force ground support against two other ZIPRA bases in Zambia that was launched this morning and which was still ongoing would be the subject in a briefing scheduled for tomorrow.

Richard's eyes glazed over as he reflected.

What the hell is all this achieving? What's it all about other than bloody politics? This bloody war rages on spiralling out of control.

That Marxist Mugabe's grab for power is all self-centred politics. If he ever gets control, God forbid, he will never let go. That bastard!

That buffoon Nkomo forfeited his chance to take the statesmanship high ground and bring this all to an end.

The promise of peace from the internal settlement brokered by Smith with these inept so-called internal black leaders looks like it will disappear as quickly as that concept had any legs – bugger all.

What has been achieved? Fuck what a mess!

CHAPTER THIRTY FOUR

April 1979

The port engine of the Dakota spat out a dark exhaust cloud as it coughed to life. The lines of paratroopers quickly dwindled as they boarded the four ParaDaks at FAF 7 Buffalo Range in south eastern Zimbabwe – Rhodesia.

"Green Section, you are good to go," informed the lone air traffic controller.

"Roger that tower," replied the pilot commanding the two Canberra bombers that were on the runway.

Rob watched as the pilot spooled up his engines before releasing the brakes to speed down the runway. He waited until the second Canberra was airborne before he picked up his kit to make his way across the hard stand to board the ParaDak.

Jesus this kit is heavy, he thought to himself as he lifted the MAG. He had elected to also carry15 ammo belts given that this op promised to be a full on battle.

Having climbed the metal steps into the aircraft he shuffled along towards the belly of the plane and finding his spot he fell heavily into the seat.

"I see you my friend."

"I see you to," replied Rob.

"Again we go together to shoot pigs."

"Yes. And many of them."

Simon's crooked smile reminded Rob that his friend nearly met his maker when an AK round past through his mouth during a firefight.

"I will watch your back my friend," said Lieutenant Simon Mutambara.

"As you have done before and as I will do for you my friend."

377

Rob cast his eye over Simon observing that his Marksman Badge and Parachutist Patch were proudly displayed on his camouflage uniform.

The Dak rolled forward signalling to those on board that this next incursion into Mozambique to kill ZANLA terrorists was at the point of no return.

"May God be with us," muttered Simon.

God has nothing to do with it, thought Rob while he searched for his vomit bag anticipating he would soon need it.

CHAPTER THIRTY FIVE

June 1979

The old man's face was etched in his sadness.

Sitting barefooted and hunched on an upturned square tin can under a tree off to the one side of the village, he looked through tired eyes without seeing. He wore an old chequered shirt that was missing two buttons and short khaki trousers which carried several holes in them. Too large for his skinny legs, the shorts were tied around his thin waist with a rope.

Three women, winnowing grain, were close by. Dust and particles of chaff filled the air around them. Several goats lingered close by vying with many chickens to recue any grain that may fall their way.

Lifting his gaze he looked beyond the village, to the middle distance, towards a large gomo, a majestic weather beaten granite outcrop millions of years old. The sculptured rock face was interrupted by green shrubs and trees. His focus settled on the tall wire fence.

The old Batonka man reflected back over many years, recalling the trouble his village had endured as the civil war raged around them. When the tootsies first emerged from nowhere ten seasons ago his villagers had informed the local Police of their presence. Those men with guns caused much trouble for the villagers. The Police called them terrorists. Each time they informed the Rhodesians of terrorist presence, the Security Forces would arrive and invariably a gun battle would take place close by. The terrorists would either be killed or chased away. But then after a while, sometimes months, the terrorists would return and the cycle started over again.

When the guerrillas started to actively intimidate his villagers he was badly beaten many times, losing teeth, crushed fingers, a broken nose and arm. Even today he finds it hard to use the arm to lift anything. The guerrillas even burned him with logs of wood taken from the fire. At least they had not killed him. But he had remained alive to witness the horrors of the past two years. Several of the villagers were shot in the face, the bullets obliterating their skulls leaving a bloody mess of shattered bone, torn flesh and mangled brain matter. Several were beaten so badly they eventually died from their injuries, while several others in the villages suffered mutilation with their ears severed and some villagers had their tongues cut out. The mutilation was to remind the villagers not to talk to the Rhodesians and that the guerrillas had ears in the bush to hear all that was being said.

The guerrillas took many young girls for their pleasure and a few new babies had been born as a consequence. Many young women had lost their lives in the process of serving the guerrillas physical needs.

His village had supplied food to the freedom fighters even when there was not enough for the village itself. Many villagers were left hungry and a few had died from becoming very thin and weak.

The freedom fighters had given the villagers lectures that tended to go in one ear and out the other. Most villagers got the message that the white settlers had taken their land and restricted them to smaller land areas. They got the message that the white settlers had introduced their laws which were not tribal laws. However what most of the villagers could not get was the doctrine of Marxism, the struggle against the bourgeoisie and the exploitation by the white capitalist entrepreneurial classes.

The intimidation worked. The villagers lived in terrible fear finally refusing to engage in any way with the Rhodesians. But that brought its own separate hardship upon the village. The Rhodesians were displeased that their source of bush intelligence had stopped. The Police and Army took some villagers away and after beating them to tell the whereabouts of the freedom fighters they were returned to the village. The Rhodesians were angry to learn the villagers supplied the freedom fighters food and shelter and so the beatings increased. The villagers feared the RAR troops in particular because they metered out very rough physical justice. Two villagers had died from that justice. But in the balance of things the villagers feared the freedom fighters more.

The Rhodesians then built Protected Villagers. They were forced by the Rhodesians to leave their home and take up residence in the PV. Their old village was burned down by the Rhodesians. They were told this was necessary so that the freedom fighters would not use the huts as shelter.

The old man and his villagers resented this forced move. It meant they had further to walk to their fields. They were forced to live with people from other villages, some of whom were of a different tribe. The regime of tribal hierarchy was placed under stress in these circumstances causing many disputes to arise. The villagers were forced to return to the PV by dusk or face the prospect of being shot by the Rhodesians. Many villagers had already met that fate because they remained outside the PV after the evening curfew set in.

He acknowledged to himself that since occupying the PV the level of physical violence against his people had subsided except, when on a few occasions, the freedom fighters had mortared the PV. The first mortar

381

attack, one night soon after they had moved into the PV, was uneventful other than the loud explosions which caused them anxiety. No mortars actually landed in the PV. They fell outside the fence line. The same thing happened with the second mortar attack that took place a few months later. There was a long period after that where their PV was not subjected to attack, but recently it had started up once again. On the third occasion some mortars exploded inside the PV killing some villagers. The people inside the village now feared they would all die when the freedom fighters next attacked the PV. The freedom fighters had sent the message to the villagers that if they went into the PV then they would die. This last attack was the evidence that the threat given by the freedom fighters was real.

Either way it seemed to the old man that they were doomed. If they stayed in the PV then the freedom fighters would attack them or if they leave they would get shot by the Rhodesians.

He recalled the day many months ago when he had walked to a field of his neighbouring village. He was told by a visiting man from that village that a terrible thing had occurred there when metal fell from the sky and so he was curious to see this thing for himself. What he saw shook him. There was a large piece of metal in the middle of the field and all around it were fragments of metal and debris. He could see that there had been a ferocious fire all around.

He was told that the freedom fighters had used a strong weapon to bring down the plane and that it had crashed in this field. All the people on that plane had died. He recalled staring at the large metal tail of the plane and although it was burned he could make out the blue and white markings. He thought this was the plane he used to see each day flying over his village.

His sad eyes filled with water and a droplet fell from his eyes to the soil at his feet. He watched the moisture from the drop seep into the soil and he wiped the wetness away from his eyes with his left hand.

The sound of an explosion in the far distance jolted him back to the present. Sporadic gun fire followed. Not long after he heard the sound of a helicopter in the distance. He searched the sky, catching a fleeting glimpse of it. Looking towards the women he saw they continued to winnow grain regardless. His eyes glazed over once more and he wondered where all this was trouble was leading them to, when all this trouble would end.

He wondered whether he would actually live long enough to see it end.

Can any comfort come to those who suffer

while evil goes unchecked?

What words must we utter

while those in pain wept?

When peace finally comes

will forgiveness follow?

Or will it succumb

to another dark shadow?

Only time will tell if good shines through

Only time will tell if people hold true

Abbreviations and Glossary of Terms

AK 47 – Kalashnikov rifle. The main assault weapon used by ZIPRA and ZANLA. It was also used by the Selous Scouts and Rhodesian Special Forces in cross Border raids

Alpha Bomb – bomb that exploded after bouncing into the air

amaNdebele – tribe who now inhabit Western Zimbabwe migrated from Natal in South Africa when Mzilikazi's led his band of followers north between 1828 and 1838

Ammo – ammunition

AP – anti personal mine

BDF – Botswana Defence Force

BSAP – name of Rhodesian Police Force (British South Africa Police)

Callsign – Radio identification number

Camo – Camouflage

Casevac – casualty evacuation

Chimurenga – Zimbabwe nationalist word used for "War of Liberation"

CIO – Central Intelligence Organisation in Rhodesia

Clicks – Slang for Kilometres

CO – Commanding Officer

CT – Term used for terrorists by some Rhodesians meaning Communist Terrorist

ComOps – Combined Operations Headquarters. The nerve centre of the Rhodesian Security Forces coordinating all parts of the Rhodesian military.

Dak – Dakota aircraft

FAF – Forward Air Field. Airfields in the operational arrears used by the Rhodesian Security Forces to mount anti-insurgent and external cross border raids.

Fireforce – Mobile troops mostly airborne delivered by helicopters directly to the battle zone

FN – Fabrique Nationale Belgium weapon used by Rhodesian Security Forces

G-Car – Alouette helicopter used to transport troops which carried twin machine guns

Gomo – Rocky outcrop

Gook – Name often used for terrorist

Hot Spot – term used by Rhodesians to describe a part of the country where insurgency activities were high

Hot Pursuit – term used to describe a cross border operation in pursuit of fleeing guerrillas

INTAF – Rhodesian Internal Affairs

Ja / Ya – Yes with a South African and Rhodesian accent.

JOC – Joint Operational Command. Field operational centre Joint Security Force command

K-Car – Alouette with 20 millimetre cannon called 'kill car'

Kaffir – The word is derived from the Arabic term Kafir, which means 'disbeliever' or literally, 'one who conceals'. While originally a neutral term for black folk living in Southern Africa, it became an offensive term for black people

Kaunda – President of Zambia

Kopje – Hill usually rocky

Kraals – Name of African village

Long-drop – A bush toilet usually consisting of a toilet seat suspended over a hole in the ground

Maningi – Derogatory and offensive name for white folk

Mujibas – Youths who assisted nationalist guerrillas

n'anga – Tribal medicine person sometimes referred to as a 'witch doctor'

Ndebele – Tribe occupying western part of Rhodesia

OAU – Organisation of African Unity

Op – Military operation

ParaDak – Dakota carrying paratroopers

PF – Patriotic Front, an alliance between Mugabe's ZANU and Nkomo's ZAPU

R&R – Rest and Recuperation

RAR – Rhodesian African Rifles, predominantly black Rhodesian soldiers

Recce – Slang for reconnaissance

RLI – Rhodesian Light Infantry, predominantly white Rhodesian soldiers

RPG-7 – Rocket launcher

SAS – Rhodesian Special Air Service

SB – Special Branch. Intelligence section of the BSAP

Shona – Tribe occupying the central and east of Rhodesia

Sitrep – Situation report

SKS – Simonov 7.62 millimeter semi-auTerryation weapon

Slot – Slang for shoot

Stick – name given to one helicopter load of six troops

Strela – SAM 7 Soviet heat seeking missile

Sudza – tribal food

Terr – Rhodesian name for terrorist

TF – Territorial Force. Non-permanent soldiers on military call ups

Tootsie – Slag name for thug, trouble maker, thief

Tonk – slang for battle

TTL – Tribal Trust Land. Land set aside for sole use by Rhodesian African tribe people

UDI – Unilateral Declaration of Independence from Britain by the Southern Rhodesian Government on 11th November 1965

WO – Warrant Officer

Vultures – slang for media reporters. Media always swoop on a bad story

ZANU – Zimbabwe African National Union. Political arm for Robert Mugabe (Originally Sithole)

ZANLA – Zimbabwe African National Liberation Army. ZANU's military arm supported mainly by the Chinese and Maoist in training

ZAPU – Zimbabwe African People's Union. The political arm of Joshua Nkomo

ZIPRA – Zimbabwe People's Revolutionary Army. The military wing for ZAPU and supported by USSR

About the Author

John Frame was born in Salisbury, Rhodesia (Harare, Zimbabwe). The early years were spent in the peaceful pre-bush war era of Southern Rhodesia.

He became acutely aware of the political turmoil facing his country when his father became involved with the Rhodesian Front party; which held Government from 1963 through to the late 1970's.

After high school, John went to South Africa to attend Rhodes University where he succeeded in gaining an Honours Degree in Commerce.

He became aware of the seriousness of the bush war from observing how his sister and their family took anti-terrorist protective measures on their farm. This was reinforced when working with Price Waterhouse during the long University breaks he often found himself carrying an automatic weapon as well as the mundane stationary and papers in order to safely attend the more remote auditing locations.

Unwilling to sit on the sideline while his friends and family were increasingly embroiled in the conflict, John entered the Rhodesian Air Force, assigned to Airforce HQ, where he gained valuable insight into the conflict.

Surviving the war and after qualifying as a Chartered Accountant, he left Zimbabwe and resettled in Australia, where he and his family consider it one of the best places to live!